RED
HERRINGS

DONALD DEWEY

MILFORD HOUSE

an imprint of Sunbury Press, Inc.
Mechanicsburg, PA USA

MILFORD
HOUSE

an imprint of Sunbury Press, Inc.
Mechanicsburg, PA USA

For information about special discounts for bulk purchases, please contact Sunbury Press Orders Dept. at (855) 338-8359 or orders@sunburypress.com.

To request one of our authors for speaking engagements or book signings, please contact Sunbury Press Publicity Dept. at publicity@sunburypress.com.

ISBN: 978-1-62006-043-8 (Trade paperback)

Library of Congress Control Number: 2019940317

FIRST MILFORD HOUSE PRESS EDITION: April 2019

Product of the United States of America
0 1 1 2 3 5 8 13 21 34 55

Set in Bookman Old Style
Designed by Crystal Devine
Cover by Lawrence Knorr
Edited by Lawrence Knorr

Continue the Enlightenment!

For Joel Doerfler

He opened his eyes in a hotel room. It took him a moment to remember the hotel's name as the Global and his room number as 321 next to the ice machine. It had been more than a week since he had awoken to familiar surroundings, longer than that since that feeling had been a normal part of his life. Anonymity had accepted his invitation.

He threw off his sheet and got up before he began feeling sorry for himself. He took it as a good sign that his toes came down within the area carpet.

He used the sink for pissing, brushing his teeth, and shaving. After smearing a coat of after-shave over his face and throat, he emptied the remains of the bottle down the drain and tossed the bottle into the green plastic basket under the sink. The razor he put back into his leather traveling case before dropping it in the basket so the cleaning lady wouldn't cut herself while disposing of the garbage.

It took him less than five minutes to scribble the letter he had memorized falling asleep. He had always been good at preparing his thoughts, right down to commas and periods, even in foreign languages. The pen managed the words without deep concentration, his attention flitting over the curlicues of the printed blue lettering at the top of the hotel stationery. He thought them a sign of self-indulgence for such a modest hotel, and himself self-indulgent for wasting a thought on them.

He hesitated over the red-covered journal one last time, draining every possible reassurance from it that there could be no misunderstanding about its entries. Then he slid both the journal and the cover letter into the stamped and addressed packet waiting for them. As he dressed, he could only hope Sylvester's address was still valid after so long, or that at the very least the postal authorities in America had some forwarding location. It was too late to worry about that now. When he was ready to go, he slipped the packet into the inside pocket of his jacket. Going out the door, he imagined that the buckles on his opened suitcase on the chair shook. He didn't like imagining things like that and pulled the door closed behind him more emphatically than necessary.

He went directly from the hotel to the letterbox on the corner. There was something more trustworthy about it than the mail slot next to the front desk in the hotel lobby. As soon as the packet left his hand in the narrow aperture, he felt a relief that nothing more could be done.

The walk to the embassy was through quiet, already hot morning streets. The entire population seemed to have gone off on holiday, leaving only temporary help behind store counters to deal with the tourist armies descending during the day. On a language level alone, were there truly that many substitutes fluent in English, French, and Spanish? He didn't understand that kind of planning and was sure there wasn't much intelligence behind it.

Across the street from the embassy, he paused at the sight of the open, unguarded gate. For an instant he was baffled by the thought that for almost everyone else he had passed in the streets a normal day was beginning, then he didn't know why he should have been surprised. For a special moment to be special, it should have been special in every one of its features.

He caught the encroachment of a personal thought just in time, quickly listing the names of people around the world he fancied existed but had never met. He walked across the street thinking of Aurelio Virgilio in Italy, Georges Bonmarche in France, Lars Bjornstrand in Sweden, Myron Gobbledegook in America, Istvan Broz in his own country. As his feet crunched down on the gravel path winding toward the stately embassy building, he glanced up at the wide windows over the entrance. Somebody—maybe Glauber?—had been there, then gone away, probably to report him coming. It made no difference. Once he had crossed the street and stepped on the grounds, he had become their responsibility.

He wanted no messy scenes, however. Shrillness was not the last thing he wanted to remember about himself. The birds chattering in the trees—blue jays, he guessed—were about as loud as he wanted things to be.

With one foot on the front step and the other still on the gravel, he removed the small pistol from his pocket, blanking out any more doubts that it was still in working order after so many years. He told himself not to feel the cold of the nozzle on his temple or to hear the rush of excited voices behind the door as he pulled the trigger. He remembered he had never met a Xuan Kai-Shek from China, either.

ONE

Berlin.

Informant MG reports that the German authorities have been fully cooperative in releasing the body of JC to his homeland, no further investigative steps foreseen at a local level. Media coverage has been minimal, responsive only to neighborhood eye witness accounts and explained as an individual psychological crisis. Embassy officials have informed JC's widow of the situation. She has not indicated any opposition to the present disposition of the decedent.

Informant MG also reports no trace of item mentioned in his last report. An inspection of his hotel room turned up nothing. Lacking any indication the item was destroyed by JC prior to his death, it must be assumed that he passed it on to an as-yet-unidentified second party. Initial concentration will be on his widow and son, but other potential recipients are being pursued.

TWO

Charley Sylvester had spent a restless night. Between the voices in Nick's room across the hall and thinking about his flight to Italy, he had been tossed around on a middle-aged man's Sea of Anxiety until the four o'clock news. Standing under the shower, he wished he hadn't nodded off at all. Four hours of sleep had done nothing for his mood except numb it. Instead of guessing the name of the girl Nick had been rolling around with and getting melancholy about the years when the creaking of the kid's bed had been from wrestling with a school mate, parental responsibility was waiting to know what he intended saying to him over breakfast. Instead of pretending to prepare himself for the changes he would find in Rome—and in himself—after seven years, he sighed before the prospect of a full day at the office, an irksome cab ride to Kennedy, and seven hours in an uncomfortable airplane to a later time zone before putting his feet back on solid ground. It was bad enough setting off into one hot summer day with four hours of sleep, but he was actually setting off into two of them.

By the time he walked into the kitchen, Sylvester had graduated to four-star irritation. Irritation that his shower had done little for his druggy body. Irritation at the rap coming full blast out of Nick's room. Irritation at the mellow aroma of the coffee Patricia was percolating for him as a going-away present. It was more than a year since he had asked her to stop playing house for him in the morning and that she had agreed with an air of filial tolerance, but this morning she was determined to make an exception because of his trip. She stood at the stove in a blue housecoat, her long brown hair tied loosely in the back with a green ribbon. It was exactly the way her mother had never stood, Sylvester thought. Mornings in Rome with Felicia had been about one of them stumbling out of bed to answer the door for the waiter with the *espresso* from the bar downstairs. It wasn't that he and Felicia had been unable to light water for coffee, but they had shared a self-deceiving sense of logistics, forgetting that while the telephone for calling the bar had been closer to the bed than the kitchen had been, the front door had definitely not been.

"The party still in full swing?'

Patricia smirked as though she had expected just that question to be his idea of a greeting. "Good Morning to you too, Charley."

He saw that the paper lay untouched on the table. Unless she had developed the deftness of a pickpocket, she hadn't been curious to see if the Arts section had run her dance piece. He was disappointed by that. "What's her name?"

"None of my business."

"I didn't ask you her source of income, just her name."

He separated the paper's sections before he had to see another expression of long suffering. He had always hated that look in her mother, and it hadn't grown more charming in the next genera-tion. He found her item on the dance group beneath the fold on the third page of the Arts section. That made four days in a row and seven in the last eight for her. It also made for four days in a row and seven in the last eight when her story looked like it had been laid out by a blind man. "Hey, look, you have a whole half-sentence in a column all by itself! Wow! There's exclusivity for you!"

Patricia dropped bread into the toaster and went over behind his shoulder to see what he was looking at. "Looked more impor-tant on my screen."

"Too many of these verbs they teach you in journalism school. *Weave. Skid. Collide.* They were dancing, not having a car crash."

"The Metro desk must have gone to the same school."

"The Metro desk is a piece of furniture. If you mean Descalso, say Descalso. He doesn't need you to defend him for two reasons.

One, he's not here. Two, he knows as much about layout as he does about Chinese pretzels."

"Yes, Charley."

He put the Arts section aside before he was tempted to find something else that irritated him in the dance piece and made sure Descalso hadn't been given an extra assignment with the Obituaries. He breathed easier at the simple layout: the football announcer and Nobel Prize winner above the fold, the French Socialist Party leader below it. He had been right not to cram the cowboy actor into the bottom of the page. He would still be home on the range today.

"Radio said Congressman McCauley died."

Nick slopped in wearing nothing more than his jeans. Sylvester was struck as never before by how much his son looked like a newer and more muscular version of himself. He might never have had the kid's iron stomach or his fanaticism for keeping it that way with all his bars and weights, but the long shock of black hair over his right eye, the hawk nose, and the jaw always set for either a one-liner or a punch had stared back at him from mirrors for years. "Glad to hear it."

Nick grabbed the container of orange juice from the refrigerator and walked it over to the counter to get a glass from the cabinet. Sylvester smiled to himself. It had been years since he had made his one and only scene about drinking from the carton, but for some reason, the lesson had stuck. He had never been that responsive about it with his own mother. "So going to introduce us or is she slipping out the door right now?"

Nick kept pouring. "She's in the bathroom."

"*She.*"

"Joy. You met her."

"I would remember a Joy. There aren't that many of them in the world."

"Right, Dad."

He pretended not to see Patricia's warning look. "Well, tell Joy for me to wear something besides boots and chains. Sounded like De Sade's dungeon in there."

He had said wittier things and had said more sensitive things, but he wasn't all that regretful when Nick slammed the orange juice container back into the refrigerator and stalked out. Going on the record could be its own reward. What he could have done without was Patricia's disapproval. "What, I wasn't supposed to say anything?"

"Maybe something besides a crack."

"And maybe I'd like Good Morning instead of 'Congressman McCauley's dead.'"

"He was just trying to . . ."

"Relate to me, I know. New stiff in the morgue? Tell my father."

She had also inherited her mother's look of surrender: a what's-the-use-of-trying-to-get-through-to-the-mentally-challenged? "Yes, sir."

"Good. We got that clear. Think yet about what you want me to bring back from Rome? There's got to be something."

"Really, Charley. Nothing."

"It won't contaminate you, you know."

"What's that supposed to mean?"

"You know damn well what I mean. Your mother gets around, but not even she's had the time to go around the whole city and touch everything."

"That's not fair."

"Okay, it's not fair. And when something occurs to you, call me at the Reggio. Cynthia will have the number. And what about your mother? Any message?"

She kept her back turned. She had hovered over the counter long enough to repaint it. "Just hello."

"I can say that on my own."

She peeked around at him, a suddenly sly grin on her face. "But not with my permission you can't."

He had never minded being outwitted by her, but that didn't mean he had to admit it. "Watch that toaster. It's like a nuclear oven."

She was too late. By the time she popped the machine and scraped some of the black off, there was no toast left to his toast.

THREE

As he pressed for the elevator next to his apartment, Sylvester scolded himself to be a glass-half-full guy in honor of his trip. Didn't he have plenty to be grateful for? Patricia and Nick had grown up to be recognizable human beings, hadn't they? She might have used too many journalism school verbs and was maybe getting a little too comfortable in her off-off-Broadway niche, but she had never brought home a boyfriend he wanted to choke, had never been arrested, and had been involved in only one fender bender. Nick might have still been ricocheting back and forth between one so-called social science and another at Columbia, but none of his charlatan teachers had kept him off the Dean's List. What else did he need to know—or want to ask? And the world at large was also in there pitching to give him a glow for the day. Who was the genius who had invented rollers for suitcases? Who was the other wizard who had given his building one of the few functioning elevators in the city? And most of all, how had he earned the favor of the U.S, Post Office so that his building received the first delivery of the day rather than the last after midnight? What *wasn't* there to be grateful for?

The pile of envelopes waiting in his mailbox proposed candidates. Those with windows Sylvester immediately tossed back, leaving it to Patricia to decide if it was more important to subsidize the city's museums or pay the cable bill. He could have done without the offer of a nice plot in a Staten Island cemetery and of another Amex card, but those he dispensed with in the garbage can of the mailbox alcove. What he didn't have a clue about was the letter and red diary-looking thing from a hotel in Mainz called the Global. In Manhattan, he thought, a hotel called the Global would have been a flophouse near the West Side Highway.

The name Cicut descended a fraction of a second before he read it as the signature on the hotel stationery. Sylvester was astonished. Outside of a random moment when the old Yugoslavia had been mentioned, he had seldom thought of Josef Cicut recently, and that in itself was strange considering how much time they had once spent in each other's company. That seemed like a reason to be astonished twice over. He had first met Cicut at Salvador Mundi Hospital in Rome after Felicia had delivered Nick and Cicut's wife, Elena, in the other bed in Felicia's room, had delivered . . . Peter? Paul? He was annoyed and then flabbergasted he couldn't remember. He was sure they had bought the kid Christmas or birthday presents along the way, but if there had been a card with the boy's name on it, he had no picture of it. Of Cicut and Elena, he had plenty of pictures—of the never-quite-at-ease ex-diplomat who had always said he preferred his new life in Italy as the head of a translation agency and the potato-cheeked wife who had tossed in her fluency in a zillion Balkan languages to the family enterprise. Somewhere upstairs in his closet, he had Polaroids of all of them at the tables of Trastevere restaurants, on the tiny balcony they had off the living room of their apartment behind the Chiesa Nuova, from a Sunday outing in Velletri, from another to Umbria. For a few years, the Sylvesters hadn't been closer to anybody than to the Cicuts. There hadn't been a world crisis around the turn of the century they hadn't debated or acted supercilious about. Standing now in the alcove, Sylvester was surprised by how close he felt again to those times—and by how easily he had let them recede from his mind.

None of which explained a Mainz hotel called the Global. Or the worn notebook that had been included with the letter.

Puzzled as he was, he had to postpone his reading of the letter when the doorman Henry reminded him a taxi was waiting. Only after Henry had helped him stow his bag in the trunk and the cab had started its snail's progress downtown did he read:

Dear Charley, Our paths have not crossed in several years, but I am hopeful you have not forgotten me. By the time you read this, you shall have undoubtedly learned of my death. I leave behind my wife Elena and my 18-year-old son Philip who will have need of a friend and of someone in whom they can confide. If you can find the time, I would appreciate you contacting them. Their address is Vicolo del Moro 2 in Rome.

I address this last appeal to you in the name of fond moments spent together in the past and in the hope that your esteemed position in the American journalistic world has brought you personal satisfaction and the utmost happiness. Naturally, I leave to your discretion the disposition of the enclosed. My regards to your children. Your indebted servant, Josef R. Cicut.

Sylvester was dumbly aware of the street noises going past. He needed the driver to cut back even on his crawl through the Broadway traffic until he had put his head back on. Cicut dead? Making it sound like suicide? No, he hadn't heard anything of the kind so how could it have happened? Ask Nick: His father—the one with the "esteemed position in the American journalistic world"—was the expert on every stiff in every morgue on every continent. Was that supposed to be some kind of taunt? And even if it wasn't, how could somebody he had known so well have just disappeared without leaving a ripple? He knew about the deaths of every asshole who had run for Congress and of every brainless Miss High School who had appeared on a TV sitcom, but of Josef Cicut's nada, nulla. Was he even reaching to presume suicide? Maybe the guy had had some disease he didn't want to burden his family with and thought it more appropriate to share his end with the Global Hotel. The whole thing was ridiculous.

Sylvester took a deep breath as a green light moved the cab past 72nd Street. The driver misunderstood and grumbled something about the morning traffic. Sylvester dropped his eyes back to what he was holding. Philip, that was easier to grasp; not Peter or Paul, but Philip. That he definitely should have recalled because he had once asked Cicut about giving his son such a non-Slavic name. Had the man told him why? Who cared? He had plenty of other reasons to be agitated by Global Hotel stationery.

Had it really been necessary for Cicut to wonder if he had been remembered? That was too stiff even for somebody who had always been crammed into a dress shirt and creased pants; stiff, cute, and arrogant. And lest he forgets: self-important to a theatrical degree. Josef Cicut had pontificated, had shared the ridicule of others for his pontificating, then had wrapped it all up with more pontificating. The whole letter was like that. Charlie Sylvester might not have remembered who Josef Cicut was, but could Charlie Sylvester be sure to contact his wife after so long to . . . To what? Say hi, I just heard Josef was dead, in fact, he himself told me? He sends final greetings from Germany?

So much for his glass half-filled. He wanted the diary to irritate him as much as the letter, and it did a pretty good job. He didn't speak Serbo-Croat, Serbo-Croatian, or whatever the hell it was called, but he knew it was sometimes written in Cyrillic and sometimes in Latin and that in neither one of them could it have consisted only of three- and four-letter words exclusively made up of consonants. Shorthand? A code? Whichever, the dates at the top of each page went back years before he had met the man in the Salvador Mundi hospital room. The cramped hand, similar but not identical to that of the letter, betrayed a young Josef Cicut, one not given to as much discursiveness, a man in a hurry, maybe even in a panic, to catch up to his thoughts. And the thoughts themselves? Who knew? Whatever they had been about, though, they had been sitting in a drawer of the Cicut apartment before the two families had ever traipsed through the vineyards of Velletri or bought tons of oranges from piazza markets in Umbria. And only *now*, with Cicut declaring himself dead, they were worth sharing?

And for what? They had to be the "appeal" he was talking about, but appeal about what? Helping him publish his memoirs?

The cab suddenly sped up. The driver had found maneuvering room and was proceeding down Broadway as if on a street made for cars. Sylvester was sorry for the progress. He had really been working himself up past a stage of petty irritation to absolute fury, and the clearing Manhattan traffic was spoiling it.

FOUR

Sylvester had long since accepted the criticism—first voiced by his ex-wife Felicia but restated by any number of people in one form or another—that his inner agitations were seldom inner enough. He saw no reason to undermine expectations arriving for work. The good news was managing to get off the elevator with only two people asking where he was going with his big suitcase. The bad news was that was two too many. At bottom, he really didn't know why he was going to Italy instead of to, say, Malaysia, and questions reminded him of that. Once he had looked up Bruno Lepri and a couple of old hands at the Correspondents Club, how was he planning on spending the rest of his time? He couldn't say. The idea of getting away for a few days seemed to have started and stopped at the idea of getting away for a few days. There were just so many side trips from Rome he could have taken without remembering he had already taken them and hadn't been all that impressed the first time. Genetic bells? Curiosity about how one Carlo Silvestri generations ago had ultimately morphed into Charley Sylvester? That kind of navel-gazing had never interested him. If he was being realistic, he would have been counting on nothing more than eating and drinking himself into months of dieting when he came home. Who did he thank for *that* thought? The letter from Cicut?

The walk through the bullpen to his office in the back corner had never felt more like running a gauntlet. Ellington had been keeping score on Patricia's published pieces and expected to be appreciated for his attentiveness. Morandi wanted him to bring back truffles from Italy. Lopez wanted to know if he had heard that Congressman McCauley had died. The editorial secretary Jean needed his signature on a couple of vouchers. The intern Mark Something had a scoop on the latest corpse, a congressman named McCauley. By the time he reached his office, he had run out of gratitude toward the guy who had invented suitcase rollers.

Cynthia was sitting at his desk sorting agency dispatches. She was wearing her gauzy lime green number showing off her tanned freckled shoulders, and that felt like the first sign of progress since he had opened his mailbox. Nobody had sexier clavicles. "Morning, Charley," she singsonged, trying to be furtive about registering his suitcase as a final confirmation he really was going off later. "Give me a second and you can have your desk back."

"Keep it."

"We'll have to fix up this McCauley background a little."

"You will. I've heard more campaigning for him today than when he was alive."

He dropped down on the black leather couch he had rarely used since they had wheeled it in as a symbol of his importance. He had never encouraged other people to use it, either, since that threatened longer visits. But every so often it had its value, now giving him a view of Cynthia's solid calves and green toe polish under the desk.

"You look all set."

"I thought I was. What do we got besides McCauley? Actors? I wouldn't mind some dead actors today. The more famous the better."

"Bad Netflix movie last night?"

He had intended sharing his correspondence from Cicut with her as soon as he had walked in, but having to get up from the couch right away again and going over to close the door suddenly felt paranoid. He preferred staying where he was and watching her curl her big toe up from her sandals. "Anything come through in the last week or so about a Josef Cicut?"

"Josef Cicut? Nothing I remember. Why?"

"Rumor has it the man is dead."

"And this is important because Josef Cicut was celebrated as . . .?"

At the World News desk, the debate had been over whether a train wreck in Pakistan was worthier of reporting if nine had been killed instead of eight; now it was what made a corpse enough of a celebrity to earn more than agate type. "He was a diplomat for a country that no longer exists. How's that?"

She dropped her shoulders against the back of his chair with a suspicious look. He had always liked Cynthia Glass's looks of suspicion. They seemed to elevate him in her priorities. "I hear something personal."

"Yes, you do."

He wrestled gravity and his belt buckle to stand back up, close the office door, and hand her the letter. He smelled her minty shampoo as she bent forward to read. If he had been more daring, if the office hadn't had a window facing out on the bullpen, if she wouldn't have swatted him for it, and if a warlock descended to earth and transformed him into somebody other than Charles Lawrence Sylvester, he would have jumped her. He didn't feel like waiting for the lunch they had planned at her apartment to see the rest of her freckles.

"Obviously you knew him," she said, baffled.

"Years ago. After his diplomatic career was over. As the head of a translation agency in Rome. Our families were pretty close at one time. We're talking back when you were in high school."

"No, we're not. But moving right along. And you haven't been in contact with him since? Pretty presumptuous of him even if he is dead."

"Think of it as progress. Now the dead are writing to us."

"Did he know you were going to Rome?"

The question hadn't occurred to him, and it made him queasy it had occurred to her. That kind of paranoia required more than a closed door. "And then this," he said, giving her the diary. "Some kind of journal from what looks like the Balkan war years."

She leafed the pages deliberately with her long fingers, her frown growing deeper with every page. He hadn't realized how much he had been counting on her laughing off the whole thing until she didn't. "And you think . . ."

"I don't think anything," he said, his anger from the cab stirring again. "I don't *want* to think anything. Here's a guy who . . ."

"Who was a friend for a long time and had all these stories or whatever they are that he could tell you about only after he was dead." She blinked at him in her best this-is-reality-Sylvester innocence.

"They could just be shopping lists."

"Sure they could."

"Okay, they're probably not. They're probably a chronicle of something the world doesn't know, Joe Cicut didn't want the world to know, but now wants me to tell the world what it hasn't known."

She nodded quizzically. "That sounds pretty good. Hot stuff. And meanwhile you're feeling betrayed about something, but you're not sure if it's only personal or if you'd prefer it being only personal."

"Go to hell."

"Yes, sir. But before that . . ." She turned into the computer at the side of the desk and went hunting for Josef Cicut. She wasn't sure of what she had found even when the screen glared back at her. Either was he when she swiveled the screen around to him. There were old items from Cicut's diplomatic days in Denmark and as a negotiator with the Vatican on some bilateral commission. Then there were two entries mentioning his translation agency in Rome that had little to do with him personally. Then, for some reason three-quarters of the way down and earmarked LATEST NEWS where it didn't look like LATEST anything, there were reports from two Mainz newspapers—*General Anzeiger* and *Rheinische Merkur*—saying Cicut had died of a heart attack during a visit to the Croatian embassy and that his remains had been shipped to his home in Italy. Nothing at all hinting at suicide. On the other hand, even Sylvester's rudimentary German was good enough to see that the two papers had done little but copy the essentials from some official communique issued by the embassy. "So I guess he's dead all right," Cynthia said for him.

"And nothing from the Italian papers? The body arriving from Germany? The death of a foreign entrepreneur in Italy?"

"Maybe he didn't live in Italy anymore."

That made so much sense he wondered how he hadn't noticed leaving his brain back in the mailbox alcove. Just because he had left Rome didn't mean everybody else had to wait there for his return some day. For all he knew, Cicut had left Elena and the kid years ago. "Look anyway."

She pressed the key to the second screen, then to the third, but nothing new came up. "Looks like he was bigger for his heart attack in Germany than he was for this language thing in Italy."

"That would please him no end. Try our morgue."

He was sorry he had asked. There wasn't even the paraphrasing from the two Mainz papers of the official communique. So much for the thoroughness of the electronic library. Worse, the lead item was the interview, a good ten years old, that Eddie Roenicke had done with Cicut when he had made the mistake of going off on vacation to Tunisia with Felicia and the kids. Eager beaver Roenicke had decided the paper always had room for a melancholy feature about ex-ambassadors who must have been puzzled by events back in their abandoned homeland. The piece had been absolute garbage and had introduced a note of mistrust in his relationship with Cicut. The man hadn't wanted to be bothered, and Eddie Roenicke, the colleague of Charley Sylvester, had bothered him for two thousand words, suggesting that some ex-ambassadors were as self-dramatizing as Gloria Swanson in *Sunset Boulevard.*

How come Charley Sylvester hadn't headed that off? Because Charley Sylvester hadn't known about it and had been preoccupied showing off Carthage to Patricia and Nick, that was why. But Cicut's understanding of that explanation had never quite equaled his acceptance of it. What had always been a cold fish, relatively easy to ignore because of his wife and son, had become a frozen fish. In Josef Cicut's regimented instincts everyone was responsible even for what they weren't responsible. Punishment: Estrangement over the last few years in Rome between the Sylvesters and the Cicuts. And that kind of thing, Sylvester realized, was why it had been so easy not to think about the man lately. There had always been an aloofness—a detachment that said the Sylvesters were really no more important than anybody else he might have been spent Sunday afternoons with. Down to it, Cicut's theatricality was the man's most sympathetic quality.

"Keep going?"

He was about to say it was pointless when he saw Claude Applebaum at the far end of the bullpen. "I thought Applebaum was in Europe."

"Came back yesterday. On vacation, I think."

He liked that coincidence even less than the one about getting a letter to look up someone in Rome the day he was going there. Or maybe he had just never gotten used to adults wearing bow ties.

FIVE

ylvester assumed there were solid geological reasons for the existence of the Atlantic Ocean. But they weren't as important as the fact that the Atlantic had kept him separated from Claude Applebaum—first with him in Europe and Applebaum in the States and then with him in New York and Applebaum on the other side. Ellington and others had been content to snicker at the paper's roving European correspondent as its raving European correspondent, but he had found that cattiness wide of a dozen marks. Snakes didn't rave. What Claude Applebaum mostly did was slink from one continental capital to another for his foreign affairs column to hiss at anyone between the Irish Sea and the Urals deemed to be working against State Department interests. Because of his press credentials, he was seldom denied access to those with portfolios; in the columns that came out of those meetings, he could make Belgian liberals sound like either the best friends Utah ranchers ever had or the worst threats Connecticut insurance companies had ever feared. Was he a useful vehicle for the CIA? Anybody exposed to a month of his sententious musings had to consider the possibility. But then anybody exposed to a month of his sententious musings also had to admit the possibility that he was also a useful vehicle for Geico, the American Dairy Association, and the Minnesota Twins. Whatever the specific pimping occasion, his column could always be headlined FOR SALE. Sylvester had learned that the hard way with Sergio Polimeni.

Polimeni had been as much in demand as any certified public accountant in Italy ever had been. Banks had asked him to take a second look at what their auditors had come up with, small Mediterranean governments had quietly asked for his expertise with state balance sheets. Then Polimeni had made the mistake of taking on a similar troubleshooting assignment for the smallest government of all, Vatican City. What he had discovered had confirmed the suspicions of the cardinal who had brought him in, but then that cardinal had been succeeded by one who abhorred the idea of outsiders looking at Holy See books, especially an outsider with an authoritative reputation like Polimeni's. It had taken months to tear down the man's credibility, to preempt anything scandalous he might utter at any time about anything, but torn down it had been and so relentlessly that Polimeni had finally traded in his professional discretion for an interview with Sylvester to give his side of the story in the hope of salvaging his livelihood. But barely had the interview reached print than Claude Applebaum had come along to "analyze" it in the name of good relations between the Vatican and whoever his sponsor of the moment had been. Sergio Polimeni had ended up a suicide—at least for those who didn't think it likely he could have gone walking across the Ponte Garibaldi one night and accidentally stumbled over a chest-high railing into the Tiber.

Reclaiming his desk from Cynthia, Sylvester didn't like the Polimeni parallels with Cicut. He had absolutely nothing but an ambiguous phrase in Cicut's letter even to conclude suicide, but the comparison still beeped in his mind. What he liked just as little was the thought that the shortest shortcut at hand for understanding Cicut's cryptogram was Claude Applebaum. The man might have been malignant, but he was rarely uninformed about European matters, especially if there was an embassy and attendant gossip somewhere in the middle of them. If Cicut had done anything but keel over from a heart attack, Applebaum would have been the first to know.

"Don't, Charley. Don't go near him."

He was sorry he had done so much whining about Applebaum to her. As she sat in the corner of the couch, her legs crossed and her fingers steepling her temple, she might have been X-raying his brain and squinting at the tumors she had uncovered. "Thanks for the vote of confidence."

"You're going on vacation. Go on vacation."

"And while I'm over there drop in on Cicut's widow and tell her I got some stuff from Josef but can't figure out what it is?"

"That's one possibility."

"Why can't I see the others?"

"You don't drop in on her at all," she said severely. "Doesn't sound like you've been all that tight the last few years anyway. Or option three, you give her that journal and let her take it from there. It was her husband's, so legally that should make it hers now. Anything but Charley Sylvester sitting down to a game of Stratego with Applebaum just because he wants to prove he isn't all that rusty at some things."

Sylvester was embarrassed—by the accusation and by how transparent he was to her. Outwit Applebaum? What could be more appealing? Sergio Polimeni's wasn't the only casket the son of a bitch had helped carry to a cemetery. But Cynthia was also right about his vanity. Pulling the tiger's tail just because he had been feeling creakier in the joints for a long time didn't seem like a particularly smart move.

But when had he ever been particularly smart?

He looked at the diary on the desk in front of him. Some of the red cover was so thin from wear it had no color at all. He hadn't noticed the remnants of the store price on the lower left corner of the back before. He couldn't read the number but he could definitely make out the old symbol for Yugoslav dinars. The book had indeed been laying somewhere in Cicut's house while he and Felicia had eaten there, while the kids had played in Philip's room, and while the ex-ambassador had tried to sound more interested in the histories of Italian dialects than in events back in the home he had fled. Maybe *betrayal*, as Cynthia had said, was too strong a word, but he didn't see an endorsement of trust between friends, either.

"You're going to say something to him anyway, aren't you?"

"Joey Bacsik down in the mail room today?"

"He didn't give me his schedule."

He wasn't in the mood for her snippiness; he had enough of his own. "I'll be back in a few minutes. You take care of McCauley, okay? If I hear his name again this morning, I'll kill his corpse."

"Jesus, Charley."

Sylvester couldn't have agreed more as he crossed back through the bullpen toward the elevator. He would leave it up to Jesus to put the right words in his mouth when he talked first to Joey Bacsik and then to Applebaum.

SIX

There might have been a newspaper before Joey Bacsik. The question divided the old-timers. What they could agree on was that Bacsik had already been perched in his captain's chair in the center of the mail room when they had been hired and that the first time they had made the mistake of venturing there, he had assailed them with questions about how serious they were about being journalists. His litmus test for deciding how sincere they were was one question: what was the difference between a reporter and a correspondent? Sylvester had passed the test by saying that a correspondent was a reporter who had kissed his editor's ass. That might not have been especially original, but he had hit Joey Bacsik on the right day because the mail room supervisor with the thick sideburns (then brown, now white) had not only accepted it but had gradually moved from there to deciding that Sylvester was his favorite in the news department. To prove it, he had dragged his endlessly complaining wife to Rome on a vacation some years afterward, boarding with the Sylvesters for a week. They had continued on to Florence on their tour of Italy without grasping that their hosts would have built Florence for them if it that had been the only way of getting rid of them.

But that had been a much younger Joey Bacsik, and Sylvester had to strain his memory to relate him to the feeble old man who needed to get rid of his glasses and practically put his nose on the page to make out the letters in Cicut's journal. There was in fact little left of the Bacsik as The Man Who Came to Dinner and

Who Brought Along His Pain in the Ass Wife. The wife Beatrice
had died, the fanaticism about turning down every other Italian
dish for weight reasons had become 30 or 40 pounds too many
for his dwarfish stature, and he barely paid attention to the mailroom assistants he had always driven to despair with his micro-
managing. About the only thing that had remained intact was his
querulousness. "This looks like old shit," he said.

"But it's Serbo-Croat abbreviated, right?"

Joey Bacsik never agreed even about the obvious without
making it sound like a major concession. "I guess so."

"What do you make of it?"

He flattened his nose back against the pages with the sigh of
the severely tried. "These initials BN and BK look like Bosanska
Novi and Bosanska Kostajnica. They're pretty close to each other
on the edge of Bosnia-Herzegovina. Not a very clever code if that's
what it is."

"Make any sense of what he's saying?"

Joey Bacsik leaned his head back from the diary, restored
his glasses, and eyed Sylvester sardonically. "Do I have to read
it to know? What did people keep journals of from those days?
Not how many sausages they bought in the morning. No way you
don't have a lot of bodies in here somewhere."

That made it unanimous with himself and Cynthia, Sylvester
thought. Did he want to know more, find out he had been sent a
confession by Cicut of some outrage committed before the days
of translation agencies in Rome? What would that have resolved?
Cicut's bad conscience in sending him the journal as a last act
couldn't have counterbalanced what he had had a bad conscience
about.

Bacsik was still peering at him. "And so what? You know how
many diaries like this there are around the world? I bet there are
a couple of people in this building who have them. That's what
slaughterhouses do, Sylvester. They turn out a lot of meat for a
lot of people. What makes this one so special?"

The answer seemed ridiculous. "This is my slaughterhouse."

Bacsik was unmoved. "Really? You feel the same way about
Send-a-Dollar-for-Cancer-Research when you get it in the mail?"

"You're losing that warm heart you're famous for, Joey."

The little man sighed; he had tried. "Okay. Leave it with me a couple of days and I'll see what I can get out of it for you. Who knows? I may be wrong."

"Better idea," he said, plucking the book back. "I'll get a copy of this made and have it sent down. I'm going to need it when I take off tonight."

Bacsik thought about being offended at having the diary yanked away from him, then opted for a better target. "Why go back to Italy? You'll just find people you don't know anymore. Go to France instead."

That too seemed like a unanimous opinion, Sylvester told himself. It already had been when he alone had thought it.

SEVEN

He should have figured on finding Applebaum in the office of the managing editor Kevin Porterfield. The smell of waxy shoe polish hanging over the broad square room could be shared only by favorites, and nobody was more of a Porterfield favorite than Claude Applebaum. It had been Porterfield who had given him the roving correspondent niche and Porterfield who had repeatedly nominated his columns for Pulitzer Prizes. Surrendering a desk for a few minutes was hardly a sacrifice anyway with Porterfield's routine of going out to some fine French restaurant for lunch while most people were still burping from breakfast.

Applebaum was hunched over Porterfield's 24th-century computer for little reason since the monitor was about the size of an I-Max screen. At first glance he belonged to a university campus—green bow tie, black-framed glasses, stooped shoulders making him shorter than he was, distant eyes roaming for a reason to deny the world an A-Plus. But the professor wasn't a professor. There was no pinch of self-doubt, no reservoir of wry benevolence that he himself deserved a C as much as anybody else; the sallow hunger in his expression was mainly impatience with the borrowed technology that wasn't living up to its promises.

"Helluva way to spend a vacation."

Applebaum needed one second to accept he was being disturbed, another to get over his annoyance, and a third to work up a smile. "Charley! I hear we just missed each other over the Atlantic. Not going back to your old beat, are you?"

"Take your guns off, Claude. Just looking up old friends for a couple of weeks."

Applebaum convinced himself he could relax; he had picked up a volleyball of a paunch since his last visit and his short-sleeved white shirt did nothing to disguise it. "It's not the same anymore. Rome, Madrid, Paris—they all look like Omaha. Line up over here for your Cokes and fries."

There was a green file next to the computer with the crayoned name CICUT on it. That Sylvester could remember, the paper's morgue had yellow, red, and blue files in addition to the standard manila cream; green he had never seen before. But then he had never seen Applebaum's private files, either. "Doing a column on Josef Cicut?"

Applebaum had to remind himself he wasn't hiding anything. "For the Sunday edition. Then it's a month in the Rockies with mountain lions and rattlers and pretending I like roughing it. I didn't know you knew him."

He sidled close enough to the screen to make out the article title "Fish Out of Water." Cynthia had called his impulse Stratego; she should have called it Lying. "He called me. Apparently, a day or two before he died."

Applebaum wasn't sure he had heard a joke. "That's right! That piece from Rome a few years ago . . ."

"That was Roenicke, not me."

And Applebaum knew it; odds were, Roenicke's interview was in the green folder. "Right. But you were close? I mean, if he called you . . ."

"Not that close. Why I found his call so weird."

"To say what?"

"Just how are you, what've you been up to? Like we'd seen each other last week. Would you believe it?" No, Applebaum wouldn't. "You seem to have kept up with him. Why was he this 'Fish Out of Water?' And why do we care if he was? We didn't even get a wire service line on him."

"But you knew he was dead."

"Friend of a friend."

"Right."

"You're a bad interrogator, Claude."

He grinned. "I've been told just the opposite."

"Everybody has a fan club. The secret is not listening to it. So why was Cicut this fish out of water?"

Applebaum wanted to hear ignorance and glibness so he heard them. "What else would you call him? At one time he was one of the best brains in the European diplomatic service. Head of the European Community desk in the foreign ministry, ambassador to Denmark when things got a little tender with Scandinavia. The little junket with the press when he recreated the trail taken by the Jews escaping the Nazis during the occupation. Who in Denmark could have a better, more understanding friend? And then that consular agreement with the Vatican. What was that little scene he pulled when the cardinals were getting obstinate about Clause 7 or Codicil 45? Suspicion of the Orthodox church? Oh, no, he didn't mean that. Somebody must have misunderstood. He knew the Vatican wasn't still back in those ancient days, was more open-minded than that. How many headlines did he get out of that? Mister Drama. Performance Art with a diplomatic sash. And all that when he was barely in his thirties. He had everything in front of him. Just climb the staircase. Next step ambassador to London or Washington, then deputy foreign minister."

"I think he lost his country somewhere in there, didn't he?"

"Okay, he did, and he didn't want to go back to the little fiefdoms that took its place. No question, it wasn't all his fault."

"What fault? He looked content enough to me when I'd run into him."

"C'mon, Charley. One day he's negotiating with the pope, the next he's signing contracts to translate agricultural reports in Swahili."

"Seemed happy enough to me."

"You get a taste of it like Cicut had, you never really lose it."

"*It* was losing a lot of family and friends in all those massacres." He knew it was a mistake as soon as he blurted it. Applebaum couldn't nod sympathetically fast enough. "At least that was the feeling I got from him."

"But that was how many years ago now? From what I hear, the man had changed. Became despondent. The language stuff wasn't doing it for him anymore."

"He was thinking of going back home?"

Applebaum shrugged. "That's the scuttlebutt. He went to Germany because there was a friend of his who worked in the embassy there and he wanted to be sure there wouldn't be complications if he decided to repatriate. After so much time, not everybody remembers what uniform you wore back in the day."

"But why decide to go back after all this time in the first place?"

Another shrug. "Might've been Milovan Jelic running for president and looking like a winner. He was pretty tight with Cicut once upon a time. If you're going back, why not when the new president can get you the best seats in the soccer stadium?"

Sylvester didn't like that explanation: It was too logical, and when logic came out of Claude Applebaum's mouth, something was wrong with it somewhere. "Yeah, that would make sense," he said anyway.

"To me, that just adds up to he got something less than a reassurance from this friend of his in the embassy, that the word from home was that Jelic wasn't all that big on memory lane. Cicut couldn't take it. One stress too many."

"That's a big leap."

"Got a better theory?"

He thanked the picture of Cynthia sitting on his sofa with her warning for not only keeping his mouth shut but about not showing he was keeping it shut. "You're the one writing the column. I wouldn't know where to start. Well, say hello to the mountain lions and rattlers for me."

"Isn't there something else you wanted to ask?"

Sylvester didn't have to pretend to be dumbfounded, he *was* dumbfounded, and that in itself felt worth a few points with the prick. But Applebaum was also enjoying himself too much as he poked at the bridge of his glasses and turned back to the screen. "Why of all the subjects I could have pulled out of my hat to get something in for Sunday and get out of here with a clear conscience, I picked Josef Cicut."

"I think I already asked you that."

"You did? I mustn't have heard it. *Buon viaggio.* And if you see Mrs. Cicut, pass along my condolences."

Outside Porterfield's office, Sylvester reassured himself he hadn't given away anything. Either that or he couldn't even beat himself at Lying.

EIGHT

Zagreb.

Informant MJ has reluctantly confirmed the existence of item mentioned in last report. Says he personally witnessed its compilation. Also voiced intemperate suspicion that we are more than aware of its existence and may, in fact, have it in our possession at the present time. Assurances to the contrary appeared to have little impact. Status quo where item is concerned threatening to present relationship. Recommend further reassurances from the highest level.

NINE

Applebaum knew he was flirting with postponing his departure, but he didn't know what else to do. The last thing he needed was Josef Cicut's name popping up on the front page, reminding everyone it had last been seen in a column written by Claude Applebaum. He dared not risk that. But at what cost did he call Bell? The buttoned-down robot never did anything over the phone, always insisted on a face-to-face meeting, and in this case that meant missing his plane for Portland. And for what?

Applebaum took another bite of his ham sandwich. He hadn't missed the paper's cafeteria. Not every commissary had to have the oysters of the German Foreign Ministry or the Farnesina's minestrone in Rome, but there had to be some middle ground between them and the Goodyear rubber on his plate.

He knew he was procrastinating. He didn't want any surprises from Josef Cicut from the cemetery, but calling Bell would also be bringing a lot on himself for so little evidence. What exactly could he say that would justify the queasiness in his stomach and still get him out of the city in time? He took out his Platinum Parker and notebook and made one of the lists that had a way of calming him.

One, Sylvester had been too coy by half. More than that, he had deliberately sought him out, had lied about a call from Cicut, and had asked too many questions about the Sunday column. What would Bell have said to those suspicions? *"If he knew the man, Claude, of course he was curious after hearing he was dead,"* Bell would have said. *"What's unnatural about that?"*

Yes, Claude, what was unnatural about that?

Two, Sylvester's freckle-faced assistant had come into the mailroom with a sheaf of printouts while he had been talking to Joey Bacsik. She had looked uncomfortable to see him there and to all appearances hadn't turned and walked right out again with her papers only because Bacsik had been expecting them and had reached out to take them from her hands. What would Bell have said to that? The first thing he would have asked was whether he had gotten a look at the papers passed to Bacsik, and he would have had to say no, he had gotten no more than a glimpse of widely separated paragraphs, the format he associated with diary entries. And there had been more than one rumor about Cicut's diary-keeping habits, hadn't there? And Bell? *"So you really didn't see what the papers were about. They probably weren't a last will and testament, right? Why would Joey Bacsik be interested in that and why would Sylvester want him interested in it? But suppose Sylvester and Bacsik are in one of these rotisserie baseball leagues and he was just passing along the latest stats or something like that?"*

Yes, Claude, suppose it was just something like that? Suppose the rumors about Cicut's diary had been produced by the same people who swore to UFO sightings?

Applebaum cleared his mouth of the dry ham and bread with another swallow of Sprite. He had every practical reason to side with the objections he could anticipate from Bell. That he knew, Cicut and Sylvester hadn't been in touch for years. Hadn't Sylvester said as much? Or had that just been another of his lies?

He regarded his list with disappointment. He still didn't know what to do. He had less than five hours to make his flight and get away. There wouldn't be another one until the next morning and he had already given back the key to his sister's apartment. He could despise Sylvester just on the grounds of making him indecisive.

"I thought you guys ate in four-star restaurants?"

Applebaum couldn't believe his luck. Joey Bacsik had a tray with enough plates on it to feed three people; no wonder he had ballooned up. "Sit down, Joey."

Bacsik shrugged why not, and spread out his chopped steak and potatoes, carrots and peas, two kinds of rolls, chocolate ice cream, and (just in case a doctor was watching?) a bottle of water. His goggle-like glasses made it a major exercise. "All you people coming and going today," he said, finally stuffing a napkin under his chin. "Like an airport around here."

Applebaum couldn't have hoped for a better opening. "That's right. Sylvester's off somewhere too, isn't he?"

"Sylvester. Martin in Fashions. Klein in Sports. Maybe I'll finally get this building to myself and show everybody how to run it."

"Martin and Klein going to Europe, too?"

"Just Charley. I told him, I said don't go back to what you knew. You won't know it anymore and that'll bug you the whole time you're over there. Go somewhere different. Save yourself the pain. Think he'd listen?"

"Charley Sylvester? No."

Bacsik waved his fork and shot it down in the general direction of his potatoes. "He's a good guy, but I'm talking from experience. When I went back to the old country after 20 years, I kept waiting for people to be the way they were last time I'd seen them. I'm still waiting."

"Czechoslovakia?"

He was offended; not as much as he showed, but a little. "What Czechoslovakia! I was born in Belgrade. My old man got me and my sister out when we were kids, so we might've been a little blank in the head, but we never called ourselves Czechs. Funny people the Czechs. They think everything's a joke."

"I didn't mean . . ."

"Forget it. Czechoslovakia don't exist anymore. Nothing exists but what you keep up here in the noodle. Keep that in mind."

"I'll do that."

"Make sure. Meanwhile, I told them to keep an eye out for any of your packages. They got your Oregon address up on the cork board."

"Thanks."

"Hey, it makes us all feel useful. Won't be long before they're closing that mail room and putting in one computer the size of your thumb to do the same stuff. I tell the young ones, consider yourself lucky you got in before the door closed. Half of them look at me like I'm nuts, the other half is thinking, 'he don't know the half of it, I already got my degree on the next turn of the screw and I'm gonna have his job.' Don't matter to me. I've had mine. Time for somebody else."

"We're all running out of time, Joey."

"You got that right, but I think you got more left in the bank than me."

Applebaum tried to be subtle about glancing at his watch—to no avail. Bacsik hardly raised his thick lenses from his plate as he said: "Don't let me hold you up. You got to catch a plane, get going."

"No, no, I've got a few minutes." But not so many that he could afford another oafish attempt at subtlety. "You doing some special job for Sylvester while he's gone? That was a helluva pile of papers what's-her-name gave you before."

The old man needed a second to remember what he meant. "Oh. The diary. Yeah, some journal Sylvester got. Serbo-Croat. I told him I'd look at a few pages and see if it made any sense. You can imagine what it is."

Applebaum stiffened so quickly he was sure he had given himself away. "No, I can't, Joey. What?"

Bacsik was disappointed in him. "If it's in my lingo and it goes back to the Nineties," he sighed, "what's your guess? Somebody confessing his fucking bloody sins, that's what. Slaughters, massacres, genocide, whatever fancy word they give it. If you were there, you saw ugly. If you saw ugly and wrote it down, it's not something you'd drag out to read your kids around the Christmas tree. Come on, roving correspondent. Maybe you need a few weeks back here in the Style section."

The blind man's laugh was meant as a sympathetic chuckle but felt all the more patronizing for that. Applebaum resigned himself to making two calls—one to Bell and the second to the goddamn airline.

TEN

Sylvester had never confused himself with a sexual Olympian. He had known more women than reception office magazines decreed represented the national average, but most of the women he had known sometimes seemed to have been with different Charley Sylvesters, beguiled by whom he was no longer or by whom he could barely recognize as ever having been. Every time he had felt the itch to count up his conquests over the years (usually after he had been told he wouldn't be adding to the list), he had been diverted by the naivetes, fantasies, and vanities of Those Sylvesters back there; the memory of who had shared his acts of love, one-night stands, and everything in between had never been as mesmerizing as what Narcissus had seen in the pool. The simple act of remembering had rippled him off into some rushing order of names he was glad to have known but also making him as fugitive as the woman he happened to have been with specifically then and specifically there. Even in his marriage with Felicia, as he had been forced to accept belatedly, he had come to go.

He didn't have to tell any of that to Cynthia. And because he didn't she had been taken off guard by his prolonged passion, by his need not to let her orange blossom sweat go even after she had begun to smile up at him and rub his back with frizzy, self-conscious sounds meant to return them to bemusement with their attraction for one another. He held on a moment past that, too, telling himself he wouldn't roll off her until one of their hip bones or thighs demanded it. When he finally conceded that was already too much negotiation for sincerity and lay down next to her, her eyes were waiting for him through the sun from her big bedroom window. "Going to miss me *that* much?"

"You could have come with me."

"Sure."

"I mean it."

"No, you don't. You've been waiting to be alone since you bought your ticket."

"So I should shut up?"

"Good idea."

"I'm sorry."

"You're in the wrong place, Charley. I don't have illusions about that or even that it's just about me. You didn't see yourself this morning. A lunatic letter from a suicide across the world and you were on the scent."

"There's a difference of opinion about the suicide part."

"People don't assume you're about to hear of them dying of a heart attack."

He knew she was right, whatever Applebaum had said. But he still didn't want to accept suicide so easily. "You didn't know Cicut. He listened to his own breath for signs. Most superstitious guy I ever knew. He crossed against the red light, he was convinced he was doomed for the rest of the day."

"And I was talking about you. You've been working the graveyard too long. You should be back doing what you want to do."

"Sounds wonderful. What would that be?"

"Can we be serious for a second?"

"Sorry."

"That's twice. But moving right along. You don't have the excuse of Nick and Pat anymore and you know it."

"Nick's still in school."

"And would you be any further away from him if you sent him checks from where you'd be happier?"

"I'm not far away from him."

"Okay, he's the one who's far away from you."

"That's crap, Cynthia."

"Stupid Cynthia."

He didn't want her withdrawing—not when she was so right. But then he didn't want her antique clock on the bureau across from the foot of the bed to remind them it was time to get back to the office, either.

"That's all you have to say?" she tried again.

He surprised himself. One second he was thinking she was right about everything—about Nick, about Cicut's letter, about his weariness of working on obituaries every day and pinning that on the need to be in New York and not fail the kids. Then he was falling into an even more brittle place where his job as a reporter (and that's what he was, not a compiler of dead names) justified his silence. Let others like Cynthia put their version of the truth on the record. A reporter's job was simply to pass it along, not interject himself personally into the thoughts of others.

"I hope Bacsik can make something of that diary," he heard himself say.

She immediately sat up and showed him all the freckles on her back as she reached down to the floor for her underwear. "Why I'll get through the next couple of weeks," she snapped. "I don't ask for *all* your parts when we're together, but it'd be nice if the one ticking up there showed up once in a while."

"Cyn . . ."

"Three strikes. C'mon, we've got to get back. Or are you telling me you weren't looking at the clock all the time I was talking?"

He didn't tell her that.

ELEVEN

Applebaum was grateful to Walter Bell. Not only wouldn't he miss his flight to Oregon, but Bell had volunteered to come out to the airport to hear what he had to say about Joey Bacsik and the Cicut diary. It was a rare act of grace by the bureaucrats Applebaum had to deal with. Was it due to the regard Bell and his superiors had developed for him? He liked thinking so. He liked thinking he had never been just one more number in some Washington computer file, that he had been appreciated for the good sense he had always tried to impart in his columns. He might not have been right a hundred percent of the time, but if presidents and prime ministers in Europe respected his insights, was it so outrageous to expect some of the same deference in Washington? Claude Applebaum didn't think so.

Bell had taken a lounge divan right up against the panoramic window over the airfield. The huge nose of the Delta 747 was all but poking him in the neck from the other side of the glass, but he had made sure of his isolation; the closest waiting passengers were two Japanese businessmen three divans away. As usual, he was in his pressed blue suit, blue shirt, and dull red tie: as much of a uniform as braids and epaulets. Even his impeccable haircut trim looked like it had come out of some academy. "Good to see you, Claude," he said, half-rising and extending a firm hand. "I appreciate your call on your way off. Get you a drink?"

Applebaum shook his head at the club soda Bell pointed to as his idea of a drink. He hadn't meant to give the impression he was off on an assignment rather than a vacation, but so what if he had? A plane trip was a plane trip, wasn't it? He hated the way Bell had a talent for dropping him into fluttering thoughts without even trying.

"So what's this development you think is so significant?"

Applebaum talked so he wouldn't have to think. At first, Bell nodded and looked eager to hear about Joey Bacsik. Applebaum had never doubted the man had some kind of bionic recorder behind his pale blue eyes. More than once Bell had surprised him by throwing up a minuscule detail from a months-old conversation despite never having overtly taken notes at the time. Joey Bacsik and Charley Sylvester were now on Walter Bell's hard drive. But then after a couple of minutes, Bell seemed more interested in his club soda than in what he was being told. The Cicut diary might have been just another soda bubble evaporating under his eyes.

"That's interesting, Claude," he said, a second too long before the silence between them. "Definitely worth a follow-up."

Applebaum hadn't expected a victory parade, but he had definitely expected more than a "worth a follow-up." "Contain your elation, Walter."

Bell gave his smile to his glass, then changed his mind about that, too. "It's a journal, all right," he said. "We've heard talk about it. Certainly, our friend in the East has. Seems to make him nervous."

"Then he's going to be twice as nervous if Charley Sylvester has it."

"Don't like the man?"

"I didn't say that. I just . . ."

Bell nodded too quickly. "Got it. One of these Woodward-Bernstein types? Only the facts, ma'am, the way Sergeant Friday used to say?"

Applebaum could have done without the combination of sarcasm and fixed stare at the soda. "If you want to be trite, Walter, that's your prerogative. But your superiors might be interested."

"Absolutely. I didn't mean to suggest otherwise. Sylvester—married to an Italian fashion model or something?"

"Long divorced from her, and not a model. One of those magazine style writers who knows too much about couches and settees."

"Right, right."

"The journal, Walter."

"No, no, you're absolutely right. I know for a fact that our European friends would like to know what happened to it."

"They've been in touch with you about it?"

Bell seemed to chide himself for saying too much. "In a way. But the important thing for us at the moment is for you to stay out of it. That column we discussed last time about Cicut . . ."

"Already written. For the Sunday edition."

For the first time, Bell looked uncertain. "Well, that might be a bad idea, Claude. The situation has become somewhat fluid in the last few days, and it might be better for you to keep away."

"What're you talking about, *fluid?* I told you it's already written."

The man couldn't imagine why that was a problem. "Can't be the first time you've asked for your column back. What's his name—Porterfield? Tell him you've come into possession of some new facts since you wrote what you did and you'd rather wait a few days. Isn't that the way you do it?"

Applebaum felt his heat coloring his ears. Now he was being told how to do his own job? "It's not that simple. They have schedules. Sometimes they promote specific pieces. It's a whole organizational . . ."

Bell wasn't impressed. "Promote a piece on Josef Cicut? Really think so? I read your Op-ed page all the time. This one is on vacation. That one's column won't appear today. Book tours. Illnesses. C'mon, Claude. You know you can kill that piece. And I'll bet you it doesn't leave a big hole on the page, that they'll find something else."

Applebaum had missed it: the turn from the amiable to the unpleasant. But there was definitely something unpleasant in Walter Bell's expression as he finished off his club soda without moving his hard drive eyes from him.

TWELVE

Leonard Warneke hesitated over the coins in his hand. He had only two half-euros, a euro, and a two-euro piece. He would have sworn he had picked up smaller change during the day, but apparently not. The question now was, was even half a euro a little extravagant for the Trevi Fountain? He had nothing against tradition and nothing against one day returning to Rome, but a half-euro seemed a lot for a superstition. If he could think of anything to buy at the kiosk behind him that would leave him with 10- or 20-cent pieces, he would buy it.

The giggling French couple with their miniature camera decided for him. By stepping in front of him to block his direct view of Oceanus, they all but delivered a criticism of his stinginess from the gods. To right matters again, he penalized himself by ignoring the half-euro in favor of the one-euro piece, kerplopping it in the water and watching it settle into the United Nations of coins on the floor of the basin. Instantly, it went from being his to being nobody's. The French woman with the short auburn hair smiled at him for fulfilling his obligations.

Warneke put a spring in his step walking away from the fountain; tossing the coin made him feel ceremonial. Depending on how he looked at it, he had paid his way into the ages or ingratiated himself with the petty thieves who waited for the tourists to thin out so they could go scavenging in the fountain. He could have passed muster on either count. It might have been a few years now, but he could still hold a conversation with anyone in

the piazza about the deleterious effects of the Age of Enlightenment on ancient Attic thought. The weathered university card in
his wallet might have barely shown his name after so many years,
but it had still gotten him into two days of conferences without
having to pay an admission. Nobody had challenged his credentials, at least once the unctuous organizer had declared his "understanding" of how niceties like intelligible university IDs had
been an afterthought in the Balkans for some time. The man had
been so insufferable in his assumption of administrative chaos
in Zagreb that Warneke had been tempted to tell him he hadn't
been inside a classroom for almost a decade. But instead, he had
only nodded politely as the great Italian understander suggested
he get new credentials when he returned home.

What he might have also told the pompous fool was that
he had dealt with more than his share of the gutter types who
scavenged for coins in fountains. He hadn't asked to know them,
might never have left the university in the name of a "more authentic" life if he had known they were waiting up the road for
him, but known more than one of their kind in more than one
city he had. Thanks to growing up in a *lumpenproletariat* district
he could speak their lingo whatever the language; thanks to the
muscle tone he had developed in sports he had never had to back
away when somebody hadn't liked what he had to say in the lingo.
Warneke the troubleshooter, as Franjo and the other party lead-
ers called him, and when he was honest with himself, he could
accept that he had been better at that than he had ever been
in front of a classroom talking about Plato and Aristotle. Within
his university department alone there had been three more per-
ceptive instructors when it came to something like Plotinus, but
where were his rivals when it came to intimidating goons to leave
cities (Dubrovnik and Budapest), planting documents with refugee groups that made them vulnerable to the local police (Tirana),
or looking into hostile professional associations abroad (Belgrade
and Bucharest)? He didn't have any rivals, at least within his
own party, and he had managed his movements without leaving
behind his name. Down to it, the "authentic life" he had once

wanted so urgently had little by little made him not so much a troubleshooter as an invisible man.

Warneke shook off that thought as he made his way back to his hotel; it was invariably the prelude to a fit of despondency. Already, he had to admit a sliver of guilt that he would be returning home with more information on the "Giovanni Battista Vico and Human History" conference than on the movements of Elena Cicut. The reminder that Franjo had not expected much from his surveillance of her didn't help, it just made him feel absurdly, squeamishly defensive. And about what? He had warned them before leaving Zagreb. What was he supposed to have done if he saw the mailman delivering the famous diary to the widow—knock the man over, grab it, and run to the airport? Only the prospect of a few days vacation in Rome had stopped him from laughing aloud at Franjo's reply of "Just knowing she has or doesn't have it will be sufficient for now. Once we know one way or the other, we'll take the next step."

The next step to what? More knowledge for itself?

Sometimes he wondered how far he had traveled from the abstractions of the classroom, after all.

The vibration of the phone in his pocket offered two possibilities: the French woman with the short auburn hair from the fountain had decided to leave her husband and camera for him or Franjo wanted another useless report. Why wasn't he surprised when the voice in his ear wasn't that of the French woman?

"I told you I would get back to you if . . ."

"That's not why I'm calling, Leonard. We have further information that will require you to remain in Rome a few days."

Warneke was taken aback by the tone. There was humorless Franjo, and then there was super-humorless Franjo who might have really had something important to convey. He walked his phone over to the entrance of a toy store so he could have the super-humorless Franjo all to himself. "I'm listening."

Franjo grunted as though that in itself was an accomplishment. "The widow doesn't have the diary yet because from what we have learned it wasn't sent to her. It was sent to an American journalist who happens to be arriving in Rome today."

"Where did you get that information?"

"Irrelevant, Leonard. The point is that the journalist . . . do you have a pen?"

Warneke was astonished by the array of electronic toys in front of him. Nine-year-olds were apparently now expected to be able to do everything from solving rhomboid puzzles to launching rockets to Mars. What had happened to simple galactic wars between alien races? Play station and movie violence was one thing, but shouldn't there also have been the imaginative kind connecting mind to hands to palpable plastic or metal? Had he been born too early or too late?

"I asked if you had a pen."

"If I answer, will you promise not to ask again?"

THIRTEEN

Sylvester had prepared for all the changes he expected to find in Rome after seven years except for one—him in the middle of them. More spacious passageways in the airport, flashier billboards with unfamiliar actors for new movies, recently white-washed statues, freshly sanded *palazzi,* repainted corner kiosks promoting magazines he had never heard of, supermarkets in place of grocery and convenience stores, the latest Fiat models for taxis—he had noticed some of those changes in the Italian movies he had ordered from Netflix, but that had not been the same thing as taking them in in person. Instead of the director of his expectations, he felt like the lowliest of extras trying to grasp why everybody had been busy shifting sets around him. The Fiumicino customs officer regarded him as just one more American tourist with zero knowledge of what he was about to encounter. The cab driver from the airport to the city ignored his still good Italian to speak in tourism English. And once they were ensnared by the inevitable morning traffic jam around Piazza Venezia, he was just another cartoon foreigner in the back of a cab for the children gaping out at him from the blue Audi alongside. He might never have lived in the city at all.

The Albergo Reggio behind Piazza Navona he tried to accept as a compromise. He was still a visitor living in a hotel, but it was a hotel he knew, one where he had put up years of acquaintances while he had been living in the city. It didn't hurt that the cueball-head manager Romolo remembered him and asked

polite questions he might have asked after one year rather than
seven. The man's only blunder was in asking about Felicia, bringing various shades of red to his face when he got the answer.
Sylvester considered that a tradeoff for the small fact that Felicia
had apparently not been using the Reggio—*his* hotel—for her own
acquaintances.

He sized up his first-floor room directly above the entrance
awning as a mixed blessing. The good part was that he hadn't
been stowed away for a view of alley drain pipes, in fact, was close
to getting wet from every splash of the fountain outside the front
door. The bad part was that he was also on top of the bronchial-
motored scooters that ripped up and down the street. He knew
from past open windows that he would get a lot more of both the
good and the bad in the early morning hours when the water
sprites babbled serenely in the quiet between descents by every
dirt bike racer on the continent.

When someone knocked on the door, his first thought was
that it was Romolo to tell him that a mistake had indeed been
made and that his reservation had been for a broom closet on the
top floor. He was still working out this abrupt attack of insecurity
when he opened the door to Eddie Roenicke. He stood hobbled.
He had seen Roenicke in New York a few times, but then he had
just been another correspondent dropping by the office during
his holiday. On his own turf, where he had once been callowness
personified and was now beginning to gray above the ears, the
spindly giraffe dated both of them.

"Charley!"

Sylvester was helpless against the bear hug so didn't resist it.
"A reception committee?" he got out.

"The electronic age. You were being tracked every mile across
the Atlantic. I thought I'd pass up an hour or two of official
communiques."

"No sacrifice too great, huh?"

Roenicke took in the room looking duty-bound to show his
approval of it. The first time Sylvester had seen that expression
had been in his own home when the ages-younger substitute Eddie Roenicke had dropped by to get the keys to the office and

ask a lot of questions about Tunisia he couldn't have sounded less interested in. It had occurred to him only later that Roenicke might have been confirming how far away the Sylvesters would be in North Africa so he would feel free to do his little story on Josef Cicut. "I know you're jet-lagged, but that's not going to get you out of something tall and cold in the Navona. C'mon. You can unpack later."

He didn't argue. He couldn't think of a better tonic for his cramped legs than walking the few yards over to the Piazza Navona and then sprawling them out under a sidewalk table while he sank into something with ice cubes. On the way there, Roenicke kept up a monologue that needed only a polite grunt or two for response—about his wife Myra and her involvement in a church theater group, about the small dinner party she had planned for him, about the office secretary Claudia's orders that he drop around to see her (implying she wouldn't be invited to the dinner party). And mention of Claudia led to the nuts and bolts of the job—the office computer that needed a geek's attention every week, New York's habit of consigning his dispatches to the website and giving print preference to anything from the Middle East, his frustration with Porterfield's return to the old policy of swatting aside anything to do with Italy except the Vatican or some sex scandal.

"In the old days there wasn't even a website. You're ahead of the game. I thought you were big on the electronic age."

Roenicke snorted. Somewhere inside his practiced weariness he was still the kid who didn't care what toes he stepped on. Sylvester had always admired that quality in him, and didn't really care that it had been helped along by generations of Roenickes on the paper's board of trustees. "When you get down to it, Charley, the paper is still the paper, as in P A P E R."

"And I thought I was the relic!"

He wouldn't have minded a protest ("Who would have ever said that about *you*, Charley?"), at least for show. But back within the piazza's towering demands from Bernini and Borromini, he offered Roenicke's missed opportunity up for the comfort that quickly came over him to be back where he had spent mornings baby-sitting Patricia and Nick, afternoons meeting sources for his stories, and long nights having one drink too many with friends. That he could tell, the major changes were more Indians and Slavs selling the chains and cheap jewelry that had once been the monopoly of Somalis and Ethiopians and another bar in the northern corner across from the center island. It was there that Roenicke headed. "Sun doesn't hit here for another hour or so," he said, sounding very much like the home team.

He waited for his gin and tonic before gearing up for Josef Cicut questions. That Roenicke hadn't already mentioned the man he didn't consider especially suspicious, he just would have liked the name to have come up the way other things had.

". . . The economy, the economy, the economy. For entertainment there's going down to the bar and playing the slot machines. The whole damn country is turning into Atlantic City. That's mainly what they mean by . . ."

"The economy, the economy, the economy."

"Right. You got out of here just in time, Charley."

"How about you? You're here a long time now."

"I know. They make sounds about moving me. I pretend not to hear them. They pretend they never made them until somebody brings up the contract again. But Myra loves it here and . . . Well, I do too, I guess."

"You guess?"

Roenicke smiled haplessly and gazed out to where a mother was chasing after a tot about to lose his shorts. "So what do you think about this Cicut business? Sad ending for him, huh?"

Sylvester felt a beat behind. If Roenicke had been trying to avoid the topic, he had apparently found another one—his long stationing in the city—that appealed to him even less. "Applebaum said it was a heart attack. That he wanted to return home and couldn't take being told he couldn't."

"You saw Claude?"

"Before I left. He seems to have been here a lot lately."

"No more than usual."

"Then he's been playing fast and loose with datelines."

Roenicke didn't smile; "We don't bother one another," he said. "But as for Cicut, the Italian papers have stayed away from the widow and so have we."

"*We?*"

"Correspondents."

"I'd have thought you would be especially . . ."

"Never going to forgive me for that? I thought it was a story, that's all."

"That's not what I'm asking, Eddie. I just thought you might have some extra insights others wouldn't. Applebaum, for instance."

"What do you mean?"

"When I left, he was doing a little thing on Cicut called Fish Out of Water."

"You're kidding." He shished like a kid half his age.

"I can't figure out why the Great Man would devote one of his Sunday sermons to somebody like Cicut."

Roenicke shrugged; he had no idea, either—the way people didn't have ideas about what they had very clear ideas about. And then he had an even clearer thought: "You used to be close. Going to see the widow while you're here?"

Sylvester took a sip of gin wondering how long that question had been warming in the oven. Since they had started talking about Cicut? Since they had been walking over from the hotel? Or had it been since Roenicke had decided to drop by the Albergo Reggio to welcome an old colleague? "I might. Any objections?"

"Of course not. You were friends."

He had been careful not to tell Applebaum about the letter and diary sent from Mainz. He hadn't expected it to feel equally instinctive not to tell Roenicke about them.

FOURTEEN

As soon as Roenicke had left with a reminder of the dinner party, Sylvester took Cicut's letter from his jacket pocket to confirm the address where Elena and Philip were living. Vicolo del Moro was across the Tiber in Trastevere, not behind the Chiesa Nuova, the place where he and Felicia had known the family. He remembered Vicolo del Moro as a dowdy street, a narrow, cobblestone slip of dusty shops and cheap *trattorie* with crow's-nest apartments crowding the sky. After the sprawling place behind the Chiesa Nuova, that didn't sound like there had been too many profitable days for the translation agency, if it still existed at all.

He couldn't find out sitting at his sidewalk table. When he walked inside the bar to ask for a phone directory, the two bartenders looked at him as though he hadn't heard the blacksmith shop had closed a century ago. "Everybody has a cellphone," one of them shrugged toward a space where there had once evidently been a pay phone and directory, "so we used the space for something better."

He didn't know how an elaborate display of the weekly soccer lottery results and a poker machine were "something better," but Roenicke seemed to have had a point about national priorities. He returned to his table outside for planning his next move without knowing if the agency still existed. The choices were two: Go back to the hotel to look at its directory (assuming it still had one) and then take a nap to rest his legs but also prolong his jet lag for another day or drag himself immediately over to Trastevere to see Elena Cicut and cut off a lot of empty conjecturing. He consulted the tall character with the sandy crewcut and black leather wrist bands sitting on the stone bench on the piazza's island directly in front of the bar. The man had shown only his muscular back since camping down. His big hands grasped the bench as he rocked gently back and forth and kept an eye on the nearest chain sellers, a blond husband-wife team with Eastern Europe written across their pouchy faces. There was something exacting about the crewcut's vigilance that said he didn't trust the vendors. If he wasn't a cop on the lookout for peddling violation, he was the king of the chain sellers making sure his underlings weren't ripping him off. Did such a man of the world recommend going back for a nap or yoking his legs then and there over to see Elena Cicut?

He heard the answer and couldn't have agreed more. On the way over to the river he ignored the whining of his legs to discipline them into good behavior. He sank into the Basilica of Sant'Andrea where Patricia had always wanted to go to see the frescoes, into the Campo d' Fiori market where he had once gotten into a slapstick fist fight with a clumsy pickpocket, and into the State pawn office where Felicia had once marched their cutlery to dramatize her insistence that he demand a raise from New York and where he had had to spend the rest of the day trying to retrieve the stuff. He wasn't sure he wanted his thoughts to overhear his laugh at Felicia's theatrics and the pawn shop scene. But yes, sometimes he *did* miss brawls like that with her. Her rages had almost been worth her snooty Parioli airs. And he too had been less worried about practicalities in those days, and not always for the worse.

So why had everything turned so serious? Why had she one day not only wanted to be free of him, but undo what they had created together in Patricia and Nick? That was a gene he had never understood, right down to the final morning when she had whirled around the apartment making sure the kids hadn't left anything out of their suitcases they would miss in America. He had watched her in trickling horror that morning, having to accept that not only wasn't she going to back down before the confusion on the kids' faces but surrendering to the hateful idea

that she was in such a hurry to get them out to the airport because she wanted to get to a buyer she had already lined up for
the apartment. It had never been career with her, no matter how
many times he had used that as shorthand with other people;
having a family had never compromised her mobility in the ritzy
magazine world, and she had always said as much. What having
a family had threatened was something much simpler—the *next*.
What was around the corner. What could test her in a way she
hadn't been tested before. What might have been a disaster or
might have a triumph, but what one way or the other would have
had her name on it, would have been hers and hers alone. For
a few years he had been the first to profit from that obsession,
and then the kids had. But then, more finally than he had ever
wanted to acknowledge, husbands and children were no longer
the next, couldn't offer her that promise.

There was a tepid breeze off the Ponte Sisto, and Sylvester
paused in the middle of the bridge to watch the Tiber move tur-
gidly under him. The labored movement toward the sea struck
him as senseless, familiarly so. He remembered what Joey Bacsik
had said about going to France to meet new people instead of
looking up those in Rome he hadn't seen in years. When he got
right down to it, who was there besides Bruno Lepri he could have
done without running into again? With the charter members of
the Correspondents Club, like Maitland and Barfoed and Billy
Pope, he could already hear their greeting to one another and the
instantly trailing sensation that the reunion hadn't been worth
it. By comparison he might have looked forward to seeing Felicia.

Feeling suddenly exposed standing above the sludgy river, he
walked faster to the other side of the bridge.

There had been a few changes on Vicolo del Moro since he
had seen it last. The restaurants didn't look so cheap anymore,
for one thing. They were still tiny, all but shoehorned into claustrophobic spaces, but with the kind of elaborate window lettering
that advertised vaguely foreign gentility. Number 2 was a textiles
shop with stacks of canary yellow and rose Asian silks cramming
the single window. Next to it was a sliver of a doorway for two
upstairs apartments. One bell said MARTINI, the other nothing

at all. He rang the nothing, waiting so long for a response he had visions of his great transatlantic mission ending right then and there. But then the intercom barked, and he recognized Elena Cicut's voice even in her single wary *si?*

"Elena, it's Charley Sylvester."

"*Chi?*"

"Charley Sylvester. You remember. Nick's father."

This time the silence felt personal, and he scratched his memory, as he had on the plane, to recall if there had been some specific spat with the Cicuts that had produced their gradual estrangement before he had returned to New York. Aside from the coolness over Roenicke's article, he couldn't remember anything. Even Felicia had been careful around them, partly because she had liked Elena, partly because an ex-ambassador might always introduce her to someone with pedigree. "Charles?" the voice relented through the static. "Nick and Patricia?"

"Right. Can I come up a second?"

A skinny brunette in jeans and a black training bra came out of the dress shop with a cigarette and a plastic lighter in her hand. She smiled blankly, then got down to the serious business of lighting up. He wouldn't have minded a whiff or two from the cigarette to remind him of how he had been smoking the last time he had been in Trastevere, but the buzzer chose that moment to open the front door. The wall flanking the inside staircase had water stains and lumped plaster it had probably had for a couple of centuries, and the rickety steps under him couldn't have been much newer. Cats might not have lived in the hallway, but they had dropped by on occasion.

Elena Cicut stood wedged into the door to the left of the stairs on the first landing. There was a stray curl hanging down over her forehead from her short, reddish hair. Her lumpish face had always made Sylvester think of someone who had awakened with a start, and now she looked to have been stirred from a nightmare. She might have accepted who he was but that didn't earn him a totally open door. "Charles?" she asked, holding on to her doorknob.

"Who else would go around claiming to be me?"

She didn't have to resist smiling very hard. "I am sorry you came now," she said, accent on every word. "This is a very bad time for me."

"I know, Elena. I heard."

There was a flicker of hesitation, about something besides a dead husband as her idea of a bad time. He handed her Cicut's letter through the door space, wondering how the years had reduced them to that to be more at ease with one another. She took the letter suspiciously, but kept one hand on the doorknob against him. He didn't want to watch her reading it, he already felt enough like a process server, so he looked off at the soot-covered bulb in a corner of the landing. It annoyed him that it was on in the middle of the day and he was tempted to do the landlord's job for him by unscrewing it. The apartment belonging to MARTINI was another flight up.

"Come in."

The door was wide open when Sylvester looked back. There was a strong mint odor in the vestibule, and the hall wall was covered with dull prints of stick figures hunting ducks in marshlands. He followed her through the dark hallway toward the back over checkerboard red and black tiles, only her chunkiness seemed the same. Her print dress fit badly, practically tilting off her left shoulder, and she scraped along on tattered slippers. He had never known her indoors when she hadn't been traipsing around barefoot, to the point that Cicut had been a nag in his warnings about the splinters, nail heads, and other nemeses on their wooden floors lurking in ambush to jab her.

She led him into a small, square room, about half the size of the living room at the Chiesa Nuova. The only window was over an alley; a clothes line with nothing on it stretched over to a scrawny post. "Sit down. Please."

He recognized the Balkan wall rugs, the brown and rust slip cover thrown over the divan she directed him to, and the needlework on the back of the tall armchair she took. There had to be another whole living room of pieces from the old place somewhere in storage or (was it possible?) in the State pawn shop.

She reached over the wicker table between them to hand him back the letter. She didn't want to hold it longer than she had to and he took it back not knowing what use it had now. And how could she not have been curious about Cicut's allusion to the diary? "You look well, Charles," she said, a strain in her voice. "How are the children? Nick must be studying at the university by now, yes?"

"Columbia."

"That has a very good reputation. And Patricia? She must be in her twenties. Out of the university, yes?"

He could sense her trying out her English sentences after a very long time. "She works at my newspaper."

"That must make you happy."

He seldom thought of it so simply. "Yes. Yes, it does."

There might have been less furniture, but there were a lot more butts in the ashtray on the wicker table between them than he had ever associated with her. At most, she had bummed a cigarette or two from him after dinner.

"You do not have to apologize," she said, finding her smile, but more weariness with it. "You are afraid you will look astonished if you look at me too directly."

Sylvester would have been embarrassed if he hadn't remembered she had fished for compliments even when her eyes hadn't had so many rings under them and her hands hadn't looked so weather-beaten. "I imagine you've had a rough time lately."

She dropped her gaze to the ashtray. "No, it has not been easy."

"I didn't know Josef had heart problems."

Either had she; she had to look deeper into the ashtray before that particular lie disappeared. But she took his opening. "We all get older."

"Why would he write to me after so long, Elena?"

"You were friends."

"Who hadn't communicated in years. And this letter makes me wonder. Are you satisfied Josef died of a heart attack?"

She had to order her attention away from the ashtray. "Why would I not think so? You mean what he says there about being

gone by the time you read it? Have you forgotten Josef's hypo-
chondria? A cold was pneumonia, a cut on his hand a reason to
amputate the hand. Surely, you remember that."

He should have; it had been part of the man's endless super-
stitions. "Were there many at the funeral? I didn't see any reports
about the body being shipped down here."

"It was not."

"You and Philip had to go up there?"

"No. We were separated, Charles. After the agency went . . .
There is so much you probably do not know. The agency went
bankrupt. Another victim of the Internet. So many things these
days are easier for people to get, or think they are getting. The few
translations that came Josef and I had to do ourselves to survive.
That took its toll on all of us. Josef was never a man who adjusted
easily. You remember that at least?"

Sylvester heard the reprimand or the warning or whatever it
was, and nodded. He was sure she hadn't missed the allusion in
the letter to the diary. But as with Applebaum and Roenicke, he
had a strong feeling he was better off not mentioning it.

"We finally had to give up the place on Governo Vecchio and
move here. But practically the day we moved in, he was moving out again, at least in his mind. Worrying about money just
never entered Josef's world. As far as he was concerned, that
should have been behind us once and for all. There were too
many arguments about nothing, then he said he needed time
away by himself. He had an associate from the agency who was
away for the summer, so he took that apartment. In exchange
for watering the man's plants! Can you imagine! Hamlet taking
care of plants?"

"Hamlet?"

She shrugged; she was past defending at least one corner of
their marriage. "It is what I called him when he went on as though
there was an audience listening to him. All great sorrow and evil
fate."

"But things were so bad between you you couldn't go up to
the funeral?"

Something clever came into her eyes—clever and bitchy. "You could not imagine yourself in such a mood when you broke up with Felicia?"

He had left himself open for that, but also realized his answer was no. "I was told he went to Germany because he planned to repatriate and there was a friend up there in the embassy."

Finally, a piece of the facade crumbled. "Who told you that?"

"Somebody from my paper."

"This Roenicke?"

"No, somebody else."

She was surprised. "Josef's affairs were more public than I knew."

"So it's true?"

"He spoke about that like he spoke about a lot of things when our situation became difficult. He certainly did not mention that reason specifically when he called before leaving for Germany."

"He must have given you some reason for going there."

She pretended not to hear his skepticism. "He had a friend from school up there in the embassy. Sima Glauber. I just assumed he wanted to get away for a few days and have Glauber tell him everything would be all right."

She said it so facilely he didn't think he owed her politeness. "And who would be taking care of these plants while he did that?"

She didn't like being jabbed, but at bottom she didn't care too much about that, either. "Do you have a cigarette, Charles?"

"Sorry. Gave them up a few years ago."

"The health worries of Americans." She regretted it as soon as it came out of her mouth. But it also gave her an opening to dismiss him. "This really is a bad time, Charles," she said, standing abruptly. "I am sorry that letter got you to come so far, but there is nothing I can tell you about it. Perhaps if you are going to be here for . . ."

He had to stand up with her, but he didn't have to tell her he hadn't come to Italy just because of the letter. "I'll be here a couple of weeks." She hadn't wanted to hear that. "Why don't we have dinner the day after tomorrow? I'd say tomorrow, but I've been drafted into a dinner by Roenicke and I don't think you'd like it too much."

That much she was sure of. "I think not," she said, moving more quickly around the wicker table to lead him back to the door. "Why not call me and we will see what we can arrange in a few days?"

She was so insincere that he was distracted by it all the way back through the gloomy hallway to the front door before an obvious subject occurred to him. "And the invitation is for Philip too, of course. How's he doing?"

She pulled back the front door lock with a force that said she had lost a bet with herself. "Fine. He is not in Rome right now. He is at school."

"Summer school?"

"Yes, a special studies program. I'm afraid he has taken after his parents in his obsession with languages." She extended her hand stiffly. "It was very nice seeing you again, Charles. Please do call."

Sylvester ignored her hand and took her by the shoulders to kiss her on both cheeks. She smelled of soap and cigarettes, and didn't want to be kissed. He didn't give a goddamn about what she wanted. That was the way they had done it in the past. "I *will* call you, Elena."

FIFTEEN

Sylvester was glad he had insisted on the kiss. It was custom, a minor thing, but as he went down the stairs to the street he wanted to believe it had taken her so off-guard that he had recovered something from his babbling to her. With his goodbye he had reached back into his past with Elena Cicut—acquaintance who had become friend, to his children as well as to him—and declared that whatever had been going on since they had last seen one another, he wasn't going to just disappear.

When he stepped out into the street, he almost fell back again from the blinding sun. His memory of how dim Vicolo del Moro was clearly needed work. The blaze seemed focused over the fountain at the end of the block. In the middle of it a green sedan was screeching off up toward the Lungotevere for no good reason.

Until he saw a reason in the driver—the sandy crewcut who had been sitting on the bench in front of his bar in the Piazza Navona.

He watched the car speed away for too many passive seconds. But then a couple with a black poodle crossed in front of it, and the driver had to brake. The seconds came back, giving him time to read the license plate. The only piece of paper he had was Cicut's letter. It felt appropriate he use that for his jotting as the crewcut got back into gear and continued up to the Lungotevere and out of sight.

Appropriate enough almost to overcome his shaking hand and trace over the number 8 to make it more intelligible.

SIXTEEN

Warneke had overreached, and he knew why. Whatever illusions he might have entertained to the contrary now and then, he had never dealt well with more than one situation at a time. He was a plodder, a soldier ant, a grader only of the paper in front of his eyes. That had been true as far back as the procrastinating years when he had tried to go on teaching while spending more and more time on politics, usually botching both. His parents might have said it had even been true when he had ignored their birthday gifts until he had derived all the pleasure there was to be gotten from those of his grandparents and uncles. His ex-wife Monika would certainly have said it of a doting on her that had finally become indistinguishable from possessiveness even for him. Now again, he had been fine as long as his target—dubious as it was—had been the Cicut woman. But the additional responsibility of keeping an eye on the American Sylvester had made him careless. And that was without counting the lull he had put himself in thinking that dumb surveillance of the widow, good restaurant meals, and philosophy conferences had added up to more of a vacation than work.

With what result? With the result that not only were the widow and the American aware of him, but that Sylvester had had enough time to copy down his license plate. So unnecessary practicality number one: return his rental car before Sylvester tracked it down to the agency. And unnecessary practicality number two:

call Franjo to tell him what had happened and to admit he had to be replaced.

But Franjo didn't want to hear that. "So you don't get so close to them."

"I don't think you're hearing me . . ."

"I hear you very well, Leonard. But we have no one to send in your place right now. This is your job."

"And if Sylvester tracks me down through the car agency?"

Franjo laughed; superciliously. "He works for a newspaper, not the CIA."

"If you think it's funny."

He didn't, not that much; Franjoe didn't think anything was funny that much. "One way or another, this master detective has to get license information from the police."

"And from there go straight to the rental agency with my hotel address."

Condescension. "Well, I could suggest the mammoth step of changing hotels. But instead I'll just give you the number of somebody who will inform us immediately if there have been any inquiries with the police about your license."

"It would really be much easier if I came home."

"We already discussed that point, Leonard. Give it until to-morrow morning and then call this acquaintance of mine. He will have no trouble remembering me."

"This is a mistake, Franjo."

He had stopped listening. "Do you have a pen?"

Warneke knew he had become as humorless as Franjo when he said yes.

SEVENTEEN

ylvester knew where to find Bruno Lepri.There were thousands of *ristoranti, trattorie, osterie,* and *bottiglierie* in Rome, but Bruno Lepri could have counted on one hand the number of times he had eaten lunch anywhere but at Giuliana's near the big Sunday flea market at Porta Portese. The place was barely visible from the Viale Trastevere thoroughfare--- a dumpy fettuccine and wine cantina three doors off into a side street, no sign anywhere announcing its name or even what was being sold inside. If not for a couple of mineral water decals in the corners of the smoked window, it could have been a tailor's shop or a second-hand bookstore as much as a *bottiglieria*. The first time he had gone with Bruno, it had been with a what-the-hell-anything-once attitude. After that he had looked forward to whatever pasta the severe owner Giuliana had decreed was going to be the single item served during the day. The white wine with the consistency of an oil slick he had never gotten used to, though drinking it straight rather than following Bruno's habit of mixing it with Coca-Cola had allowed for the illusion of being a connoisseur.

Because he had decided to walk to the *bottigliera* from the hotel, to shake the overlong sleep his jet lag had insisted on, Sylvester was sodden with sweat by the time he walked in the door. But he was relieved instantly by the coolness reeking of the wine soaked into the walls and floor boards. Little had changed since his last visit. The ceiling fan still squeaked and still looked on the verge of spinning off its axis down onto one of the seven or eight spindly tables under it. Most of the customers were still those who worked the counters of the nearby shops now closed for lunch; two others were from the state power company, apparently taking a break from fixing a street line. With one exception all of them were bent busily over their plates, conversation all but non-existent, looking intimidated about signaling approval or criticism to Giuliana about what they were shoveling down. Giuliana, an ageless 50 a decade ago and sure to be the same age a decade from then, stood vigilantly in front of the freezer in the back, her big forearms folded over one another, equally ready for any attack on the bottles of soda visible behind her or for some foolish comment from one of the tables. The exception to the eating was a table against a side wall where three men were in the middle of a *scopone* game. Bruno, whiter in his mustache and wearing one of the inevitable plaid sports shirts he found in the cartons he loaded and unloaded for a living, was seated backwards in his chair kibbitzing. He was the last one in the place to notice the new arrival. "*Dio santo!*"

As the little man jumped up from his chair and rushed over to hug him, Sylvester was sorry Joey Bacsik wasn't there to see why looking up old friends was better than going to France. He himself was surprised by the depth of joy he felt in being back again with the odd-jobs hustler who had never been capable even of laments (and they were constant) without sounding enthusiastic about them.

"*Sei invecchiato, Charley!*"

"*E tu, no?*"

He recognized some of the faces they passed to a deserted back table and he knew they recognized him, but nobody volunteered a nod, let alone a hello. He had always been *l'americano*, the dubious source of Bruno's endless tales about New York and Chicago, and they didn't easily forgive the hours of torment he had been indirectly responsible for. Giuliana recognized him, too, enough to give him her usual greeting of waiting impatiently until he had stopped mopping his face with his handkerchief and cleared his arms completely away from the table so she had room to bang down two glasses and a half-liter of house white. Bruno had hardly launched into the wonders of her latest marinara sauce when she pivoted around and scraped back to her guard post in front of the freezer. Bruno whinnied a laugh, but low enough so he didn't invite trouble. "You can see she's had a personality transplant . . . *Cin-cin.*"

Sylvester was perversely glad the wine was as bad as ever; what he didn't see was the Coca-Cola. "Doctor says no more," Bruno said with a frown. "He probably meant the wine too, but I got out of there before he told me. The more you let people talk, the more you wonder why you did."

"That go for you, too?"

Bruno cast a grin over at the other tables. He really didn't have freckles or even acne on his face anymore; the spots had become so substantial they looked like brown berries. "The day they stop listening to me, they'll have nothing left to think about but their own ideas, and that's the last thing they want. But tell me about you. What are you doing here? Coming back to work?"

He made sure to stick the word *vacation* up front, not to repeat the false impression he had left with Elena Cicut the day before. He told him about Patricia and Nick, both of whom Bruno had drafted one time or another to help set up flea market tables for his employer of the week. (What he didn't tell him was about the shiver he had felt the evening Nick, mad about having to go to a high school class on a Saturday morning, had sulked about going back to Rome and getting a permanent job as Bruno's assistant.) He told him about the office cracks that came with being the obituaries editor. (What he didn't tell him was that, as Cynthia had said, he had begun to suffocate under the cracks and, more than he had ever admitted to himself on the other side of the ocean, needed to move on.) What bothered him after so long was that he didn't have more to tell, that he listened to Bruno's accounts of the same weekly flea markets, same maybe-serious-maybe-not-serious affairs, same dreams about getting out of the city, almost as if he were doing the talking and Bruno the listening.

Bruno pretended to be diplomatic about the next question. "And the *Signora*? You see her yet?"

"I'm barely landed, Bruno."

"But . . ."

"Of course I'm going to see her. It just takes a little working up to."

Bruno grinned. He and Felicia had never liked each other, both aware from their first meeting in a Trastevere cafe that he wasn't the kind of person who was going to help the Sylvesters in Rome society. The showdown had come when she had heard he frequented the underground gambling joints in the old slaughter house section of the city and had dragged her husband along there one night on the pretext of getting a feature story for the paper. "And if the police had raided while you were there?" she had demanded to know the next day. "They don't raid those places, Felicia," he had said with more self-assurance than he had felt at the time. "That's how they stay in business. The cops get their cut . . ."

Which brought him back to the license plate he had jotted down leaving Elena Cicut's. "That cop friend of yours still go to the *bische*?"

"The *bische* aren't what they used to be. Too much legal gambling. But yeah, if you mean Badalamenti, he still goes to Restivo's places. Likes that sense of being cheated, I guess. Just don't call him a friend. What he is is a loser who needs more than his pension to get by. What about him?"

Sylvester took out the letter and showed him the plate number. "A beautiful woman?" Bruno asked gleefully.

"An ugly man I think."

Bruno pulled a dog-eared pocket notebook out of his shirt pocket and copied down the license plate. "I thought you were on vacation."

"It's for a friend."

Bruno smiled wanly. "Like old times."

Sylvester returned the smile, but couldn't recall those kinds of times.

EIGHTEEN

Walter Bell didn't want to grow old. Watching Joey Bacsik hobble down the street, he told himself again that the best way to go was to be seated directly atop a terrorist bomb planted in an airplane. His last sight? Something outward, maybe some wisp of cloud. Certainly nothing inward, like maybe Joe Average American reclining across the aisle with headphones on and watching some cops and robbers movie. His last piece of consciousness should have been as abstract as the abstraction awaiting him on the far side of the bomb that blew him immediately and unconsciously to pieces. No one more thing, Lieutenant Columbo. No one more thing.

Joey Bacsik, on the other hand, looked like he would have been hard pressed to enter an airport on his own power, let alone pick the right seat. The squat old man took the stoop of his brownstone resting at every step. The records Bell had consulted said he had been eligible for retirement four years ago, so why hadn't he gone off into the corner that the years had prepared for him? Bell didn't understand people like that, starting with his own father. It wasn't as though they had been artisans, not wanting to deprive the world of the flutes or chairs or painting frames only they could make. His father had worked for a life insurance company and Joey Bacsik worked in the mail room of a newspaper. What was so unique about their work that would have ended with the retirement they had earned? They were nothing more than robots, just carrying on because they had been trained for their tasks. It was ridiculous that they kept at them until they could hardly walk.

Bell waited until Bacsik had closed the street door behind him, then crossed over to the brownstone. He walked slowly, to give the old man time to get up to his second-floor apartment. There were a few people on the street coming home from work, but nobody sitting around for a long look at him. He had struck the right clothing balance: a dress shirt outside his pants, but not sloppy to the point of conspicuousness. If he was lucky, that wouldn't matter. It would all be in his tone and in his ID. Nothing he had read about Joey Bacsik had suggested a ball-breaker.

The file hadn't been all that accurate. Still wheezing from his trudge up the inside stairs, Bacsik wouldn't even press the intercom button without cross-examination about Charley Sylvester. What was the sudden rush about looking at the diary? Sylvester was in Europe, wasn't he? His secretary hadn't said anything about it when he had run into her at the office that day. And who exactly was Walter Bell, anyway? He knew everybody at the paper, past and present, and had never heard of any Walter Bell. Maybe he should call Sylvester's secretary and check him out. No problem, Bell assured him. In fact, he had Cynthia Glass's cell number because she had warned him that Joey might be suspicious. Did he have it? Did he want it?

Bacsik didn't. It had been a long day for the old man, and he wasn't in the mood for games. He pressed the intercom button.

NINETEEN

Sylvester was proud of himself for his lack of conscientious-ness. For two nights he had slipped off to sleep knowing Cynthia was responsible for dealing with the political hacks who demanded full-dress articles for obscure party bosses in the Adirondacks, the publicists who wanted to use some character actor's death to promote a movie, and distant cousins of bro-kers trying to turn the Obit section into a court of last resort for the Ponzi schemers in their families. But when his room phone wouldn't shut up, his immediate thought was that she had blink-ed first, that she was sure to be calling for office nonsense. He was half-right: It was Cynthia, but not for office nonsense. Even in his drowsiness he heard that in her voice at once.

"It's Joey Bacsik," she said. "He didn't show up for work this morning, and that was a first for everybody in the mail room. They called his place a couple of times but got no answer. Gabby Schwartz went over to his apartment at lunch time. Joey is dead, Charley. Beaten to death. And the apartment looks like a cyclone hit it. The cops are saying it's a robbery gone bad."

For him or for her, for one of them, while he got a grip on what she had said, Sylvester told himself to answer something diver-sionary. "That's a beat cop talking to a TV reporter. Detectives don't jump to conclusions that fast."

Annoyance. "Yes, sir."

He looked at his watch. He was six hours behind all the living and dying in New York; behind all of Joey Bacsik's dying. "Okay,

okay, I'm just taking it in. The old son of a bitch deserved better." There was nothing on the other end of the line, but he still heard something. "What?"

"Nothing."

"What, Cyn?"

"Maybe it's just a coincidence. The timing . . ."

She didn't have to say more. And he didn't like anticipating what she was going to say. "You gave him that copy of the diary, that's what you're thinking?"

"Yes," she relented. "You're thinking it, too."

"The hell I am. For Christ sake. He went to an ATM machine and thugs followed him home. Or they'd been casing his place for weeks."

"And you're not even a beat cop!"

"Let's not get carried away, okay?"

"I don't like the coincidence."

"What coincidence?"

"All of them," she said testily. "You get that crazy letter just before you take off. Applebaum's writing a column about this Cicut. . . ."

The last things he needed to mention were his visit to Elena Cicut and the crewcut who had been following him. "Two things. What you need for a coincidence."

"Three. He was in the mail room when I brought down the copy."

"Of course he was. How else could you give it to him?"

"I don't mean Joey, I mean Applebaum!"

Sylvester didn't know what he was doing—lifting his hand for a cigarette on the end table; it had been years since he had grabbed for a Marlboro to put off thinking about something. "He followed you down to the mail room?"

"No. He was just there. Talking to Joey about mailing things to Oregon. If I'd kept my mouth shut . . ."

"What did you say?"

"Nothing. Like 'Here's the stuff Charley mentioned, Joey. Thanks.'"

"So?"

"So Applebaum was still with him when I left. And you know Joey. He'd jabber about anything to show you what you still had to learn from him."

A church bell tolled down the street. From the historical safety of Rome, Italy, it mocked her paranoia—and his for even listening to her. "Agreed: Joey has . . . had a big mouth and Applebaum's a shit. But do you hear what you're saying?"

The strain was still in her voice. "It's those . . ."

"I know. Coincidences. We need to focus here, Cyn." The shabby man in the T-shirt and boxers staring back at him from the closet mirror couldn't have seconded the motion more heartily. "Make sure everybody in the city knows about Joey tomorrow. More than the usual long-time employee crap. Get a couple of guys from the mail room and some of the editors, too, to say something. How Bacsik put them through the ringer when they were first hired, that kind of thing."

"Why not you?" The tartness was back. "You were as close to him as anybody. Let's get a quote from you."

"I can't . . ."

"Why not? If it makes you feel better, I'll run it past the pharaohs. Shoot."

She enjoyed his discomfit, but at least it got her to think of something besides her coincidences. He wouldn't have minded forgetting them, too, or—second prize—being able to take his eyes off the closet where he had stashed his suitcase with the diary inside. He had to be as spooked as she was to think about getting up and going over to make sure the journal was still where he had left it. "Try this," he said to shut himself up. "'Orientation for new reporters meant surviving the Joey Bacsik test. Others with fancier titles did the hiring and the assigning, but it was Joey who, in between all kinds of instruction on postal zones and what it would cost the company to cross too many of them too fast . . . '"

"Too fast is right."

"Sorry. 'It was Joey who had a knack for drawing you out on personal questions to see if you had the mettle to do the job you were being paid to do. If he passed you, you were a brother for life. If he failed you, you stood a pretty good chance of looking for other work in a very short time.'"

When she came back, it was more airily. "That *fancier titles* thing should go. They *like* their fancy titles, Charley."

"Then change it or drop it. But relax, will you?"

"I'm just . . ."

"I know. I'm upset, too."

"I'm going to ask about it, though."

"Ask what?"

"See if that copy of the diary pages is downstairs in his desk. Or if it's not there, get the cops to look for it in the apartment."

"Cyn . . ."

"It would make me feel better, okay? I don't like the idea of you running around Europe with the original if somebody wants to get his hands on it. Call me irrational."

"Irrational."

He would have settled for a bada-bada-boom laugh, but she wasn't up for it. Instead, it was "Be careful, Charley" and with more sincerity than he wanted to hear. Only when he put down the telephone did he feel a missed opportunity to say the same thing to her.

He got off the bed and over to the closet before he wallowed another second in her voice. There weren't enough motorcycles in the city to drown out his sigh at seeing Cicut's diary exactly where he had left it under his shirts. Then a thought he could have done without: Any hotel safe would have been better than his shirts.

TWENTY

The world had run out of novel flavors, Cynthia thought; or maybe she had. Or was it that she didn't want yogurt at all, but wanted to splurge on the chocolate puddings lined up in the freezer next to the Yoplait like snakes in the garden? She couldn't imagine spooning the puddings without picturing her waist expanding in protest. But if she had ever earned a splurge, tonight was the night. It had taken more than nine hours to lock everything into both the paper and the website, to persuade Erdman in Science that readers needed comprehensible English to understand the importance of the death of a physicist, and to hold off running a notice on a British guitarist until Spencer could file from London in the morning. And on top of all that, there had been the shock at Joey Bacsik's killing, her futile search for the diary copy in the mail room, and the non-answers she had gotten from the police about what had been found in his apartment. The detective named Calderon had begun to sound like she had had something to do with killing the old man.

And yet for all that, she still recognized Cynthia Glass. Instead of going for the puddings she talked herself too easily into grabbing two plain yogurts and then going over to the fruit section for a couple of peaches that weren't rocks from the Grand Canyon. She assigned herself the task of consulting her family tree when she got home to see if the phrase *easiest way out* had originated with one of her ancestors.

There was only one customer ahead of her at the counter of the convenience store, and he didn't act like all that much of a customer. The Korean clerk Shin stared blankly as the man, the kind of slight mustached figure she associated with knife-throwing acts in old movies, sputtered away in a language that wasn't getting through. Both of them turned to her for rescue— Shin because he wanted to deal with somebody else, the knife-thrower because he had some wild hope of being understood by somebody. "You American?" he got out thickly.

"Yes."

"You talk the Serbian?"

Cynthia thought of it as synchronicity: It was Slav Day. The day before Minnesota had been a common theme, a week ago pine trees. "I'm afraid not."

The man squeezed his eyes in disappointment. "No Serbian?"

"Sorry," she said, as Shin grabbed for her yogurts and peaches to have something to do. "No English?"

"No English." He took a wrinkled newspaper out of the back pocket of his jeans and showed her a circled item from a want ad in an ethnic paper. She assumed the words were in the same Serbo-Croat he was speaking. "This? Where this?"

She looked for an address or telephone number in the box, but there was nothing. "Sorry, I don't understand."

The knife-thrower looked at Shin, who just shrugged again. "Can't help you, friend. Don't understand a word you're saying."

The man went from one of them to the other one more time, finally believed how hopeless his cause was, then smiled awkwardly and marched out. "I thought all those Eastern Europeans spoke English," Shin said, running up her tab. "How does a guy get this far without it?"

Cynthia didn't know. What she did know was that she wouldn't want to be part of the knife-thrower's act. His eyes said he wouldn't consider it a total loss if he missed with a throw and got his assistant in one of his performances.

TWENTY-ONE

Four people, himself included, was not Sylvester's idea of a dinner party. Walking into Roenickes' apartment, he had expected seven or eight, maybe double that. Instead, he walked into a Myra Roenicke blonder, thinner, and a lot tipsier than he remembered, an Eddie Roenicke grinning through a hovering apology for something, and a small round man in a clerical collar named Minic who might have passed for Robin Hood's Friar Tuck except that there was no hint of the comical within his self-importance. There was nobody else in sight, and the three of them took him in through clumsy seconds of silence less as the special guest for the evening than as the roasted pig that could now be set in the middle of the table.

Finally relieved of the bottle he had brought, he was led into the living room by Myra. Silliness in her eyes and a glass of white wine attached to her hand, she insisted he appreciate their possessions. He saw why Roenicke would have a brawl on his hands if he ever came home to announce the paper had reassigned him. What passed for air came through open French doors off a terrace where a table had been laid; otherwise, the room would have been claustrophobic with its things and more things. An intricate network of recessed lamps gave off a bleary but smart amber glow fit for a Broadway theater. Showrooms didn't have as many plush armchairs, different-shaped throw cushions, and wall tapestries. Fussily framed paintings competed for wall space, and not all the prints turned out to be prints. "Rubbings," Myra explained in a

Southern drawl fighting to survive, approving of his attention to a black field spotted with silver Hebrew lettering. "The Wailing Wall in Jerusalem. And over here she's done the Great Wall of China. Friend of ours. I guess you'd say she's into walls."

Roenicke emerged from the kitchen with a gin and tonic. "Say you're impressed, Charley, and she'll let you drink this."

Sylvester didn't miss Myra's flash of pique. Minic, sitting like Humpty Dumpty on a couch cushion, didn't miss it, either. "Eddie says you worked here a long time, Mister Sylvester," he said, advertising his tact. "Very different from Manhattan, isn't it?"

He thought about correcting the *Mister Sylvester*, then decided not to. "You know Manhattan, Father?"

"The main office of our publication is there, so yes, I go a couple of times a year." He covered his wine glass from Roenicke's attempt to refill it. "Enough, Eddie. I know you want me to turn into one of those drunken Irish priests, but not tonight."

Roenicke backed off with a nervous laugh; the crack had come out a little nastier than intended, or maybe it hadn't. "You're talking about a magazine?"

"We have several. Nothing on a scale like your employer, of course. Two monthlies and a weekly. Their titles wouldn't mean anything to you."

"A lot of *j*'s and *z*'s," Roenicke volunteered, doing his best to ignore the empty glass Myra held out to his bottle.

"How does the IRS pronounce them?"

Myra giggled; it almost made her forget that she wanted more wine and that she didn't like Roenicke for denying it to her. "For tax purposes," Minic said, "we are presumptuous enough to call ourselves Freedom Press."

"Got to call yourself something," Roenicke shrugged.

"And to anticipate your next question, most of our readers are people who fled the chaos to the east of us in the Nineties hoping for a freer and safer life. You and I know the world isn't that black and white geographically, but a name like Freedom Press has its reassurances for some."

Sylvester sipped his gin and tonic—except it wasn't gin and tonic. Roenicke had apparently been in such a hurry to get from the kitchen back to the conversation that he had mixed up the tonic with club soda. "So Eddie tells me you knew Josef Cicut."

"I told you . . .?"

"Maybe not in so many words."

Not even Myra found that one funny, and she immediately excused herself to check on what was cooking in the kitchen. At least he had confirmed what play they had all been rehearsing. "A shot in the dark and a good one, Mister Sylvester," Minic nodded. "Yes, we ran into one another on occasion. Tragic end."

"I thought he had a heart attack. Something like a suicide, *that* would be tragic."

"Language," Roenicke said, not liking Minic's frown. "Let's just call it a bad ending. That's what it was. Just bad."

The priest didn't need an interpreter. "I think Mister Sylvester is referring to those rumors that Cicut took his own life. Of course that's absurd. You're suggesting an enormous coverup involving more than one government. I'm afraid, Mister Sylvester, my region of the world attracts stupid rumors like flowers attract bees. And you can imagine how much worse that has become in recent years with so many people cut off from what they had assumed was home."

"And what exactly is your country, Father? Croatia? Bosnia?"

He smiled humorlessly. "I was born in Dubrovnik, actually. I prefer to think of myself as a Dalmatian. All those others came later. What did you say about Dalmatians, Eddie? They assist firemen in your country?"

It was Abbott and Costello, and Sylvester hadn't laughed much at them, either. "So what were your impressions of Cicut?"

"To be frank?"

"Or just tell me a lie."

Roenicke winced, but Minic understood a gag when somebody else disapproved of it. "On the rare occasions we met," the priest said evenly, "he looked lost to me. I wasn't surprised. Many who choose to emigrate find that matters become harder, not easier, the longer they are away from home. Sometimes there can be open bitterness or just the stress from not surrendering to that bitterness."

"The kind that would lead to a heart attack."

"Exactly."

He wondered who had written the script—first for Applebaum, then for Elena Cicut, now for Minic. The jangling telephone from the table near the terrace and from another room somewhere in the back of the house made him stop wondering. A hot nerve in his chest understood how Roenicke could come out of his chair as if catapulted. "Let's hope it's not some journalistic crisis that will spoil our dinner," Minic said. "Myra's cooking puts the Italians to shame."

Sylvester wouldn't have bet against the Italians. What the buzzed Myra in the kitchen seemed most capable of was dumping gallons of brandy into all the pots on the stove. Then Roenicke was handing him the phone. "For you."

He took the receiver as Minic set down his wine and headed off for a hallway where he obviously knew the bathroom was. What he didn't understand was why Bruno hadn't used his cellphone number. "Because you didn't fix it for Italy, that's why," the man chortled. "We're not all that global yet, Charley. You said you were going to that *stronzo*'s house so I . . ."

"Okay, okay. You're just faster than I thought."

"You made it sound important."

Roenicke sipped his wine like somebody who wasn't curious— like at the Piazza Navona bar when he'd had no idea about things he'd had plenty of ideas about. Sylvester tried to be casual about going over to the terrace to inspect the table setting for dinner. "So you already talked to your friend?"

"Write it down. W-A-R-N-E-K-E. What kind of a name is that? L-E-O-N-A-R-D. Like Leonardo, no?"

He caught himself from repeating it aloud for Roenicke's benefit. He hadn't realized how truly stuffy the living room was until the soft night breeze on the terrace hit his face. The lights of Monteverde glowed in the distance. He pictured normal people sitting down to dinner behind some of the windows. "Nothing else?"

"Like what? You asked for a name."

"Okay. Thanks, *amico*. I owe you a dinner."

"You already did. This is for the night club after."

Roenicke was waiting with a wary smile after he had returned the phone to its cradle. "Don't mind Minic," he said. "He can be a little stiff."

"That why you're walking around with a walkie-talkie?"

"He wanted to meet you."

"Did I want to meet him?"

The clatter of something metallic hitting the kitchen floor stopped him from another shrug. "What're you asking, Charley?"

"What the hell do you think I'm asking? Why did he want to meet me and why did you think that was a great idea?"

The callow kid who had once liked his shrewdness in getting his interview with Josef Cicut shifted uncomfortably in his chair. "You got ghosts in your head, Charley. While you've been sitting over there burying your Nobel Prize winners, a lot of new shit has been happening here. The old rules don't apply. The problem is, we always seem to be behind knowing exactly what does apply. Anybody who has an idea is worth listening to, even hotheads like Minic and his Freedom Press. They can be useful for basic intel."

"*Intel?*"

"Information."

"I know the word, Eddie. What I don't know is why it's coming out of your mouth like some fucking Washington spook."

Roenicke reddened in anger, but then remembered where he was. First his eyes darted toward the kitchen, then toward the hallway where the bathroom was. "This isn't the time," he murmured.

"You sure as hell set it up like it was."

The flush of the toilet cut off any more debate. "Tomorrow, okay?"

Sylvester didn't want to say yes, but the kid who was no longer a kid was openly appealing to him. The idiot was in more muck than even Father Minic. "Tomorrow. But in the meantime, get me a real goddamn gin and tonic."

He tried not to feel righteous as Roenicke grabbed his glass, tasted the club soda, made a face and another apology, then scrambled out to the kitchen. He gave up the struggle and enjoyed feeling righteous.

TWENTY-TWO

Badalamenti didn't miss the look as he closed the door behind him. They recognized him, then they remembered he had taken his pension and sneered into their chests as they went back to their balls and cues. He was used to it by now, and he pitied the weasels. The closest they would ever get to making up for their years of being intimidated by him was a private smirk that he couldn't threaten them anymore. The house manager behind the register, an elephant named Gigi, might have seen a cockroach walk in. They were all so spineless he wondered what would happen if he announced he was back in uniform and was there to fine them for filling the storefront with cigarette smoke.

But Badalamenti had no time for the weasels scattered around the billiards and boccette tables. It was enough effort for him to stride with an air of authority to Restivo's office in the back. The last thing he needed was them suspecting he was there because he had been summoned. He knocked and opened the office door so quickly that Restivo was still in the middle of his *Avanti!*. As usual, the fat swine was splayed over his chair as if he hadn't been able to get up since being dropped into it years ago; his width seemed equal to the desk in front of him. What Badalamenti hadn't counted on was the second man sitting on a straight chair against the wall. There was none of Restivo's pig greed in the second man's eyes; he had cleared them of any feeling a long time ago. He had to be near 50, but was athletically spare, the impression strengthened by his crewcut, pressed jeans shirt, and black wrist bands.

"Orazio! Always punctual! I told you, didn't I, Leonard? After serving the State for so many years, Orazio certainly has his faults, but being tardy has never been one of them. How are you, Orazio?"

Badalamenti knew Restivo's enforcers, and the "Leonard" on the straight chair wasn't one of them; he didn't even look Italian. "There's a limit, Restivo," he said, wishing his mouth hadn't sounded so dry. "You know you've been getting your money. These calls to my home won't get it to you any faster."

The one called Leonard thought that was funny; at least the twist he gave to his mouth resembled a smile. "No money, no money," Restivo said grandly. "I know you can be relied on to meet your debts. If I didn't, I would leave you to the legal games and the tax man. No, what we want to talk about is your willingness to do favors."

Badalamenti didn't understand the words, but he didn't like how Restivo slid his eyes over to Leonard. It was the first time he had ever seen the man not completely in charge, and he didn't like it. He was so taken aback that he needed a moment to catch up with the hushed, broken words coming from the stranger. It was a passable Italian with some kind of Russian accent. "You made a request for a license plate number," he said. "Why would you still be interested in such things? Silvio here says you are retired."

Badalamenti knew he was reddening, visibly so even inside the dark shadow cast by the desk lamp that was the office's only light. He thought about explaining it as his indignation that he hadn't even been offered one of the other wooden chairs in front of the desk, that a man of his stature should have been shown respect and not treated as some naughty schoolboy being called to account, but he couldn't convince himself of such a feeble ploy. What he was embarrassed by was how he had agreed to be putty in the hands of that *buttafare* Bruno Lepri. "Maybe you could be more precise, Signore?" he asked to gain a few seconds.

Badalamenti knew thinned patience when he heard it in Restivo's sigh; he had been on that side of a desk too long in dealing with petty felons not to know it. But Leonard only twisted his mouth again, his stillness in the chair seeming to drop down to yet another level. "Good," he said. "We have gotten that out of the way. Now would you answer my question, please? Who asked you to look up a certain license plate?"

Badalamenti wished they were back talking about the euros he owed Restivo from too many bad nights at the *bische*. Those debts were easy to figure out. But for a moment he stood stymied working out what he owed Bruno Lepri, what he owed an arrogant shit like Leonard, and what he owed himself in deciding whether or not to surrender Lepri's name. Lepri was the easiest: He owed the *buttafare* nothing. Leonard? He knew he didn't owe him anything, either, but the man was too coiled in his spareness, too much of an opponent for somebody out of condition if he tried to get rough. The foreigner was a violence waiting to happen. But he also owed himself more than just collapsing before a threat. "I don't see why it's any business of yours," he managed. "Who is this, Restivo? And why is he asking all these questions?"

The fat man shrugged. "A friend. What he asks you, consider it a question from me. Who asked you to check up on this license plate?"

Badalamenti realized he had a better question: Who at the Questura had a private phone line to Silvio Restivo and to the foreigner with the sandy crewcut? And an even better one than that: Why was a street bum like Bruno Lepri interested in the same things as Silvio Restivo and the foreigner? That suddenly felt like negotiating room with the two of them. "Like you say, Restivo, I can do a favor here and there. But it's common courtesy to return that favor, don't you think? For instance, this little money question between us . . ."

Restivo laughed as he did most things—like a drooling pig. Leonard, on the other hand, didn't seem to have a twist in his mouth left as he shook his head sadly and hoisted himself to his feet only by contracting his stomach muscles, not touching either arm of his chair.

TWENTY-THREE

Sylvester stubbed his toes on yet another raised cobblestone. Rome's street pavers were costing him a fortune in shoe leather.

If he had to slap a headline on his dinner with the Roenickes, he decided, it would be MYRA ROENICKE, 38, FABULOUS COOK, SHREWD CONVERSATIONALIST. Granted that might have been premature since Myra Roenicke was still alive and in no need of a headline on the Obit page, but considering how she had lived up to Minic's advertising with her vodka penne and glazed veal and had then sabotaged every attempt by the priest and her husband to wheedle more out of him about Cicut by jabbering away relentlessly about her church theater projects, she merited the only award he was capable of conferring on another soul.

And he was also indebted to her for more enlightened relations within his own family. By conspiring with his hostess, in being able to stifle more Cicut chat and to evade mention of red diaries, he had to have made Patricia proud (at least in some extrasensory spiritual sphere) of how he had spoken so expertly about basement and loft plays in Manhattan he had never seen; there couldn't have been a phrase from her reviews he hadn't pulled into the chatter to reinforce some eloquently fraudulent argument. Before having to summon up those reviews for the Roenicke table, he had never realized how much Patricia's writing had stayed with him. Journalism school verbs or not, she had a definite flair for the concise put-down and the illuminating

historical reference. He would have to sneak in that compliment
somewhere when he returned to New York. In the meantime,
though, he had managed to ingratiate himself on both sides of
the Atlantic while dining on a Rome terrace. Even if Myra hadn't
already been obsessed with her church group, his reports from
the off-Broadway front would have certainly inspired her at her
next rehearsal for *Who's Afraid of Virginia Woolf?*.

He just wished she hadn't kept refilling his glass while Minic
had tried to look tolerant of a subject he had no interest in and
the simmering Roenicke had been working up themes for domes-
tic discussion after the guests had left. He had taken too long to
say no more refills to her, and now was weaving far too much on
his return to the hotel. Since when had his left leg been incapable
of the same firm strides as his right? The cobblestone streets
had ruined his shoes from all his rutting steps. If none of the
evening revelers he passed shot censorious looks at him, it was
only because they were tourists too busy with their cackling (and
maybe a few wobbly steps of their own). He didn't know why he
had discouraged Roenicke's idea of calling a cab and had insisted
on walking back to the hotel. Had it been nostalgia? If he peered
down at the cobblestones, would he find traces of loafers he had
worn through the same streets while he had been living in the
city? He had certainly navigated the same *vicoli* and *vicoletti* more
than once while making every effort to persuade his legs he still
stood erect above them.

He made it into the shimmering lights from the noisy Piazza
Navona bars, past a temptation to drop down at one of the tables
to calm his head, and across the square without stumbling. The
last obstacle was the concrete bench where Leonard Warneke
had been sitting—---- that creep his assignment for the morning.
Full relief came with the dark alley of the side street connecting
the piazza to the hotel. Once there he knew he was safe, that he
had only to behave relatively coherently with the night clerk while
asking for his key before getting up to his room and vanishing
from society. The leisurely splash of the fountain strengthened
his purpose down the home stretch. His thought in seeing Elena
Cicut hurrying out the front door was that she wasn't needed,

that he could get upstairs and into bed on his own. Then he reminded himself he shouldn't have been seeing Elena Cicut at all.

"Elena!"

She whipped her head around with the mix of alarm and arrogance Sylvester S. Sylvester had always given him when he had
interrupted Patricia's Siamese clawing the furniture. Elena too
was plotting how to scamper under a bed. "Hello, Charles."

The words "what's wrong?" escaped from his mouth.

"Nothing," she lied, gripping her shoulder bag tightly. "I was
just seeing a friend. I didn't know you were staying here."

"Where else would I stay? You want to talk, let's talk."

He pushed it too far, lurching toward her with a Frankenstein's
monster move that almost toppled him over. But she thought
he was just funny; for the first time since seeing her again, she
smiled freely. "You do not look so good, Charles."

"How about a coffee in their little bar here? I could use one."

"They were closing when I looked in."

"Then we'll get them to reopen."

He wanted to take her hesitant nod as their pact, so he did.
She wouldn't say any more about his condition and he wouldn't
point out how quickly she had dropped her lie about coming to the
hotel to see somebody else. Besides, she had already given herself
away in remembering what hotel he was most likely to be found in.
That had taken a pretty good reach going back years on her part.

She had been right about the house bar in the back closing
down. The barman had already upended the handful of stools
around the small counter and had extinguished the lights over
the surrounding tables. But the man was also a hotel employee
at the service of guests round-the-clock more than he was a bartender so he put two of the stools back down and took Elena's
order for a grappa with no fuss. Sylvester didn't bother asking
for the coffee he needed. She could drink his grappa as well as
her own. And just requesting the drinks relaxed her, seemed
to remind her of the things people did when not cooped up in
grim apartments all day. She didn't pass up the invitation of the
Cinzano ashtray on the bar, either. He remembered her Nazionali
cigarette brand as the cheapest in the country, the kind found on

every table at Giuliana's *bottiglieria*. Just about everything about her except her moon face was economical. She had given her hair the quickest of combs, her lips the thinnest of glossy swipes. The plaid sports shirt she was wearing might have come out of Philip's closet, the plain gray skirt with the small stain on the hem from a flea market. And closer to it, he saw her crocheted shoulder bag was pretty frayed, either a favorite she refused to throw out or the best of what she had left.

"I did not tell you the full truth yesterday," she said, exhaling her smoke as soon as the barman had left their grappas and gone away again.

"Start with Philip." She drew back from his peremptory tone, and he didn't blame her. "Sorry. It's been a long night."

She only had to look at him to see that. There were a lot of objections—to his tone, to having been caught leaving the hotel, to the world at large—in her stark black eyes. "He is not in any school," she conceded.

"Where is he?"

"I do not know."

He knew his astonishment showed. He couldn't imagine saying "I do not know" if someone asked him where Nick was; not with her finality.

"He is older than his years. The last months have made him much older."

"When you say you don't know. . . ."

"It is what I mean," she said curtly. "I do not know."

"How long are we talking about?"

She hunched over the ashtray with her cigarette, keeping her eyes averted. "The day after we received word about Josef. More than a week now. He said nothing at all that afternoon, just went into his room and remained there all day. It was just as well. I could not have said anything useful to him. Then he was not there. When I went into his room to see if he had left some sign of where he had gone, I found only what I did not find. A pistol from Josef's collection. Josef gave it to him for his 16th birthday."

Sylvester remembered the guns, but it hadn't been a collection so much as a grab bag of old pistols and automatics that might have been rounded up from pawn shops. They had looked so worn and neglected they had to have been more dangerous to the shooter than to a target. Cicut had kept them behind glass in a corner of his Chiesa Nuova living room, but in such helter-skelter fashion he had been underlining their worthlessness, the way old campaign buttons were thrown into a desk drawer. He hadn't understood why they had been given even that small space, and Cicut had only smiled that "they should always look like that." Only now did it occur to him that he should have pressed for a less cryptic reply, that maybe he just hadn't wanted a better explanation. "Those things are antiques," he said, wishing he knew for sure. "They probably don't even work."

"I do not know."

"Is there ammunition for them?"

Another shrug. "There were some bullets in a drawer. There may be some gone, I really did not count how many there had been,"

He didn't know who was the most bizarre—Philip for taking the gun, her for being so cavalier about the bullets, or Cicut for making sure his little arsenal had made the move from the Chiesa Nuova apartment. "And I guess you haven't told the police."

"Is that what you do in America when a teenager goes off—alert the police?"

"If he goes off with a gun, probably."

She accepted that, but little more. "I am used to dealing with difficulties, Charles, but for a long time now I do not understand my feelings. When I heard about Josef, my immediate thought was that it was just a confirmation of what I knew had to happen. Since Philip has disappeared, I refuse to think of the worst. I have just told myself he will be back. Is that what they call self-preservation?"

"Help me out here, Elena. From the beginning. I don't understand what happened in Germany. None of it. Why Josef was there. How he died exactly. Why you and Philip weren't allowed to attend a burial of some kind."

She was irked he hadn't answered her self-preservation question. "I never said we were not allowed."

"You don't just get a phone call from another country telling you your husband is dead and say, 'Oh, okay, you take care of things.'"

She went back to the ashtray. She had been the one to order it, but she didn't seem to want the grappa any more than he did. "They told me it would be best for Philip," she said, all but whispering. "They would ship the body back home to a family plot with Josef's parents and relatives. What was I to say? I have no money for such things. Could I be anything but grateful to them?"

"*Them.*"

"A very officious man at the embassy there."

"I thought you said Josef knew somebody up there. This Glauber. He wasn't the one who called you?"

"No. I asked to speak to Sima, but the one on the phone said he had gone home for a vacation. He might have been sitting right there listening to the conversation. Glauber always seemed to me to do things like that. Everything a little furtive even when it was not necessary. But what difference does it make?"

"A lot if he'd talked to Josef."

The last thing she had come for was criticism. "I told you, Charles. Josef had not been himself for some time. He insisted on things being just so, and if they were not, he could not deal with it. I can only assume that whatever relief he was hoping to get from Glauber he did not find."

"Meaning he didn't have a heart attack?"

"I did not . . ."

"Yes, I think you just did."

She sighed and narrowed her eyes before another exhale. She had been fighting too many big battles lately to get stuck on a skirmish. "No, there was no heart attack," she said, announcing it to the bottles behind the bar as much as to him. "The one on the phone said he shot himself in the head on the front steps of their embassy. It happened so fast they could do nothing to prevent it. They gave out the heart attack story to save themselves a scandal. The German authorities were informed, but since it happened on embassy grounds, their interest was not high. Of course the man on the telephone said it was handled that way for my benefit and Philip's."

He was dismayed by how steadily she said it, and didn't know if she was barely holding herself together or had envisioned the scene she described too many times to feel it anymore. One way or the other, somebody had finally admitted the suicide, and he had an impulse to swivel around to see if Minic and Applebaum had overheard. But then he suddenly felt short of breath. Cynthia had warned him to stay away, and now it felt too late. He had been told too much, had no right to have heard it, but couldn't just forget it. "The man who wrote me that letter was no hysterical bundle of nerves. He was purposeful. He had some crazy idea killing himself would accomplish something."

She smiled wearily. "Yes?"

"He had to have said something."

"About what?"

He hadn't seen where she was pushing him until he was there. "About something that preoccupied him more than even his wife and son."

She would have congratulated him if there had been anything to congratulate. "You knew Josef. He was never an especially warm man, was he?"

Nor had he married a woman so different, Sylvester thought. How many times had he and Felicia gone back and forth on that one, debating which of the Cicuts was the colder fish? He had always voted for Josef and Felicia had said it was only because Elena was a woman, and there the debate had usually ended. Until he was sitting only a few feet away again from the co-cold fish in the Cicut family. "He was making a goddamn statement, Elena. With his own life! For the love of Christ, what's in that diary he sent me? What was he guarding for so long?"

"Yes, I assumed he was referring to that diary in your letter."

"You've read it?"

"The diary? No. But I saw it in his drawer a couple of times."

"You were never curious . . .?"

She finally recognized the grappa at her elbow and took a sip of it. She seemed to think that was enough of an answer. Diaries, bullets—whatever was in a drawer wasn't worth her interest.

"I can't believe you weren't curious. Just a little bit?"

"Have you read it?"

"It's in Serbo-Croat."

"But you suppose enough from the paper or ink to assume some guilt."

Her sarcasm was better than nothing, seemed closer to a normal human reaction. "In my place what would you assume?"

"Of course," she said, braving a direct look at him. "Another genocidal atrocity. Josef was not only a cold man, he was a brutal one. And he told me about it all and I have kept it a secret all these years as part of our marriage."

"That's not what I'm saying."

"Then what are you saying?"

Exactly that, Sylvester thought. And hadn't Joey Bacsik said the same thing?

"You don't have room in your imagination for any other kind of human being, Charles? Was that the Josef you remember?"

He didn't know whether to curse or thank all the wine he had drunk on Roenicke's terrace. He really didn't know what a sober answer would have been. "I don't seem to remember him at all," he said, hearing his dithering. "The man I knew certainly never struck me as someone who would shoot himself."

She looked genuinely baffled. "And you are criticizing what exactly?"

"What brought you here tonight, Elena?"

"I told you: I wanted to apologize for not telling you the whole truth yesterday. You were a friend for a long time. I should not be lying to my friends." She smiled bleakly. "I do not have many."

That much he could believe. The Cicuts had always been an island unto themselves, as if never trusting others to appreciate their lives and lacking the patience to enlighten them. "That wasn't the only reason you came."

She rotated her cigarette slowly over the ashtray, sending up thicker smoke. For once he seemed to have asked the right question. "No," she said finally. "I need help, Charles. I need to find Philip. Nothing else matters. I do not care about diaries. Forgive me if I shock you, but I do not even spend much time thinking about Josef and what he did. We did not have easy years recently, and I was relieved when he finally went off. He could have come back, he might not have. I would have accepted either. But about Philip I cannot think that way. And I suppose I was hoping . . . well, when you rang my bell, you reminded me of the happiest times of my life, right after Philip was born, when he was a little boy, when Felicia and I took the children out to the piazza and sat there chattering like hens while they dug at the stones and got themselves filthy dirty. I do not know how you can help in any practical way, but this afternoon I suddenly thought that if I did not ask for your help, I would have been a terrible mother."

"I understand, but I don't know how I can help, either. Even some people I might have called years ago, they're long gone."

"Yes. I suppose I did not want to think that far ahead."

He would never find an easier opening for his own piece of truth. "I might have left the impression yesterday I was here only because of Josef's letter . . ."

She gave him the same smile she had in the front of the hotel, when he had almost fallen on his face. "You are here on some assignment for your newspaper?"

"No. Just a vacation."

No concept was more foreign to her. "I see."

One apology felt like enough. "What about Philip's friends, schoolmates? You must have called some of them."

"Of course," she said, recollecting her attention. "Either they have not seen him or are just saying that."

For all the years that had elapsed, he found it hard to see Philip painting her as an ogre to his friends. If the kid had any Cicut genes at all, he would have found that beneath him. "Why would Philip take a gun with him? Is there someone he might be blaming for what Josef did?"

She shook her head; she had settled that question for herself.

"And you have no idea why Josef went to the embassy in Germany aside from the possibility of seeing this old friend."

"That is what I said."

"Just to reminisce about the old days? You don't believe that, Elena."

"I know nothing that would contradict it."

"You don't seem to like this Sima Glauber."

"Not particularly. Did you like all of Felicia's friends?"

The second time she had taken that kind of gratuitous shot irritated him in its very emptiness. Unlike the first time back in her apartment, not even she looked confident about it. "What about you and Josef? Things started getting difficult economically. You got on each other's nerves. But was there something worse than other things, the straw that broke the camel's back?" She shook her head; too fast. "You're sure?"

"I said I was."

"Any more dead ends you can think of?" He got a facsimile of a smile from her. Then he remembered what wasn't a dead end. "Did you ever hear of somebody called Leonard Warneke? Somewhere in his forties, sandy hair?"

"No. Who is he?"

She was waiting—hopefully—for him to tell her. But he couldn't tell her anything. "Not important. But we can clear up one mystery anyway. I have the diary upstairs. I brought it here for you. It belongs to you."

"For what?"

"Because it's yours now. And it could also tell us why it was so important to Josef, maybe had something to do with what happened."

"I told you, I am interested only in finding Philip," she said, extinguishing her cigarette with two hard pounds into the ashtray. "That has nothing to do with some old diary Josef kept."

She was up on her feet before he accepted how serious she was. "You're not making sense. It'll take five minutes to see one way or the other."

The endless objections were back in her eyes, this time with a layer of anger. "I am not looking for history, Charles, I am looking for Philip."

"And if Philip was more curious than you were? If he knows exactly what's in that diary and that's why he ran off?"

"He never touched his father's things."

He could have taken her as sincere and been flabbergasted or he could have been getting as angry as she was. "He's a teenager, Elena. He's been through every drawer in your house. You did at his age, didn't you?"

Soldiers lined up for a dress parade didn't draw themselves up more rigidly. "No, Charles, I did not."

He was caught off guard by how quickly his laugh—and the relief under it—came over him. But why not? She wasn't being adamant in some culturally primitive way, she was simply lying to him about not knowing what was in the little red book. He felt back on earth. "What's in there, Elena?"

He could see the tremors in her upper arms as she stood in front of him. She was deciding to hurry on out of the bar and the hotel, then she was deciding to continue standing exactly where she was, then it was greater fury with him for keeping her suspended between those choices.

Then she just blinked. "To you it is only a book," she said. "To me it was the picture of my marriage."

TWENTY-FOUR

"They thought of themselves as the Three Musketeers—Josef, Glauber, and my brother Milo. Perhaps I had no sense of humor, as Milo said, but to me they were typical university students more interested in playing pranks than studying. Who could drink the most. Who could get the most women into bed. How to embarrass some unpopular professor. According to Josef, Glauber was the one who usually came up with the schemes and he was the one who refined them, turned them into public spectacles. If they didn't have an audience for their jokes, what was the point of them? My brother—well, Milo never said no to anything if it meant a slap on the back and getting people to buy him a rakia. He always had a little of the politician. The worst of their nonsense was when they bribed the keeper at the district zoo to join a holiday parade with an elephant. What they did not know was that the elephant had been acting dangerously and should never have been allowed out from his bars. The keeper did not care as long as he was paid. The elephant was brought down to the parade, was panicked by all the music and people, and ran wild. The reviewing stand was destroyed and the mayor and nine other people were hurt before the keeper could gain control of the animal. Josef and the others were very proud of the commotion they caused. Not only the keeper, but the director of the zoo was fired. Even when Josef was once telling the story with dinner guests here in Rome, I could hear the triumph in his voice. I said nothing. He was seldom so exuberant about things in the past.

"After university Josef and Glauber entered the foreign service. Milo could have too, but he preferred teaching in the same school where I was. He said he was more interested in young minds than bureaucratic ones, and never missed an opportunity to say that to Josef and Glauber. The more he said it, the less amusing Josef found it. It did not bring out the best in him. When he became successful, he could not hide an air of superiority where Milo was concerned, as if to say Milo had made his professional choice and it had been the wrong one. In any case, Josef and Glauber both did well and were given important tasks. As he must have told you, the biggest decision Josef made was to remain at the Foreign Ministry at home instead of accepting what would have been a glamorous but minor posting in the Paris embassy. I liked believing I had something to do with his choice because I could not hide my reluctance to leave my students. We were very much in love then. But by staying home he also managed to remain under the eye of the right people and was soon being sent abroad for very delicate assignments that would have never been within his reach if he had gone to Paris. An agreement he made with the Scandinavians was the talk of the ministry. He said Glauber, who had chosen to go to Switzerland and then Belgium, joked about it, but it was never as simple as that. Milo taunting the two of them about teaching instead of working in a bureaucracy was nothing compared to the rivalry between Josef and Glauber. Sima had to have been jealous of Josef's success, it was in his nature.

"When we decided to get married, Glauber said he could not come from Brussels because of work or something. Josef was very disappointed, called him three times to change his mind. He had Milo call him, too, but to no avail. At first I thought it was spite on Sima's part, but later I wondered if it was not more, if he saw what was coming and wanted to stay out of the country. Josef hated me for thinking that, but I still believe it. As my grandmother used to say, Sima Glauber was somebody who sniffed the air before he put on his hat. It was a week after we were married that the trouble erupted. The animals came and ransacked every store and building with the wrong name attached to it. If you were not one of them, you were beaten or shot. The shooting and screaming went on all day. But the worst of it was when there was a long silence at night between gunshots. You knew they were hunting for somebody in particular. There was something worse about that than about the random killing that went on all day. Then finally the silence ended with a short, ugly burst of gunfire and you knew they had found who they were looking for. Just listening to the silence and then the shots made me feel so helpless, like an accomplice.

"At first, they stayed away from the women and children so I remained behind to take care of my mother. There was no question that Josef was on their list, and so was Milo because he was both a teacher and on the town council. The two of them had to get out. I thought they would somehow get to Bucharest or Budapest, but they had never intended to do that. From the beginning they had planned just to go into the hills and fight. Milo told me that later. One of a hundred things that Josef thought it important to keep secret from me. And about that one he was probably right. I could not imagine him fighting. There was no way he would not have gotten killed the first time he found himself in a battle. I would have carried on like a witch if I had known his intentions, probably insisted on dragging my mother with us to the hills if he did not change his mind. He was right not to want me and my tantrums around his neck.

"But Josef the fighter was not the only thing I was wrong about. I do not know how we could have convinced ourselves the swine would leave the women and children alone. Maybe it was because we knew so many of them. One had been our pharmacist, another a clerk at the bank we dealt with every week. We had been neighbors for years. We had depended on the pharmacist slipping my mother extra pills when her doctor was off on vacation. He had been welcomed at our dinner table. He had gone to football games with Milo! But that was before the madness, before everyone saw themselves worth only what a piece of paper said their names and religion were. Always it was *blood* this, *god* that. The right veins were highways to paradise.

"It is a cruel thing to say, but I have thought it often enough: My mother saved my life by having a heart attack. With her gone

I had no more reason to wait for a crash at the door in the middle of the night, to stay away from the window so some animal passing by outside did not get an idea. We were out of food anyway. We had survived that long mainly because of a young priest at the church down the street. Even in their hatred, at first anyway, they were too superstitious about what Father Stela represented to move a hand against him. Superstition has always run very deep with us. Father Stela was the one who smuggled me out of town with two neighbors and their children. It was only after I was gone that the slaughters became uncontrollable, women and children no safer than the men. The pharmacists and the bank clerks stopped seeing us as human beings altogether. I suppose they needed time to reach that point, to convince themselves of their delirium.

"I found Josef and Milo within a few days. I must have seemed like another person to them because that was how they seemed to me. They were weary and dirty, and had become accustomed to speaking harshly to one another and everybody else. Most of all, it was their eyes. There was nothing in them. *Nothing.* They smiled when they first saw me, but after that, nothing. I had come into their world, they embraced me, and then I was immediately swallowed up in their reality. The first time Josef and I made love, it was . . . numbness. I had to keep touching his body not in passion but just to be sure there was one on top of me.

"We lived like that for months. There was fighting, but mostly it was moving from one encampment or village to another and sitting in cold, wet places trying not to get pneumonia. That was when Josef started keeping his journal. He said it passed the time, gave his mind something to focus on besides the endless coughing around us. I envied him. When I was not cooking or holding classes for the youngest children, I seemed always to be gazing off at the sky or the clouds or the strange formations of the rocks on the horizon. It was not a healthy way to pass the time. Others looked up in the hope of seeing bombers coming to help us, but all I could think of was how insignificant we were, how we would soon be gone while the sky and the clouds and the mountains would still be there. I made the mistake of saying that to Josef, and he got very angry. It was not the moment for poetry, he said, and then he went back to writing in his little book. I knew he was right, but I hated him for being so.

"Of course I was curious about what he was writing. When I asked him to show me, he said he was only making jottings that would not interest me. What he meant was that it was his private domain and he did not want me violating it. I did not ask anymore, but I knew I was going to look the first opportunity that came. Then one night we were in a town that still had hot water for baths. When Josef went off to get clean, I saw that he had left behind the journal. I had underestimated his need for privacy. The first few pages were in a clear language, describing where we had been that day, what visiting advisers we had talked with, the funny little things that somebody said. But then around the time I had asked to see what he was writing, he began using a code. Stems of words, obscure associations only he could have connected to their meaning. It took forever just to work out the names of some of the people he was referring to. It was as if he was telling me his diary was not for me then or ever. He could have died, that code said, and I would still never know what he had written. I hated him for that too. It was an emotion that came very easily in those days. But maybe you will understand why the sight of that little red book did not fascinate me, why it did not make me impatient to learn something about Josef I did not already know. I already knew more than I wanted to.

"When the fighting finally stopped and we returned home, we recognized only shells. Homes and stores were more what they were in our memories than in what our eyes saw. After the elections the new state offered Josef a very prestigious position in foreign affairs. He tried hard to believe in what he was doing and he had diplomatic successes with the Vatican and others. But there was an emptiness about it for him that was very much like the eyes of the man I had seen when I had first rejoined him. Hardly a week went by that he did not come across some new hole in his life—a place that had been bombed out of existence, a colleague or an acquaintance who had been killed or, even worse, never accounted for. Then there were the reports of new trouble stirring to the east. He refused to go through it all again. When he said he wanted to come to Rome, I was not totally surprised. He had been dropping hints for weeks about this one and that one he had met while he had been negotiating with the Vatican, how they would have helped us settle if we ever decided to leave home. The truth was, it was something I wanted to hear. The school where I was teaching, every day one of the instructors or some student would be talking about *their* blood and *their* god. Milo told me to be patient, but I could not believe in those open minds he wanted to see. Maybe I was also still being poetic, as Josef had said. Perhaps if we were in new surroundings, I told myself, we might also have a new marriage. Then Philip came along and it did not seem so hard to believe in that. I *liked* being with Josef again and I could feel he liked being with me. There were days when I thought of it as a small miracle, what that priest Father Stela would have called a 'turn in the divine plan.'

"The next years you know. In retrospect, I suppose even the Internet and the other translation services that put us out of business were amateur compared to the hatreds and the malaise we had gotten away from. At least I wanted to think so in quiet moments. Still gazing up at the sky and the rocks on the horizon, yes? And Josef still did not welcome that attitude. I could see him slipping back to where he had been. The need to choose between selecting the best school for Philip and maintaining the apartment behind the Chiesa Nuova was the first big crisis. And then there was Milo.

"One night we were watching the Telegiornale. And suddenly there is my brother on the screen. Fatter and older, the sleek black hair he had always preened about now some kind of gray stubble. We had spoken on the phone often and e-mailed one another, but we had not seen each other in years. All I knew about what he was doing when he was not teaching was that he had become close to a so-called Independent Alliance party that I did not like the sound of. They used the word *homeland* quite a lot but were otherwise very vague. What they did seem to have was a great deal of money behind them. And now here was Milo standing in front of a lot of other people who looked just as overfed as he was and he was announcing that he would be a candidate for the presidency in the next election. Milo Jelic a chief-of-state? The idea overwhelmed me. It was ridiculous. I wanted to cry. Or maybe I wanted to laugh, I did not know. Then I looked over at Josef. He was so white he looked ill. He did not hear me. He just kept staring at the screen until I turned off the picture."

TWENTY-FIVE

Bruno caught his howl before he got looks from everyone in the market. But he was still staring at a piece of skin hanging off his finger and still wanted to kill Menghini. What would it take for the bastard to spend a few euros for new display tables? He had been pinching his fingers on the same catches Sunday after Sunday since Sundays had been invented and the damn hinges had only gotten rustier. They didn't need a greasing, they needed a sledge hammer. But that would have meant replacing them, and it was cheaper for the hired help to cut up their hands. There wasn't a counterfeit watch or DVD Menghini wasn't making a thousand percent profit off from the tourists and the bargain hunters. Why spoil that with a new table or two?

"You get slower every week."

La Regina sat on her canvas chair with her fat pink legs squashed over one another while she sent out as much spittle as smoke with every exhale of her fancy English cigarette. Bruno couldn't tell what she was focused on through her thick *Star Wars* sunglasses: Maybe she was mocking his caution in opening the tables, maybe she was taking in the first customers wandering through the heavy furniture aisles down toward them. Either way, she cared less about his problems than her husband did. "You could get off your fat ass and give me a hand here, you know."

"Boh!" She clamped her meaty hand over her cigarette again and looked down in the other direction where Menghini had gone to get more cartons out of his van. "Maybe you should go help him unload the truck," she said behind another small shower.

"Yeah, maybe I should do that." He upended the fourth table and settled it on its frail legs, then went over to the pile where four more were waiting to be opened. He wished the sky would make up its mind, rain or not rain. Having to wrestle with the tables was aggravating, but on top of that to have to close them right back up again in a downpour? Sometimes he thought he was better off passing up the few euros Menghini gave him and stay in bed Sunday mornings.

"Rain clouds and everybody hides under the bed," she muttered. "There can't be fifty people here."

Bruno picked up the worst table of all. A drop of his blood was still on one of the hinges; its linoleum cover had rips from one end to the other. "That's where Menghini is too—hiding in the van."

Her small even teeth were something like a smile, but she really didn't think he was funny. Her father had worked the market for years, back in the days of tattered record albums and discolored bracelets, and she had never hesitated accusing Menghini of not being up the old man's standards. But she also drew a line where the weekly help was concerned. "Do what you do, Bruno. You *can* do it, can't you?"

He was glad to see Menghini finally laboring over toward them from the parking area with two more cartons. There were times when La Regina's hostility seemed like a flirtation, and he had little trouble imagining himself squeezing into her fat thighs. The trouble was, she knew that, too.

"Tables aren't up yet?"

Bruno didn't bother answering. If Menghini wasn't already a *cornuto*, it wasn't because he didn't deserve to be. Only an idiot walked around in white T-shirts every month of the year so he could show off his biceps—and also his cannon ball of a belly. "You got somebody looking for you, Lepri."

"Yeah? Who's that?'

"I don't know. Foreigner. You promise him some of this shit behind my back? I told you, I'll give you a discount, but no fucking around."

From Menghini's mouth the word *discount* sounded hilarious. But he wondered why Charley Sylvester would be up so early wandering around looking for him without simply coming over. "An American?"

Menghini made an effort at getting the DVD pile he was holding in some right side up order. "I don't know. A foreigner."

Bruno looked over to the parking area. He didn't see Sylvester or anybody else he knew. The skeleton couple with the little boy looked like they were there to price coffins and didn't know why Angelina sold only salt and pepper shakers. The blonde curled around the arm of Romeo was still piling up her gigolo adventures before she discovered her traveler's checks missing. The only other candidate appeared to be in his mid-forties; he had the build of somebody who had once played football and maybe still coached it. He might or might not have been an American, but he was definitely not Italian. "You mean that one?"

Menghini took his time turning away from his Hong Kong rip-offs. "Yeah. I told him to come with me, but I guess he's shy, don't like walking up to big celebrities. You doing these tables or what?"

Bruno had a familiar feeling about the football coach. For sure he didn't like it when the guy looked in his direction and then immediately darted his eyes back to the old timepiece in his hand he had been examining at Tresca's table. The list of people who didn't want to be seen being interested in him was far too short. He really wasn't in the mood for more cops trying to make a name for themselves by using him against Silvio Restivo. And the coach had that kind of air about him—somebody with one thought too many in his head

He jumped from the sudden pelting of the rain on the linoleum tables he had set up. They could have been gunshots. He didn't know where his edginess had come from. La Regina didn't care as long as he was there to entertain her. "It can only make you wet," she smiled nastily. "And it'll pass. Don't put up the umbrella, Carlo. They'll think it's worse than it is."

Menghini didn't have time to tell her it *was* worse than it was. One second the drops were heavy but distinct, one shot at the tables at a time, the next second the sky opened up in a barrage.

Everybody in the market was running or opening up umbrellas or cursing at somebody to cover up faster. The old bitch looked dazed as everybody and everything around her moved. The rain parted her hair and drenched her English cigarette so fast that she still had the remnant of her nasty smile as an expression. Menghini didn't wait for her to issue any more orders. With a hard swipe he cleared the table of the DVDs he had just laid out into the carton standing below. Bruno had to admire the shot. Except for one DVD that hit the top flap of the box and fell off it was 100 percent accurate. He told himself that even the football coach would have to admire it. But he couldn't see the coach's face anymore because the man had opened a portable black umbrella over his head as he continued inspecting Tresca's goods. Bruno felt better to see the umbrella. He had never heard of any cop, undercover or not, who went slinking around with an umbrella. The coach was definitely not a cop.

TWENTY-SIX

Sylvester told himself not to worry about the deluge coming. He hadn't packed an umbrella, so it simply wasn't going to rain. Better to think about the diversion in front of him. It was the oldest gag among the foreign correspondents in Rome, but he still smiled at it as he turned into Via Propaganda. Where else should most of them have offices except in a *palazzo* on a two-block strip down from the Spanish Steps called Via Propaganda? The street had been named after a Vatican department having nothing to do with reporting or its facsimiles, but who cared about that? It was more fun thinking that there had once been a sardonic imp from a Paris or London paper who had moved into the first office, savored it so much he had attracted others to the building, and pure fact had never again been transmitted abroad.

But two steps into the street made fantasies less appealing. Why was there a police cordon and why, on the other side of two dozen or so curiosity seekers, was Roenicke leaning up against a police car and looking numb as two uniformed cops with notebooks took turns trying to get through to him? As he drew closer to the corner, he saw that Roenicke was staring off at the *palazzo* doorway for something his bleary expression said was never going to appear there.

He started to call out, then thought better of it and inched further up the window of the corner Japanese restaurant so he would be directly in Roenicke's sight line. He was surprised that the guard on the barrier didn't notice—and by how quickly his move worked. Roenicke spotted him, said something to the cops, and both of them turned around to look at him. The taller cop had seen more dangerous animals in the zoo so nodded reluctantly, and Roenicke leaned off the patrol car to come over. He didn't walk so much as lurch.

"It's Claudia," he said, ignoring the hovering faces eager for a payoff to all their waiting in the damp morning.

"What about her?"

Roenicke stepped closer to the restaurant window so as not to be overheard. He had been eating garlic. "I think it was a letter bomb," he said, near stuttering. "I was just turning into the hallway when it went off. I could barely make out her face, Charley."

Sylvester heard the words. That was better than focusing on the wrinkles and spots on Roenicke's face he hadn't really noticed before. He knew the words had to be true, just as Cynthia's words on the phone about Joey Bacsik had been true. But he still didn't know what they were supposed to mean. There were too many practicalities for him to raise before he could accept what he was being told. A letter bomb on a Sunday? There were no mail deliveries on Sunday, in Italy or anywhere else that he knew about. Claudia? Who would want to hurt Claudia Ricci? The woman had been working as an office manager for the paper for more than 20 years and, truth be told, had never glowed with enough personality to make enemies. He hadn't even known what to get her from the Duty-Free shop except the usual Chanel. With somebody who had worked with him for so many years, shouldn't he have been able to think of something more personal? The perfume in his pocket could have been for any one of the women straining to hear what Roenicke was saying.

"She should've been home today. But I had a lunch with that goddamn congressional delegation and she volunteered to cover a few things for me."

Sylvester was saved from blurting something inane by a fluttering near the building entrance. The cops standing there clicked to military attention as a bald, knobby man in a rumpled tan suit and with frameless glasses stepped outside lighting a pipe. He was practiced in ignoring the respect shown him by underlings.

But what caught him unawares was looking up from his lighter and not seeing Roenicke with the cops who had been taking his statement.

"The one in charge," Roenicke said. "Gaetano. You better come over with me. In case Porterfield wants a record."

Sylvester understood the pieces, but not the whole. He knew Porterfield liked records of everything, including supermarket shopping lists from correspondents if one of them was half-witted enough to send them. He knew that Roenicke had learned how to cover his ass from his father and generations of Roenickes on the paper's board. And he could see the son of a bitch was still trembling about what had apparently happened upstairs in the office. But he still felt at cross-purposes with the street around him as Roenicke introduced him to the Inspector named Gaetano as "my colleague from the home office." Gaetano eyed him as somebody unlikely to have broken the time barrier getting from New York to Via Propaganda because of Claudia Ricci.

"You would be of great assistance, *signori*," the man said with an odd buzz in his throat that might have been from a bee he had swallowed, "if you would accompany me to my office. It will only take a few minutes, and it's best to resolve as much as we can before we have feeding time." His baggy eyes slid over to the barrier at the other side of the block where a matched set of him-and-her redheads looked very much like local reporters. "This way, please."

Roenicke held back. "I left my phone upstairs and I should call New York to tell them what's happened."

Gaetano made the sacrifice of taking his pipe out of his mouth. "I thought you had already informed them through Signor Sylvester," he said drily. "But no worry. There are telephones where we are going."

He didn't know why Roenicke pouted for having to follow over to the blue sedan parked outside the barrier; if anyone had anything to gripe about, it was the Obituaries editor who was supposed to be on vacation. Then he wondered if he had another grouch coming over the little razzamatazz Gaetano worked at the car. With a uniformed cop already behind the wheel, the inspector quickly locked in the rest of the seating arrangement by taking a back door and nodding for him to take the other, leaving Roenicke no choice but to sit up front with the uniform. Somewhere in a police past that must have covered a good 30 years, he thought, Gaetano had made the mistake of letting two witnesses to something sit next to one another in the back and communicate to each other. People like Gaetano didn't make that mistake twice.

They had barely set off when the rain thundered down. It took only a second for the windows to turn into a smear. The driver searched for the wipers on the dashboard as if he had never used them before. This amused Gaetano. *"Petrino, per la mor' di dio.'*

The driver named Petrino finally found the right button. *"Eccolo!"*

"You were here some years ago, were you not, Mister Sylvester?" Gaetano asked abruptly, no longer mesmerized by his driver and not caring who he was bathing in his caramel tobacco he relighted.

"It's nice to be remembered."

"Ten years or so ago? I was in Milan then. Though I think we actually ran into one another during one of those bloodless European foreign ministers meetings."

"I'm sorry, I don't recall."

He thought that funny, in an unfunny way. "So you can remember those meetings but not me! What does that say about *my* bloodlessness?"

Sylvester looked out the window with the discomfort he had apparently been meant to feel. They had to be going to the Viminale Palace of the Interior Ministry, but from what he could make out through the window Petrino was taking the scenic route through Naples. Had he missed a signal between the driver and Gaetano as they had all been climbing into the car?

"There's no reason for this, none," Roenicke said from the front, mainly to himself. "We haven't had any kind of threats."

"When we arrive, Signore. I'm sure we'll work it all out."

Sylvester told himself to take that advice. By himself he would have connected so many dots—the Cicut journal, Joey Bacsik, the skulker named Leonard Warneke, Roenicke's creepy behavior around Father Minic—he wouldn't have left any of them visible. Just because he had been drafted into things against his will didn't mean he had a license for losing his objectivity.

"And what about you, Mister Sylvester? What brings you here?"

"Vacation."

"Ah! Seeing old friends."

"One less now."

Gaetano looked surprisingly offended by the answer and turned away to open his window and empty his pipe out into the rain. "Yes. One less."

When they finally arrived at the Viminale, Gaetano stayed put for a second to scan the cars parked nearby. "Your embassy appears to be slow about getting to the latest news bulletins," he said. "Well, good for me. You can fill them in later."

The policeman didn't let the glistening of the entrance steps stop him from taking them briskly. Inside the portico he looked at the two of them to confirm that he had less rain to dry off his head and forehead than they did, appeared satisfied, then made for the screening booth. "None of us is exempt," he said over his shoulder as he emptied his pockets of keys and change into the tray. "Better that way, don't you agree? Nobody gets used to thinking of himself as more worthy than anybody else just because of a title or an employer."

Sylvester didn't know what the smile on the guard's face meant. That Gaetano made the same speech every time he entered the building? That nobody resented the security precautions than he did? Or was it the first time in memory the man had ever submitted to the X-ray machine, seeing it more important for the moment to deliver a homily to the two journalists from the big-time American paper?

He wondered what the X-rays would do to Claudia's Chanel as it rode the conveyor belt into the machine.

TWENTY-SEVEN

There was nothing of the we're-all-equals about the castle hall Gaetano called an office. The desk in front of the floor-to-high-ceiling window was wide enough to accommodate three dais VIPs and just low enough not to make the policeman the cartoon character who disappeared except for his big nose when he sat down behind it. "*Pazienza, signori,*" he said, waving them to the tall episcopal chairs in front of him and opening a file envelope he had been handed on his way inside.

From the modern furnishings he had seen in the outer offices they had passed through, Sylvester decided Gaetano must have had a personal nostalgia for his medieval trappings. They infected him with his own nostalgia for his cave back in New York, superfluous couch included. Everything around him was too chilly, too somber, and especially too empty. The air conditioner above the door rattled indifferently before the rain pelting the window, not caring what temperatures it blew as long as it was louder. The only items covering the arch mousy brown walls were a conveyor-belt photograph of the President of the Republic, a print of some greenish tubal pasta kind of thing, and a cork board stripped of everything but a few red and green push pins. Even the long desk was bare except for a telephone, computer monitor and leather-bound date book. It was the ambiance of somebody who had caught a jacket thread in the door stepping out of his time machine.

"Perhaps the vintners of Reggio Emilia?"

Roenicke needed a second to realize the question hadn't come from the lint on the knee of his pants. "Excuse me?"

"Your recent stories for your newspaper," Gaetano said, waving the computer printout in his hand. "Any angry vintners in Reggio Emilia?"

Roenicke didn't know what irritated him more—the flip tone or the evidently easy access to his filings. "I told you, Inspector. There's nothing controversial lately that could have caused this."

The policeman shrugged and returned his glasses to the printout. "Is that good or bad for a journalist? How can you interest readers if you don't upset somebody?"

Sylvester was disappointed Roenicke could bristle so easily. Then again he hadn't been the one working with Claudia Ricci lately. "Are you sure this bomb was really intended for Eddie's office? You can't have analyzed what's left of the envelope yet. There are plenty of other correspondents in that building."

Gaetano gave him the same spoilsport look he had back in the car. "And your employee Signora Ricci opens envelopes addressed to others as a matter of course? No, Mister Sylvester. We have no doubts on that question. The *portiere* who brought the envelope upstairs confirms it was addressed to Mister Roenicke."

"So you know who delivered it."

"Unfortunately not. Probably by design, the *portiere* was not at his station when the envelope was left on his desk. Life isn't always so elegant."

Sylvester told himself to shut up. The only thing clumsier than not knowing something was making the mistake of assuming others didn't know it, either.

"And what about your newspaper in New York, Mister Roenicke? Has it been editorializing in a way to aggravate temperamental people?"

"You mean terrorists?"

"I don't know what I mean. That is why I am asking. *Has* there been some problem with a terrorist group? Threats? Warnings?"

"Not that I know. Charley?"

"Nothing I know about. I might not know anyway."

"Really, Signore? I thought you worked in the main office."

"Not in Editorial. What you call Necrology."

"A correspondent of your experience?"

The bait flapped around so obviously Sylvester couldn't even work up a fantasy to throttle the little bookkeeper. "So what's next, Inspector? Something useful?"

At least Gaetano had a sense of humor. "Next will be to move on to other possible motives. For instance, something personal in your life, Signor Roenicke."

"That's ridiculous. I know nobody who wants to blow me up."

"Not quite accurate. There may be at least one person. Perhaps if we were in New York, we could attribute it to the wrong Edward Roenicke. But I cannot imagine there are too many Edward Roenickes in Italy, can you?"

Roenicke didn't bother giving him his answer and Gaetano was left to sigh and let the printout collapse on his blotter like a last felled tree. "Well, then we must hope that where two trails end, others open up. Where would you suggest we begin looking?"

Sylvester wouldn't have minded if the desk *had* been a little higher to make Gaetano a cartoon character on the other side. He didn't like sharing his sensation that there was something just a little too twitchy about Roenicke. The guy's jitters should have been about losing Claudia so brutally or about Gaetano's skepticism toward him or about a dozen other natural things, but what it felt like was Roenicke's awkwardness in his living room when they had been alone and the questions had been about the exclusivity of the guest list for the dinner party.

"So you can suggest nothing, Signor Roenicke?"

"If I had . . ."

"Of course, of course. But we know that trail is out there somewhere, do we not?" The telephone rang with a buzz like the one in Gaetano's throat. "Excuse me."

The call was the last straw for Roenicke. He gave up trying to control his fidgets and stood up with a sigh a ham actor couldn't have improved on. It had finally dawned on him that somebody had tried to kill him, and his breathing came with more of an effort. Gaetano noticed by not noticing. Whatever was being said into his ear might have been nothing at all, the other party might have already hung up, but he sat back in his chair with just enough monosyllabic replies to justify his prop while he furtively studied Roenicke pacing up and down the length of the office.

"We have to call Claudia's sister, Charley. We can't let her hear this from the television or the radio."

Sylvester remembered the sister—a tall woman with a chipped front tooth who was a doctor and had three or four kids. "Marisa? Mara?"

"Letizia. Lives somewhere near the Piazza Vittorio."

"I don't remember where she lives."

"Well, I'm telling you. Near the Piazza Vittorio."

"Sit down, Eddie. You're making us both nervous."

Gaetano seemed satisfied to have arrived at an effect he had been awaiting. "Yes, please do sit, Signor," he said, hanging up. "I understand how this episode can unnerve you, but you are still the most likely person to point us in the right investigative direction. We've eliminated your dispatches and you have no personal enemies. That would seem to leave us with your other activities."

"What activities?"

Another patronizing shrug. "You tell me."

"This is intolerable!"

"More for Signora Ricci, I would think," the policeman shot back, new iron in his voice. "So let me state it as clearly as I can. If you cannot provide an arrow or two for us, we will have to find them ourselves, no matter how intrusive that will put us in your life. An Italian national has been murdered in the center of the city, and *that* is what will not be tolerated."

Roenicke looked so miserable Sylvester was tempted to throw in Minic's name for the hell of it. Then he thought better of it—because, he was suddenly sure, Roenicke had been thinking better of it since Via Propaganda!

"Something you can contribute, Mister Sylvester?"

Gaetano smelled it, too, but he hadn't been there for Myra's penne and veal and wasn't quite sure what the odor was. "Claudia was a friend of mine, too."

The policeman waited for more, and so long that Sylvester was on the verge of throwing in Leonard Warneke's perambulating habits just to relieve his awkwardness in front of the desk. But then Gaetano accepted there wouldn't be more. "I believe I heard you say there is a sister of the deceased," he said, turning back to Roenicke. "I would appreciate your leaving her name and address in case it is not among the victim's belongings. And of course, as of now you will be escorted by two of my men everywhere you go until further notice. That is not negotiable. In case it has slipped your mind, the envelope was addressed to you, not to the unfortunate Signora Ricci."

Roenicke's gloom said he wasn't so convinced who was the unfortunate one.

TWENTY-EIGHT

Bruno made up his mind to confront the football coach. The cat-and-mouse game had gone on long enough. First there had been the market where the creepy stranger had been eying him while standing under his umbrella at Tresca's table. Then there had been the two hours at Giuliana's when the coach had been nowhere in sight while he had been listening to Menghini and the other rained out dealers grousing about the money they had been spending on bad wine instead of making it on cheap merchandise. Then the creep had appeared again, standing in the rain in front of the cinema half a block away, as they had all gone down to the Sette Bello bar for a decent coffee. Had he been standing there the whole time? What kind of maniac did that? Now, as he shivered in his shirt sleeves as he made his way home through the heavy mist, Bruno glimpsed the wiry man again through a store window, still a half-block or so away but bolder in his stride. He was still under his little umbrella, but didn't look as harmless as he had back in the market or as weird as he had in front of the movie house. If he was a cop, he had clearly decided to get down to the harassment he had in mind.

Bruno would have taken any other day of the week. The perfect corner for an ambush was at the Via Clio up ahead. It offered a sharp turn that gave him the benefit of surprise against anyone coming up after him, and also sprawled out openly into the fruit market where dozens of witnesses could protect him against anybody who overcame the surprise to get the better of him. Except it was Sunday, and there was no market, no housewives ready to lift their eyes from oranges and carrots to protect him, just a desolate little square being soaked to a glitter. Even the tables at the bar down on the next corner had been pulled in because of the rain. If he was going to surprise the coach and find out why he was being followed, he was going to have to do it without another body on the street watching.

He had to do it anyway. The nearest he had to a weapon in his pocket if things got ugly was his sharp *portone* key, but if the coach was really a cop, he didn't want things to get ugly. He felt like a fool standing still against the wall next to the closed wine shop. He wouldn't have been any less wet if he had kept walking, but that wasn't how it felt. He blamed the sudden hot growling in his stomach on the oily *carciofi* he had eaten at Giuliana's. He could have dropped some *caca* on the street right then and there. And what should have been the first words out of his mouth when the coach reached the corner? Should they have been something threatening? Something innocent? The simple curiosity of somebody who wanted to know why he was being followed?

He needn't have worried. When the coach reached the corner, he did so all the way over near the gutter, fully expecting to see Bruno waiting for him. Under his umbrella he grinned. "You're going to get a cold standing there like that, Bruno," he said in a heavy accent that might have been German or Polish. "Best way to get a cold."

"What do you want?"

The coach eyed him up and down, like a cop who was used to being sure others didn't have hidden weapons. "Talk to you. What else?"

"About what?"

"We could go somewhere dryer."

"Say what you have to say."

"I was referred to you by a mutual friend, Officer Badalamenti."

Bruno wanted to kick himself. He should have never asked a favor of that fat slob Badalamenti. He had been too eager to help Charley Sylvester after so many years. And what had he gotten for it? Now the rain had even penetrated his shoes. "Don't you people ever give up? I don't play *piccione* for you with Restivo. Don't you have enough little mice already doing that for you? Get your promotion or your payoff or whatever it is you're after without me."

Bruno couldn't believe it happened so fast. He couldn't have taken more than three or four steps away from the wine shop when the man's fingers were on his wrist. Every bone he had there felt like it was splintering. And even as he continued to hold the umbrella over his head with his free hand, the foreigner's eyes shone with a cold finality. "Wet or dry, it makes no difference. But you will tell me, Bruno."

Bruno knew he had been wrong. There was something too bare, too unapologetic about the strong hand around his wrist for the coach to be just another cop on the make. He didn't want to look too long into the man's eyes. It would only confirm he wouldn't find anything familiar there. "Whatever Badalamenti told you . . ."

"Was the truth. Just like what you will tell me."

Bruno remembered he had a free arm, much freer than the coach had with his umbrella. He could have swung it around and broken the grip on his wrist without a problem. But the coach's expectant smile said that would have only made bad worse.

TWENTY-NINE

Zagreb
   Informant MJ completely incommunicado. Aides cannot commit to date for meeting. Not surprised by events in Rome.

THIRTY

Roenicke finally ended his tap dancing. He knew they had a conversation—a long conversation—coming and he at least had the grace to skip saying he had to run off to repair the Coliseum. As soon as they were back outside the Viminale, he pointed to a bar across the street and loped down the steps without a word. Sylvester followed obediently but slowly, wishing he had the confidence of either Gaetano going up or Roenicke going down for negotiating the sodden concrete. His vertical agility didn't seem to improve with age.

The bar was a retreat for the cops and clerks assigned to the Interior Ministry. Even on a Sunday afternoon there were enough uniforms in the place to police the center of the city; the most casual conversations at the cluster of tables in the back rang with volleys of harsh, authoritative voices.

"You asked me about Applebaum, about all his visits here," Roenicke said, trying to conceal his shaking hand by stirring his spoon through his cappuccino.

"That was before . . ."

"Let me do it in order, okay, Charley?"

"Okay."

Roenicke nodded; he needed reassurance he had won at something. "Yeah, he's been coming through more than normal," he said, working to keep his eyes on his spoon. "And it's not just for the paper. A word here, a word there. You know what I mean."

"No, I don't, Eddie. I told you that. There's a little bit too much of 'You know what I mean' when I don't. What else has Applebaum been doing here?"

He hadn't really expected a pass. "He's the one who introduced me to Minic. He said the guy was worth cultivating as deep background for the Balkans."

"Okay. So he was worth cultivating and he has his own agenda with his Freedom Press crowd. When's that not been part of the job? You listen to Minic, you listen to the anti-Minic, and you try to write facts. Every once in a while you trip across the truth."

"That simple?"

"Unless you got a better system."

He took his cappuccino in both hands to siphon off the foam. He kept looking at the cup after all the foam was gone. "Minic acted like some kind of pilot fish with the paper as the whale. He was by the office or on the phone two or three times a week. Even started calling me at home. I should meet this one, I should meet that one. Always with an Italian angle, of course, otherwise why bother me with it. Refugees from the Balkans. A poet who couldn't get his work published at home. An undersecretary at the Farnesina who was practically a lobbyist for Minic's friends. I don't know how many dinners and lunches I had to say no to. Overall, I got useful background for maybe two stories. Just for the Web, of course. You never saw them, I bet. Thanks to Porterfield."

"Let's stay on track."

He should have resented the tone, but he was too deep into making up for neglected confessions. The pain in his eyes made him look younger—stupefied younger. "A few months back Applebaum dropped in. Said I wasn't taking as much advantage of Minic as I should have. Ruining his middleman reputation."

"And you told him to go fuck himself."

He smiled feebly. "For a long time now, I've felt like I was at a dead end here. One that was going on and on. Can dead ends run on and on? I don't know. But the paper was running about twenty percent of what I was filing. Myra didn't want to hear about moving, didn't want me even mentioning the subject, so forget about enthusiasm for asking for a transfer. With Berlusconi gone there wasn't even a squalid orgy or some arrogance of power story to write. Like I told you the other day, economy, economy, economy. And I'm not an economist. I know: the whole world is collapsing under those red numbers or inflated numbers or whatever the hell they are. But it wasn't something you ran down to the Treasury Ministry or Labor Ministry in the morning to get excited about. And how many times can you write about Vatican hypocrisy or the decline of some ancient custom to fill in the gaps? 'Whatever happened to those guys who caned chairs like Dante wrote poetry? Oh, here's Giuseppe, the last of his breed, in his little Trastevere shop.' I needed something . . ."

"Sexy."

"For my own sanity. I mean, we can feel like hacks sometimes, but Christ, can't we at least entertain ourselves every once in a while, hold on to the illusion that we're the only ones who have access to something nobody else does?"

"And that was Minic."

"You weren't entertained by him?"

"What's it all about, Eddie?"

A couple entered the back and took the last available table. The woman had made a stab at being a blonde, the man at shaving that day. They took their chairs in a smoothly autonomous way: not a husband and wife, but like police partners who assumed the other could do the appropriate social thing. When the woman gave him a half-nod, Sylvester knew they were the escort Gaetano had arranged for Roenicke. He nodded back to the woman and she immediately looked away from him.

"Things started heating up with this Croat election campaign." After Elena Cicut's tale, Sylvester knew what name was coming. "Minic and his friends think this Jelic guy is the Second Coming. For the Good Father he's the only one with a shot at bringing the Serbs and Bosnians into a real functioning coalition with the Croats. Minic said he could get me an interview with him."

Sylvester had a curdling reminder of being immersed in the New York bureaucracy too long: Turfs were supposed to be turfs. A Rome correspondent, not one from Zagreb or even Belgrade, talking to a Croat politician? He could see Porterfield charging down the hall to ask the Foreign Desk what was going on. "That must've gone over big with some people."

"I told Minic ahead of time. I said, I'll see this guy without any guarantees. But even if I do a piece, I'm going to identify him as a radical nationalist who probably has the *least* chance of bringing everybody together around the campfire, and I'm also going to identify you as the one who arranged everything. No problem, he says. He's not ashamed of his beliefs, and Jelic certainly isn't. Let the world in on the secret."

"And that was enough for Porterfield and his sense of turf?"

Roenicke shrugged. "I guess. He didn't stop me."

"Sorry, but I missed that on the Web, too."

"Because I didn't write anything." He still wasn't sure whether he was proud of it. "I met the guy in a restaurant in Trieste. His praetorian guard didn't frisk me, but they had X-ray eyes when they stared at my pockets. The restaurant had been a warehouse in another life, and the people I saw eating there looked like they liked thinking their fathers had once broken their backs lifting crates in the place. That's Jelic's line, and he wasn't wrong. Place still smelled of sawdust. Anyway, he thought I was funny for trotting along with Minic. Ten seconds with the guy, and I wanted to be out of there. He spoke English, but all he used it for were these little speeches he had memorized. He was everybody's friend, especially in the West. Minus the thugs around him. I could have gotten the same shit off his website. It was a big waste of time—for me, anyway. Not for him, of course. He'd gotten the paper to come to him. And Minic, he was in clover! The Pope didn't have more accomplished diplomats."

"And your accomplishment was not passing along his crap. That's not why you're jittery, Eddie, or why somebody sent you a letter bomb."

He hadn't held out much hope of getting that by, either. "No. A couple of days later Minic called. I thought he was going to ask when he could expect to read the interview in the paper. But it was just the opposite. He suggested holding off publishing anything. When I asked him why, he said there had been what he called *developments*. I told him I'd seen that movie, too. When I asked about these mysterious developments, he said he'd get back to me. I spent the rest of that day reading every wire service I could. I even called Griffith in Belgrade. Nothing direct, just how have you been, what's new at your end? Nothing. He didn't have anything that would have added up to a *development*. Nothing in Zagreb, either? Griffith didn't know. Our stringer there was off on safari in Tanzania for a vacation. Nothing he had heard anyway. I got off the phone before he started getting suspicious."

"And this development, that turned out to be Cicut?"

He nodded. "I didn't know anything about it for a couple of days. Then Applebaum dropped in again. Just kind of slipped it in: 'Didn't you once do an interview with Josef Cicut?' People who ask you questions they know the answers to . . ."

"Should be trial lawyers."

"Right. But there was more than that. He started to talk about the rumors around Cicut's death. Was it a heart attack? Was it suicide the Croats in Germany were trying to cover up? You didn't know what to believe, did you? And the whole time he was waiting for me to volunteer something he thought I knew."

"But you didn't."

"Like what? I didn't even know the guy was dead before Applebaum told me. If you add up what all of us over here seem to know before the lemon vendors on the corner, the paper would have a case for closing half its offices in Europe."

"But Claude wasn't to be discouraged."

He shook his head. "He thought it might be a good idea to contact Cicut's widow and get her take on everything. I told him I didn't think so. One, whatever happened or didn't happen in Germany was what happened or didn't happen in Germany so go bother the Berlin office. Two, my last little foray outside of what should have been my territory had only gotten me a roller coaster flight to Trieste. And three, I wasn't exactly bosom buddies with the Cicuts after the first interview. I guess you never told him the background to that little piece."

"Must've slipped my mind. But we're still not to Claudia."

"No." He looked around restlessly for the bartender who was doubling as a waiter, but the kid was too busy with a cycling race on the TV set. "That shouldn't have happened, Charley," he said, his voice barely above a cringe. "It shouldn't have happened to her and it shouldn't have happened to me."

Sylvester had been premature back in Gaetano's office: Only now was the full force of the letter bomb descending on Roenicke. His eyes stared blindly into the table cloth pattern of oddly purple roses. His long fingers couldn't even hold a steady strum on the rose he had focused on. "We should've ordered something stronger."

"I'll buy you every drop in the bar. Just tell me how it got this bad."

He nodded without agreeing. "Maybe it hasn't. I'm still not sure. Maybe it *was* those vintners Gaetano was talking about. Maybe Myra's got a secret lover and he's tired of being a secret. What do you think?"

"You wanted to take it in order. Go back to that."

"I did say that, didn't I?"

"Yeah."

He turned in more tightly to the table, trying to forget the bartender he wanted a drink from. "You must've still been on the tarmac at JFK. Applebaum called me from New York, said there was this rumor about a diary. It might or might not be true, but if anybody knew for sure, it would be Minic and maybe there'd be a story for me in it." He smiled forlornly. "What Minic mainly knew was that you were probably the one who knew the most about it and that you were on your way to Rome."

Sylvester didn't know why he had ordered a Campari. He had never really liked Campari. And he wanted to believe what Roenicke did: There was no real proof the bombing had been the work of people connected to Minic and Warneke. Least of all that it might have been connected to a nitwit who had insisted on asking an old man to translate a copy of what he had then carted across the Atlantic. Via Propaganda was infamous for breeding fantasies like that. Ask anybody.

THIRTY-ONE

Sylvester thought of the Oxford philosopher John Warren. Warren hadn't been Plato or Hegel or Nietzsche, but he had been a prolific author of scholarly texts in which the word *positivism* had figured prominently in the title and which had been praised by his fellow British academics as classroom-shattering in their implications. Sylvester had never heard of the professor until he had had to put together his obituary on one of his first days at his new position in New York. He would have bet not a single writer, editor, or maintenance man on the paper had ever heard of John Warren. And the lights at Piccadilly Circus hadn't exactly been dimmed in honor of his passing, either. But that hadn't mattered. He had been determined to write the don's death notice himself, to show his staff that there had to be a new direction on the Obit page even though he hadn't had the slightest idea if that meant east, west, or simply down a different rabbit hole. He had collected every word he could find on John Warren in the clips (mainly reviews of the books of other philosophers) and on the Internet, then had sat at his desk for most of an afternoon daring the snippets of thought in front of him to answer his criticisms of them. What criticisms? He couldn't recall. The important thing was to argue with a philosopher philosophically, as he would have argued with a pitcher about his pitch selection or with a plumber about his choice of wrenches. He had shot the day that way, at best finding reasonable grounds for quibbles, more often resigned to not being able to follow the logical processes that had led John Warren to conclude whatever the hell he had concluded. He had obsessed so long over what should have been a simple rewrite that he had missed the deadline for composing the Obit page and had been forced to shelve the notice until the following day, when it had appeared as a two-paragraph item that suggested the paper's new Obituary Editor had been no more familiar with Professor John Warren than the *Post* or *News* editors had been. That impression hadn't been wrong, it had just been ignorant of how much effort had gone into verifying it.

Now he thought Roenicke's stare—an admission of too much passivity but still with a demand for information—could have been from one of John Warren's relatives. What had he been wasting so much time for? He wanted to tell the idiot he knew more than he gave the impression of knowing, but he couldn't because what did that add up to aside from a lot of futile and not especially learned speculation? He possessed more than Roenicke knew back in the safe of his hotel, but he possessed absolutely nothing. His voice sounded out of practice when he said, "You've become awfully open to story ideas from Applebaum."

"I told you."

"Right. The scoop of the century. Because he'd been so right about so many other leads. Like your little jaunt to Trieste."

Roenicke didn't retreat; his expression seemed even hungrier. "You win some, you lose some, right?"

"And Minic, too? You've been taking your leads from a couple of pretty B-movie characters, Eddie. Why's that?"

He didn't like that question. He preferred getting back to his own. "Is it true, Charley? Is there some kind of diary the family told you about?"

"Who's asking—you or Minic?"

For what seemed like the first time all morning Roenicke backed off from himself, could even scoff at a distance from Eddie Roenicke's world. "You don't have to worry about that. After you left the house, the Good Father got into a snit about how I'd been less than the perfect host. What he meant was that I didn't do enough to shut you and Myra up with all the theater talk. Too bad for him Myra heard him and told him that if he didn't like the conversation at her dinner table, he should find his free meals somewhere else. By the time he was giving me a stiff *Buona Notte* I figured Myra had gotten her wish, that he wouldn't be around anymore, that I had outlived my usefulness to him. So no, Charley, I'm asking for me, not for Minic or Applebaum."

"Why?"

"That sounds like the answer."

He had been so busy with the pathetic Eddie Roenicke that he had lost sight of the professional Eddie Roenicke. "But you should be working on another one—what Gaetano asked you. You have to have *some* idea of who sent you that bomb."

A spear of sunlight suddenly shot through the window and directly into his face. He had too many lines under his eyes for his age, but he had thrown them into the pot of things it was too late to deny. "What do you think I've been thinking about ever since it happened? You have to be a fanatic to do that, right? How many fanatics do I know?"

"You've mentioned two since we sat down here."

"And what sense would that make? Jelic is taking time out from remaking Eastern Europe so he can blow up this correspondent who let him practice his speeches? I don't think so. Minic has taken an extra vow to get rid of anybody he decides isn't useful to him anymore? Tell me that makes sense, Charley."

"You made an enemy somewhere."

"*Enemy.* You mean the kind of guy who'd come up and shoot me or stab me? Letter-bombs aren't that kind of enemy. They're impersonal, neon signs for everybody to see. I can't even claim almost being killed is the sexy story I was looking for. I might have been the target, somebody else might have been the target, Claudia *was* the target. If Gaetano's half the cop he acts like he is, he'll figure out that whoever sent that bomb is probably just as satisfied right now he took out Claudia instead of me. Message delivered. Whatever it is."

Sylvester sat up straight. He was sure Roenicke was right, in a way. The *message* was the key. But it couldn't have been to Roenicke because he would have been presumed already splattered all over his office. The special delivery had been meant for someone who would have been told about Roenicke getting killed—whoever that was. "Is that what you'll tell them at the embassy?"

Roenicke glanced at his watch, then looked up with a wink. "Let's hope they're interested to hear it."

Sylvester tried to look sympathetic, savvy, and anything else that wouldn't give away his awareness of their profound conversation in half-truths.

THIRTY-TWO

Bell knew the shrilling bird in his pocket was his fault. If he wasn't secure enough to leave his phone in the car, he should have at least turned it off before entering church. There weren't many excuses for being out of contact with Broderick, but being in church headed the very short list. Anybody who went off on a religious retreat every September as Frank Broderick did couldn't hold the privacy of Sunday Mass against an underling. But Bell had neglected to take advantage of that, embarrassingly so, and now Catherine's glare was spreading along their pew and all the way up to the altar boy who turned back at him with a snotty expression. Bell mumbled an apology to whoever could hear him at mumble level and got up the aisle to the back of the church as fast as he could. Looking through the frowns (and one expression of glee) from the back pews, he traded off on another couple of rings so he wouldn't have to answer until he was out in the vestibule. Finally through the swinging doors, he pressed in Broderick. He expected to hear annoyance for a call at such an hour, and he wasn't disappointed. But at least it didn't sound directed only at him. "We have a problem in Rome."

That was hilariously appropriate, Bell thought, glancing at the blown-up photo of the Pope's visit to New York next to the door: Where else but in Rome? Then he had a second, more troubling thought as Broderick went tersely into detail: He had been too quick to think that sending off the copy of Cicut's diary would resolve the situation. With the official agitation in his ear he knew it mattered little that he had even gone the extra mile by making sure Sylvester's secretary hadn't understood what she had copied. "Now we have the body of an Italian national in the middle. A secretary, for Christ sake. They're totally out of control, Walter."

Bell had never forgotten his first lesson at the Academy from the acne-faced agent named McClellan: *"When the situation gives every impression of being black, make doubly sure it isn't white before you proceed a single step,"* McClellan had said over and over. "Or trying to tell us they're completely *in* control," he ventured. "Which we can disabuse them of by quoting a few lines from the diary."

"That's not in the cards right now."

He could have done without the bruiser with the bloodshot eyes coming out through the vestibule doors and heading straight for the street exit in a race with his stomach or bowels. It was bad enough the slug didn't have the staying power for an entire Mass with his hangover, but what could the asshole have thought of somebody fielding business calls during it? "Well, get a new deck, Frank," he blurted as soon as the street door banged closed. "They're pushing to tell us they're in charge, that they can wake up every politician and editor on both sides of the Atlantic. But they won't be so cocky when they realize what we have. Why are we delaying?"

"It's a question of timing."

Bell was sorry he had answered the phone. At least one hour a week he was able to put complications out of his head, feel perfectly secure following the step-by-step ritual of Mass he had known since his days as an altar boy. But Broderick and the procrastinators he never seemed able to shake up were now making him furious. "We've invested in this, Frank. Heavily. *I've* invested in this. Personally. If they don't know we have what we do, they're going to keep going after the original. And that's going to give you more headlines you don't want."

"I wish you'd tell me something I don't know, Walter."

Left up to him, Bell thought, he could have watched the Jelic people blow themselves up for their overreaching and not missed a meal. The worst to come out of that, at least if his name wasn't

Charley Sylvester, would be a finer appreciation of the long view—that the only lasting cure for lunacy was letting the lunatics destroy themselves. But he knew no one wanted to hear that. Catherine didn't want to discover his monthly paycheck hadn't been deposited in the bank. Broderick didn't want to admit he didn't have two or three alternate scenarios for their next move. Even the church he was pacing within didn't want to abide that kind of cynicism. One way or another, the game had to go on.

"It wouldn't have to come from us, Frank."

"What wouldn't?"

"What your people have translated."

Broderick sounded like he moved his mouth closer to the receiver. "Meaning?"

"There's a police investigation going on here about this Bacsik. Why couldn't something come from them?"

"Because I just told you they don't want . . ."

"Yeah, I heard that. And you know it. But the NYPD is the NYPD. They stumble into something and tell the wrong reporter about it and it gets out, that's not our fault. And Christ knows they invented leaks down at Police Plaza. Didn't you ever watch *Kojak* when it was on?"

"You're playing with fire, Walter."

"More than everybody else is? You said it yourself: They've got a dead Italian national over there. Who were they really after? Roenicke? Applebaum? They've declared war, Frank. What's the worst that could happen?"

"The people who sign your checks might not like you dicking around with them."

He had noticed it before: Bravado had a bad habit of not wanting to be withdrawn. "Like I say, what's the worst that could happen?"

Broderick had already worked that out. "This Sylvester, for one thing."

Bell congratulated himself for having the answer to that objection so readily. "Yeah, well, that's more of that timing thing they're so preoccupied with. The cops say too much before midnight, Sylvester's okay. They say it afterward, he's not okay, but our friends over there realize they have a handful of flies. One way or the other, they're back in their cages."

Broderick made a sound like a moan: He had already decided. "With one extra."

"What?"

"I want the original, too."

"We don't need it."

"We need it, Walter. When you're buying a Rembrandt, you don't brag to the world how you've got an authentic copy. Can you take care of that?"

Bell didn't understand why that had to be his job. Hadn't he already contributed enough with Bacsik? But he seemed to have won enough arguments in the last five minutes to throw in a freebie. "Okay."

He knew the silence meant Broderick was looking pleased with himself. "How's Catherine and the kids?"

"I better get back to her. You got me at Mass."

"Oh. Sorry. Thought you went to an earlier one."

Bell told himself to be magnanimous and to chalk it up to Broderick's ignorance, not his indifference. "I'll keep you posted."

Bell clicked Off before Broderick could disconnect them. He liked doing that with Frank Broderick and everybody else. A vain little act, he couldn't deny it and he had mentioned it in his confessions for years, but he still felt better dismissing others before they dismissed him.

So why wasn't he feeling altogether content? Why did he have the sudden feeling that Broderick had maneuvered him in some way, and for more than having to get the original of the diary? Had it been something said? It had to have been, but he couldn't zero in on what exactly.

Or had it been something unsaid?

How did you locate something unsaid?

He physically shook his head, as if expecting to see all the defective and insufficient parts of his thoughts tumble out on the vestibule floor. He didn't recognize any of the deformed pieces, so he went back inside before Catherine began wondering what he was doing. He arrived just in time for the Communion.

THIRTY-THREE

Sylvester stood in the doorway as if accomplishing something. The bed was made, the light rose blanket pulled tightly up to the pillows. The weed-like flower stood at attention in its tiny glass vase on the bed table next to the telephone. The numbers and letters on the telephone buttons didn't look like they had been tinkered with; from his distance anyway. The wastepaper basket under the bed table, the bureau, the closet—they were all where they were supposed to be. The morning papers were stacked on the dresser with the same *Il Corriere* on top that he had left on top before going out to see Roenicke. On the other hand, they were stacked evenly, fold edge flush against fold edge, and that he definitely had not done. Was that the work of the hotel maid or of some intruder? Would an intruder bent on killing him the way Claudia Ricci had been killed also have paused to vacuum the carpet? He didn't think so.

He closed the door behind him, committing himself to whatever booby trap would blow him to pieces. The crawly feeling had been with him since he had left Roenicke and the police escort outside the bar. Watching the would-be blonde and the Five O'clock Shadow bundle Roenicke into their blue sedan for the drive to the embassy had made him feel alone, unprotected. He was the one the diary had made most vulnerable, wasn't he? Granted he hadn't shared that information with Gaetano, but if the inspector was as insightful as he pretended to be, shouldn't he have figured that out without help? Why assign both cops to Roenicke? Couldn't he have had the blonde for himself?

There was no answer except from the fountain burbling outside.

Sylvester shucked his jacket and kicked off his loafers. He shouldn't have been surprised by his determination to be depressed. With or without diaries and letter bombs, he hated late Sunday afternoons. He always seemed to be walking alone through strange cities at that hour, knowing nobody, watching other people who knew everybody. Even stretching out on the bed of a hotel he knew in a city he knew felt like walking through strangers on Sunday afternoons. Did it go back to his school days, when he had had to acknowledge that the weekend was over and that he had to do his homework? He had never come up with a better theory, but whether because of that or something else, on Sunday afternoons he felt too early for some things, too late for others. He wanted to give in to crying out for a new start for everything. Then the urge receded again. There were the practicalities, including some like Pat and Nick he didn't want to give back, so he had to accept that starting over would never happen.

He picked up the phone before he had to put up with himself anymore. He had no reason to expect to find Cynthia at home on a Sunday, but she was there anyway. "It's my puzzle hour," she said. "The theme is football. In the summer!"

"Call a time-out and answer me something."

"Make it personal, Sylvester. If it's about the office, I'm hanging up."

"Almost personal."

She thought that funny despite herself. "Okay. What?"

"That copy of the diary you gave Bacsik . . ."

"I have no idea," she said immediately. "Either the police have it and aren't saying or . . . . .well . . ."

"Right. The coincidence conspiracy."

"What's going on, Charley? You called just for that?"

For once he had an almost tenable lie. "Well, I was with Elena Cicut, the widow, and gave her the thing, like you suggested.

But then it occurred to me that copy is floating around there and that's not exactly gracious gift giving, is it?"

She wanted to doubt him. *He* wanted her to doubt him. But she let it go with a promise to call some woman cop named Calderon and inquire again about the diary copy. He was perspiring from more than the heat when he hung up. He wasn't even sure why he had lied about giving the diary to Elena. Was there such a thing as meta-paranoia—being paranoid for the sake of being paranoid?

He wished he hadn't spotted the sleeve of his powder blue jacket sticking through the jamb of the closet.

And wished the telephone hadn't chosen that moment to give off a ring like some pneumonia case clearing his lungs.

He didn't like the timing. It pulled him in two directions. Was the telephone a distraction for the jacket sticking through the closet or was he supposed to have picked up the phone without thinking because he was suspicious of what he saw at the closet? Or had both things been planted merely to discombobulate him?

He sat up in amazement at how persistent was the temptation to lie still and crumble like stale cake. He had been the one to criticize Roenicke for taking so long to accept what had happened to Claudia? He didn't have the right to criticize anybody.

"Hello."

"*Amico!*"

He was grateful to hear Bruno's voice. And with the telephone no longer a danger, he could also look over at the closet more clearly, blame the protruding jacket on the maid. When were they going to start giving courses on closing closets at hotel service school? "*Come stai?*"

But Bruno wasn't Bruno, not the Lepri he was used to. "Come over to my place, Charley," he said anxiously. "It's important."

"What is?"

There was a hesitation, then: "There's somebody here who says he has to see you. I think you should come, Charley."

He tried to remember, *wanted* to remember, other times that Bruno had sounded as he did now and it all turned out to be about nothing. But he drew a blank except for the image of some-body unpleasant sitting near Bruno. "What somebody?"

"The one . . . You know. The one you asked me about."

"Warneke? Leonard Warneke?"

There was commotion on the other end, then another voice—calmer, icier than Bruno's. "Yes, Leonard Warneke, Mister Sylvester. And Signor Lepri says you know where he lives, so please come immediately. And bear two things in mind. One, do not come empty-handed. Bring that item with you. Number two, if you inform the police of this conversation, it will end badly for everybody. Please do not take too long."

The receiver clunked down in Sylvester's ear. He had been feeling alone? Now there seemed to be a mob in his room.

THIRTY-FOUR

A s the taxi took the Ponte Garibaldi over the river, Sylvester thought of baseball things. He and Roenicke were tied 1–1 in people their obtuseness had gotten killed—Claudia Ricci for Roenicke, Joey Bacsik for him—but he was staging a tie-breaking rally thanks to Bruno. One wrong move, like maybe the one he had already made by leaving the diary in the hotel safe, and he would forge ahead 2–1. It might even go to 3–1 if Warneke decided Charley Sylvester was more bother than he was worth and that a safecracker could just as easily have gotten to the thoughts of Chairman Cicut. Let Roenicke overcome that kind of a lead!

The red light at the Lungotevere intersection scolded his whimsy. Where had he earned the right to be so flippant? Was he numbing himself to reality so he wouldn't have to think he was responsible for anything? The possibility alone made him feel small. He didn't like himself; in fact, his whole trip had been an exploration of how much he didn't. Foreign intrigue, and the most foreign and least intriguing thing of all was himself. How could he have lived so long without suspecting himself of such colossal vanity? Cynthia had never felt so right about him. He had been a fool not to call Gaetano. Were Pat and Nick supposed to think better of him for rushing straight toward Warneke to prove how much of a match he was for that character? Were they supposed to be consoled by assurances from Bruno that he had done what he had done only because it had been his fault for getting a friend into trouble in the first place and he had needed to make it right?

What nobility! If he had a cellphone in his pocket, he would have called Gaetano right then and there.

But he didn't have a cellphone in his pocket; he still hadn't gotten the damn thing fixed for Italy. Or, if he didn't count the bottle of Chanel he had been lugging around to no purpose, anything else in his pocket to reflect smartly on a middle-aged man (assuming he counted on living to 100) in the 21st century. Like all Sunday afternoon things, he was too late for what he had once upon a time been only too early for.

He slipped the perfume onto the back seat for the next lucky passenger and stopped the driver before they turned into Bruno's narrow Trastevere street. It made no practical difference where Warneke was concerned, but he felt more in control approaching Bruno's building on foot rather than being dropped off in front of it as if on a social call. His sports jacket was too much and too little. The air wanted to stay dank from the rain, but the returning heat wouldn't let it and the glaze of surviving sun couldn't make up its mind. The stores he passed were all closed for Sunday; even the bar that had probably been open in the morning had shut down. The cars looked more abandoned than parked. The only sign of life was a sullen kid kicking a soccer ball against the metal shutter of a *drogheria* and being lectured by an older kid sitting astride a motorcycle. Every stern word from the older one brought an angrier bang to the shutter and an echoing clatter of flimsy metal over the street. If they weren't older brother handing down the law to younger brother, they were reasonable facsimiles. He had a pang of loss for not having eavesdropped more on the conversations between Pat and Nick when they had been growing up.

The scarred *portone* to Bruno's building had never locked because of a faulty catch, and nobody had found a locksmith in the years since Sylvester had last been there. He dragged his feet up the stairs to the third floor waiting for some argument to convince him to turn around and run back down to the street. Instead, he spent too many seconds thinking about how the aerosol used for the hallway was a sign that Bruno was living in a higher rent district than Elena Cicut. By the time he decided the scent was

raspberry he was knocking on Bruno's door and out of alterna-
tives even if they had existed. The Bruno who answered didn't
look like somebody in danger, he was just a Bruno who acted
ashamed of having screwed up. And the rail-tall Warneke sitting
erect on the divan next to an old pile of newspapers wasn't showing a weapon, or even any special menace; he was just making
faces at the wine he was drinking. He was also the only thug in
the world with two pens and a leather ink shield clipped to his
shirt pocket.

"Sorry about this, *amico*," Bruno said, closing the door behind
them. "I forgot to warn you Badalamenti has a mouth bigger than
his stomach."

Sylvester needed a second to remember who Badalamenti was
and another one to see that the fan on the table that took up the
middle of the room was turning so slowly and generating so little
power it couldn't even flap the page of Bruno's crossword puzzle
book directly in front of it.

"Thank you for coming, Mister Sylvester."

He could have believed Warneke meant it, that he had intended no irony; or, the man might just have been totally humorless
and didn't know himself if he was being sarcastic. He was open to
any suggestion at all until he felt the blood return to his legs and
the heat subside in his chest.

Bruno scampered over to the table and poured a third glass of
wine to go with the one at his elbow and the other in Warneke's
hand. Whatever had been going on between them hadn't stopped
him from acting as a host. He looked older, more derelict within
the peeling walls of his apartment, and for the first time in decades Sylvester remembered what his mother had once said about
his uncle Richard and his seedy apartment in Flushing: "He has
one of everything and none of most things." He was annoyed for
remembering such an uncharitable crack after so long.

"It's piss, but it's better than nothing," Bruno said, handing
him his glass. "That's what I always say to Giuliana, and she
don't know if it's a compliment or what."

Warneke thought Bruno's attempt to sound conversational
was amusing. "Why do I not see your pocket thick with that item,

Mister Sylvester? It would not be because you do not have it with you, would it?"

The wine, the labored English enunciation, Warneke's posture on the divan, just the pens—they pressed a relaxation button in Sylvester. He didn't want to be where he was, and Warneke was still as taut as he was at leisure, but he was suddenly confident there would be another room with the man somewhere down the road. (He had to have been insane to have come so far without having taken that for granted!) "I'd sure as hell like to know what this precious item is you're all interested in."

He didn't expect to be believed, and he wasn't. But he had apparently also given away something: Warneke sat up alertly, played back what he had said, consulted his English a second time, and then frowned. "Who else has asked about the diary?"

Sylvester drew a blank. Elena had known about the diary and not been interested in it, but who else? He couldn't remember if Roenicke or Minic or Applebaum had specifically asked about it or whether he had just been too absorbed by not mentioning it to them. His legs felt weak at the idea of once again having been clever only for himself. There was a wooden chair with a broken slat in the back, and he took it. It wasn't the decrepit chair he had once warned Nick about staying away from, but it could have been. Bruno was still furnishing his place from discards on the street. "That's news to you?" he asked anyway. "I thought you worked in relays."

Warneke needed a moment to understand, and didn't like it when he did. "At least you came alone, I hope?"

Bruno took the other straight chair at the table like a guest in his own home. "I told you," he said. "When Charley gives his word, he means it."

"You're going to a lot of trouble for something you've never seen. You haven't actually seen it, have you, Warneke? Like a copy somewhere?"

"What copy?"

"Just a thought. Things in print sometimes get copied."

He wasn't tantalized; Joey Bacsik wasn't in his universe. He was still back at the last bend. "And I am not the only one, you say. Yes, I am sure what you say is true. I could not imagine otherwise."

Sylvester hadn't expected the man's dithering; it was as bad as his own and almost caused him to drink the wine Bruno had handed him. But then he smelled that it was the rotgut served at Giuliana's and put aside his glass. Even with the street window open the room was close to steaming, and it was the kind of oily house white that would have made his stomach rumble. But somewhere in the last few seconds, to see Warneke's reaction, he had gained even more leverage than he had brought walking in the door without the diary. Whoever the man was working for, it evidently wasn't Minic's Freedom Press. "So we have what—two teams on the field? And which bunch of heroes sent that letter bomb to my newspaper this morning and killed a woman?"

Warneke was so indignant his forehead turned red. "I happened to hear about that on the radio sitting here with your friend," he said. "Tell him, Signor Lepri."

Bruno didn't like having to agree. "Maybe you're a good actor. Maybe that's what you wanted me to think."

Warneke couldn't hide his hurt at the answer. "I did not come here to kill women, Mister Sylvester," he said stiffly, standing to get rid of his glass on the table. "It is that kind of thing I am here to prevent."

"But you were too busy watching Elena Cicut's house to manage it?"

"I am sorry to say I was too late there, too." He winced with what seemed like sincere regret and went over to the window that faced on the street. There was another smash of the soccer ball against the *drogheria* shutter downstairs and he looked toward it anxiously. Even with his hands in his slacks pockets and rocking back on his heels, his whole body seemed cocked for an attack. But his voice had a new somberness. "In case you have not grasped the situation, Mister Sylvester, they have the boy. As soon as they found out Cicut sent his diary to someone, they made his son a hostage for it."

"Phillip!!??"

"Perhaps we should have foreseen that, but we did not."

Sylvester didn't want to believe Elena had lied to him not only in her apartment but also in the hotel bar. She had been candid about so many other things, why not that, too? Hadn't she come right out and asked for his help in finding the boy? "*We. They.* Somebody likes this Jelic?"

Warneke nodded calmly to whatever was going on between the brothers below him. "Jelic is a butcher, Mister Sylvester, and the only thing that might stop him from gaining dangerous power is to publicize a record of his butchery. Something Josef Cicut had for years and, apparently, has now passed along to you."

"I don't believe that." He didn't know why not; his nerves seemed to accept it, and so did Bruno's queasy expression. "If what you say is in that diary, he held on to it for a long time without letting it bother him."

Warneke turned back into the room; in just a few seconds his eyes had lost their alertness. "The butcher feels no guilt for what he has done," he said, sounding as though he had said it before. "We have heard from Nuremberg, the Hague, how many other forums, that he can be a trumpet of self-righteousness about it. But that is not always true of the individual who was not personally involved in an atrocity, who perhaps received a confidence about it only after the fact and kept silent about it. It is there where you find the guilt of self-justifications. For some their indecisiveness degenerates into an excruciating pleasure in itself. And all that, mind you, even when your wife is not the sister of the person who confided in you about his bloody hands."

Sylvester knew any word out of his mouth would be one too many. But he also hadn't come running across the city just to hear a sermon. "I ask again. Nobody has read this diary, but everybody seems to know what's in it. How is that possible?"

Warneke approved of the question. "Cicut's miscalculation. Have you not wondered why he found himself in Germany?"

On that at least Elena had apparently not lied to him. "His friend at the embassy, someone named Sima Glauber."

Warneke winced again, but this time not at himself. "Glauber does not have friends, Mister Sylvester, he has opportunities, and it was Cicut's error not to recognize this. When Cicut told him what he had in his journal, undoubtedly because of nostalgia for some tie the two of them once had with Jelic, Glauber immediately contacted anyone and everyone who might benefit him in the future. It is a delicate art, always threatening to alienate one side or another, but Glauber has been very adept at it his whole career. He informed my associates of his talk with Cicut, then he informed Jelic's people of it. We should not be surprised if he has also informed the government of Micronesia. Who knows where the next opportunity will arise?"

"Nobody is that nimble."

"Ask him his formula when you meet him. I have other objectives. The first is to get that diary. The second is to get the Cicut boy back." He managed to keep a straight face, not just in saying it but in awaiting a reaction.

"You don't give a goddamn about Phillip Cicut. You just want the diary."

"It is the same. They would have no further purpose in holding the boy if they knew the diary was beyond their grasp."

"Really? They don't seem to mind killing people just for the hell of it. Or weren't you listening to the radio before?"

There was another blast against the grocery store shutter. Sylvester liked thinking it was Warneke's head.

"I am aware of that," he said stolidly.

"You're *aware* of it. That's something, I guess."

"Indignation will not help the boy."

"Telling the police who these patriots are might."

"There is no mystery about that. You yourself had dinner with one of them at your colleague's house the other evening." He stepped over to the wine bottle on the table as smoothly as he had obviously been patrolling Roenicke's house.

"Watching me now, too? You have a very busy day. But if you're talking about the priest, he's a clown."

"Really? Was that the Widow Cicut's opinion of him, too?"

"What would Elena . . .?" But he knew. It had been there all the time in the tales she had told him. "The one called Stela!"

"Stela Minic," he nodded. "He has been close to the Jelic family for years. She didn't tell you how he once saved her life by smuggling her to safety? He was a younger, less complicated priest in those days. But not a clown then and not one now."

Sylvester pressed his back into the broken slat, but it refused to crack altogether. "But if she knows Minic has the boy, why ask me to help find him?"

Warneke thought for a moment, then threw down his wine the way some people swallowed Alka Seltzer. "Perhaps she has finally developed doubts about Minic. Or perhaps she is just desperate and she is willing to ask anybody. Children in danger are an ideology in America, no? One that appeals to the heart as well as the head? Worth championing to any end?"

Sylvester had no better answer than the silence and then another rattle of the shutter downstairs that descended between them, and Warneke didn't surrender his advantage. "Do not look so betrayed, Mister Sylvester. She was not lying to you. She was . . . well, sharing the layers of the onion she thought she could share with you. Do not forget she too had years when she had to learn about people in life and death circumstances, when she could not think only in terms of private rules of morality. She has more at stake than your good thoughts about her."

Bruno too was looking at him to say he should have understood. His plane had brought him across the ocean to one Europe, but his cab to Trastevere had brought him across to an older, more cynical one. He felt ridiculously naïve saying: "Philip Cicut returns home and only then we talk about the diary."

"The diary is what will get him home."

"No, just the opposite."

"That is foolish. Right now they know this book can only be in your office or home in New York or here with you in your room or your hotel safe."

"He may be right, Charley."

Every berry on Bruno's face was another crusty vote against him. And what was behind them—thugs forcing their way into his apartment with Pat and Nick there? Into his office with Cynthia there? Just exactly how much had that secretive prig Josef Cicut made him responsible for after so many years?

"Mister Sylvester?"

What did he say? That his apartment building had Henry on guard as a doorman? That his office had a security desk in the lobby?

"You are wasting important time, Mister Sylvester."

"And you and your friends—how do I know who they are? Maybe you're just as bad as Jelic. For all I know, you *are* Jelic's man. Nice little speeches about butchers, but what else you got, Warneke? Why should I just hand the diary over to you?"

At least Bruno was back on his side waiting for an answer to that one. But Warneke was unfazed. "The only thing Jelic and I have in common is that we were both teachers in a simpler life. Me at the university, him at the grade school level. I have never really decided which position is more important to a child's education. Can we even speak of a child at the university level?"

"I asked why I should hand the diary over to you."

"Who would you have endorse my credentials? Somebody in your embassy? I would be careful about that. The Italians? Until this morning they preferred to think we did not exist on their territory. Or maybe your newspaper? I am certain your correspondent in my country would tell you there are political forces opposed to Jelic, but that would not ease your concerns about me personally. I do not know your correspondent, he does not know me, and for all you know my name is not even Leonard Warneke at home. I am afraid it must be you and you alone who decides to believe what I have said to you or not."

He felt the vibration from Bruno: Somebody so bare-faced, Lepri was thinking, had to be telling the truth. But wasn't that why it was such an effective tactic? "If you think I'm just going to hand you that diary, you have another think coming."

"Charley . . ."

He didn't need Bruno's belated warning or the tiniest mouth twitch Warneke tried to suppress: A nanosecond after the words were out of his mouth, he was chasing after them futilely. "Okay, I do have it with me. But that still leaves you needing something to trade, and that's Philip Cicut. You're the one wasting time, Warneke. If I don't get help from you, I'll get it from a cop named Gaetano."

He wanted to be gratified seeing Warneke waver, and for half a second, the half a second before he reminded himself they were bartering over a kid Nick's age, he was. And then he was just relieved when Warneke moved decisively toward the door. There was a violence in the man that even he seemed reluctant to acknowledge. "You will hear from me within forty-eight hours," he said. "I warn you even that may be too long. You are dealing with matters beyond your competence, Mister Sylvester."

Sylvester told himself to nod in agreement as Warneke hurried out and clapped the door closed behind him, then to nod some more at another crash of the *drogheria* shutter downstairs, accepting the reprimand he deserved.

"Charley . . ."

"I know, I know," he said to Bruno, not knowing anything.

THIRTY-FIVE

Elena disliked the Cucina and disliked Father Stela's insistence she meet him at the smoky soup kitchen. It was the third time he tried to impress her by showing how he supervised the sour-smelling hall, and she really didn't know why. Weren't charities like the Cucina part of his vows anyway? And why would she of all people need evidence of Stela Minic's good works? As she sat at a back table watching the sad-eyed Albanians and bone-thin Africans shuffling along at the counter for their soup and pasta, she wondered if he wasn't reprimanding her for not taking his unsubtle hints and volunteering to come down in the evenings and help feed the homeless. She could think of no other explanation for not meeting him elsewhere and avoiding the odor of what could have been months-old kale.

She sat up as the door behind the counter swung open, then subsided back on her bench again as a young black nun hefted another huge tinfoil tray of food out from the kitchen. The woman muttered to the red-faced nun ladling out the minestrone, then both of them looked annoyed about something happening behind them in the kitchen. Elena couldn't imagine being further away from people than she was from the two of them—from the conversations they had with one another, from the tasks they performed, from the holier-than-thou thoughts they each must have had during the day. They might as well have inhabited different planets. She was sorry if it displeased Father Stela, and maybe it meant she was colder than she wanted to think of herself as being, but she could never feel any great urge to feed poor people while telling them everything was fine because *ultimately* they would be rewarded. She had never had time for an *ultimately*. She had been in the hills too long for that. Wasn't the whole idea to avoid an *ultimately*? Josef might have forgotten that, but she hadn't, and she knew Philip had never learned it. Philip could never believe in something so fantastical that he would think it forgivable to raise a gun to his own head to find some new *ultimately* existence. He was still her son more than Josef's.

Thought of Philip made Elena want to smoke, but she knew she couldn't have given in to that impulse even before the legal warnings and threats had been posted on the walls around her. Back then or now, just the sight of a cigarette where she was would have started a stampede from the other trestle tables toward her, minestrone and fettuccine be damned. She had to use plain will power, no nicotine, against the edginess she had felt taking the bus to the Cucina for the challenge not to let Father Stela get away with another empty reassurance about finding Philip. The promise the first time had sounded mechanical, the kind of thing a priest said to anybody at all in need. The second time, though, had bothered her more with every passing hour after they had parted, to her certainty in bed that night that he had been hiding something, He knew Philip was dead? He knew Philip had gotten into some trouble that made it impossible for her to see him again soon? She had known Stela Minic too long not to sense when he was being evasive; usually well-meaning but sometimes evasive because of some new "turn in the divine plan," as he was prone to putting it. She was determined not to let him get away with it again.

By the time he appeared at the kitchen door behind the counter, Elena was thinking of lining up with a tray at the front just to end her awkwardness. Her table had filled up so fast there was barely room for Minic to squeeze in next to her. It was a blessing that only one of the Africans sitting directly across from her had paused even to nod to her out of courtesy, that everyone else who had fallen in around her had gone ravenously to their food. She felt so obtrusive with nothing in front of her that she didn't know where to train her eyes, wanted to be invisible. She thought she recognized the language between the African and his friend as Somali because her student Muhammad Shermarke at the agency had once tried to teach her a poem that sounded like the same *shimbiro geed wada* she now thought she picked up—something about birds in a tree. But she might have only been making that up to give her mind something to settle on. The Albanian from the couple on her right she definitely recognized. They were talking about the refugee camp outside Formica where they had to return before midnight. There had been a time—how long ago had it been?—when she could have drifted back and forth between such exotic chattering and forgotten minor things like eating, marveled at the differences and yet sameness in languages spoken tens of thousands of miles away from one another. Now she couldn't believe she had been that same person.

"Elena!"

She was relieved when Father Stela ignored the space she had been guarding for him and waved to follow him outside: She couldn't have challenged him to tell the truth with so many strangers listening.

The Cucina's front door was across the street from the train station where travelers were still rushing around at the end of a Sunday in the city. The hulking tram up at the corner was maneuvering through a pygmy fleet of cars and taxis as it made a slow, squealing turn down a side street. For a moment she was overcome by all the traffic noise and hazy blue lights from the station, bewildered by so many people and vehicles in a hurry to get somewhere. She herself was where she wanted to be, where she had to be for Philip to find her, and she couldn't imagine what others were thinking.

Father Stela took in the commotion for a moment as if personally responsible for providing it. He was so taken with himself that he almost missed the elderly woman trying to get past him through the door for her meal. The woman practically had a hump from scoliosis, but even with that wasn't all that much smaller than Minic, who barely lifted his arm high enough on the door for her to pass under. He had seemed shorter to her lately. People got shorter as they grew older, her own mother had absolutely shrunk before dying, but he wasn't much more than fifty and already appeared to have consolidated his body into a tighter chunk of middle age that he would never be able to transform back again.

"So how are you, Elena?" he asked as soon as he let go of the door.

"I still know nothing."

He nodded. "*Pazienza*, as our Italian friends say. But I may have news."

She didn't believe him; the thought was instantaneous. Had he said something of the kind before? Was it the sinuous way he had said it? Or was it just her distrust of subjunctives? Whatever, there was something false in his voice.

"You must not get upset," he said.

"I cannot be more upset than I am right now, Father."

He heard her coldness, but shrugged it off as what he should have anticipated. "Do you know somebody named Warneke? Leonard Warneke?"

Elena told herself to keep a straight face, not to betray that she had already answered that question when Charles Sylvester had asked it. "Who is he?" she asked as she had the first time, but now concentrating her mind on the tram that finally disappeared around the corner. "A friend of Philip's?"

Minic lingered a moment on her face, waiting for her to say something else, then finally had to accept her answer. "As you know, I have spoken to as many people as I can about Philip," he said. "This morning I received a telephone call from this person identifying himself as Leonard Warneke. Do not be upset, Elena." She instinctively pulled back from the hand he wanted to put on her forearm. "The gist of it," he said, pretending not to notice her reaction, "is that this Leonard Warneke claims to know where Philip is. In fact, he says he has him."

"*Has* him? What does that mean?"

"Unfortunately what it sounds like—if he is to be believed. Mind you, I am not certain he is to be. I am already checking into that. But if he is credible, then I'm afraid we have an abduction situation."

He said it so gravely she felt a sudden pity for him: It was either that or giving in to the hysteria she felt nibbling on her nerves. "I have no money," she said with contempt that he or Leonard Warneke or anybody else could have thought otherwise. "That is ridiculous. You told him that, yes?"

"Calm, Elena. As I say, I am not even certain this man really knows where Philip is. I have spoken to quite a few people since he went off, and they in turn have spoken to many. It is hardly out of the question some small-time thief heard of the search for Philip and is trying to exploit the situation."

"And is that what you think?"

Minic frowned against the blare of a car horn up the street. "What I think is that I wouldn't be acting responsibly if I didn't pass along everything I have learned."

"And what is that exactly?"

He weighed reminding her she had never taken that tone with him before, but then just said: "He wants to make a trade. Not for money, but for some book of Josef's."

Elena didn't have the tram anymore, but a taxi driver at the corner came to her rescue by stepping out from behind his wheel to rant at a young couple who had crossed in front of him and made him miss the light. Only deep inside the man's raving were Charles Sylvester and Josef's diary. "Josef had a lot of books. What kind is this man talking about? Poetry? A novel?"

It was too much, and his skeptical look said so. But he couldn't call her a liar, either. "Some kind of journal, apparently. Josef kept one, did he not?"

"There was nothing like that in the books we packed up before moving. But if you would like, we could go to where we stored them."

"Elena, Elena."

The game was up—that was what her father had said when she or Milo had exhausted all their alibis for some wrong they had not wanted to admit. Now *Elena, Elena* had the same ring of irritation. "Yes, Father?"

"I think you know very well Josef kept a dairy during the bad days," he said evenly. "Milo spoke to me about it more than once."

"Yes, I think I do remember. But he must have thrown that out years ago."

"Not according to this Warneke. He had it with him in Germany. But I think you know that. And I think your American friend Sylvester knows that, too."

"Charles . . .?"

"Please, Elena. I'm trying to help you. If this man Warneke is what he says he is, I am ready to deliver the journal to him to get Philip. And it's Philip we should be thinking about right now, isn't it?"

Stela Minic hadn't just grown shorter, Elena realized; he had become completely different. There was nothing at all well-meaning in his eyes. "That sounds ugly coming from you, Father. Why is that?"

He had no answer except to let another horn blast up at the corner behind him. But then he reached under cassock to his pants pocket and came out with a cellphone. She might not have been there as he punched out a long-distance number, muttered something into the receiver, then handed her the phone. He looked so smug she was sure she was about to hear Philip's voice—and to resign herself to the fact that he was no longer in Rome.

But it wasn't Philip. *"Zdravo, Elena,"* Milo whispered in her ear from some place very far away.

THIRTY-SIX

Sylvester could hear Joey Bacsik cackling from where dead Joey Bacsiks ended up. The gnome had predicted trouble that day in the mail room with his warning not to go to Italy, to go to France or somewhere else instead. But he had brushed off that idea, hadn't even considered it an idea. Too bad Porterfield was turning it—too late—into a platinum idea. "Look, Charley, I'm not asking you to camp down over there forever. But you're on the scene and Roenicke's got to come home for a little bit and explain what the hell has been going on over there."

"You mean take a breather, don't you? The guy was almost blown to pieces."

"Sure, that's part of it. But I'd be lying if I didn't tell you some friends upstairs seem to be sharpening their knives against him to get at his old man for boardroom crap. Like the bomb couldn't have been such a complete shock to him if he was playing at the wrong games." The pause was deliberate—Applebaum One, Applebaum Two, Applebaum Three. Only when he didn't fill in the silence was the test over. "Upstairs is on the phone with Washington more than with me since this thing happened."

"I thought you were the Upstairs, Kevin."

"I can't tell you how long, but no daily shit work," he said, rumbling on deafly. "The agencies can handle that. But just in case something breaks over the bombing, say. We'll look pretty bad if we don't have one of our own coming in first on that. And it goes without saying we're resetting the clock for your vacation time."

Ask Porterfield to say it anyway? He was too irked for repartee.
Another few seconds and he would have been through the lobby
without Romolo stopping him with the phone. Another few seconds of thought on Joey Bacsik's advice and he could have been
strolling along the Seine to visit Notre Dame. "I can't even get into
the office," he tried anyway. "It's a crime scene. Who knows when
that ends?"

Porterfield knew surrender when he heard it. "The *Post* will
give you any hookup you need. I've already arranged that. Of
course if something urgent comes up, you can always stop somebody with a laptop on the street and ask to borrow it. You can't
miss them, Charley. Most laptops look like attaché cases. They
have them everywhere, even in the Gobi Desert. Give the guy a
tip, though, okay?"

He clicked off before he was the one on the receiving end of all
the repartee. Romolo maintained his manager's solemnity in taking back the phone, but seemed smug about having intercepted
him to pass on the panicked call from New York. Which brought
to mind more important duties than Kevin Porterfield's telephone
manner. "That package I gave you for safekeeping, Romolo . . ."

"Signore?"

"Could you check it's still there?" He felt smaller standing
there showing the man he was serious. "Just a glance. As a favor
to me."

The bald guardian of the Albergo Reggio looked baffled about
what personal favors had to do with doubts about his security
measures, but a guest's request was a guest's request and he
stepped away from the counter to go into his small office at the
rear of the reception area. Sylvester's eyes fell on the newspapers
fanned over the desk. Claudia Ricci had made the front pages in
Italian, English, and French. He was about to check how she had
done in Spanish when he recognized a familiar middle-aged lump
across the fold of *Il Messaggero*—Charley Sylvester. The photograph—of him with Roenicke and Gaetano—had been taken on
Via Propaganda, evidently by the him-and-her redheads the cop
had spotted. Was it good or bad that the picture didn't really give
away anything, that Leonard Warneke, Stela Minic, and every

other Croat in Europe already knew he was there and lugging around Josef Cicut's diary?

"It is where I placed it, Signor Sylvester," Romolo said primly when he came out of the office again. "But if you would feel . . ."

"No, no. I'm sorry. I'm just jumpy this morning."

The manager accepted the apology on behalf of his establishment. "I understand. When you have incidents like this . . ."

"Yeah. *Incidents*."

"Excuse me?"

"Hello, Charley."

Sylvester blinked. It gave him the illusion of controlling the vision striding in from the front door, allowed him to make Felicia even taller and statelier than the Felicia who had visited New York two Christmases ago. The powder blue shirt and skirt, the long honey blonde hair, and studded sandals were all his creation. The only thing that wasn't were her puffed out Angelina Jolie lips.

"I saw the picture in the paper," she said, taking off her sunglasses and stopping just close enough to bathe him in her violet scent while he inspected her. Her still-taut face wasn't afraid of the bright lobby light." I assumed you would be at the Reggio. How are you, Romolo?"

"A pleasure to see you again, Signora. It's been too long."

She cast an appraising eye over the lobby. "Not too many changes. As smart as ever. Good for you."

"Thank you, Signora. We try. If you'll excuse me a moment."

He had Romolo's tactful withdrawal back to his office to thank for not having to go for an awkward kiss. She seemed to be awaiting congratulations when she looked back at him. "Okay, you never miss a review."

She didn't care anymore that he didn't take her luxury habitats columns for her magazines seriously. "I was being sincere. He has kept it up quite nicely." She dropped her eyes to switch her spaghetti-string bag from one shoulder to the other. "Poor Claudia. That was a terrible thing. I couldn't help thinking about how irritated I got with her once when I called you and you weren't in the office."

"I'm sure she got over it."

"Do they have any idea about . . .?"

"If they do, they're not sharing it with me." She smiled tentatively. Either she had rehearsed just so many lines and now had run out of them or it was her self-consciousness about her teeth. The society-conscious Ferrantes had had their daughter's buck teeth filed and braced to be presentable, but she had never lost her shyness about smiling openly. "You look good, Felicia."

"Thank you. Can we take a walk or something? Standing around hotel lobbies makes me think I forgot my suitcase."

He didn't realize how much he had wanted company for stepping out into the morning sun until she was walking alongside him, the world glinting off her sunglasses. Old news or not to Warneke and Minic, his picture in the paper made him feel vulnerable. He had to keep ordering his head not to swivel around to see who was behind them while, without prompting, to head off a question she preferred to deal with offensively, she tried to make her husband more interesting to him than he apparently was to her. "I think you would like Gianni's research. The history part of it anyway. These dukes and countesses sounded like they only stopped screwing long enough to get up from bed and put down another peasant revolt. Then it was back to bed with their latest catch, sex irrelevant."

"And I'm sure the Senator reads all these discoveries to you over breakfast every morning and you go, 'Bravo, Gianni, Bravo!'"

She gave her neck the small roll she always did when she smarted from something she didn't want to admit was funny. "People who know these things at the university say Gianni is very thorough," she said stiffly. "It's how he spends his time when he's not conspiring with his politician friends, which means I have more free time. So no to the question you're not asking. No complaints. What about you?"

"They just asked me to fill in for Roenicke for a couple of weeks."

"Oh."

Oh seemed to cover it—all the way back to the last time he had been operating the Rome office and they had still been married and putting off the fact that they were through as a couple and had to make big decisions about Pat and Nick. "I didn't get much chance to say no."

"Did you want to?"

"I think so."

"You had to be clearer about it than that."

"We always left the decisiveness up to you, remember?"

She could have said *oh* again, but didn't. "And Patricia? Nicky?"

Never the *kids* or the *children*, always Patricia and Nick by name, other independent adults, so he didn't get the idea she was afflicted with any maternal longing. In the beginning he had clung to the artificiality of it, Felicia Ferrante working hard to be as emotionally remote from her children as she was geographically. But now practice had so insulated her that genuineness didn't matter one way or the other.

"I see Patricia is still making her way up the ladder? . . . Yes, I do read the paper every once in a while."

"She's very good."

"I don't doubt it. She's had a very good teacher. On a purely aesthetic level, though, I wouldn't mind her being a little less prosaic."

"She'd appreciate the review. Ask her if she wants one."

She cocked her chin toward the other side of the piazza, keeping her glasses above all the pre-school children, mothers, and babysitters who took over the center island in the morning. "And Nicky?"

"Pain in the ass."

"So he must be the creative one!"

Crossing the island and leaving the piazza, he missed Warneke, maybe on the same bench as the first time he had seen him, with news about Philip Cicut. He was startled he had been counting so blindly on the man. "We're still good at it, aren't we?"

"What?"

"Bringing up things so we don't have to talk about them. Agenda points just to be checked off. Is the Senator good at that, too?"

She focused on whatever invisible beings were standing in their path, lengthening her stride gawkily with her thin leg as a distraction against saying: "You imagine Gianni tells me about his decadent aristocrats at breakfast and I try to imagine what you three talk about at breakfast in New York. The truth is, it's easier imagining what the three of you *don't* say to one another." The worst of her awkwardness out, she pulled back her leg. "You don't talk about me, certainly. You don't talk about your great anger at closing yourself off from the world in their name. You probably don't even talk about those little men—the Porterfields and Applebaums and Roenickes—you let go ripping past you for your martyrdom. So what's left to talk about if not the real ways you've been cheated? And that you would never say to Patricia or Nicky. They figured it out for themselves a long time ago, but you would never come right out and say it. That's part of your idea of being a good father."

He could have never said it to Cynthia or anybody else, maybe not even to himself so resolutely. But it didn't seem to make any difference saying it to her. "Right."

She hadn't expected such swift agreement. "Just like that?"

"What do you want to hear, Felicia? I'm the same as always and that's why you had to find greener pastures? Or maybe I'm exactly the opposite and that's because you sent me on my way with the kids? Either way Felicia is the wisest of women?"

"People don't calculate as much as you think they do, Charley."

"No, they wake up one morning with epiphanies. And god help you if you try to work out where they came from."

"Clue: from need." She stopped in front of the main entrance to the Senate; she had had a destination all along. "See that one?" She nodded to a fat man entering the *palazzo* one scraping step at a time, aides on either side of him supporting him by the elbows. The salute from the sentries in the guard box said he had to be a senator. "Gianni says you can measure the importance of Italian politicians by the way they walk. When they first get here from their province, they're all bounce and spring, can't wait to get into the hall to introduce some pet project. Then they have some success and they walk more somberly, making sure everybody they pass sees them and is impressed. The third stage like that one, Senator Trombetta from Avellino, is when you've been a cabinet minister and the vice-president of your party. He can't walk without others holding him up."

"He's also old, Felicia."

"Not that old, not in calendar years. It's political senility you're looking at. Don't be political, Charley."

She kissed him on the cheek so quickly, overwhelming him with her perfume, that his first thought was of all the anti-kissing maneuvers he had wasted back in the hotel. And then she was whispering, as if afraid that Senator Trombetta, his aides, or the sentries would overhear her: "Gianni would like to see you."

"I'm not really interested in dukes and . . ."

"Not about that," she said, leaning back and eying him sternly. "We're having a few people over tomorrow evening. You have the address, yes? After eight would be best. Nothing formal, but no stains on your tie. *D'accordo?*"

And she was off into the Senate building—not getting a salute from the sentries, but an eye roll after her trim ass from the one on the left. He felt weak in his thighs from how sudden—and familiar—her kiss had been.

And equally annoyed that she hadn't asked if he was seeing anyone regularly.

THIRTY-SEVEN

Warneke asked for the instructions to be repeated. He didn't believe them the second time any more than he had the first time. First he had been told the Cicut diary was critical, so much so that he was to remain in Rome even after he had given himself away, now he was being told to forget it, it wasn't important, "other considerations" had intervened. What other considerations? They would be explained when he returned home. But not just yet. He was to remain where he was for a few more days, just in case he was needed there.

"You mean newer instructions to contradict the new ones?"

Franjo didn't appreciate his sarcasm. "I cannot be more explicit now, Leonard. But you will be informed."

"And what about the boy?"

"We're mindful of that situation. But when you think it through, we really aren't all that certain he simply didn't go off on his own, are we?"

"Yes, we are."

"You mean you are."

"Who's in a better position to know?"

"I'm sure that was taken into account."

"And what do I tell the American?"

"You tell him nothing. Is there any reason to see him again? We think not. Stay away from him."

Warneke tried not to personalize. It wasn't easy with Franjo, a cretin who left the top button of his shirt open because he couldn't get his pudgy fingers under his chins to close it. Was it ominous he had never seen Franjo and the Italian scum Restivo in the same place at the same time? Two big bedbugs separated only by the pieces of the mattress they were working on.

"Are you listening, Leonard? Stay away from the American."

Warneke thought about telling him he had spent most of the day sitting across the street from the Freedom Press office, moving his car only a couple of times to go around the block in case somebody became suspicious of his vigil. He forgot the thought. Franjo didn't have to be burdened with too much information. "I heard you."

He clopped his phone back into his shirt pocket and lit a cigarette. It was his third of the day, and he was ashamed he had gone over his daily limit with hours still to go before bedtime. His rationalizations flooded in: Five on a day of stress were tolerable, especially if he had only one cigarette each of the next two days to get back to his daily average. Where would he be by then? Back in Zagreb? Still in Rome? He didn't like playing games with whimsical rules. Before taking Franjo's phone call, things had been clear—not easy, but at least clear. He was to get his hands on Cicut's diary, Sylvester wanted the Cicut boy returned home, the diary would be published at home for embarrassing and (ideally) indicting Milo Jelic, Jelic's goons would be left in disarray, and things would drop back to the passable muddle they had been in for years. Nothing epic, but clear. Saving minds from Jelic's demagoguery, saving a little national pride. But now there was too much flux. All the disorder in Zagreb was agitating him beyond his own powers of recognizing his state and controlling it. In some serious way Franjo and the other party clowns were chipping away at him more than the united efforts of the Jelics and Sylvesters, and couldn't have cared less. His assignment had become a round-robin!

He was so distracted by the idea that he felt an eternity behind what was right in front of him, coming out of the *palazzo* where the Freedom Press office was. The gods had demanded he take a second portion of their worst gruel. The tall blond with the wide shoulders he didn't know, but nobody had to identify

Tomas Leszek for him. His stomach revolted like the day he had mistaken vinegar for water on his mother's kitchen table. He wanted Franjo sitting next to him, seeing for himself that their first instincts about the disappearance of the Cicut boy had been right. But then on second thought he didn't want Franjo or any other unimaginative witness to his reaction at the sight of Leszek. He wanted the hot trickling slime in his stomach all for himself. Had anyone even figured out yet the country where Leszek had been born, what native currency had so fascinated him as a kid that he could be had for hire in any other legal tender recognized by a bank? There had been rumors and counter-rumors, most of them within a tone of distaste that sometimes sounded indistinguishable from admiration. Warneke had come to despise the mere mention of the man's name. Tomas Leszek was everybody's outside solution, the *other* when those who should have known better had thrown up their hands. And where Tomas Leszek was, kidnapping was the least of it. Who didn't know that by now? And yet, with Interpol bulletins on him all around the continent, Tomas Leszek still felt free to parade in and out of Stela Minic's office.

Warneke started to reach for a cigarette before realizing he already had one going. Seeing Leszek talking to his blond friend like anybody else on the street was beyond galling. There was hiding in plain sight, then there was a defiant degree above that. He thought of those old silent comedies where one character was always slipping through a door to the right just as his pursuers were coming through a door to the left. And on and on they would go through one door after another, except in this case the doors led to whole cities and there was nothing funny about the timing involved. Even with official protection, nobody should have been that agile. There was too much of the accidental in Leszek's survival. His existence all but defied reason, and that was motive enough for despising him. Accidents were not rational. Tomas Leszek was an animal.

Warneke felt the sweat on his arms, and it wasn't only because he had been parked in the sun too long. It was as if he had needed something like Tomas Leszek to come along to make any sense at all of what he was supposed to be doing across the street from the Freedom Press. Otherwise, why not just let Leszek and his friend walk down the street, stop at their green Audi, mutter something to one another over the roof, and then get in? He had a dozen excuses for letting it happen, starting with Franjo's orders and ending in the possibility that Leszek or his friend would know him, putting the Cicut boy in even more danger than he was already. And that was without factoring in what effect any oafishness would have on getting the diary.

The cigarette in his fingers reminded Warneke he could rationalize anything. The more he thought, the less he thought lucidly. That came with his philosophical training. He waited till the Audi pulled off into the traffic, let two cars go by, then shifted into gear. If there were rationalizations, there were also super-rationalizations, and they were legion. Might not the two goons give away where the boy was being held? That would be solid information for the next call from Zagreb, the kind of solid information that changed minds. It was also what he could have told Sylvester in the hope that the American held up his end of the bargain. Who cared whether Sylvester told the police where to get Philip Cicut? With some luck he would already be on his way back to Zagreb with the diary by then.

He needed to trust Sylvester.

He was already too committed not to have that need.

He drew lightly on his cigarette; he wanted his ally in evasiveness to last as long as possible. Leszek drove calmly, leery of attentions from a *vigile urbano*. He had probably had a lot of practice avoiding every traffic cop in Europe so as not to activate computers for a minor driving violation. Even on a Le Mans thoroughfare like the Via Nomentana he drove modestly, letting one and then two cars go by him. Warneke had to hang back, to let a couple of cars pass him as well so he wouldn't be on Leszek's rear fender. He liked the paradox behind the serial passes on the big street: Leszek's biggest vulnerability to drawing attention was in trying not to draw attention. The thought gave a contemplative extra to his little drive. One day he might even return to a classroom and use the experience as an illustration of some principle or other, dazzling his students. Whenever that day dawned.

The Audi turned off at Via Undici Luglio. Something momentous had apparently happened in Italy on a July 11. He couldn't imagine it had been the construction of the pastel-colored Lego apartment complexes that sprawled out on both sides of the street two blocks down from the Nomentana. The zone could have been Anywhere, the World, the perfect place for Leszek. The Audi stopped in front of the third complex down, and the blond got out. Without anyone in front of him, Warneke had to keep going, telling himself there had to be a third and maybe fourth slug babysitting if the building was where they were holding the Cicut boy. He thought of it as luck when the red light stopped him at the corner. That gave him a natural excuse to glance back to see if the tall goon was entering the building where the Audi had stopped. The Audi windshield made it impossible to see if Leszek was staring down at him, but he couldn't worry about that. What did bother him was that he had lost Leszek's friend. Either the man was a speed demon and had entered the building or he hadn't entered it at all.

Warneke was still taking in the laundromat and the *tavola calda* at the street level of the *palazzo* when the daylight outside his window disappeared. He didn't have time to turn before the movement through the window told him it was somehow connected to the ugly sound and uglier headache that wasted no time in retreating into sleep.

THIRTY-EIGHT

ylvester felt more entitled than he wanted to feel entering the Correspondents Club. He didn't have formal accreditation, but thanks to Porterfield's call he wasn't exactly the visiting guest he had expected to be, either. Confirmation of the good and the bad came from the sleepy receptionist Fulvio, who hadn't added a wrinkle or single gray hair in seven years and who took him in through a dim recollection he labored to summon up less tentatively. "*Come va, Professore?*" was his compromise.

"*Bene, Fulvio. E la famiglia?*"

His family Fulvio recalled more confidently; confidently, but not happily. He wished the "Professore" hadn't reminded him. His daughter was still going out with a bum without marriage prospects, his older son was still picking up trash in the Villa Borghese for the *Comune,* and his younger son had gone from being a prospect in a semi-pro soccer league to a perennial patient in clinics for knee problems. By the time the man had gone down the list, Sylvester had sidled around a challenge to his credentials and into the lounge. Time had stood still there too; even the rattle of the air conditioner was the same. The bleary light still rose from huge silver clam shells that were the chief wall motif for the wide box of a room; the tables were as deserted as always between lunch hour and dinner time. Somebody turned the pages of a newspaper in one of the two corner booths off the end of the bar, but he couldn't see who. What he could see, and what he had counted on seeing, was Billy Pope at the bar, bestowing his latest monologue on two women—a heavy, middle-aged Latina with too much mascara and a 30ish bartender with ginger hair who hovered in bemused attention. The bartender, a definite improvement on the glass-eyed Mario who had worked in the place for years, had no other customer to worry about.

"They already heard that one, Billy."

Billy Pope didn't need a door to make an entrance. It took him forever to detach himself from the women, deliberately turn his orange layer cake head, and take in the intruder. His neck creaks calmed, he wasn't displeased. His smile might have been less genuine than Bruno's, but not nearly as forced as Roenicke's. "Be Jeeziz, look what they're taxin' us with in the Eternal City now!"

The affected brogue said the scotch in front of him wasn't his first of the day. "The Catholics haven't fired you yet?"

"Fired! They've expanded me, man! I'm now the New Catholic Internet Service. Your employer happens to be one of our subscribers."

Sylvester wasn't sure that was good or bad. The Billy Pope he had wanted to see was the one who shaped up for his Catholic news agency at daily press conferences with the other correspondents, suffered relentless cracks about the appropriateness of his name for his job, then forgave everybody over Jamesons while he dispensed the latest gossip from the sacristies around the city. Did he still follow that routine or was he now content to sit in front of a computer all day, forgetting even what the inside of a church looked like? The only way to find out was to meet the Latina as a Buenos Aires correspondent named Amanda, exchange hellos with the bartender Franca, and accept a prosecco at Pope's insistence. The women were fascinated he worked for the newspaper that had been bombed, but he cut that line of conversation short by sticking to the generalities Amanda had probably already written for her paper in Argentina. As an example of pushing people away, it wasn't subtle, but it only took a few minutes to work. Amanda had to go off to the store before making supper for her husband and sons at home, and Franca had to go down to the other end of the bar to serve two Frenchmen who came in and barely grunted at Pope.

"Not particularly friendly types," he said lowly, the brogue gone.

"Meaning what? They don't like your stories?"

Pope smirked and went at his glass. He had never radiated health, but the pouches of his pouchy face seemed to have been emptied. The cuts under his chin also looked like a shaky razor. "Bad business that bombing," he allowed. "Makes me wonder if there isn't some terrorist group out there opposed to plenary indulgences."

"How many times have you used that one?"

He didn't deny it. "Was the target really Roenicke?"

"They don't seem to know."

"And you wouldn't tell me anyway."

"Well, it was either him or the paper, right? The paper hasn't done anything especially different lately. Did he ever tell you he was worried about something?"

Pope liked his scotch and had never shied away from a bombastic theatrical gesture, but the Catholics hadn't kept him around just because he knew what Lent was. "And what would he tell Billy that he wouldn't tell Charley?"

"I guess that's why I'm asking."

He eyed the half-swallow left in his glass as a small hint before the big hint and grinned at his own sharpness. "What he mainly told me was that he didn't like working for your employers. Always asking if I really had an audience online or just wanted to believe I did. And so what if I did? It wasn't like having *real* readers, was it? I gather most of his stuff ended up on your website."

"Did you reassure him?"

"Some people ask questions to be reassured, Charley. Others ask them just to have it on the record they asked. As far as he was concerned, the only people reading his stuff online were the paper's webmasters. Kept saying he'd outlived his usefulness."

That was what he had said in the cop bar across the street from the Viminale, too, Sylvester remembered. He hadn't given it much thought at the time in the middle of all the rest of Roenicke's moroseness, but it *was* an odd thing to say. And it didn't quite sound like he was referring to the paper. "This new Internet service of yours, it still buries you in press releases telling you about everybody's good works?"

"It's called e-mail. Fortunately, there's also a little button called Delete. What is it you're asking about?"

"A priest."

"My territory indeed! Name?"

"Stela Minic."

He came more alert. "That Freedom Press crowd from Croatia. Have offices over near the Nomentana."

"Here, and apparently everywhere else, too."

"God bless. Maybe they're big on calendars at the end of the year. Or they just find three people who agree with them, get some stationery, and put a name on the door. There's always some monarchist or its equivalent around who'll pay the rent and gas bill for that kind. What makes this Freedom Press any different?"

"How about the religious angle? Before this Minic was into publishing, he was all priest from what I hear. I thought you might have some insights there."

He finished off his scotch, moving from the ante-hint to the hint. Sylvester caught Franca's eye and made everybody happy. "What I hear?" Pope asked as soon as he had his refill. "This Freedom Press has a lot of children. Some of them are priests, some of them are anti-clerics, and a few wouldn't know the difference between the first two. They'll take the Father, Son, and Holy Ghost if that's what gets them by, but they also have more immediate gods."

"Like Milo Jelic?"

Pope nodded. "One name I've heard."

"And how does that front work here? Minic does what he does for his propaganda press, but what's he supposed to be doing here . . . what's the word I'm looking for?"

"Ecclesiastically?"

"Right. He says Mass? He has a parish?"

"All Catholic priests say Mass, Charley. That's what separates them from you and me. Where does he say it? I'd have to check into that, but it's probably one church more than others. In return for which he pitches in with the odd sacrament. Then there's a soup kitchen over near the Stazione Termini I heard about. Lots of refugees, so that would make him right for it."

"He sounds like he's all over the place."

Pope's smile was close to a gloat. "Where do you want him to be?"

In a basement where Philip Cicut was being held, Sylvester thought. "What about superiors? The cardinal or higher-up who's supposed to see he does more than work for this political hobby horse?"

"Because you're a purist where priestly vows come in."

"Background, Billy. Just background."

"But to what? Wouldn't have anything to do with recent events, would it?"

"I met the guy the other night. He made me curious."

Pope knew a half-truth when he came across it, but could also be benevolent when the scotch hit him. "He'd be subject to the same hierarchy as the rest of us who flock to Saint Peter's Square every Sunday morning. There's a bishop or primate responsible for Zagreb and probably a few other places in that region. You want his name, that what you're asking?"

"Couldn't hurt."

"You're teasing me, Charley."

"I just want to understand the mechanics of it. This guy has a superior in this hierarchy over in his home country, but he spends all his time with this propaganda outfit here, New York, and wherever. So is he doing all this with the knowledge, maybe even with the approval, of his superiors or not?"

"And you'd like to ask this bishop that question?"

"You can take the reporter out of the office, etcetera etcetera. Maybe I'm not used to having a vacation. But sure, that would be a pretty basic element of any background I did on this guy and Freedom Press."

"Except you'd probably have to go to Zagreb. Porterfield writing blank checks like that these days?"

"You're saying it's not my turf."

"That's what I'm saying, laddie."

"Then whose is it, Billy?"

Pope finally found a reason to pause before downing another slug. There was definite admiration in his eyes when he said, "You son of a bitch!"

Sylvester thought the same thing.

THIRTY-NINE

Warneke recognized Warneke. It had to be him who was thinking because he hadn't surrendered his being to anybody else. But that still didn't make sense of things. He was subjectively Leonard Warneke, but not objectively Leonard Warneke. Leonard Warneke, the one who showed up in mirrors and windows, didn't have spasms over his left ear that swamped his whole head. That Leonard Warneke didn't feel as woozy as a drunk. He had always been careful about that kind of thing, rarely having more than a single glass of wine at dinner. He had always been on guard against alcoholic excuses for not being in control. And yet here he was, himself and not in control and he couldn't deny it. He had to take his own word for it, didn't he?

He opened his eyes all the way. The aching didn't get any better or worse, it was just his. Floors and windows looked like floors and windows. The wooden floor he was in the middle of gleamed from waxing. Everything else—chairs, tables, curtains, shades, the smallest knick-knack on the walls—was missing. The closest thing to furniture was the black knob on the door at the end of the floor. He might have been in an apartment waiting to be rented. The traffic noises outside were muffled, sounding many floors down. What else was there to think than that Leszek and his blond friend were using one of the apartments in the Lego building as his prison?

He was ashamed he had been led so gullibly. For how long had they been aware of him? When he had been going through the charade of driving around the block a couple of times during his watch on the Freedom Press office? When they had caught a glimpse of him coming out of the building and walking down to their car? When he had gotten too close to them along the Nomentana? Whenever he had made his mistake, it was an embarrassment that had almost certainly killed any chance for getting the Cicut boy. How did he tell Franjo what had happened? Just the thought of that blimp taking it in and reminding him he had disobeyed instructions made him nauseous. Or maybe it was just the bang on his head waking up his stomach.

But first there was getting to having to call Franjo. Oddly enough, they hadn't left him with his phone to do just that. Bad sports.

They hadn't tied him down to anything, so even as he got to his feet behind another throb to his head and took a stuttering step toward the door he knew he was going to find it locked. But he walked on anyway, at least feeling his legs under him again. His brain went from useless mini-seconds ahead of what he was doing to dumb mini-seconds behind what he was doing: The knob turned easily, the door not at all locked. On the other side was another empty room, a little smaller but otherwise identical to the one in which he was standing. It too was waiting to be rented.

Warneke froze. He really didn't know what the game was. The light in the front room was weaker, especially over in a vestibule pocket that had to be the front door to the entire apartment. Was that where they were waiting for him—behind that? That didn't make sense. There had to be a building hallway outside the front door. Why would they risk being seen by some other tenant using the stairs? They wouldn't. They hadn't just caught him unawares and knocked him out, they were mocking him, making him think stupid things and stand petrified until he could think of more stupid things There was a philosophical term for his kind of situation. He could see only too clearly his ex-wife Monika standing at the stove and throwing it at him back over her shoulder. She had always been stealing words out of his books and classroom notes and without the slightest idea of what some of them meant using them against him. He was grateful he couldn't think of what this particular one was. *Asshole* had to do.

He moved his legs over to the door and opened it. He had been right to dread what he would see: It *was* just a hallway of the building, with absolutely nobody lurking in wait for him. A radio was playing in the apartment across the hall, and he could make out Bach. Leszek hadn't imprisoned him, he had just warehoused him for . . . He looked at his watch. Unless they had played with it while he had been unconscious, he had been out less than an hour. They hadn't wanted to attract attention with a corpse? That certainly hadn't stopped them from sending their letter bomb to the American journalist. He wished he understood what they were playing at. When had Leonard Warneke suddenly become a more sensitive issue than a reporter for a big American newspaper? As much as he hated to think it as he jabbed his thumb into the elevator button, that didn't make much sense, either.

He found the final mockery across the street from the entrance to the *palazzo*: his car parked very neatly and legally. From where he saw it, he couldn't even make out his smashed side window.

FORTY

Rome.
　The item will be purchased today.

FORTY-ONE

The cardinal regarded Sylvester as if he had uncovered the source of sin in the western world. Then again the finance minister had looked at him as though he had traced inflation back to its origins and the celebrity chef as though he had found the reason for so many flies in his kitchen. Circling the Proietti salon wasn't exactly being out of his depth, he decided: He had felt that way sitting in his own living room listening to Nick talk to his friends. This was more like swimming in a drained pool: The more form he put into it, the more ridiculous he was.

Felicia did her part by bestowing one insincere smile after another as she recited names for him. His own he recognized, the others he was sure he would find by going back to the hotel and Googling them on the lobby computer. "It'd be easier if you just gave me the list later," he said after the cardinal had swept his cape off to a soul still savable. "I'll be impressed in one fell swoop."

"You're not supposed to be impressed by them, Charley. They're supposed to be impressed by you."

"So one for two."

She guessed a sports metaphor, and that was enough for her to raise her gaze to the next group. She was in full brittle jaw mode. The next circle was two short turtles hemming in a sun-scorched blonde with too much silver jewelry on her fingers and wrists. For all that, the blonde looked more genuinely entertained than the hostess.

"We don't really have to, do we?"

"You didn't have to come at all, but you did. What do the English say? In for a penny, in for a pound?"

He spent his pound. The turtles were president of this and director of that, and the blonde was an executive from the Food and Agriculture Organization. Which reminded Felicia of the time Sylvester had arranged a hush-hush lunch for the director of FAO and the visiting American Secretary of State. The blonde was impressed, the turtles eyed him as competition for her attention, and Felicia evaded a question about how she knew that story. She wasn't concealing their marriage exactly, they could find out about it soon enough from someone else in the muggy room, but she wasn't handing out personal details as party favors, either.

Sylvester could have done without noticing the sulky cigarette-slim gigolo type retreating into a corner to make a call on his cellphone. A hot stab reminded him of the phone call he hadn't received. Or had he just been naïve again in expecting Warneke to get back to him within the forty-eight hours he had promised? Where Warneke and his crowd were concerned, even going through the motions in a drained pool would have been a lap forward.

"Charley! Just the man I want to talk to!"

Gianni Proietti came over so exuberantly that Felicia stopped in mid-sentence with the FAO blonde. There was cordiality between her husbands, her expression said, and then there was overdoing it and attracting attention from everybody in the room. Proietti's self-satisfaction said he would have been disappointed with any other reaction. Which was one of Proietti's problems, Sylvester thought: The man had a lot to be satisfied about. He was a walking superiority complex. He had the rough features of an action movie actor, he had an attractive wife born to glide through VIP gatherings, he had family money that thousands of families could have lived on, he owned land for backing up the money both inside and outside Italy, he was reverently addressed as *Senatore* by the political hacks and as *Professore* by the toady academics. And even that wasn't the worst of it. Gianni Proietti had apparently never gotten up in the morning without immediately going into the workouts that made him leaner and more toned than just about anybody who came into contact with him. So why did he also have to have a thick field of jet black hair and a breezy sense of humor?

"Or do I take that surprise to mean you were hoping to get out of here without that happening? What do you know about pirates?"

"They have a baseball team in Pittsburgh and a lot of followers in Somalia."

"No, no, the old-fashioned kind. Blackbeard, Captain Kidd, those buccaneers who operated out of the Caribbean in the 18th century."

"Not much."

"But they were up and down the East Coast of America."

"Before my time, Gianni."

"Well, good. There's something I can enlighten you about. Come on."

Proietti didn't wait for permission from Felicia, so he didn't, either. He had second thoughts about it when, the champagne glass in his hand feeling increasingly useless, he had to trail along past a Madame Tussaud's gallery of waxworks pretending not to notice them, out of the salon altogether, into the marble hall, and then over to a thick burnished door that had PURPOSE OF THE INVITATION written all over it. The loud rush in the salon suddenly didn't feel so innocent. "Who's waiting for us, Gianni—Blackbeard?"

He had the grace to almost blush. "A deception. I admit it. But if I had just led you off quietly, they would all be whispering to themselves right now about what Senator Proietti was plotting with the American journalist."

He pushed open the double doors into an amber-lighted den of wood and leather Sylvester had sometimes dreamed about having when he was having stupid dreams. The book shelves ran from floor to ceiling against three of the walls, framing a blond oak desk against a patio door. The desk was a litter of small and large electronic junk; standing next to it like obedient altar boys were two book stands, each supporting an encyclopedia-sized tome. And taking in some of the titles on the near shelves behind the door, his pipe spouting his caramel tobacco, was Inspector Gaetano.

"Arm's length from the books with that pipe, Piero," Proietti said, not all that jovially as he closed the doors behind them.

Gaetano turned to them without looking especially chastened. Whatever kind of cop he was, he was at ease smoking up the den of the country's richest senator. "A pleasure to see you again, Signor Sylvester."

"Go ahead, Charley. Tell him it's good to see him, too."

"Is this the reason I was invited to this shindig?"

The Italians looked at one another: *Shindig* wasn't in their vocabulary. But they weren't going to be bothered by it. "The inspector thought it would be better to have a few words without curious listeners."

"Meaning at the Viminale?"

Gaetano bit down on his pipe stem to avoid a comment. As subdued as it was, the lighting still glistened enough off his glasses to mask his eyes. "Let's not get into comparative leaks around the world, Charley," Proietti laughed too heartily, going to his desk chair. "I think Washington would be in first place. But what the inspector wanted to impress on you—excuse me for stating the obvious, Piero—is that this Cicut business has been on what you call the radar for some time. And unfortunately for all of us, it goes well beyond these Slav groups. Piero?"

Gaetano took his cue with what might have built into impatience in another second. "The other day in my office," he said, ambling toward a leather chair, "Signor Roenicke was in a state of panic. Either he was totally bewildered by what had happened or he knew just enough to be bewildered by how far whatever knowledge he had had been allowed to degenerate into that act of terrorism."

Proietti poked a letter-opener into his desk blotter. "Excuse the inspector's syntax. He is a student of the speeches of Aldo Moro."

Gaetano sat down heavily; he didn't think that was particularly funny. In fact, he didn't seem to like being talked about in the third person at all.

"Yeah, I guess that was my impression, too."

"Your impression? All right, your impression. But what I was getting to was that you, on the other hand, seemed to be trying to act in command of matters you really knew nothing about. Would that be an accurate conclusion, Signore?"

Sylvester wondered when he had clocked enough time in Rome to go from Gaetano's *Mister*, as he had been addressed at the Viminale, to the new *Signore*. But he would have to ask that later. Proietti was waiting for his answer, too.

"What do you think, Signore? Did I read the situation correctly?"

"If you did, I don't see why I'm here. I wouldn't be of much use to you, would I?"

Proietti turned a smile on Gaetano. The policeman didn't bother acknowledging it. "If you had not had your intense conversation with Roenicke across the street from my office, no. But you did have. You wanted to know what you had been dragged into. What was your *impression* after that little talk, Signor Sylvester?"

"Your escort time us, too?"

Proietti gave another light stab to his blotter. The bonhomie was wearing off. "We are talking about a homicide, Charley. That is the inspector's immediate concern. But you must have also understood by now that there are other matters involved. Roenicke has gone back to America, and we had no juridical reason to detain him. But that also means you have to be the source of whatever light we need to go forward."

It sounded like a compliment and a threat rolled into one, and probably deserved a crack and a fast exit. But if he wasn't going to trade off for some information from them, with whom? Leonard Warneke of the 48-hour reassurances? So he took the other comfortable upright chair next to Gaetano's, placed his glass on the edge of the desk, and told them about his conversation with Roenicke. Most of it, anyway. He still wanted them to be the first to mention the diary. Gaetano listened without blinking, Proietti with a superciliousness that he wasn't hearing anything he hadn't already known. "And I guess you know about the priest, right?"

Gaetano had to puff a little harder to get smoke. "Minic? Yes, we are aware of him. A man of strong convictions, apparently."

"That was my impression, too."

Gaetano didn't like digs. "And this diary?" he retorted blandly.

Win one, lose a few hundred. "Yes, Roenicke mentioned that, too."

"In what way?"

"The way you're thinking. A lot of people seem to think I have it."

It sounded too evasive by half even to him. "Please, Signore."

He sensed the same dwindling patience from Proietti. "And I do. It's in the safe back in my hotel. I brought it here for the widow. It's her property now."

Proietti's sigh ran around the room and up and down every bookcase surrounding them. "Thank you, Charley!"

"You have read this diary?" the policeman pressed.

"I don't speak the language."

The pipe had gone out, and Gaetano wasn't about to relight it. "Then I suggest we get it and turn it over to people who do speak the language."

There was really nothing he wanted to do more, to get his inheritance from Josef Cicut out of his life. But the cop's peremptory tone was also getting on his nerves. "It was sent to me and it legally belongs to Elena Cicut."

"And it might also be evidence in a homicide investigation. If you and Signora Cicut require a receipt for it, you will have one."

Proietti stood up, the bonhomie back as diplomacy. Sylvester was grateful for the timing: It made it unnecessary to procrastinate over whether he should mention Joey Bacsik. "Somebody owes you an apology for getting you in this mess, Charley, and not just Cicut. But once you give the inspector that diary, I have a feeling you won't be bothered anymore. Then you can get back to the vacation Felicia says you came for."

He didn't want to linger, he should have stood with Gaetano, but with every word out of Proietti's mouth he wanted to sit longer. What had Felicia said about being in for a penny so in for a pound? "And what about Cicut's son?"

The two of them looked blankly at one another. They were back at *shindig*. "I don't understand," Proietti said.

"I think Minic or somebody like him is holding the boy as a hostage as the price for getting that diary."

Gaetano took the dead pipe out of his mouth to rifle through his mind for all the files that had passed over his desk recently. He couldn't locate the one he was looking for. "Why do you say that?"

"Elena Cicut." It seemed like half the truth anyway.

And it explained everything to Proietti. "Well, of course. A mother having nightmares about a son who has run off."

"Could be."

Gaetano wasn't as convinced as the senator. "But you don't believe that."

Directly in front of the question, Sylvester was surprised by how much he still wanted to believe Warneke's promise.

"We don't have to go through the salon to get to the front door," Proietti said, filling in the silence by opening the doors. "I'll say good night to Felicia for you, and then pay for it after everybody has left. But we'll have a quiet dinner before you leave, yes?"

FORTY-TWO

"**A**sk."

Sylvester squirmed as Gaetano braked down too short of the light, guaranteeing they would be stopped at the corner. Gaetano driving was not Gaetano sitting in the back seat being driven. He had to surrender most of his ruminations to the night traffic and keep worrying that his glasses might fall off his face if he let a few seconds go by without tinkering with them. Behind the wheel he was as jumpy as a student driver.

"Tonight was your idea or Proietti's?"

The policeman nodded in approval. "The essence of cooperation is making everyone feel it's been a mutual decision." Another tap at his glasses as he somehow made it through the traffic light. "Are you truly on vacation, Signore?"

"An awful lot of people don't seem to approve of me being here. They think I would've been better off going to Patagonia. Why do you think that is, Inspector?"

He shrugged. "You used to live here, you went away, now you are back to renew acquaintances with people you used to see regularly. Perhaps some people view you as a visitor to a zoo. You have come and gone, but they have remained in their cages all this time. What they really do not approve of is their own immobility."

"I'll accept that."

"Good. But why I asked is that other people from your newspaper. . . ."

"Applebaum?"

"Applebaum."

"We have different jobs."

"Yes. Yours is the dead and his is what—be careful or you'll be dead?"

"I think I heard a joke."

A scooter came out of nowhere to cross between the car and the motorcycle to get over to the right lane, almost taking his headlights with it. "*Cafone!*"

Sylvester couldn't help blurting a laugh at the cop's outburst. "We are all equals before our Maker and these morons," Gaetano conceded.

It seemed like as much of an opening as he was going to get. "You really didn't know about Philip Cicut?"

"Are you sure you do? That his mother does? Parents, Signore. Sometimes we envision dire situations as a response to some lack in ourselves. Resolve this one little crisis and that will atone for all the crises with the child when we were inadequate."

"Spoken like a father."

"A 20-year-old son and two teenage daughters. You?"

"Your printouts must have told you."

He shrugged unashamedly. "One of each, I believe. And you were married to Signora Proietti for thirteen years. How did it work out that you received custody? That detail isn't in my printouts."

"It's a long story. I think Minic has the boy."

"That would not be very clever of him."

"What I didn't say before is that he left his mother with a gun."

Gaetano had to catch himself from looking away from the road. He even forgot about his glasses. "I see."

"I wish I did."

He didn't know what else to say, and neither did Gaetano. Traffic or not, the policeman sank into a thoughtful silence until they arrived at the hotel. He made a guttural sound of displeasure at the sight of the police car parked next to the fountain. Sylvester knew they were too late. "Let us wait for a moment. It is probably nonsense."

"Like what? A master jewel thief going through the rooms?"

"What is it they say about the hammer seeing everything as a nail?"

"If the diary's still there, I'll buy you a cognac."

"You act astonishingly sure of the importance of this diary in everything. Is there maybe some other detail you have omitted?"

Sylvester didn't know what he thought he had accomplished by not telling Gaetano about Joey Bacsik back at Proietti's. Whatever it had been didn't seem relevant now, so he told the policeman about Cynthia's call. Gaetano tried to affect a granite expression, but there were too many flickers of irritation and even anger to pull it off. Finally, he sniffled behind another look over at the hotel entrance. "All right, here is what we will do. We will go inside because we want a drink in the bar. I will stop off at the desk to ask what is happening because the officers there will know me and expect me to do that. But you will not break stride. You will continue on into the bar. If the officers or anyone from the hotel address you, keep going. Understood?"

Sylvester understood. He understood so well he had invented understanding. He understood why it was the first time he had ever seen Romolo without a tie (because he had been summoned from his nearby apartment by the night man for a crisis). He understood why the two uniformed cops gave Gaetano the stiffened attention the cops on Via Propaganda and at the Viminale had given him (because out from behind the wheel the man was Authority). And he understood Romolo's apoplectic expression as the manager saw him (because of all those sniffy assurances about hotel security).

"Signor Sylvester . . ."

Gaetano nimbly cut off the man's line of vision. "Get me a cognac, Charley. I'll be inside in a second."

He did what he was told, proceeding on into the bar with at least four pairs of eyes on his back. This time there were customers in the place, even faint piano Muzak under the rattling laughter of a fat woman entertaining a couple with the story of her shopping adventures on the day. He took a table as far away from her as he could find and ordered two cognacs from the bartender doubling as a waiter. He waited for some new sensation—guilt,

relief, anger, he didn't care which. There had been a big movement around the object he had carried across the ocean, so there
should have been a correspondingly big movement somewhere
inside his chest now that it had been carried off away from him.
But there wasn't. The diary might as well have still been safely in
the safe under the safekeeping of the safety-first Romolo. Taking
it hadn't affected him in the least.

Except when he thought about Warneke. Over him he could
get angry, work up even to a fury. Minic might have been the
creep he was, but he would have only been guessing that the diary was in the hotel safe. Warneke hadn't been operating with that
handicap. Some asshole had actually *told* him that was where the
diary was.

By the time Gaetano shuffled in, Sylvester had drunk most of
his cognac and was eying the cop's. He hadn't missed anything
out at the front desk.

"It would be nice to narrow down the time," Gaetano said, but
not sounding especially perturbed.

"I don't know that night man, but he can't be as meticulous
as the manager."

Gaetano was amused. "And if you were twice as meticulous,
what would you do if the fire alarm went off on the third floor?
Leaving the desk unattended for a few minutes would seem the
lesser evil, no?"

"That's how they got him away from the desk?"

The policeman nodded. "There were at least two of them involved. One guest upstairs to do the distracting, the other to come
in and get to the safe. That is why your meticulous manager is
making a copy of his register for me even as we speak."

"You're talking about awfully slick people."

"Your Father Minic doesn't strike you that way?"

"No," he thought aloud, and neither did Warneke fit that
description. "I mean, more than professionals. Practically . . .
acrobats."

"Something like that," Gaetano said pensively. "People with a
touch." He swigged the cognac as if announcing one end of his
evening. "I think it is time you take the Senator's advice, Signor

Sylvester, and concentrate on that vacation. Whatever tenuous connection you persuaded yourself you had to this business has just been stolen."

"I think there's still the matter of Philip . . ."

Even in the dimness of the bar Gaetano's glower was on a level of darkness all its own. "There is only one matter—the murder of your former assistant," he said sharply. "Human life. One second here, the next squeezed out like a candle. All the rest of this—our famous diary, this teenager who may or may not have gone hiking in the Dolomites, whatever may have befallen that colleague of yours in New York—is of less interest to me. If they help shed light on the demise of the unfortunate Signora, fine. We will fit the pieces together. Until then please don't confuse what you think are my priorities."

"You're the one who was in such a hurry to come here."

The policeman had no answer to that, and he didn't seem to mind.

FORTY-THREE

Elena couldn't believe she had procrastinated so long. Milo was her brother, but Philip was her son. How could she have sat around balancing them, first loading this scale and then the other? The one and only truth was that Milo had lied to her, that Philip had *not* gone to Father Stela to ask for his help to go back home and join his uncle. Zagreb wasn't even his home; Rome was. Milo had always lied to her, even as children, and always with that twinkle in his eye that said don't listen to her doubts, she was too bright to suspect he could fool her, leave everything to him. But now the everything was Philip. She could never trust Milo again. She hated him for making her so hesitant. But she also had to get the diary if she expected to see Philip again. Milo hadn't really come right out and said it, but for sheer spite against her he was capable of evil. What did she dare put past the fat, middle-aged man she had seen on the television?

If it wasn't already too late.

She stepped back behind the fountain as two policemen came out of the hotel and went to their *pantera*. They had barely driven away when a sour looking man in glasses and filling a pipe came out and walked to a private car parked in the side street. She thought of pipe smokers as contented people, but there was nothing serene about this one. Even his walk had a protest—an odd hitch that seemed to leave his right heel behind after the rest of his body had moved forward. She didn't like the way he yanked on his driver's door, flounced in behind the wheel, and attacked the dashboard like it was a mortal enemy. As meek as he might have seemed on first glance, there was violence in him. She was sure he was connected to the two policemen, probably a policeman himself. The street felt lighter after he had gone off.

She counted to ten in case there were more policemen leaving. There weren't, but she had done well to hold back because she recognized the bald manager and the night desk clerk from the first time she had gone to find Sylvester. As they came out the door, the manager was barking over his shoulder at the slumping clerk. Something bad had happened, and the manager was blaming the clerk for it. She wished the clerk would argue back, but he merely shook his head and shrugged and then shook his head again. She knew why Josef had been so appalled the night they had seen Milo on television: There were too many passive people like the clerk waiting to be stepped on. She didn't want her brother gaining too much power over them, either.

The bald manager finally stopped his scolding, took a theatrical breath, and then clomped away. The clerk lingered at the door until the manager disappeared inside the third *palazzo* down the street, then felt safe enough to mutter to himself and go back inside. Elena had never thought before how courageous—not just foolish or determined or insane, but *courageous*—Josef had been to put a gun against his temple and fire a bullet there. A sheep like the clerk could have never done that.

The thought was her last excuse for standing still. Through the revolving door she saw it all suddenly coming together in the lobby—the clerk going directly to the hotel office behind the desk and a couple stepping out from the bar and going over to press for the elevator. Elena was inside before she had to question her sense. The couple, who had been speaking German, smiled and nodded to her, and she did the same, asking if they were enjoying their stay, grateful for the rusty German she had used on her calls to Mainz about Josef's body. Out of the corner of her eye she saw the clerk peering out at them. He was dubious but apparently didn't speak German because he accepted them as three friends having a conversation, then returned inside. The German woman was telling her more than she wanted to know about the Trevi

Fountain and the gigolos who fished there for single women, but the man thought it was funny. He was all courtesy in letting her precede him into the car and press the button for the first floor. As the man pressed for the fourth floor, the woman complimented her German in a patronizing way. Elena tried to look flattered.

As soon as she stepped out into the carpeted silence of the first floor, she had an urge to jump back into the elevator car to hear more about the predators at the Trevi Fountain. The candelabras gave off too much light for the narrow hall of white doors. They made her feel more naked than she had felt back in her bathroom when she had been making a cartoon of choosing the right underwear, telling herself it would never come to that with Sylvester, deciding on her good lacy black bra but her old cotton panties, scolding herself for thinking of trying to seduce Sylvester in the name of getting the diary, daring him to make of her old underwear whatever he wanted when all he would really be interested in was her sucking him off, despising Milo for making her think of reducing her and Sylvester to play objects, choosing her good bra and black silk panties, remembering the time in their Chiesa Nuova living room when she had caught Sylvester staring at her lewdly with Felicia and Josef sitting there, getting furious with herself for dithering over any of it when he was now divorced and she was a widow.

She knocked on the numbered door the night man had told her on her first visit—the visit when she had blithely waved away Sylvester's attempts to show her the diary. She felt like a pyramid of a fool, so many blocks painstakingly put in place so she could be down to seeing whether she had to fuck to get what she wanted.

"Elena!"

He was more astonished—and louder—than she had pictured when he saw her at his door. His voice echoed up and down the hall, threatening to bring out the guests from every room. "May I come in a moment, Charles?"

She had never imagined him saying no. He stepped back in his stockinged feet, then frowned at the mess of clothes and newspapers he had exposed her to. "The maids refuse to come in three times a day," he said, clearing the only chair of papers. "Got to talk to their union about that. What is it? News about Philip?"

She cringed at the sound of Philip's name in the room as she sat down. "I need the diary, Charles. It is the only way I will get him back."

He clenched his jaw; he wasn't at all surprised. "Who told you that?"

"My brother."

He nodded, but so vaguely he might have forgotten who her brother was. She could have gotten the same response from him if she had said the King of the Gypsies.

"I think he is serious, Charles. I also think he is capable of harming Philip. Maybe only to hurt me. I do not know. I have been trying to tell myself he is just an older version of Milo at his most swinish, but on the telephone he sounded like a stranger who had been my brother only in the past."

He flopped down on the end of the bed with a glumness like that of the clerk downstairs. She had expected him to be a dozen other things—sympathetic, stubborn, lascivious—but not that.

"I don't have it, Elena," he announced. "It was stolen."

She thought of the policemen and the man with the pipe leaving the hotel, but this time they felt like they were leaving through her chest. She opened her mouth, but nothing came out. She wanted to hit him for letting what he said had happened happen, but her arms weighed too much.

"What else did your brother say?"

"What else would be important?"

He pretended not to hear her tone. "You have to go to the police."

Her anger finally started returning usefully. "That seems to be your only advice, Charles. And what exactly would I say to these police?"

"Not the Questura. There's an inspector who knows the whole background to this. I can take you to him."

She knew he meant the one with the pipe: Another man who wanted everyone to think he was in total control, then slammed dashboards or fired bullets into his head as soon as he thought he was alone. "It was a mistake coming here. Excuse me, Charles."

But her body refused to move. Her legs stayed planted on her feet on the floor, her arms felt like part of the chair as she lifted them. Then he was in front of her with a glass of water. He had to have gotten it from the bathroom on the other side of the head of the bed, and she had not noticed. She had lost seconds—minutes?—of her life. And she had returned to it to have water being fed to her the way she had once fed her mother while the animals had been roaming around in the streets outside.

"This is ridiculous," she said.

"Drink," he insisted.

He was right: The water seemed to go directly from her throat to her brain. Parts of her insides came awake.

"You're staying here tonight," he said. "You're not going home."

She wanted to laugh. She had counted on her pitifulness as seduction.

Then she wanted to cry.

FORTY-FOUR

Gaetano had the name. It had taken patience before the computer printouts Govoni had mercilessly kept piling on the work table set up next to his desk, but he had found the inside man at the Reggio he had been seeking in the hotel register. Too bad he had been so successful: a classic example of being careful what you wish for.

The families and the trysters in the register he had eliminated immediately. He hadn't dared entertain the thought that his target had come with an entourage; there was no time to consider that kind of elaborate planning. Which had left six singles who had checked into the Reggio in the last 48 hours. One was Sylvester. Two Germans and a Pole were in the city to attend a United Nations conference at the Food and Agriculture Organization. The fifth was a Chinese woman in Rome to visit her son, a monsignor in the Vatican bureaucracy. Which had left Emilio Tepedino, who, according to Govoni, already had an apartment in the Monti district of the city.

"Maybe the exterminators were spraying his place and he wanted to get away from the smell for the night." As usual, the sergeant waited to see if he had said something relevant or would be appreciated for his wit. He could go either way.

And Gaetano would have settled for either. Instead, he had the printout on Emilio Tepedino identifying an employee of the Italy-United States Chamber of Commerce. There were other positions that would have alarmed him more, but outside the American ambassador to Rome, he couldn't think of any immediately. "They must have been in a great hurry to draft somebody local like Tepedino. It was a big risk."

Govoni was at sea, but wasn't about to admit it. "Which they should not have taken if you've figured it out. Should we bring him in?"

"And hear what, Matteo? He was woken from a sound sleep by the alarm just like everybody else on the floor?"

"But we could ask why he was in the hotel in the first place."

"You already told me. They were fumigating his apartment."

He didn't realize how tightly he had been holding the report on Tepedino until Govoni slumped out of the office, his efforts to be of help once more rejected. Gaetano promised himself (for what, the third or fourth time in the last month?) to make it up to the man, but right now Emilio Tepedino was a bigger concern. And one he had done his best to suppress even with Senator Proietti's interest in the whole affair of the diary. All the prattle from Sylvester and Proietti about the precious journal had sidetracked him. He had sounded so sanctimonious in the hotel bar telling Sylvester he was primarily interested in the homicide, that all the other business of Croatian white rats and Croatian black rats circling each other in their political saraband had been secondary. But Emilio Tepedino and the Italy-United States Chamber of Commerce announced in neon lights that he had been a fool in his professional piety.

Gaetano restarted his pipe; he didn't deserve the pleasure, but anything at all to postpone having to think about his next move. How could he possibly have criticized himself for not seeing the obvious when the smoke fogged his glasses? He wanted to concentrate on the letter bomb? All right, concentrate on this: It had been a message, a lethal message but still a message. And who had needed a message? It couldn't have been Roenicke: He was supposed to have been dead, in no position to appreciate messages. There had been a bigger target than Roenicke the Casbah-level tool, so big that the people behind it—and it was almost certainly the same people who had been busy at the Reggio—had thought it worth the risk of drafting somebody transparent like

Emilio Tepedino for the diversionary work. The message had been meant for the only people who would have taken an attack on an American correspondent seriously—the Americans themselves. And what that message said was . . .

He could tell from Govoni's hushed voice on the intercom that somebody like the President of the Republic was calling. The sergeant insisted his superior be of the most respectful frame of mind when he picked up his phone; otherwise, who knew how many transfers tomorrow would bring?

It wasn't the President of the Republic, but Proietti. "Problems last night?"

Gaetano had never considered anything but the truth until he was in front of the choice. And an evasive Thomism from his university classes—usually handy at moments requiring tact—wasn't an answer, either. "We should meet," he compromised.

Proietti sucked in some air. He had already made up his mind about the answer he had wanted to hear. "Will it wait until tomorrow?"

"Probably not."

Silence, then: "I see," sounding very much like somebody who didn't see and didn't want to see. "My house at five."

"Fine."

Gaetano held the receiver an extra moment. Force of habit from the old days when listening devices had been cruder. He was sorry he had been the one to spearhead the installation of what the Americans and Germans had been using for years.

FORTY-FIVE

Warneke was put off by so many people in the billiards hall before noon. He had counted on privacy at such an early hour. But games were going on at three of the tables, and a Filipino was practicing his technique at a fourth table. The flabby manager he remembered being called Gigi was standing behind the counter and eying him alertly. The back door to Restivo's office was closed, muffling what sounded like an argument inside. Whatever else had made the man so obscenely fat, it hadn't been lounging around in bed all day. So much for privacy.

"He's busy right now," Gigi volunteered without moving.

Warneke wasn't in the mood for what was supposed to sound like the final word. It wasn't the day for last words. Leszek and his friend were still an embarrassment. And more than even that, he couldn't shake that moment of coming awake in the empty apartment and almost—almost, but close enough—wondering who he was. He would have as soon fired the *boccette* ball under his hand at Gigi as said, "Tell him I want to see him. Now."

One of the *boccette* players looked up at the tone, then over at Gigi. Gigi considered an extra moment, then seemed to remember he had more hair than muscle protruding from his Cinzano T-shirt. He hated himself for stepping out from behind the counter and walking over to the office door. He knocked lightly, opened the door, then went inside, closing the door behind him, barely time for Warneke to glimpse a gray-haired man sitting in front of Restivo's desk.

The *boccette* player and his opponent both stared at him—two more who seemed to believe in their silent menace. Warneke bounced the ball in his hand on the table but looked around at the faded pictures of old tournaments on the walls so the two of them wouldn't get more ambitious. He wouldn't have minded bashing in their heads if it came to that, but it wasn't what he had come for. The ball in his hand was a fraction of the size of the shotput he had last heaved in Bucharest, and there would be no little Rumanians disqualifying him this time for not pausing before letting it fly.

He was relieved when the two players went back to their game. He didn't like feeling so close to being out of control. Again.

Gigi opened the office door, and the gray-haired man scuttled out from under his arm and didn't raise his eyes from the floor as he hurried over to the entrance. Gigi waved to him like somebody used to seeing Restivo's visitors hurry away with thanks they still had their limbs. Warneke slowed himself down on the way to the door, making sure the goon saw the billiard ball and could think about its possible uses.

Restivo was splayed out behind his desk as he had been the last time; not much air had been let into the stuffy box since then. The main difference was that, instead of the desk lamp that had given him an extra chin or two at night, the daylight coming through the high wall window now emphasized how fast he was losing his hair on top. There were three empty *espresso* cups on his desk amid a clutter of envelopes and papers.

"My Eastern friend! Back so soon for help?"

Warneke could have done without Gigi closing the door behind him and then leaning against it. He really didn't want to have to use the ball in his hand. "And you're the man for that! Who else did you help after our little talk with that cop?"

Restivo understood, but gave it one try anyway. "Why do you look so irritated, *amico*? I don't owe you money."

"The people you told about our talk with Badalamenti."

Restivo hadn't heard anything funny, but he smiled anyway. "So many people, so much business to conduct. You really expect me to remember every little detail from what happened . . . when?

Last week? Yesterday? *Il logorio della vita moderna*, like it says on Gigi's shirt there."

Warneke didn't know the Italian, but he knew he was supposed to turn around and remember why Restivo felt so secure having his goon closed in with them. He didn't want to do it, but it seemed like the only way to avoid more fencing. Suddenly, he was back to being a second—a half-second—ahead of when he should have let go of the ball. In Bucharest the little Rumanians had disqualified him for not pausing, but he didn't have them watching now. That alone made up for the lightness of the billiard ball, and it was out of his hand—neither spin nor glide, just hurtled—before he had to think about all the other differences that probably would have kept it glued in his palm as an empty threat. It thwacked Gigi so perfectly above his left eye that he was too panicked yelling to get his hand up in time to stop the hurt. There was the arrogance of a bull in the way he stomped his foot even as his eyes started rolling and he sagged, first against the door, then into the chair next to it. The goon didn't know what he had done to deserve so much pain. Life was so unfair.

Restivo's dismay restored the balance in the room; he came completely out of his chair, his suspenders straining with the abrupt move. "You're crazy!"

Warneke agreed, but also made sure to step off sideways so he keep an eye on both of them at the same time. "I asked you a question. Who else?"

Gigi's moaning persuaded the fat man he was without help for the moment. He flopped back down on his chair heavily enough to crash the springs through the floor. "Who? Everybody, that's who."

"Names."

A slyness came and went in Restivo's eyes. "You think you're special because you walk in here with the name of somebody in Zagreb I haven't seen in five years? Like that makes us friends? I hardly remembered the man. You don't sell fish like that and you don't sell information like that."

"Freedom Press?"

He thought about denying it, then saw no reason to. "Maybe. There are some people there that appreciate me. They pass along this, I pass along that."

"Like my name?"

The fat man shrugged. "You were grateful to me for Badala-menti, they're grateful to me for you. What's wrong with a world like that? Everybody knows everything. Like with computers and all these spy people. Only on a personal level and maybe with a few euros of profit here and there. Right now, for example, I prob-ably know something that could help you. But in your state. . . ."

"There's no end to it with you, is there?"

Restivo found nothing wrong with that, either. "I have had to improvise in the new gambling reality like everybody else. But no great sacrifice. We branch out. At bottom we are always chasing our tails, no? You, me, the next idiot who walks through that door? No great shame in that."

Warneke suddenly felt very tired. The hippopotamus might as well have been sitting on his chest. "*How* can you help me?"

Restivo nodded approvingly. "Let's just say that not all the tail chasers speak Italian or that goulash you speak. They like Pepsi-Cola, you understand?"

He should have known. "Americans."

"Not everybody drinks Cinzano." He looked over to where Gi-anni was rising to a second level of moans. "Put some ice on that. I can see the swelling from here."

Gigi wasn't sure which one of them he wanted to strangle first, but he lumbered to his feet and went out without a word, still du-tiful enough to close the door behind him. "You made an enemy there, Warneke. And for what? To demonstrate to me how serious you are. I never doubted that."

"What Americans?"

"How should I know? They don't show me their birth certifi-cates. Some of them have names, some just letters. Some come here to play *boccette*, some go to the *bische* to play roulette. It's all about playing. You should know that. Or have I misjudged you?"

Warneke thought he should have known the answer to that.

FORTY-SIX

Sylvester was glad Myra Roenicke had beaten him to the call. His questions couldn't help but be doubly awkward if he had had to phone her with them. But he also could have done without the little deceits of the lunch invitation, the *prosciutto e melone*, and the soft breeze on her terrace fending off the worst of the afternoon heat. The casualness was as forced to her as it was to him. She was all edge in addressing her small talk to the floors, ceilings, and anywhere else not in his vicinity, transparently with her own agenda—payback for how she had been his accomplice against Minic the first time he had sat on the terrace. He didn't have to be a psychic to figure it had to do with Roenicke's recall to New York.

"Tell me another city where you can feel so cosmopolitan eating cantaloupe," she said, following her fork into her mouth. "Why would anyone want to go anywhere else? Can you tell me that, Charley? It had to be hard for you to leave, wasn't it?"

"There were special circumstances."

"Yes, I suppose," she conceded too quickly. "I never really knew your wife. I got a feeling she didn't like me very much."

"I don't think that's true."

"You don't know the vibes between women. Felicia always seemed to be looking past me to the nearest pair of pants."

He wanted to laugh at the clumsiness of the insinuation, but that wouldn't get him to a couple of things he wanted to ask her.

"So it couldn't have been anything personal, this feeling you had that she didn't like you. She was that way with everybody."

She looked at him quizzically. "That would seem to follow, wouldn't it?" But she didn't give up that easily. "Or are you still just making excuses for her? I always thought you did. Like you felt grateful for the time—and the children—she gave you and refused to complain when it was time to move on."

"That's really not the case, Myra."

"Okay. Just an outsider's opinion. I sure as hell wouldn't just let my kids hop a plane across the ocean. But then I don't have any kids, do I? So Myra doesn't really know what the hell she's talking about, does she?"

She heard the shrillness in her voice, shut up, and refilled her glass with mineral water. There would be no blaming wine this time.

"You've heard from Eddie?"

"This morning. The talk shows didn't get him to sleep."

"And?"

"They haven't told him how long he's going to be there."

"I don't know any more than you do if that's what you're asking."

She smiled at being caught out. Her black polo shirt and jeans made her starkly pale and thin. "Sort of."

"And you're afraid they're going to reassign him."

"I must sound incredibly selfish. Your husband almost gets killed and you're thinking of what *you*'d like to happen."

"What do you want me to say, Myra?"

About that she had no doubts. "That there's still a chance they won't pull him out of here and send him to some godforsaken place."

"The paper doesn't send you from Rome to godforsaken places."

"You sound like you've drunk the Kool-Aid." She immediately bit her lip. "I didn't mean that, Charley."

"With or without the Kool-Aid they'd be crazy to send him back here after that bomb. Porterfield's not crazy."

"I know, I know."

"Then you have these mysterious extensions the last few years."

"Eddie's good at his job. What's so mysterious about that?"

He was in front of the questions he would have asked her on the phone, but now with her fragility staring back at him. "We both know there's been more involved than how good he is," he plunged ahead. She gave up staring back at him. "What I'd like to know is if it's his father who's been pressuring Porterfield to keep you here."

"Why is that important?"

"It might make sense of some things. Has old man Roenicke been handing down assignment suggestions from the boardroom?"

"Hah! Ask him to interrupt dusting his Tiffany lampshades?"

"He's still Eddie's father. If he knew you wanted to stay here, he could've been doing it on the sly without saying anything to you two."

"You have a sentimental opinion of fatherhood, Charley. The Roenickes don't."

"All right. Then who?"

"Why are you so sure somebody has been pressuring Porterfield?"

"Eddie may be good at his job, but that hasn't stopped Porterfield from making him the Web's favorite correspondent. Not the paper's, only the Web's."

She nodded to herself. "He's complained to you?"

"Practically the first words out of his mouth the morning I got here."

"Yes."

"So if it hasn't been his father . . .?"

"Applebaum."

Sylvester didn't know why he was surprised: Applebaum had been his backup thought. "You're sure?"

"He told me right at this table he would take care of New York if we wanted to stay here so much. He even wrote it down right in front of me. Claude likes to make lists. I think not reassigning Eddie was right under buy some grapes."

"You don't sound very grateful."

"Of course I am. But since when has Claude Applebaum ever done something without benefiting himself?"

"Since never. But who cares? In this case . . .?"

She thought of an answer, dismissed it, then went back to it. "When one of my actors, usually the ones who read Stanislavsky in Cliff Notes, when they say they can't *find* their character, I have them look to their left, then to their right, then behind them, then out in front of them. When they still can't find their character, like they say, I point out to them that can leave only one possibility. *Where they're standing! That's where it's hiding!* For some reason, what's profited Applebaum is just Eddie being here."

She wanted him to smile with him, to share her bafflement, so he did. But he knew she was right, so completely right he suddenly craved a scotch instead of mineral water for washing it down. "He told me about the trip to Trieste to meet Jelic."

She nodded. "With that creepy Minic. And when he didn't write anything about it, I thought, oh, oh, we've outlived our usefulness to the priest and Applebaum."

"Eddie used the same phrase—*outlived his usefulness.*"

"I actually made a scene with him over it, told him to write the damn story. But he refused, said it was a crap trip, there was nothing there but propaganda for Jelic, and he didn't give a damn what Applebaum said to Porterfield. And then the strangest thing of all happened, Charley—nothing! Nothing at all! Nobody held it against him and we didn't get any calls from New York asking how we liked the food in Mali. So we hadn't outlived our usefulness after all. Claude was all forgiving."

"Eddie told me just the opposite: Minic didn't want him to write anything."

"There you go, then. Everybody was happy."

"But when Eddie used that phrase about usefulness with me, he wasn't referring to not writing up the Jelic interview. It was to something more recent."

"I don't know."

"Josef Cicut, maybe?"

She went back to her melon. "Could be. I didn't pay much attention to all that until you came here for dinner. That's all anybody seemed to want to talk about. You seem to know why it's so important."

"I think I'm getting an idea." She shrugged; resentfully, for getting away from what she wanted to talk about. She was back to thinking about packing up the furniture and the glassware and the Wailing Wall rubbings. "Eddie never talked to you about it?"

"You came in on the second act the other night. Should I have paid more attention, Charley? Is that why somebody tried to kill him?"

"I didn't say that."

"But you're not saying it was some lunatic who just doesn't like the paper's Sunday magazine section, either."

"What did Eddie say about Cicut?"

"Nothing I really remember except there was some question about how he died. What you and Minic were talking about. But you haven't answered my question."

"I'm still trying to put the pieces together. So are the police and everybody else."

"Where's Applebaum when you really need him? . . . Joke, Charley."

And he wouldn't have minded being able to laugh at it. But how off was she? Was it so absurd to think that something like the trip to Trieste had mattered only as a gesture, had never been important for itself? That Applebaum had merely been demonstrating his role as an influence over the Rome correspondent through Minic? But it wasn't a robotic influence, either. It hadn't been old Claude's fault if Jelic had needed to step up his game to impress Roenicke as newsworthy.

"I don't know what I'll do, Charley, if they reassign him. I really consider this home. And then there's the theater."

"There are community theaters everywhere."

"You're not being very sympathetic."

No, he wasn't. She had her cocoon, he had his. Jelic *had* stepped up his game. The bomb had been addressed to Eddie Roenicke, but its message had been meant for Applebaum and the people he was in bed with across the Atlantic. The Cicut diary threat had shaken the status quo that everybody had grown comfortable with.

Everybody except Milovan Jelic.

"It may seem silly to you, but when Eddie and I go out, I have more to talk about now than the politics of your office . . ."

She went on until she stopped going on and looked at him for agreement. He managed a nod, but she was still right: Between her cracks about being overly grateful to Felicia and what she had said about Applebaum, wasps were buzzing around in his head, and he wasn't at all sympathetic.

FORTY-SEVEN

"I really have to apologize, Inspector. But I have seen what happens in that Senate chamber the moment they have been dismissed. Before Gianni can take a step toward the door, he's totally surrounded. The first one wants to talk about the issue being debated, the second one has a relative in the university he would like to send to Gianni for an academic reason, and the third one just wants to gossip. It takes him forever to get through the gauntlet and out into the street. But if you would like, I can call him on his cellphone and remind him you are waiting."

Gaetano would have liked, but also knew what Felicia Proietti would have liked. "No need, Signora. I'm sure he will be along."

She gave him an approving nod and another bob to her crossed leg. She had very thin legs, a model's from a magazine, and she didn't mind flaunting them from her corner of the couch. The straight-backed chair she had ushered him into across the coffee table made him think of an interrogation chair where the suspect was unable to turn his eyes. "You didn't stay very long the other evening and you whisked off one of our special guests with you. Was it that important?"

"I'm sure the senator . . ."

"Oh, he never tells me anything. Do you tell your wife what you don't want her to know? I'm sure you don't."

"I don't think it was a question of secrets, Signora."

She laughed; insincerely. "With Charley Sylvester and this tragic bombing at his newspaper and a police inspector in the house for our reception without Gianni telling me ahead of time? Oh, come, Inspector. I may appear frivolous, but some of the neurons in my brain are still functioning."

"I never doubted it, Signora."

She didn't need the empty reassurance; she just wanted her question answered. "I really hope Gianni isn't being dragged into something that will distract him. His day is long enough as it is."

"I can't imagine the Senator would allow that to happen."

She threw her arm over the back of the couch and rolled her neck up at the ceiling as if waiting for an angel to descend and help her with the dense visitor. "And wouldn't life be easier if we only had to deal with what we *allow to happen*! Is that what a policeman wakes up in the morning expecting during the day, Inspector?"

"I see your point."

"Which gets me back to my question," she said, returning from the ceiling and leveling her stare from a new distance. "Why would the police want to involve Senator Proietti in what appears to be some random terrorist act?"

"If only." Her glare said he should have left his tongue outside the front door. "I was just thinking of the concept of terrorist acts and randomness. Unfortunately, most of them are carried out as part of a definite scheme with a definite objective, nothing in the least random about them."

She didn't appreciate the dictionary lesson. "No doubt you're correct, Inspector. But I was speaking about involving the senator."

Gaetano said something reassuring; about jumping to hasty conclusions. He was intrigued by the possibility that the attractive woman in front of him, the attractive woman who worked at being attractive with her short hair and pastel green summer sheath and fashionable rhinestone sandals and looking less than her 50 years, might have had fewer objections to his presence if Sylvester and his newspaper were not *involved*, if she didn't have to wonder about both her husbands in the same place at the same time. Felicia Proietti struck him as a woman who preferred compartmentalizing her life.

When Proietti finally arrived, announcing his presence with a heavy slam of the apartment's outer door and then a loud sigh in the vestibule, she started to sit erectly, then caught herself with a wince of a half-smile and remained in her slump. Her second thoughts were *their* secret, her eyes said to Gaetano.

Proietti rushed into the salon. "Pardon me, Inspector. The usual imbeciles proving how flappable the unflappable senator could be. Ciao, *cara*." She didn't move as he went over and pecked her on the cheek. "You didn't give the Inspector an *aperitivo*? A coffee? Nothing at all?"

"He didn't want anything. Just you."

"Right," he said, pulling his tie down from his collar and taking off his suit jacket. "We'll just be a few minutes. Take care of the phone, okay? Come, Piero."

Gaetano felt like a schoolboy trooping after Proietti across the marble hallway to the study, listening to his plaints about having to shower and shave again to return to the Senate for an evening session: He made sympathetic sounds to stay on the right side of his teacher but really didn't care what he was going on about. He was just glad Govoni wasn't there to see his scurrying.

The door to the study was open, and inside a maid was dusting the shelves of books Gaetano had ascertained on his last visit amounted to a rare collection of rare volumes on 18th century history. He had counted four languages—Italian, French, English, and Spanish—before Proietti had walked in with Sylvester.

"You can finish later, Adrianna."

The wilted woman with an ugly birth mark near her nose nodded meekly and hurried out with her dust rag. "*Si, Professore.*"

"Note my patience before a dilemma, Piero," he said as soon as the woman named Adrianna was out of earshot. "I have told her a hundred times to do it in the morning before the sun delivers more dust for the day. But her argument is that by doing it at the end of the day she also wipes away the dust gathered since the morning. So she simply ignores what I have asked her. Is she right or am I right?"

"The dust seems to win one way or the other."

"So you don't believe it's a dilemma."

"Maybe another illustration of our reluctance to submit to nature."

Proietti considered like somebody who didn't want to consider, then fell into his desk chair, "So what happened at the hotel?"

Gaetano didn't feel like taking a chair but he was tired of appearing subordinate, the schoolboy now reporting to the principal, so he sat down and recounted what he and Sylvester had found at the Reggio. He had yet to get to Emilio Tepedino before Proietti's eyes wandered to his desk calendar. "That is unfortunate," he interrupted, not all that worried about sounding indifferent. "Do you see it as crucial for your investigation of this poor Ricci woman's death?"

Gaetano had danced around so many answers to that one he wondered if he was being mocked. Sylvester's information about the murder in New York had not helped his decisiveness. "I see it as a curious coincidence," he temporized. "It was in this very room, was it not, that we were optimistic there *was* a connection?"

The Senator satisfied himself with what he had found on the calendar, then settled back into what seemed like only more indifference. "So we were wrong then or we can assume there is no connection and risk being wrong now. One way or another, I don't believe that gets you any closer to telling the poor woman's survivors that you have arrested the people responsible for this hideous crime. Or have I missed something?"

Gaetano knew he was the one who had missed something. And if he had to guess what, he would have said it was a moment during Proietti's long day at the Senate where so many people, according to the Signora, were used to approaching him with their agendas. Why did they all have to have Italian as a first language? Common sense told him to leave it at that, to get up and bid them all—the Senator who had had a trying day and faced a more trying evening, the Signora with her legs and one too many husbands in the same place at the same time, Adrianna with the mole she should have had cut off years ago—bid them all a pleasant rest of their lives. But he hadn't tolerated Govoni burying his office in paper all day just to pause before common sense. The murder business in New York alone seemed worthy of a tactical lie. "I should also mention," he said, wishing he had his pipe in his hand, "that we have received some odd calls about the progress of our investigation. Perhaps the oddest has been from the Italy-United States Chamber of Commerce."

Proietti hesitated the slightest fraction of a second before shrugging. "And why is that odd? An Italian national killed in an American office? Anything involving the two countries gives those public relations drones nightmares."

"I just found the timing of their interest odd. Not after the death of Signora Ricci, but after the robbery at the hotel."

Proietti had so many tells that Gaetano was glad the man wasn't part of his weekly poker games at his brother-in-law's: One twitch seemed to contradict the previous one. "You can be sure a great many self-important meetings went into that phone call to you, Piero. Somewhere in their bureaucracy, they are probably still working on a response to the fall of Mussolini."

"No doubt, Senator."

On the other side of the desk, Gaetano knew, he would have been as amused as Proietti was. "But you think there is more to it."

"A thought."

"Like what? The Americans have an interest in this famous diary? They might have even been the ones to take it? No, no, no false modesty, Piero. It was entrusted to this American journalist. I don't think that makes either one of us particularly imaginative in voicing that suggestion."

"No, sir."

"And that is exactly what you have never impressed me as being, Gaetano—a man of banal suggestions. But now I really have to get ready to go back. Obviously, if I can assist your investigation, please contact me immediately. You have my cellphone number, yes?"

Gaetano had no choice but to stand up.

And get nowhere.

He was already to the door before Proietti called after him. "There is one factor we left out of the dilemma about Adrianna and her dusting, Inspector."

"What is that, Senator?"

Proietti's eyes were down on his stomach where he was un-buttoning his shirt for his shower. "She is in my employ," he said. "*Buona Sera.*"

FORTY-EIGHT

Sylvester didn't know what he had expected to see in the office, but whatever it was hadn't been as ugly as the crater with the green metal legs that had once been Claudia Ricci's desk, the shards from the blown-out window all over the floor, and the soot covering the walls like some repulsive fungus. A clump of dust under the radiator made him think of a neglected body part. What was the minty odor trying to resist the police aerosol? And was it from an aerosol or from the bomb? Should he even be breathing it in?

The young cop who had passed him through the Crime Scene tape shook his head at the chaos. He had wanted it on the record he had been at his post since early morning waiting for the *"giornalista americano"* to show up and was miffed Sylvester was a half-hour late, but he also now had his first opportunity to share what he had been gazing at from the hallway. *"Che casino! Chi fa pazzie del genere?"*

Sylvester didn't return the sharing. *Who* had done it? There he would have bet on Jelic and Minic and whatever they were supposed to represent. *Why* had they done it? Something to do with the diary, but what exactly? The massacre that Joey Baccsik had instantly assumed was in it? *Where* was that diary now? The logical answer didn't seem so logical, not with the elaborate production at the Reggio for getting it out of the safe. *What* had made it seem so important to get Gaetano's permission to drop by the office? He didn't know that, either, and that left him out of journalism's *W*'s. Except for the *When* anyway. Gaetano had given him only ten minutes to find whatever he needed for carrying on with his new job.

As though the thought had materialized in the room, the cop got over his stupor at the mess in front of him and tapped his watch with a new authority in his tone. *"Dieci minuti, professore. Solo dieci minuti."*

Sylvester glanced around on the chance something useful struck his eye. The office computers had been hauled away, and that he had anticipated. The desk drawers had been emptied of everything but unused notebooks, ballpoints, and an extra computer mouse still in its box. The bulk of the ancient file cabinet had probably discouraged the cops from taking that away, as well, but the top drawer was halfway out and the visible files looked like they had been ransacked. How many times had Claudia asked him to trash that antique, or at least digitize what he considered important in the files, and how many times had his most profound answer been along the lines of "I'll think about it?" Apparently, Roenicke had been just as decisive in answering her.

The smell of waterlogged, deteriorating paper hit him as soon as he slid the top drawer all the way open. He didn't have to guess about the odor: Whatever else had changed in the office since he had returned to New York, the ceiling pipes directly above the cabinet were still the work of the original plumber from the Roman Empire. At least three times he had gotten an unexpected shower.

He hadn't counted on finding the Cicut file he remembered had been created after the interview with Roenicke, and that was just as well: It had been either computerized or taken by Gaetano. Jelic? Minic? Maybe even Applebaum? The same thing. Down to it, there was little left in the top drawer but tabs alphabetizing Italian cities and a bulging one marked THEATER with old programs from Myra's church productions. He was about to slide the top drawer closed when the tab marked TRIESTE gave him pause. Would Roenicke have consigned notes about his meeting with Jelic there? He didn't know what it would tell him even if Roenicke had, but it seemed worth a look.

But without the cop looking over his shoulder. For all he knew, Gaetano had left orders to make a list of everything taken. So why make it easy for them? He grabbed a handful of files taking in most of the T's and U's and put them atop the cabinet while he went down to the second and third drawers. Not being in the market for old sneakers, last year's directives from Porterfield, and yellowed copies of newspapers in which Roenicke's stories had made the front page, he found nothing worth a second glance. But the clutter made for a reasonable tradeoff: When he figured he had wasted enough time to then retrieve the files he had placed atop the cabinet and started for the door, the cop only exhaled with the relief of not having to give him another time check. If he had been told to list the items taken, he had forgotten. He was only too happy to accompany his ten-minute charge to the elevator, wish him a good rest of the day, then go back to his solitary ruminations on the disaster of an office until he was relieved.

Sylvester toted the files down to the English tea room three blocks away across from the Spanish Steps. He would have bet against having a treasure under his arm, but he still didn't like the idea of examining the Trieste file at some tiny bar table while being observed from who knew how many directions. With its cushioned booths, ubiquitous wall mirrors, and steady clinking of spoons and crockery above a tide of genteel conversations, he felt more secure not only personally, but culturally, in the tea room. Gentlemen didn't pry into other gentlemen's mail or some other genteel tea room sentiment where file cabinet folders were concerned.

He gave the waiter his order of a pot of tea and a scone, then dug out the Trieste file. A second later he could congratulate all his furtiveness with the cop back in the office: It had gotten him a pot of tea and a scone. The only things in the file were clips dating back to the days before Yugoslavia had crumbled, when the residents of Trieste had thought this, that, and the other thing about what was threatening to happen. Not only did the collection include two pieces he had written, but there was a third one written by Sara Hodges, his predecessor in the Rome office. Claudia had been right: There had been absolutely no reason to keep so much trash around.

He looked at the Theater file for lack of anywhere else to focus his eyes. He was surprised at how enthusiastic Myra's church was for the plays of Tennessee Williams and Langston Hughes. Or maybe he was still stuck back in his old St. Teresa's days when even *Mary Poppins* had to be analyzed for potential apostasy before being presented. The programs were little more than Xeroxed sheets of heavy paper printed on both sides with brief biographies of the people involved in the productions. Most of them seemed to have been moonlighting teachers of English or translators from the States, England, and Australia—Myra's Cliff Notes Stanislavsky actors. He wondered why Roenicke had kept the collection in his office. Because he was proud of Myra but didn't want her to know it? Certainly he had never thought of stashing away copies of Felicia's reviews anywhere. Or was it just Roenicke being a packrat, saving anything at all that had to do with him and his marriage because it had to do with him and his marriage?

He started as the waiter arrived with his tea and scone. He didn't have to sit back in the booth to give the man more room to lay things out, but he did anyway so as not to show how he had been startled. In a booth across the way a woman and presumably her mother were going through the motions of fighting about who was going to take care of the bill. It was drama for drama's sake since the daughter already had the bill and a credit card in her hand and had caught the eye of their waiter.

So many people were theatrical, and without needing the kind ol stage Myra Roenicke was proud of.

Like Josef Cicut with his dramatic finale in Mainz, for example?

None of that had added up when he had been reading Cicut's letter in the back of a cab on Broadway and none of it added up now in the shadow of the Spanish Steps. Everybody—from Elena to Warneke, from Minic to Proietti and Gaetano, even Cynthia and himself—had adopted the same posture toward the diary, that it contained testimony about some slaughter, but nobody, not even Joey Bacsik with his off-the-cuff reaction in the mailroom, had seen what was in it. Might not Bacsik really have just been killed by a burglar?

Sylvester stared at the teapot as if it had arrived at his table without being asked for. Forget all those journalistic W's. What about the cardinal rule of reporting that came even before them— *not assuming*? Suppose the diary didn't contain anything like the bloodbath everybody had been taking for granted? Suppose the diary's importance had been something far more personal, Josef Cicut personal?

But that would have required a theatrical, a desperately theatrical, Josef Cicut. The kind of Josef Cicut who kept useless guns around the house, who shared nothing with anybody except what had sounded, to hear Elena, like a deepening gloom at his fall from professional and financial, even marital, grace.

And that Josef Cicut, Sylvester realized with a strange mixture of excitement and foreboding, wasn't nearly as unfamiliar as he should have been.

FORTY-NINE

E ven with Restivo's directions to the cul-de-sac behind Largo
Argentina, Warneke might have missed the *bisca* if not for the
barrel of a man at the deepest recess of the dark cobblestone
street. The man's head all but swiveled off his neck in dread of
lurking police as he waited for an answer to his knock on the
portone under the barber shop sign. When he saw Warrneke, he
reared in panic and was on the verge of retracing his steps altogether to get back out to the neon lights of the Corso and scamper on home. But then the door opened and he shoved past the
woman opening it to go ahead inside and throw away his money.

The severe-faced woman's glare (she reminded Warneke with
a chill of his Aunt Natalia from Ivanic Grad) was still in place
when he stuck his foot in the door to prevent her from closing it
on him. "*Restivo. Bianco.*"

She didn't like his face, but he had the password for the evening and she wasn't there to make her simple job complicated;
a few euros were a few euros. He picked up a scent of lavender
as he shouldered in past her, but lavender mixed with an odor
of leather. He didn't know what that combination made for, and
didn't want to dwell on it. A rear door to the right was just closing,
so he assumed that was where the nervous man had gone and
made directly for it without any objections from the woman. He
wondered if the place had been laid out for some special appeal to
the perverse who still preferred unauthorized casinos. The other
side of the door was a long, kerosene-smelling corridor with yet

another door at the end; an arena of voices sounded ready to welcome him as he turned the second knob. He needed a second to get over the welcome. His lungs lurched up into his throat within the thick smoke that enveloped him two steps inside the gimcrack walls of what had apparently once been an enormous walk-in store room or servant's annex. The only air came from an open window high up on one of the walls and facing out on what seemed to be an alley.

If he had ever wanted an argument for eliminating even his two or three cigarettes a day, he had found it. He paused in the smoke and din to take in the 30-odd people gathered around three tables—two of them for roulette, one for American dice. The round man from outside had already squeezed into the dice table. Even in the cacophony the roulette balls and whirling wheels preserved their clatter. In their tense suspicion of the numbers about to come out, the players made him think of storekeepers on guard against being shoplifted; one ruffian with a scar down his cheek at the dice table probably wouldn't have stopped at shoplifting. There were about half as many women as men, and one resembled the gruesome drill sergeant who ran the cheap restaurant where he had followed Bruno Lepri the day of the flea market. A pretty redhead in jeans and a mustard T-shirt for a German band couldn't believe her luck that she had just won at the dice table and broke her stiffness by giving a hard swat to the chest of the boyfriend standing next to her. The boyfriend looked used to being pummeled.

He was gazing around too much for a first-time visitor. He moved to one of the roulette tables before he became conspicuous, impressed that Restivo could operate so confidently that there weren't any obvious security people. He handed 20 euros to the croupier with too many teeth, getting back four green chips and a sneer that said such a big gambler should stick to the football pools. He put one of the chips down on number 7, then felt freer to glance around at the other players. Restivo had described a tall man with close-cropped blond hair and cold blue eyes. His name was Jackiw or something ("who remembers such names?"), and he did odd jobs for the Americans and everybody else in the city. He might have been a Pole, he might have been Ukranian; the important thing, according to Restivo, was that he wasn't the nationality of the people hiring him in case he got caught while working for them. "We are all messengers in life, my Eastern friend," Restivo had relished saying, probably for the thousandth time to somebody in his claustrophobic office, "and this one is a very good messenger."

That might have been the important thing to Restivo, but not to Warneke. Sketchy as Restivo's physical description had been, it fit the goon with Leszek who had smashed in his car window. Did he dare believe in so much luck that Restivo's messenger and his friend from the Nomentana were one and the same?

He dared, and he won. The number 12 that came out cost him five euros, but the one called Jackiw or something and the goon from the Nomentana were standing in the same gray work shirt and brown jacket at the other roulette table behind the croupier. He didn't have cold eyes, they were absolutely glacial, making him the perfect partner for Leszek. But his eyes also gave away things, weak things. Now they were fixed fiercely on the little silver ball rolling around in front of him, and Warneke couldn't imagine that he had raised them to notice the newest arrival from the street. Both his hands were clenched fists. He radiated sweat. The desperate attention to the ball might have explained why he didn't discriminate about employers for staying solvent.

Warneke had no reason to linger. The noisy, airless casino was nowhere to conduct a conversation, especially if it cost him every euro in his pocket waiting out the addict. The smoke choking him wanted him to have a cigarette outside anyway. He put down his three remaining chips on the 7 again, drawing mild surprise from the croupier. That lasted only as long as it took the wheel to come up with 32. As he backed away from the table to start back outside, the croupier returned to his low opinion of 20-euro players. The woman at the door gave him another disapproving look as she ushered him back into the summer night.

He didn't like the cul-de-sac any better than the den for confronting the blond: There was too much risk of another shopkeeper coming along at the wrong moment. So lighting his first cigarette

since 2:20, he wandered back down to the corner of Largo Argentina and took up a strategic position at the railing over the pit of
fragmented pillars and broken rocks that had been whole when
the Caesars had been reigning. Stationed where he was, there
was no way he could miss the blond leaving the cul-de-sac.

He had never seen so many stray cats in one place as were
under him in the pit of ancient statuary; it might have been a cat
garden. All sizes and markings, they roamed regally through the
splintered monuments, slept, or gnawed at food scraps thrown
down to them during the day. A couple of them stood their ground
with raised tails on a slab hissing at one another. He decided the
marmalade one was Franjo and the black one Jelic. It didn't really
matter which one won their clawing contest. Both underlined the
mockery of their surroundings. One of the world's most imperious
powers now reduced to monument pieces good only for cat shit.
What else was Rome good for than for lessons in futility?

Warneke blamed the whimsical thought on the nicotine going
to his head. It wasn't the first time lately his mind had drifted in
that direction. Since when had he become so detached? He might
not have believed in shortcuts to paradise, but that wasn't the
same as posing as some superior outsider to those who swallowed their party propaganda straighter than he did. That kind
of hubris had been one of the ingredients of Jelic's popularity. He
was angry at himself for such a gratuitous thought with the cats,
and he blamed it on letting hours go by between one cigarette
and another. Each time he lit up now brought the kind of rush
he had once had only with the first cigarette getting out of bed in
the morning before going off to teach. He either had to go back to
his two-pack-a-day habit or quit completely. Enough intellectual
alibis for what he was doing!

He hoped the cats didn't mistake the butt he threw down as
another food scrap. He didn't look to see if they did. Instead, his
eye caught a coil of copper wire on the ground a few feet away
from where he was standing. He picked it up, noticing at once
how cleanly it had been clipped off at both ends. What remained
was about two meters of unused material that could have cut into
his hands with the slightest encouragement. Whose wire had it

been? How had its owner dropped it or why had he gotten rid of it? Most of all, why did he think of it as some kind of sign that had just been laying out in the street for him to find? The discovery had to be connected to the blond, didn't it? Wasn't it the gods saying they knew he didn't have any weapon for confronting Jackiw or Something and that he might need one?

Warneke saw no reason to put the wire back on the ground, so he shoved it into his back pocket. He owed the blond for the Nomentana.

Jackiw or Something apparently didn't have much to lose, coming out of the cul-de-sac after less than a half-hour. He had a slight hop to his gait, as though favoring an ankle or heel. Whatever he had lost absorbed him totally as he turned down the Corso Vittorio toward the river: He pretended not to hear the tourist couple who approached him for directions and who looked miffed when he kept walking past them. As he followed along, Warneke liked the idea that the man was fuming because it made him angrier, as well. In that anger he not only wanted to know where the Cicut boy was, but found it easier to admit he wanted to get even for what he had lost at the Lego building.

Was he letting vanity get in the way of his judgment? Yes, he was. And it didn't feel wrong.

Two blocks before the river, the blond crossed the Corso and entered a small street of shuttered shops and recently sanded *palazzi*. He stopped in front of the second apartment building and pointed the key already in his hand at the *portone* lock. Warneke sped up his pace, annoyed for having lagged too far behind. But then he won his second bet on the evening: The blond dropped his key and by the time he had retrieved it from the ground and stuck it back into the lock, Warneke was on him, pushing him and the door together into the hallway. The man fell to one knee, allowing Warneke to kick the *portone* closed behind them while kneeing him in the back. The Pole fell the rest of the way down on his face. Restivo had been right about one thing: the cries were in Polish. They got louder when he tried to roll over to see who had attacked him and Warneke elbowed him in the mouth.

"Quiet!"

His voice echoed too loudly around the hallway entrance, accomplishing exactly what he had tried to prevent the Pole from doing. But there was no sound from any of the apartments upstairs.

"You're too late. I have no money."

"The Cicut boy—where is he?"

The Pole seemed to collapse down to a deeper level of submission as he played back the question to himself. Warneke had expected protests of ignorance, and then they came: once, twice, three times. It was all *who, who, who,* and then that he was making a mistake. After the third denial, Warneke freed one of his hands from the back of the Pole's head and found the wire in his back pocket. It felt sharp to his hand, even to his callouses. He had it around the exposed throat before the Pole realized what it was. The sputtering under him could have been Chinese; it was definitely fear. "The boy!"

Jackiw or Something kicked his legs, but Warneke was far enough forward on his back only to be grazed by the shoe heels. "You're too late."

"He is too valuable to you. You would not harm him."

"Not the boy, Mister Warrneke. The diary."

Of course the Pole knew who he was. They had gone through his pockets after taking him up to the empty apartment. He should not have been surprised.

"You're too late for the diary," Jackiw struggled to say again, but already with an extra layer of confidence.

"I do not think so."

The gasp wanted to be a snicker. "I know who has it."

"Everybody knows."

The Pole should not have been sounding smug, not with a perfect globule of blood plopping down to the concrete from the abrasion around his Adam's apple. "The journalist does not have it anymore. And you cannot get it back."

Warneke sank back to the picture of waking up in the empty apartment, back when he had even had to wonder if he had been himself. While he had been sleeping there, had Minic gotten his hands on the diary?

"No, not the priest. He is like you, Warneke. The two of you are wasting a lot of energy for nothing."

"And you know this how?"

Too many words: Warneke himself heard the doubt in his question. "Because I know who took it," the man all but cackled, "and then left it in a post box at San Silvestro. No, no names. They just give you the number of a post box and have dollars waiting for you when you open it to make the exchange."

Warneke knew with a hot stab it was true. He was dealing with an addict, one who didn't care how many people he crossed to feed his habit. Now the hallway that he had feared being too noisy was too still. "You work for Minic," he said, fighting a rising feeling of helplessness.

"You're . . . strangling me."

He was, and not all that accidentally. The wire—the wire given to him by the Largo Argentina cats—seemed to have jumped ahead of his thought processes. If Sylvester didn't have the diary, he had no more need of Sylvester and his pledge about the Cicut boy. "You are working for Minic," he repeated.

Jackiw took a breath with the slackened wire, and then: "The priest is more of a man of the world than you. He needed assistance against you and my name was suggested. No more than that."

Restivo again? Warneke knew it had to be. Slugs under the soil didn't have a more extensive network of slime than Restivo did. "So you took the diary for somebody else? You do not seem to mind how many people would like you dead."

"Usefulness has its disadvantages. But I could be useful to you, too."

"I do not think so."

There was a sigh, but not a particularly convincing one. "Then you should press tighter and kill me. But no, you won't do that. You're the white army up against the black army. You have ideals, Warneke. You need to feel noble."

"You do not take your life very seriously."

"It will end when it will end. Do you want my help or not?"

"You just said . . ."

"Not the diary. That is gone. Do you want to know where the boy is?"

"I want the diary."

"Then fly to America."

Where else? Hadn't Restivo hinted at the same thing?

"I am offering something more practical. But I would not take too long to decide. Minic and his associates are not as noble as you."

"The boy is Jelic's nephew. He would not be harmed."

"Then no problem."

He didn't know why he was even listening. Who would miss the roach under his knee? "You know where the boy is?"

"What I have been trying to tell you."

"And why would I be interested if the diary is gone?"

"I don't worry about why people do the things they do. But if they want to do them and there is some gain for me in the process, I am available."

Warneke couldn't fault nicotine this time: Some part of him envied the man's cynicism. "What gain?"

"Might I go on living? It is hard to read you from down here. How serious are you? I don't believe completely, but I could be wrong and too bad for me. But let's put that aside. You might be able to say positive things to your people back home and that would extend my contacts. No?"

"Nobody lives that long, Jackiw."

"So far."

He knew he couldn't go any further. Assassins like Leszek were one thing, pimps like Jackiw another. There were no death penalties for his kind. Plus the key word the man had thrown up: *practical.* He would have gained nothing by pulling more tightly but greater police attention and more maneuvering against him back home by Franjo. "So I let you go and you give me some false address. . . ."

"Not false. True, I lie for a living. But only with others. For myself I keep the truth. Right jacket pocket."

Warneke started to reach for it, then stopped. The Pole laughed. "No, no poison needles waiting to strike you."

He removed a slip of paper from the pocket. It was simply an address.

"Now even I can feel a little noble," Jackiw laughed again. "My life for the boy's. Don't you think that's an altruistic trade? I do, considering I don't believe mine has ever been in real jeopardy. Don't you agree, Warneke?"

FIFTY

lena heard rudeness verging on insult. She had already told
Sylvester she had grasped next to nothing the day she had
sneaked a look at Josef's journal and his insistence on returning to the subject amounted to calling her a liar. She was sorry
she had ever let him in the door. She didn't owe him *that* much
for his gallantry at the hotel.

"I told you, Charles. It was in this despicable code. He didn't
want me to understand what he had written."

Sylvester leaned forward in his chair. He looked as heavy and
tired as she felt; haggard, squinting against the sun that was
shining through the living room window and emphasizing the
wrinkles under his eyes, but too leaden even to move a few inches
left or right out of the glare. "Yes. But when I showed it to a friend
in New York, he had no trouble making out initials for two towns.
Bosanska Novi? Bosanska Kostajnica?"

"There are such places."

He allowed himself the tightest of smiles. "I know. I looked
them up before coming here. But do you remember recognizing
them in the diary, too?"

Elena was surprised: She did. She even remembered that the
initials for Bosanska Novi had been at the bottom of a left-hand
page, those for Bosanska Kostajnica in the middle of a right-hand
page. "Yes, I think so."

"And you were in those places with Josef and your brother?
When the three of you were on the run?"

She didn't know what she had given away, but she didn't like the encouragement she seemed to have given him. "Near them, yes. How is that important?"

"Bear with me. It might help us understand what Josef did up in Mainz."

"He killed himself."

"Yes, he killed himself."

She didn't like encouraging whatever nonsense he was acting so strenuous about, but neither did she want to be responsible for his looking stymied. It was too much like Josef withdrawing into himself after he had failed to persuade her of something. "Whatever," she said, lighting another cigarette.

"I'm just trying to put the pieces together."

"Will that get Philip back?"

She hadn't expected his unapologetic stare. "It might."

"And if it doesn't?"

"One step at a time, okay?"

"You have steps to take, Charles. I am out of them."

"Literal Elena."

"I don't see anything funny . . ."

"No, that's exactly what I'm counting on," he said, instantly earnest again. "What you do best—your ear for language. That's what you do. How many times have you been forced to make sur-mises about what some student has tried to communicate to you in another language? You don't always understand the words, but you know how to use the context to get down to what they are trying to tell you. It's your profession."

"I think you mean that as a compliment."

"From someone who doesn't even like crossword puzzles."

"There was only one context as you call it to what Josef had written—keep everybody out, including his wife."

"And what I'm saying is you picked up more than the anger and sadness you felt seeing what he had done. More than you realize."

"You're talking about years ago, and only for a few minutes."

"I know, I know. But stay with me for a second, okay?"

And if she asked him how he would have felt if it was his son he might never see again? But she didn't. She had already showed him how unwelcome he was by not offering him the coffee that was outside on the kitchen burner. He had to see her own empty cup next to her ashtray.

"There were dates, yes? Each entry had a date? . . . Of course you remember. Even I could make out that much. It's what everybody keeping a diary does. Upper right-hand corner? Upper left-hand corner?"

"I do not like taking tests."

"Please."

He was right; she pictured that much. "Upper right-hand."

"And they weren't in code."

"That much he was willing to share."

"And when you were hurt by this obscure code of his, that wasn't just because you read it on a few pages. You flipped through the whole thing to be sure it was the same all the way through."

She hadn't thought of that before; she didn't know what difference it made, but she hadn't thought of it. She had in fact lingered so long over the journal trying to make some of it comprehensible that she was surprised Josef hadn't come back to discover her prying. "I suppose."

"And even through this code you recognized references. Minor things. Familiar things. Like the names of those towns."

"I already said that."

"And references to Milo?"

"There might have been."

"References you knew *had* to be to Milo."

"He was *M*, I was *E*. Unless, of course, Josef was so protective of his precious thoughts he reversed them to confuse me more."

"But you know he didn't do that."

"I know no such thing."

"Yes, you do, Elena. Because *M* was in a sentence or paragraph with other allusions you associated with Milo. And the same thing with you. You couldn't make out every word, but some of them were clear enough to apply only to you."

He was making her nervous, she might have almost offered him a coffee in order to get up and go into the kitchen to get away from him for a minute. For one who knew so little he presumed to know so much. "If you say so."

He nodded as if he had attained some plateau. At bottom, she thought, he had always been something of a scruffy man—always presentable, but not what she would have called neat the way Josef had been neat. If he closed his eyes, would he even be able to tell her the color of the tie he had put on?

"Here's the context question," he said, holding her stare more tightly. "Did you get the impression one entry was more significant than others? Maybe it was longer, followed by others just as long because Josef had more to say about a specific topic?"

"How can I remember such a thing?"

"Because you're Elena, that's how. And because every code, no matter how idiosyncratic, has a pattern. Every reference to the couch you're sitting on could be just *cvc*, but you would pick it out through repetition and consistency after a while."

"You are back to accusing Milo of some horrendous atrocity. And you want me to help you."

He didn't flinch; on the contrary, he looked relieved to hear her contempt. "No," he said calmly. "I may be doing just the opposite."

"You are confusing me, Charles."

He leaned over and touched her knee with his index finger. It felt strange and intrusive. Nobody had touched her knee in years. "Patterns, Elena. Patterns."

There had been repetitions, that much she remembered. Repetitions of word stems and entire words that almost made sense. And for the first time since that hateful day at their camp, she was sorry she had hurried through the journal pages. "Yes, there were dates that made it easier to guess at what he had written."

"Right. And you could remember that it was the day you had to do something in particular. I don't know, finding more supplies or something."

"Yes."

"And no entry seemed more important than another."

She knew the answer to that, too. "They were all in the same neat squares he wrote everything. Even when he was leaning on his knee to record something, Josef was a very neat man."

He didn't hear her criticism of him. "Exactly."

"But how do you know this? You have no Cyrillic."

"No, but I looked at those damn pages long enough to measure the entries. I'm pretty good at lengths and widths in any alphabet." He wanted her to smile with him, and she didn't feel like it was such a great concession. "And what about Milo?"

"What about him?"

"Entries that stood out from the others."

"No . . ."

"What, Elena?"

"Nothing. Josef was circumspect even to himself. You should remember that. Everything was very neat and . . . diplomatic. Or at least it seemed to be."

"For instance?"

She remembered the page. It was the left-hand side, and he had had to change pens midway down because the first one had run out of ink. Light blue ink replacing darker blue ink. She hadn't thought about it in years. "It was the reference to BN, Bosanska Novi. We were all very tired that day. We had barely eaten for days, smelled horribly. Were we accomplishing anything? Who was to say? There was a meeting for evaluating what we were doing. Milo was the one who called it."

"And this was in the diary."

"I am certain the entry was about that because there was this small waterfall near where we were camped, and Josef had joked it was our version of Niagara Falls. And the place name Niagara Falls was in the entry."

"And what was discussed at this meeting?"

She didn't need prodding; maybe for what Josef had recorded about it, but not about the meeting itself. Had she ever thought less of Milo than on that evening? "We were all exhausted. Some of us wanted to flee, get across the border."

"Some of *them* or you?"

"I felt no better. There were the children to think of, too. A couple were already ill and crying all the time. But I thought there might still be hope. Others did not. They were sure no outside help would be coming. Milo was firm about it. We had done as much as we could, he kept arguing. Face realities. The talk went on and on."

"And what did Josef say?"

"Nothing. He just listened to what everybody had to say. But when the final vote came, he voted with those in favor of staying, continuing the fight. Milo said all right, if that was what the majority wanted, he certainly was not going to abandon us for his personal safety. My god, Charles, he is the last one who could be accused of some atrocity! He wanted to give up! I was so embarrassed."

It sounded worse in the living room than it had ever sounded in her thoughts; it hadn't even sounded as shameful when she and Josef had talked about it and, true to his evasive nature, Josef had found a dozen reasons for Milo's behavior, had claimed he understood it all too well while in his own mind he hadn't understood it at all, had even been revolted by the idea of giving up. Even in that discussion, one involving her brother and what could have been their lives, she had never merited more than diplomatic reserve from him.

Sylvester nodded, and that made her immediately less sure of what she had said. An outsider who knew nothing of what she, Josef, and Milo had been through should not have been so quick to agree with her.

"Okay," he said, sitting back in the chair. "Let's forget the diary for a second. Tell me again about the evening you and Josef were watching the news and Milo came on. What did Josef say?"

"What does that have to do with anything?"

"Maybe nothing. Just tell me what Josef said."

"He did not say anything. He was stunned. We had had no idea."

"And you were already in this house? Not back on Governo Vecchio?"

"Of course. It was not that long ago."

"And the agency was already in trouble. Money was scarce."

"Beyond that. What are you getting at, Charles?"

He popped back up to the edge of his chair again, this time as if he wanted the sun to glare in his face. "One more question. You said you and Milo spoke occasionally by phone. After that night you saw him on the news, too?"

She knew where he was going; he didn't know, couldn't have known, but she did. And it felt surprisingly painless after so long just to corroborate it for herself. "He called for my birthday," she said, seeing she had smoked her cigarette down to the empty filter. "He wanted us to move back home. He knew what our financial situation was and said he could find important positions for both Josef and me in his movement. We would be what he called valuable assets. What he meant was Josef, of course. His reputation as an ambassador. And was it not time, he said, for Philip to grow up with his own people? Did we really want him to be more Italian than what he had been born as?"

"What did you say?"

"I said I would speak to Josef. But Milo would not be put off. He asked me to pass the phone to Josef. Josef was sitting where you are, pretending not to eavesdrop on what I had been saying. I told him what Milo wanted him for, and he had the same expression as when we had watched the news. Then he just got up and walked out of the room."

"Because he would never consider such an offer."

"Never."

"Because he couldn't imagine himself falling so low as to be just this valuable asset your brother saw him as."

"I just said that."

"And how long afterward did Josef move out of here?"

"You do not have to blame that on Milo, too, Charles."

He shook his head. He had become so oblivious to the sun that it had become part of his eyes. "I'm not," he said evenly. "I'm blaming it on Josef. I'm blaming Mainz on Josef and I'm blaming him for what drove Philip out of this house and what has left you in this situation. What I'm blaming Milo for is everything that happened after Mainz. Your brother wasn't part of any massacre years ago, Elena, and Josef didn't accuse him of that in this god-damn diary. What he accused Milo of was just the opposite and *that* was what your old friend Sima Glauber passed along. To quote an old friend, Milo couldn't afford to let his thugs know what happened at that meeting near your Niagara Falls because that would have made him a fish out of water."

He was waiting for her to respond—to deny it, to say he didn't know what he was talking about, anything. But Elena knew she would have been bluffing with even less certainty than he had to have had. She felt the smallest sense of reprieve just dropping her eyes from his face and lighting another cigarette.

"Josef didn't really die in Germany, did he, Elena? He was already dead."

"For Philip he died there," she heard the woman on the couch say.

FIFTY-ONE

As Bell's mornings went, it lacked something. The need to see anyone at all before noon daunted him for the long hours awaiting on the far side of the meeting before he got home. He was an afternoon-night person, over and out. The only consolation in having to be in the city at such an early hour was that Catherine and the kids wouldn't be home anyway. But then there was the charade of having to report to the Third Avenue skyscraper office, this being Frank Broderick's notice that *very* serious things were afoot and could only be communicated in person, worth even his personal sacrifice in having to fly in from Washington. For Bell, the trappings of the mutual funds suite were too plastic by half, the kind of front that was supposed to radiate bundles of money but that radiated none at all. Sherlock Holmes wasn't required for the conclusion that the only financial strategy ever devised in the sterile, too-bright conference room was for the best place to unload the rented furniture once it was no longer needed. And him playing a prospective mutual funds investor? He barely knew what mutual funds were, let alone be paraded in as a would-be client. Nobody expected personal tastes to be indulged at emergency meetings, but did that mean going to the opposite extreme?

What irritated Bell more than the time and place, though, was the news bulletin Broderick threw out as though discarding a beer cap. The man with the furrowed brows and let's-stay-cool-forever goatee couldn't have been more nonchalant about it, and it caught Bell so unawares that his first reaction was benevolent, giving Broderick the benefit of the doubt. In the long run, he told himself, it didn't make any difference if the Cicut diary contained only World Cup scores. He had been told to get the copy from the old man Bacsik, and an operation was an operation. But then Broderick reached under his jacket to scratch his chest and decreed as "horseshit" assumptions that the diary accused Milo Jelic of some Slav bloodbath. Something about the scratching— allergies, poison ivy?—wasn't good for Bell's benevolence. Would what Broderick said have changed anything for Joey Bacsik? Objectively, no. Broderick himself hadn't known what was in the diary until it had been translated and its code broken, so there was no real deception there. But the air around the man with the itch still exuded a musty deceit—if not about what had been done, about what the desk drones in Washington were scrambling to want done to cover their asses.

"I would've bet the farm on the genocide card." Bell waited for Broderick to be bored with the wiring tucked into the corners of the ceiling. "I didn't hear anything else from you, either," he said, swiveling his chair as if on a playground ride.

"That's the past, Frank, and not why you got on a plane to come here."

Broderick claimed he liked directness but not the kind that suggested criticism. It took him a second to get over it. "We can't just write off that letter bomb as miscellaneous overhead, Walter. People are bent out of shape about it. Attacks on the Fourth Estate, etcetera, etcetera. Besides, you give in to one child stomping his foot, others are going to get similar ideas. Jelic has to be spanked before we've got toys all over the living room floor."

"There was nothing at all in the diary?"

He dropped his eyes to his big hands; he had kept more than one manicurist in business. "There was a little moment when Milo wanted to give up the struggle and hightail it out of the country."

"Not too good for a national warrior image."

Broderick shook his head; he had already discounted that. "The reason he didn't scoot was because his merry little band had a vote on what to do, he lost the vote, and he stayed. Remind him of that little lapse and he comes back to show the world how he's always been a big believer in democratic principles, the majority rules. Uh, huh. That's not leverage, that's a boomerang right back in our faces."

"But you have another idea."

"A thought, maybe."

"You didn't come this far with just a *thought, maybe*, Frank."

Broderick's face said strike two against the underling, but he also had his priorities. "They still have the Cicut kid?"

"Last I heard."

"And you still have your private pipeline with your friend over there?"

Bell could have done without the *friend*. The best part of his relationship with Tomas Leszek was that he had never had to meet the gorilla. And that wasn't the only problem with what Broderick was saying. "You think the Roenicke business has been trouble? Kids trump the media, Frank."

"I thought he was 18, 19, something like that."

"If he was yours, he'd still be on your Blue Cross."

Broderick wasn't up for the argument. "Think I don't realize that? But the goal here is long-range leverage. You have any better ideas?"

Bell didn't mind admitting he didn't. By now he had learned to accept that he was most useful when he stuck to the tactical. He had long given up trying to manipulate the world the way Frank Broderick and his kind spent their days and nights doing; he didn't have the stamina and self-delusion for it. But that still left the practicalities at which he was very good. "Start with our asset over there. He'd do it, but that's going to mean one more constituency in Europe gunning for him. The kid is Jelic's nephew, for Christ sake."

"And you don't think, nephew or no nephew, Milo wouldn't do it himself if he was pressed into a corner by that diary?"

"But the diary isn't on the table anymore. You just told me that."

"Okay, okay . . ."

"I'm not finished. There's having to do it the right way, to make it look like Jelic's doing. I'm not sure that's one of Leszek's talents."

"But we'll assume it is for the sake of argument."

Bell didn't mistake the look in Broderick's eye: Not only had a course of action been decided in Washington, it was taken for granted that it had already been carried out, that nobody would slow down matters with reality. "He'll want a lot."

"Give him whatever he wants."

"Not just money. In his place I'd want a lot more than that."

Broderick finally found something amusing. "What would you want, Walter?"

"Protection, Over there or here."

The amusement passed. "No way here. All we need is some junior agent from the Pure Food Agency or some damn thing coming across his name and we'll be all over Facebook on our way up to testifying in Congress. He stays out."

"You're not leaving me with much negotiating room, Frank."

Broderick had anticipated the objection. "We can get anybody to pass along the key to the city, Walter. What we depend on you for is persuading people that being useful is more important than being wanted."

Bell knew it was the man's idea of flattery. And all things considered, it *was* a compliment of sorts.

FIFTY-TWO

The idea came to Gaetano when two emergency workers cleared the smoky dust of the collapsed building with their stretcher and a third medic in readiness threw open the back doors of the ambulance. Crass as the connection might have been, he was glad he had insisted on being taken to the disaster site; housing scandals were not his jurisdiction, but he might never have had his inspiration without the acrid smell in his nose and the moaning still to be heard from the far side of the gaping hole of a building. Realities had left him little choice but to try to take advantage of what lay before him. If he had to be as sub-standard morally as the building had been materially, so be it. The overriding fact was that he had gotten as much as he was going to get on the dead man in Manhattan without waking up sleeping lions in the New York Police Department—a stirring that would certainly spread to the home of Senator Gianni Proietti eventually. And what he had collected from Govoni's trawling on the Internet for Joseph Bacsik was next to nothing. In five or six different print measures it was the same brief report of a break-in robbery and homicide. There were no estimates of what or how much had been taken, no statements from any witness, not the most minimal description of the murder weapon aside from the unhelpful detail that the victim had been "bludgeoned to death." About the only food for thought the reports had prompted was wondering how long it would take to bludgeon the Internet to death with his pipe.

But the stretcher and the weeping woman on it suggested another avenue of inquiry—one that should have allowed him to penetrate the NYPD's den of lions without getting clawed to pieces.

"I think it is risky, Inspector," Govoni said as Petrino put the dust and hysteria from the collapse behind them on their way back to the Viminale. "Suppose one of the American papers publishes the names?"

"Whose names?"

"Of these poor devils here."

Gaetano preferred to think his impatience with the objection had more to do with getting back to his office to act on his idea than with Govoni's obtuseness. "You mean the way the international press publishes the name of every Pakistani killed in an earthquake, every Japanese who drowns in a tsunami, and every American driven into the ocean by a hurricane? Not even the papers in Milan will be printing the names of these unfortunate souls. Your caution blinds you, Matteo. As soon as we get back, we find out where to call in New York."

Govoni knew when to shut up: when he was being upbraided in front of a junior policeman like Petrino. And Petrino made sure to keep his eyes on the traffic.

Gaetano took it as a positive omen that by the time he was connected to the right detective in Manhattan he already had the names of a couple of the people who had collapsed into the street with their cardboard floors and ceilings. The New York detective Suzanne Calderon might not have doubted the stated reason for his call in any case, but the names of the actual casualties helped his credibility. In turn, she was sorry to have to break the news that a Joseph Bacsik had been killed during a break-in robbery. "We will check his personal belongings again to see if there is any woman by that name from your building, Inspector, but I don't remember any Italian or Latin name in his address book. Mostly people he worked with or Eastern European ethnics. Slavs, Serbians, that kind of thing. You have no idea how this woman killed in the house might have been related to him?"

"None, I'm afraid. Just a name in another address book. We just felt duty-bound to be sure Bacsik wasn't a relative."

"So we may not even be talking about the same Joseph Bacsik."

"That is a possibility, yes. I'm afraid I have little and nothing to offer."

She snorted a laugh. "Welcome to the club. We haven't gotten past square one since we found his body. Looks like our Bacsik resisted someone shoving in the door and got slammed on the neck for his trouble. Karate chop, according to the coroner."

So much for the "bludgeoning" the newspapers had yammered about. "A burglar who knows karate? You have sophisticated burglars in New York."

"That's one anomaly. The other is what was taken. Or what wasn't taken."

"I don't follow."

"Well, Bacsik was no hermit sitting on his millions. But he had a lot of those antique gold and silver candelabras and things from Europe any burglar worth his salt could fence easily. Not a single one taken that we could see. Cigar box in the closet with a couple of thousand dollars. Again, a pretty obvious place to look for a professional."

"Perhaps the assailant was frightened off by his violence."

"Yes, that's the prevailing opinion here. But then there was what *was* taken."

Gaetano felt his blood find another artery into his brain. At bottom he had wanted what Sylvester had told him to be irrelevant. "What was that?"

"He was apparently doing some kind of translation off the books for the people at the paper where he worked. This woman from there called to ask if we had found the thing. No, Ma'am, we did not. I asked her what the translation was about, and all she said was that it was some kind of memoir the paper was looking into publishing. She didn't sound like it was the end of the world the thing wasn't there . . . . ..Correction. She wanted *me* to think it wasn't the end of the world, but I could hear it bothered her. I invited her down to give me more particulars, but she hasn't done it yet. Maybe I should give her a ring and remind her."

Gaetano took it as a sign of his maturity: a few years earlier he would have been appalled by so much casualness in a homicide investigation. But now he reminded himself of probable statistics—of the number of homicides the woman had open files on, of the number of officers within the Viminale who had been approaching their own cases with identical zeal. Maturity was seldom reassuring. Having confirmation that Sylvester's office assistant had been badgering the police about the diary wasn't, either.

Standing near the doorway, Govoni had heard enough from the conversation to know he didn't have to be impressed. "So a risk for nothing?"

The man deserved his ounce of flesh, Gaetano thought. But why give it to him? "On the contrary, Matteo. We now know there are *two* crimes we best not be curious about. Who knows? If we keep digging, perhaps we'll find thousands more. Be able to say that the whole world is crime-free!"

Govoni didn't know whether his superior was being serious, so he decided on the compromise of a sickly grin.

FIFTY-THREE

Starting with his smelly shirt in the morning sun, nothing felt right about where Sylvester was sitting. How many days had it been since he and Roenicke had been at the sidewalk bar behind him and he had noticed Warneke sitting on the concrete bench where they were camped now? He should have had more than those few mocking yards as a measure of his progress since he had arrived in Rome. The mothers and nannies watching the children running around the fountain were the same ones from his first morning off the plane. So were the Slavs peddling their chains and picture frames. The bicycles leaning against the window of the rent-a-bike store looked to be locked down against the metal brace in the same exact order. Warneke wore the same Levi Strauss outfit and black leather wrist bands as that first time. What was it Felicia had once said about him—all motion and no movement? When she had said it, it had sounded mostly like a boast that she had mastered a subtlety in her English vocabulary. Now it felt like a sealed indictment against him that a Character Court had finally let be opened.

And it wasn't just him who was wrong. Why was Warneke suddenly so willing to be seen in a public place with him? The man had been nothing but furtive until he had called to propose meeting in the piazza, but now he sat smoking with his leg crossed, the picture of obliviousness to anyone who might be observing them. Only his compulsive taps at his cigarette before it grew serious ash suggested second thoughts about the exposure he had committed them to. How could his behavior *not* have meant something bad for Philip Cicut?

"You have nothing more to bargain with," he said crisply, "so you are in no position to complain about 48 hours this or 48 hours that. I know what I said to you. I am sorry I could not make our promised deadline. But I am also aware of the robbery at your hotel the other evening."

"Was it you?"

Warneke looked off to where the chain sellers were arguing about something. He wasn't their boss, after all, just a fellow traveler from their region who disapproved of their way of making a living abroad. For all his hard carriage, Sylvester thought, there was something primly middle-class about Leonard Warneke. "Humor?"

"If you know the diary was stolen, why are you here? Like you say, I have nothing more to trade with you."

Warneke stared beyond the Slavs. He seemed to have to go all the way down to the morning bustle at the Tre Scalini cafe tables before saying: "I think I know where the boy is. Or maybe you are not interested anymore?"

If it was a test of some sort, Sylvester couldn't imagine of what apart from Elena Cicut's stamina against another false hope. "Me yes, but why you?"

"He is in the hands of people capable of anything."

"That isn't what I asked."

"I have not gotten what I wanted. Why should Minic go undisturbed?" He came back from Tre Scalini with his slightly bloodshot eyes. "Or maybe I am just tired of futile people doing futile things. Never have that feeling?"

"All the time. But you had other priorities."

"Are you interested in the boy's whereabouts or not?"

"You know I am."

Having heard it, Warneke wasn't sure that was the answer he had wanted to hear, but he reached into the pocket of his shirt and came out with a slip of yellow paper. "Tell the police they are holding him here," he said, handing over the chit through scissored fingers. "It is apparently some kind of apartment for visiting clergymen."

Sylvester didn't recognize the address in the green Magic Marker. "Where is Via Guido Reni 34?"

"Somewhere behind Piazza del Popolo I am told."

"And you believe it."

"The person who told me has nothing to gain and everything to lose by lying."

"Has this person actually seen Philip there?"

The wiry man thought that was funny. "Have you? Have I? Maybe the boy does not exist at all. He is just out there to make us all feel presentable to our consciences." He took a last drag from his cigarette and then stomped the butt under his shoe. "One thing. If the boy is being held against his will, he has certainly been drugged. You do not hold captives in the middle of the city and assume they do not go near windows. If, on the other hand, he has made new friends. . . ."

"I don't think so."

Warneke shrugged and stood up with a stretch of his taut shoulders. "I leave that to you and the police to discover. With some luck our priest friend will be arrested for kidnapping. I wish I believed more strongly in luck. *Addio*, Mister Sylvester. I hope everything turns out the way you want it to."

He didn't know why he waited even the three steps Warneke took to call him back. "There was no massacre in that diary, you know."

"That we will never know for certain, will we?"

"*I* know."

"Really? You speak our language now?"

"I speak enough Josef Cicut." Warneke stalled. Now his annoyance with the raised voices of the peddlers nearby was personal. "There are no accusations of any genocide in the diary. There couldn't be because Jelic was never guilty of anything like that."

"You say that so positively."

"I know it's not what your people want to hear about Jelic. But it's the truth."

"The truth!"

"I have no reason to lie to you, either, Warneke."

"Really? From what I hear Americans were behind that robbery at your hotel. What passport do you carry?"

"Yeah, we're all the same. Just like you and Minic. And we make sure to carry diaries across the Atlantic so they can be stolen in Rome instead of just passed along to our favorite CIA agent in New York."

Warneke hadn't put much stock in his sally anyway. "This language of Cicut you are so expert in, what does it say?"

"Who told you it was Americans at the hotel? The same one who told you where Philip Cicut was?"

"Be grateful. You can verify two claims at once. Or discover both are false. What are these insights into Cicut you claim?"

Sylvester flagged down what Warneke had said: *Americans behind the Reggio robbery.* Gaetano had said practically the same thing the night of the robbery. He himself had come to that conclusion through Applebaum on Myra Roenicke's terrace and before that from how Roenicke and Minic had been behaving at the dinner party. Sometimes it seemed to take him forever to accept what his own brain was saying.

"Well?"

"Cicut had two qualities hard to miss. Vanity was one. And no debate, he had a lot to be vain about."

"I know Cicut's background."

"I don't mean just Ambassador Cicut. When he was living here, too. He had a thriving business for a long time with his agency. The Berlitz of translations. Then things weren't so thriving and he ended up bankrupt. Things at home weren't so great, either. Maybe they hadn't been for a long time anyway, but it got harder and harder to believe in his self-importance when he sat down at the dinner table."

Warneke caught his fingers going into his shirt pocket for another cigarette. He looked shame-faced. "So?"

"So then he got an invitation to go back home and play the stooge for Jelic. All those years adding up to political puppetry."

"You know this for a fact?"

"I know it for a fact. And why not play the puppet? Maybe that was all he was still good for. Nobody else was breaking down his door with offers. It wasn't a nice feeling."

"Jelic was his brother-in-law, his friend."

"Friend? They pulled pranks together in school. Jelic was never impressed by the diplomat and Cicut never needed reminders he ranked higher than an elementary school teacher. What kept them together was Elena Cicut. When that came apart, school pranks were all that was left. Then Jelic makes the offer that humiliates the proud man."

Warneke went for the cigarette without apology the second time. "So he found vindication by threatening Jelic to tell the world about him? Except he really had nothing to tell? Then he just killed himself? A very ingenious plan by the Ambassador. I wonder if it makes sense to him in the world where he is now."

"I said he had two big qualities. Besides his vanity there was what somebody I know called Mister Drama. He had a weakness for the grand show. A political thug who claimed the same airs the Ambassador had at least earned? No, no, no. That wasn't going to be the last act. No way. He needed to reclaim the limelight."

"Nobody is like that."

"When the only person you haven't impressed with all your successes and then your failures is the one staring back at you from the mirror, I can see where it might become a little easier."

"You are talking about a crazy man."

"A shrewd crazy man. He made a double play of it."

"A . . . ?

"Two birds with one stone. He staged this in Mainz because he could also involve another old school friend he detested."

"Glauber."

"Glauber. Glauber who didn't attend his wedding because he knew what was about to happen in his country. No warnings to his old friends, just stayed away while the shooting and persecutions started. Cicut had harbored that memory for a long time, and he knew that whatever he said to Glauber would get back to Jelic as soon as it was out of his mouth. He was a man who liked neatness."

"And I am saying nobody can be that obsessed."

"Maybe he just felt more futile about things than you do."

"It is insane."

"But Cicut is dead and for no real reason connected to that diary."

"You say."

"Yes, I say. We've all been fishing in a river of red herrings."

Warneke waited for any kind of denial at all. When it didn't come, he had only the smoke coming out of his nose. "And the widow believes all this mad egotism?"

"She's always known. The deepest layer of the onion you warned me about. You were right. Mainz was the rotten core, and she wasn't about to get down to that for anybody, especially not her son. Family values. Respect for your father. But the man who died in Germany, the one she had no desire to say a last goodbye to or let her son say goodbye to, was just an actor. The husband she knew as Josef Cicut, Philip's father, had died here a long time before."

"All because he could not teach any more Italians to speak English! That is what you want me to believe?"

"Right. Where's the nobility that would make us all feel better?"

Warneke took in the three little girls squealing as they chased each other around the next bench. His wince might have been apprehension that one of them would fall and scrape her knee. "Why are you telling me this?"

"So you can go back and tell your people they're playing the same pointless deadly games Jelic is."

"They would not agree."

"They sent you here for the same purpose as Minic had, didn't they?"

He shook his head. "That is not why you are telling me this."

Sylvester recognized the sulk on the face of the Slav peddler who had lost the argument with his partner. He had needed every ounce of restraint not to share with Elena the resentment that had been building in him the more he had thought about Josef Cicut. "Somebody has to know."

Warneke shook his head again. "No. You are a journalist. If that was your purpose, you would find some way to write all these romantic adventures so a lot of people would know. Should that not satisfy you? Is that not your profession?"

Sylvester was surprised at how easy it was to admit after somebody else had said it. "He got a woman I hadn't seen in years and an old man I got to thinking of as just local color, he got both killed. That's not futility, Warneke, that's murder. I really hate Josef Cicut for that, and yeah, I need it on the record with somebody who'll get more out of it than a newspaper story."

Warneke gazed around as if in search of a second opinion. But he didn't find it in the children or in the teenage customer unlocking one of the bikes in front of the rental place. Finally, he flicked another invisible ash and returned to the bench, reaching down for it like an old man groping for balance. "Nobility is not that common with the people who sent me here, either. They are not like Jelic's apes, but they too believe in what they call the long view—put off the unpleasant until perhaps it reeks a little less. It is the nature of the beast. For these policemen you believe in, too."

"One cop I know . . ."

"Ah, *one!* And this one operates independently, without superiors?"

"I'm really not up for more of your futility right now."

Warneke shook his head. "Not just futility. Yes, that is what the Minics and Jelics would like us to sit in a little box with. The other day they gave me a great lesson in it by overpowering me and leaving me in an abandoned apartment. Not their prisoner, you see, but my own. The sheer futility of going after them, finding out it led nowhere but to some pointless place."

"I'm not following . . ."

"It is not important. *They* want it to be all about futility. That way they win. But there is more to it than that, Mister Sylvester. There is also choice. It sneaks up on us at the most unexpected moments. Last night I came close to killing a man . . . . ..Yes, maybe your look is what I looked like while the thought was there. I still do not know if I made the right choice because this individual is now free to carry on with a life that is really to the benefit of nobody. Speak of your atrocities in diaries, Mister Sylvester. Who believes in them, who does not. But it is not necessary to fantasize about genocide or mass slaughters. I did not commit an atrocity last night merely by having to make a decision one way or the other. The rest is empty conjecture."

"What do you want, Warneke?"

"You ask the question before I do. What do *you* want?"

Sylvester knew. "Bringing the boy home to his mother."

He nodded. "Yes. One small thing. Something concrete."

"Something concrete."

"And seeing her face in that first moment. Gratitude. Joy. All those emotions that seem to be become rarer the older we become."

"I haven't got that far."

His laugh was an incredulous heckling. "There and kilometers beyond it, I would say. Have you and the boy been close?"

It would have been easy enough to lie to Warneke, he thought. But to the three girls now playing a more organized game of tag between the bench and the fountain? "I couldn't even remember his name a few days ago."

Warneke nodded; he seemed to have expected that answer. Then he threw away the remaining half of his cigarette in disgust. "Perfect," he said.

FIFTY-FOUR

Gaetano believed in fibers. Some people believed in God, some in science, and others in North Korea, but he believed in the revelations of Massimo Bettini's Forensics laboratory and he didn't care who knew it.

"No question, Inspector," Bettini said again, this time a little more warily after the excited reaction his first announcement had provoked. "The envelope material for the bomb is of Eastern European manufacture. The main source is Bulgaria, but it is used in practically every country east of the Adriatic."

"Including Croatia?"

Bettini ventured a witticism. "Unless it has moved."

Gaetano was aware of the attention he had drawn from Bettini's assistants at the other tables around the lab. It was his own fault for having all but whooped when he had heard about the origins of the envelope. "I need your report on my desk within the hour," he said, reimposing some sternness on the room. "Within the hour, Bettini."

"Yes, sir."

In the elevator up to his office Gaetano told himself he had enough—not much, but enough—to move forward against Freedom Press. It was one thing for somebody like Proietti to suggest threats over speculations, another for him to stand in the way of actual evidence. If the envelope fibers led to Minic, couldn't they just as easily have led to stolen diaries and American-Italian chambers of commerce? How dare a playboy senator interfere with the state's institutions!

Naturally, Govoni was waiting for him with objections. "Yes, Inspector, we now know the envelope came from an Eastern European manufacturer," the prattler said with a pained expression, "but we can hardly jump to the conclusion—investigatively—that it came from Freedom Press and this priest."

"Yes, Matteo, let's jump to that conclusion."

"And every tourist and businessman here from Croatia who could have brought those envelopes into the country with him? Every Italian who ever took a trip to the East and bought the envelopes there because they were cheaper than what he could get in the stores here? There are many possibilities."

Gaetano told his enthusiasm to hold on, that at any second he would pitch Govoni out the window. "All very plausible, Sergeant. And that's why the warrant you request will be general enough to cover stationery stores, business offices, *and* Freedom Press. Add whatever else you want, but I want legal paper walking into Minic's office. Clear?"

Gaetano waited until Govoni had skulked back out to his desk to permit himself the tiniest quiver of reasoning. The satisfaction of confiscating Freedom Press's stationery would at best establish nothing incontrovertibly and at worst keep his phone ringing with official calls. He knew that should have bothered him more than it did, then that knowing he knew it should have, as well.

Fortunately, his phone rang for some other piece of nonsense before his enthusiasm from the laboratory faded away altogether.

FIFTY-FIVE

"There is no further purpose in remaining there, Leonard. We expect you to take the morning flight tomorrow."

"What has changed?"

"Nothing has changed. I told you the last time the diary was no longer a priority and to be ready to come home."

"But you had a different tone then, Franjo."

"What are you talking about?"

Warneke was sorry the cretin couldn't see his smile; he had to settle for Sylvester seeing it without understanding it. "You know."

Rising irritation. "I have no idea what you are talking about."

"I thought you were sending signals between the lines last time."

"What signals? What are you talking about?"

"You know. Higher priorities of state. Understandings across frontiers."

"You are not making sense."

"My mistake, Franjo."

Others accepting blame for not being up to his standards of perfection, that much Franjo could process even in his anger. "You have not been at your best there, Leonard. Some of that La Dolce Vita?"

"What is that?"

"Enough! Your flight arrives here at eleven o'clock. We will expect to see you in the office in the early afternoon."

"And if they misplace my luggage at the airport?"

"Goodbye, Leonard."

Warneke held the clicked off connection in his ear long enough to picture Franjo tossing his phone on his desk and glaring at anyone who had overheard the conversation. Perhaps a threat to humble Leonard Warneke in some formal way?

"Sounded like you were breaking his balls."

Warneke put away his phone. Self-deception appeared to be a language requiring no translation. And now without the phone in his hand he had to return his attention to Via Guido Reni 34 across the quiet residential street. Positive: the five-story building had no *portiere*. Negative: it had street bells for the apartments, so he had to wait for some tenant coming or going to get inside.

"Maybe we should get some pizza while we're waiting," Sylvester said, staring at the pizzeria next to the apartment building.

Warneke heard the man's nervousness. He would have been alarmed if Sylvester hadn't been edgy. "We will wait until somebody from the house comes along. Then I will get the boy. You will remain here."

"That wasn't . . ."

"You will remain here. You will still have your moment of gratification when you accompany him home to his mother."

Sylvester said something apologetic or brave or relieved; it didn't matter. Warneke thought about his moves once he was inside the building. Jackiw had said the boy was being held in Apartment 8 or 9 on the third floor, but that had been from an upside-down reading of a piece of paper and he wasn't sure which. Minic hadn't trusted Jackiw *that* much. And if Leszek was in the apartment? Or a second Leszek? There had to be more than one of them watching Philip Cicut. And he had absolutely no plan at all except surprise, and even that would be gone if the apartment had a peephole and Leszek recognized him before opening the door.

"I can still call the police."

The American was sincere in his insincerity; if asked, he would go through with a call to his police friends. But he also hadn't come so far to be a bystander to official business. He wanted to be told no again. "You know what I hated teaching at the university, Mister Sylvester? The Socratic dialogues. People asking questions they knew the answers to but wanted somebody else to volunteer so they would feel a little less responsible for them."

"I thought that was supposed to be wisdom."

"For those not demanding too much from wisdom."

Sylvester smiled to himself and looked more deliberately across the street. "Ever hear of an English philosopher named John Warren?"

"No. Who is he?"

"Who *was* he. Somebody I didn't bury properly."

"Why not?"

"Because I wanted to know more than he did and then show him I did. Mind you, he was already dead and it wouldn't have mattered to him one way or the other."

"So you specialize in fool's errands."

"Something like that."

"Or maybe you just have the need to go further in your life than this John Warren did even in death."

Sylvester looked flattered. "You think?"

"It does not sound too hard. I have never heard of the man."

"And you his own kind, a philosopher."

"And me his own kind, a philosopher."

A pot-bellied Chinese or Korean suddenly stepped out of #34. In a T-shirt and shorts, he carried money and keys in his hand. He went directly into the pizzeria next door for his lunch. "Keep patient, Mister Sylvester. We will soon see how foolish this particular errand is."

He was out from behind the wheel before Sylvester said something else without importance. Since he had not seen other customers in the pizzeria, he couldn't imagine the Chinese not being served right away, so he took aim at the third doorway up the block from #34, strolling as leisurely as he could across the street, reassuring himself that this would be far enough and near enough to get back down to #34 just as the man came out of the pizzeria and opened the street door of his building. He just hoped the Asian didn't want to talk about football with the counterman.

There was no football talk. He was halfway back down to #34 when the Asian came out of the pizzeria holding a white paper bag in one hand and trying to get the right grip on his key with the other. He didn't like being accosted, drew back suspiciously, but Warneke glimpsed the name on the top bell as Lecco in time, smiled when he said it, and the man looked reassured as he turned the lock. Only after the Asian had wished him a good day and started up the stairs did it occur to him that the Leccos might have been affluent enough to have a Chinese or Korean servant.

He shook off the thought and entered the small box of an elevator. The car rose so slowly the Asian was already closing his apartment door on the second floor as he passed the landing. Again, there were positives and negatives. Positive: The apartment doors had no peepholes. Negative: As Jackiw had said, there appeared to be three apartments per floor. He had to resort to trial by error.

He could have done without the clattering the elevator made upon arriving at the third floor. On the other hand, the door to the right said Apartment 10 and CIATTINI, so he eliminated that one as a candidate. Number 9 in the middle said PEYROT, not an Italian name but not a Slavic one either. There was no reason not to focus on number 8 to the left with the empty name slot above the bell. At first he thought there was a television playing inside, but then he realized the sound was coming from a room in the Peyrot apartment. There was no sound at all from inside the nameless apartment.

He had no choice but to ring the bell, which jingled too loudly. He heard nothing from the far side of the door except the furniture inside that he imagined coming awake for being disturbed. The single keyhole told him nothing; there was sure to be an interior bolt above it and he would have been wasting his time to try to force the lock.

He rang again, this time with an unwelcome thought about Jackiw. Had the sewer rat lied to him, after all? Was he standing in the hallway of Via Guido Reni 34 ringing the bell of an unoccupied apartment?

"They went out about a half-hour ago."

Warneke blamed the television set for being surprised by the chunky woman with salt-and-pepper hair coming out of the Peyrot apartment. She hefted her bag on her shoulder as she locked her door behind her.

"You are looking for one of the priests, yes?"

He remembered his smile. "Yes. Father Leszek."

She appraised him more carefully, then dropped her eyes to her bag. She had to be about 40, but her eyes were older. "I don't know their names," she said. "There are so many of them coming and going, it is like a seminary." She blushed immediately. "I'm sorry. I don't mean to be disrespectful. Are you a priest, too?"

"No, no. I'm just visiting a nephew. He's what they call a seminarian. About 19, called Philip?"

She got over her embarrassment for mistaking him for a priest, "Yes, Philip," she said, going over to the elevator. "The priests barely say hello, but he is nice."

"So you've talked with him?"

She was amused. "Why not? It is not allowed? He helped me with my packages a couple of times. My husband is confined to bed, and sometimes I buy more than I should so I won't have to go out more than once. But Philip always gives me help when he sees me dragging all my bags."

Warneke could already hear the conversation he was going to have to have with Sylvester when he got back downstairs, and the American wasn't going to be happy with it. "Philip gets out a lot?"

She shrugged as she started closing the elevator door behind her. "I really couldn't say. I don't keep that close attention. Are you coming?"

"You said *they* went out. You mean Philip?"

She was coming to the end of her courtesy. "Yes. With one of the priests."

"Father Leszek?"

"Father Leszek, that might be his name, it might not be. I told you, I don't pay attention. Are you coming, Signore?"

"Ah, no. I want to leave a note."

She nodded reluctantly. "*Buon Giorno.*"

"*Buon Giorno, Signora.*"

The cables seemed to go through his stomach as the elevator car started its slow descent to the lobby. Her gaze stayed on him until the car dropped below the landing. So much for his noble intentions: A boy at ease with Tomas Leszek as a companion.

He took the stairs slowly. If he had actually left a note, what would it have said? Only one thing: that he preferred an aisle seat on the flight back to Zagreb.

FIFTY-SIX

Gaetano had expected his visit to make more of an impression. He had burst into Freedom Press's offices with three uniformed units, had made sure the patrol cars parked before the entrance obstructed traffic as well as inconvenienced pedestrians, and had barked so imperiously at the man and woman collating pamphlets at a front desk that they had physically backed away from him. It had been textbook. And for his part, Minic had come out of his rear office mouthing all the predictable sounds, especially after having to tell his hirelings to turn over samples of their stationery. The bantam of a priest was aghast, was offended, was of a mind to call an acquaintance at the Interior Ministry. But for all that there was a cylinder missing from his protests. As aghast, offended, and of a mind to call an acquaintance at the Interior Ministry as Minic was, he also gave off an air of distraction. A police invasion of his quarters seemed not to be his most serious worry on the afternoon. His eyes flashed most in alarm when he had no choice but to return inside to his office to answer questions. Gaetano was half-expecting to find his bomber in the back trying to hide behind the spare room's blond furniture. Instead he found nothing except shelves with more space than books on them and a faded photograph of the pope on a cracked wall. He had been in interrogation rooms with more personality.

"You understand, Father," he said again. "Evidence is like an arrow. It points, we are duty-bound to go in that direction."

"Ridiculous. There are stores in Rome, in all Italy, that sell those envelopes. Why aren't you going to them and bothering them for the names of their customers?"

"As a matter of fact, there is only one dealer in the city who has that stock. Tariffs and quotas and the European Community, that nonsense. And would you believe he hasn't sold a single envelope in three months? He told us he was going to discontinue orders, the envelopes took up too much space. Would you believe that?"

To his credit, Minic didn't. What concerned him more, though, was that the telephone on his desk refused to ring. He couldn't keep his eyes off it for more than a few seconds at a time.

"As you can imagine, the attack on this American newspaper office and the death of Signora Ricci has our highest priority."

Minic nodded begrudgingly. "Bless that unfortunate woman. But that is no reason to come charging in here like you have."

Why was it, Gaetano wondered, that priests looked more like priests when they wore white shirts and black suits than when they wore cassocks. There was a deception in that, but he couldn't put his finger on what kind. "Too much zeal, and I apologize. My people know how important the investigation is and they got carried away. I should have warned them about your special vulnerability."

More alert. "What vulnerability?"

"As a foreign enterprise, of course. You are certainly the focus of attention for more than one bureau here. I apologize if I have made that more awkward for you."

"I have no idea what you are talking about. We are registered with every bureau we have to be registered with. There has never been any issue that has made us more what you call *vulnerable*."

Gaetano pictured the line in the sand, pictured raising his foot over it, pictured hesitating, then pictured coming down on the wrong side of it. "You need better information sources at the Ministry, Father. Every indication is that our investigation is connected to a missing diary from your country you are undoubtedly aware of. And on top of that we have the son of the diarist kidnapped. Cicut, that's the name. I'm sure you are aware of all that."

The little man wanted to be more dismissive than he was. "You are speaking in riddles. Yes, I have heard rumors about some journal Ambassador Cicut kept. Everybody in our community has by now. And as for the Ambassador's son, naturally I have heard from his mother, an old and dear friend, that he has run off somewhere. She has even asked for my help in locating him. A boy grieving over the loss of his father and not knowing where to turn. But kidnapped? That is ridiculous."

Gaetano visualized another line in the sand. Why couldn't one test have sufficed? He had no choice but to step over that one, too. "We know there is a definite connection between the boy's disappearance and that journal, Father. Most likely, somebody holding the boy as a hostage for it."

Minic couldn't help glancing back at the phone; only for a second, but long enough to be uncomfortable at being seen glancing at it. "We all have our fantasies, Inspector," he said peevishly. "It is not my place to tell an official such as yourself which ones to pursue."

"That's correct, it isn't," Gaetano said, counting down to five to himself before he had to give Minic a failing grade and moved to the door. "We will of course return the envelopes if they are irrelevant."

"Please keep them. I'm not sure the district will survive another of your visits."

As he touched the office doorknob, Gaetano knew he would be disappointed again if Minic rallied at the last second to ask the obvious question. But the man didn't, and that seemed the biggest accomplishment of the afternoon. "And thank you for not forcing me to spell out everything."

"Inspector?"

'The connection," he said, making sure he didn't miss even a pore of the man's reaction. "I suggested the bombing and the diary were connected, but you didn't ask me how or even how we had arrived at that theory. For that I thank you."

Minic finally looked anxious about more than the silent telephone.

FIFTY-SEVEN

As Roenicke had said, it was the economy, the economy, the economy, and the numbers had been massaged to make the government look in control of it. Sylvester didn't know that for fact, he just assumed it from the jittery speed of the minister with the sinus trouble who was interpreting the press release figures handed out at the door. If the shaggy buffalo of a man had been a standup comic, he would have been telling a joke and at the same time insisting it wasn't funny.

He felt like something of a fraud himself. He had no reason for being in the echoing ministry reception hall with a couple of dozen correspondents. He certainly had no intention of writing anything on the claims being made; they were exactly the kind of thing Porterfield had told him to ignore. And the acquaintances he had renewed hadn't needed renewing; his memory had barely earned a passing mark for recalling that Callaspo from the *Guardian* had twin sons. For the rest it had been dancing around questions about the letter bomb and for how long he would be replacing Roenicke. Why had he let himself in for it? Because he had nothing better to do before meeting Bruno for lunch. And with what result? The feeling that he had become a spectator to his own profession. He wanted to blame somebody for that, but he couldn't come up with a good candidate besides Porterfield and that didn't seem fair. He could have always said no to the man. Inflated Fiat export numbers were the least of the hypocrisies on the day.

"Never expected to see you here," Billy Pope said as the press conference finally broke up and feet started clattering back to the street door.

"I could say the same."

Brogue time. "Ah, you never know when they'll have some pertinent figures on the volume of crucifix imports."

"In other words, you had nothing better to do, either."

Pope waved to the Argentinian correspondent Amanda he had been with at the Foreign Press Club bar. When he came back, the brogue was gone. "I want to thank you for your tip."

"About what?"

"The hierarchy behind Minic back in the homeland! Got me to a fertile idea."

Sylvester remembered how canny he had felt pushing Pope in that direction—and how long ago that canniness felt now. "A thought at the time."

Pope took his skeptical smile through the revolving door out into the morning heat. The traffic shooting by in the street below the imperial white steps made Sylvester dizzy. Life had apparently been going on while he had been entertaining himself inside with the economy, the economy, the economy.

"Naturally, I couldn't get past the eunuch guarding the bishop's contemplations, and he was all eunuch. The bishop has no problem with the extracurricular activities of his assistants, he says very primly, as long as they do not interfere with ecclesiastical duties. Was I calling to suggest that Father Minic had been less than zealous in carrying out those duties? No, of course not, I tell him. Even on the phone I could hear that answer driving his smugness meter wild. So then what exactly is your question, Mister Pope, he says like he's zippering up from a good piss. And I say, maybe you've already answered it. And that he doesn't like because maybe he's not paid as much attention to what he's said as he thought. So he throws in that the bishop is—and I quote— 'well aware of Father Minic's publishing activities and to the best of his knowledge these have never interfered with his ecclesiastical duties.'"

"So you thanked him and hung up."

"But with an inspiration for the ages I owe you, lad. What about *all* these priests and ministers and rabbis and imams doing what the eunuch calls their extracurricular activities? I got myself a series. I'll be keeping that website of mine filled for weeks, if not months. Who knows? The owner of that Japanese restaurant on Via Propaganda might be some Shinto cardinal."

"I don't think they have cardinals, Billy."

"And won't I be the one to point that out! But there's a moral here for us, Brother Sylvester. No matter how wild the goose chase, and the Lord knows I wondered if you wanted to send me off to the Arctic Circle with your Father Minic, we can always use what we're good at for profit. And that leaves me in your debt."

He decided against collecting then and there with Pope's suggestion they adjourn to the Foreign Press Club. The last thing he needed before noon was alcohol. Instead, he found himself ambling along abreast of the Tiber's widest twist past Castel Sant'Angelo, trailing Pope's good spirits into a reminder that he had also accomplished something by informing Elena of the address where she could find Philip. He had been helpful there too. She couldn't have sounded more grateful on the telephone to him; he had been completely forgiven for being in Rome on a vacation. She would get over to that address as soon as she had calmed down and worked out whether just walking in on Philip would be the best way of handling things. Charles Lawrence Sylvester had been a combination of the Red Cross and Oxfam for one and all.

As he walked along, though, Pope's gratitude for Shinto cardinals began to bleach under the sun. A grouch in his conscience warned that Elena might have overdone her effusiveness toward him. And the grouch didn't mean only because locating Philip had been all Warneke's doing, not his own. He hadn't even known of Philip's disappearance before arriving in Rome. How could reassuring Elena that the boy wasn't being held against his will at Via Guido Reni, how could that have become synonymous with accomplishing something? The question unsettled him, began to feel like an accusation. He hadn't come to Rome because of Philip Cicut, safely found or not. He hadn't even come for Josef Cicut. His ticket had already been bought, his reservation at the Reggio

already made, before he had ever received the presumptuous letter and the journal. There was something a little scabby about
accepting Elena's thanks. The more others viewed him as a god-
send, the less he thought of himself as one. On the contrary, he
couldn't shake a feeling that he had helped create the problem in
the first place. It was a ridiculous idea, of course, but it lapped
around in his mind as lethargically as the river next to him he
was never going to outdistance unless he got off the Lungotevere
altogether for an inland street. He got off the Lungotevere.

When he turned into Bruno's block, the sight of the ambulance
in front of Lepri's building immediately attacked as a mockery.
Once again, as in leaving the press conference with Pope, he felt
momentarily dizzy to see that life had been going on while he had
been communing with himself. He was aware of rushing down the
street, aware of the interested eyes on him from outside the bar
across the street, aware of the policeman turning to see him coming—but also all the time aware of turning off his mind with its
distracting expectations, cheap fears, reminders of ignored warnings from doctors and anybody else who had ever taken a look
at Bruno's spottled face. As he reached the *portone* and the cop
with the big arms barring any further advance, he compromised
by hating Giuliana for the rotgut she had been serving Lepri for
years and calling it wine.

And that turned out to be useless, too. When the stretcher
was carried from the building, it wasn't Lepri on it, but an elderly
woman covering one eye with a plump hand and moaning for the
Madonna's help. Bruno was one of several people trooping out
after the stretcher. "Fell in her kitchen," he reported. "I could
hear it next door. Took forever to get her door open . . . What's the
matter with you?"

Sylvester didn't know. As wretched as the woman's moaning
was, whatever her eye looked like under her hand couldn't have
been life-threatening. She was one less corpse to worry about.
Which was just as well since he didn't know her.

FIFTY-EIGHT

Warneke had slept fitfully. Had he ever been able to rest before going out to an airport? It was as if every nerve in his body dreaded setting off airport security alarms, his every thought a telling crime that would betray him. And what had he actually done? Nothing whatsoever. He was a man of the mind, and the most violent thing his mind had ever done was to suggest he was more than that.

Surveying his hotel room, he assured himself again that he had packed everything there was to pack in his small suitcase and shoulder bag. Nothing had been left on the bathroom sink, there was nothing under the bed, the closet had been returned to its bare hangars. Thanks to too much efficiency, he had even settled his bill the night before. Once out the door, he would have nothing to do but to proceed to a bus to the Stazione Termini for the coach out to the airport.

He accepted it as stubbornness to flop back down on the bed and take yet another look around. Just because everything wanted to push him home, that was no excuse for being hasty. A second and third check never hurt. He didn't have an especially notorious record of leaving things behind (only the silver name bracelet his parents had given him as a graduation gift, left behind in the dive the Romanians had called a hotel, jumped out at him), but he couldn't shake a hovering sense of having overlooked something. And wouldn't it have most likely been something staring right back at him from the bed or bed table or window ledge rather than something that had fallen under the radiator? One of his favorite classroom lectures had been the one entitled Hiding in Plain Sight. Rarely had he had a student sharp enough to interrupt his diversionary monologue to point out that the bagged coffee container on his desk, deliberately fitted out with extra puncture marks at the bottom, was leaking over his (blank) papers. They had come in looking to excel at Aristotle, Hegel, and Nietzsche, to share profound understanding across the centuries, but they couldn't even deal with a coffee container right in front of their eyes! The mere memory of it agitated him, made him despair for ever having thought he had been accomplishing something in a classroom. How could he have been so naïve for so long? If you didn't push things in people's faces, they refused to see them.

He all but jumped up from the scratching of a key at his door lock. A maid making sure he hadn't absconded with the blankets? The next guest already being assigned to his room? Or worse, Tomas Leszek because Jackiw had taken another twist? One way or the other, it was eight o'clock, and nobody should have been making noise at his door.

The noise was a full-faced redhead as tall as a basketball player and looking like he was returning to the hotel after a long night. The man reeked of staleness. "Oh," he said, staring at Warneke, then at the key in his hand.

Warneke tensed. After the letter bomb he couldn't have put it past Minic and Leszek to do something stupid. "I think you have the wrong room."

"Oh, Lord," the redhead said with a British accent, matching his key number to the number on the door. "Sorry about that, mate. Not 17, I reckon."

Warneke kept his eyes on the man's big hands. "Next one down."

"Right you are. Sorry again."

The redhead took an awkward step, but then righted himself. Warneke watched until he reached the next door, clicked his key into the lock, and behind another apologetic wave entered #17. Warneke felt his tension subside as he closed his own door behind him. His lungs didn't appreciate the soar up and then the plummet down, seeming to crack small carbonated bubbles inside his chest.

He gazed over his own room, now reduced to total anonymity except for his bags on the chair. The idea had been waiting for him all the time he had been at the door with the Englishman. It struggled to reach the front of his mind, but when it got there, he knew what he had missed. Jackiw had been right about the apartment numbers on the third floor of Via Guido Reni 34. He had been the one who was wrong. The apartment without a name on the bell might have been number 8, but it had been empty as advertised. Number 8 *or* 9, Jackiw had said. And number 9 had been the one with the salt-and-pepper-haired woman Peyrot—the woman who had been so fast to tell him that Philip Cicut had been free to move around. *That* had been the right apartment!

FIFTY-NINE

Gaetano took the call. He didn't want to, but courtesy had its place. "You can tell your editor that the chief of the investigation said No Comment."

"I think he's expecting a little more than that."

"If I could, Signor Sylvester . . ."

"That mean there is something to report but you don't want to tell me or you just wish you had something concrete to say?"

Gaetano brought his pipe back to life without another match. Small surprises on the morning. "Very good. I must keep you away from some of my people."

"Okay. What about the diary and the fire alarm?"

"Because you insist that is related to the death of Signora Ricci."

"No, let's pretend it's something else altogether. A hotel in the center of the city gets robbed. The policeman on the scene establishes that the thief had the help of a guest who set off the fire alarm upstairs to create a diversion. The policeman confiscates the hotel register to see who that accomplice might be. Readers around the world would like to know about the progress in that investigation. After all, they might be planning a trip to Rome and they wouldn't want to stay somewhere catering to burglars."

"In the interests of tourism."

"Exactly. Nothing to do with letter bombs and murders."

Gaetano had a naughty thought: Sylvester could go where he couldn't. It was the kind of thought not worth considering twice in case it looked like a bad idea the second time around. "Needless to say," he hazarded, "we've looked into all the guests there the evening of the robbery, starting with you. Our only conclusion is that the Reggio attracts even Rome residents for an occasional evening. And I trust it is word-of-mouth from people like you in the American community that draws in . . . What was the name of that functionary at the United States-Italy Chamber of Commerce, Matteo?" He put the phone down on his blotter, counted to three slowly, then picked up the phone again. "Yes. Tepedino, Emilio Tepedino. Somebody like that could probably give you some colorful details about the hotel management running around in circles. More than that I cannot help you."

Either his pipe was making him more optimistic than he had a right to be or he heard the right kind of pregnant pause in his ear. Finally: "An American, you say?"

"Tepedino? No, I don't believe so. Matteo, is Tepedino an American? . . . No, my assistant says Italian. He just works for the Chamber of Commerce. We allow that."

"Broad-minded."

"Never let it be said otherwise."

"And you've talked to him."

"Not yet. As you should appreciate, we have a more pressing investigation in front of us. Anything else, Signore?"

There was another pause, then: "No, thank you, Inspector."

"My regrets again to your editor."

"When you can . . ."

"When I can. My pledge."

SIXTY

Elena didn't want to bother the woman again, but something was definitely wrong. The people in the pizzeria downstairs had just shaken their heads at her description of Philip, and if he had been as free to move around as Sylvester had said, he would have lived in the place. How many dinners had he ruined by gorging himself with pizza and *suppli* just before suppertime? Who else was there to ask but the Peyrot woman? The deaf old man in Apartment 10 had gaped at her as though a Gypsy had come to rob his furniture and had slammed the door in her face. She just had to hope Peyrot would understand it was her son she was asking about and not be too annoyed.

But the hefty woman all but rolled her eyes when she opened the door. It took her a long moment to work up something like a sympathetic expression. "As I told you, Signora, I haven't seen him in a few days."

"But my friend said you saw him yesterday. Going out with a priest."

The woman's instant rigidness chilled Elena. Once upon a time Jovanka Popa had given her the same defensive look saying she couldn't come by the house anymore to help with her mother. There was lying in it and there was fear in it and there was calculation in it. There was everything in it but the truth. "Yes, I have seen the boy, but not recently. Your friend is a foreigner, yes? He didn't understand me."

"He speaks Italian very well."

"And yet he did not understand me, Signora."

"I find that hard to believe."

"I cannot help that, Signora."

In a calmer moment Elena knew she would need better reasons for reaching out through the straps of her bag to the woman's shoulders and shaking her. How Jovanka Popa hadn't cared if her mother lived or died, for instance. Or the cowardice of all her one-time friends who knew who was on the proscription list and who wasn't and wanted to stay as far away from her and her family as possible, that too. Or what about the arrogance of somebody named Peyrot or Popa in deciding who was a foreigner and who wasn't? They were all better reasons for yielding to her impulse. But then and there she wanted to throttle only the glib lie about Sylvester's Italian. After Josef's suicide and Philip's disappearance what she had left was her languages. How dare the ignorant cow not know what she was good at! "Tell me the truth or I will come back with the police!"

Peyrot should have looked startled, should have been intimidated by being handled so recklessly and threatened with the police, but she wasn't. Her body might have been separate from the eyes—wide, brown eyes—that were still in charge, reacting as if only to distant reports from under her gauzy blouse about how she was being shaken. "You are making a fool of yourself, Signora," she said solemnly.

"I know you know more than you're saying!"

"And I repeat: You are making a fool of yourself."

Elena knew she couldn't overcome the implacability in front of her. Had she reached out only to confirm as much? She felt the fury receding in her hands and then in her forearms and arms back to the junk in her bag even as it continued rising in her head. It was the same futility she would have given in to that morning in front of her house before her urge to strangle Jovanka Popa. Her angers always seemed to come to her warning they were useless.

"Would you like some water?"

Her arms were collapsed, and she wasn't sure she had dropped them or Peyrot had lifted them off her shoulders. All she could say was, "It is my son!"

The woman's expression didn't change; children didn't count for anything special. "I understand," she said anyway. And then her big brown eyes darted away in alarm to the old man's apartment. Elena had heard it, too: a scraping behind the door, the one called Ciattini eavesdropping. How much could he have heard with his bad hearing?

Peyrot didn't care how much. She manufactured another polite smile and opened her door wider. "Come in, Signora. I'll get you some water."

Elena didn't want to, didn't want to help protect the woman's reputation with her neighbors, didn't want to leave the hall in case Philip came back, but she followed her feet inside. As soon as she saw the couch in the center of the front room, she realized she wanted it more than water. What felt like kilometers of strain subsided from her legs and back as she dropped down on the cushions while the woman went off to the kitchen. She hadn't really walked that far from the tram, but she might as well have. She would be sure to include that strain in her scolding of Philip when she got her eyes on him again. He had to know how much suffering he had caused others.

She took a tissue from her bag and wiped at the perspiration on her forehead and neck. She was sharing the couch with an opened suitcase, and there was a second valise on the chair across from her. The Peyrot woman was obviously going somewhere, but alone or with the husband she had mentioned to Sylvester? If alone, two suitcases seemed like a lot and didn't say much for the woman's marriage. Wasn't the husband supposed to be sick? But if with the husband, two pieces of luggage seemed to be cutting it thin. Wouldn't they have needed an extra bag just for the medicines the husband probably needed?

She scolded herself for her dithering. The fact was, the suitcases were the most personal thing in the living room. Looking around, she disliked herself for the thought that the furniture was drab and second-hand, seemed to have been collected haphazardly from street markets. She could picture the same dowdiness behind the door at the other end of the living room and which presumably led to a bedroom or two. And she thought her own apartment was barely above the shabby? Blind people couldn't have lived more indifferently to their surroundings than the Peyrots did.

Or maybe there wasn't any Signor Peyrot. Maybe the woman was just further along than she was in forgetting about a dead husband and missing son.

"No," Peyrot said to the question when she returned with the water. "I am alone."

Elena was sure Sylvester had mentioned a husband. Then again she hadn't been paying much attention to any detail but the address where Philip was to be found. "But you see all these priests coming and going in Number 8?"

Whatever one thing had to do with the other, it decided Peyrot to hover instead of sit. "That much your friend understood," she said expressionlessly.

Elena smiled into her glass. She seemed to have had a lot of people handing her water lately. But why Peyrot's provocation with another slap at Sylvester's Italian when all that had been settled out in the hall? It was like arguments she had had with Josef. The last word had been spoken, best both shut up, but her insistence on throwing in one last, unnecessary word had stoked everything back up. She didn't want it to be that way with Peyrot; she wanted to say something that made the woman less guarded. "In the town where I grew up we lived near a church," she said, following her mouth now as she had followed her feet out of the hall. "We were very friendly with one of the priests. Socially, not religiously. We never attended the services there. My parents wouldn't hear of it. But one of the priests, he seemed to understand, and that never bothered our friendship. We would see each other in the street. At the cinema. He liked to go to the cinema. You may know him. Stela Minic?"

Her eyes showed nothing. Had she prepared herself for the question?

"That's funny because I'm sure he's the one who's sent most of those priests to the apartment next door. Small man? *Very* small man?"

"As I have been trying to tell you, Signora, as I told your friend yesterday, I have had very little traffic with those people."

Elena hated her confusion. She hadn't meant to talk about Stela Minic. Hadn't she intended to talk about Jovanka Popa? Or maybe she *should* have been talking about Stela from the beginning? She was sure Minic had always known where Philip had gone. And now she was at that place, wasn't she? Where was her mind when she needed it most? "Anyway, we would have these little jokes sometimes about how he expected to see us in church the following weekend. But it was never much more than that."

"Signora . . ."

"No, this is interesting."

Peyrot had to stop herself from glancing over at the closed door at the far side of the room. In the name of whoever was behind it she resigned herself—for a few seconds, anyway—to listening to what was supposedly so interesting.

"Every Sunday from our windows we would see all the people in the town coming and going to the church services. They looked so self-important going and even more self-important leaving. They had done their duty and wanted everybody to notice it. I always said this to our priest friend, and he just shrugged. You can't start all over and rebuild the human race, he would say."

"I'm sure your priest friend is right."

"But then one day, after the trouble had started, I asked him, I said, 'Stela, how can these people be so religious but so immoral? How can they follow you through your rituals every week feeling so saintly for it, but then drag people out of their homes and shoot them in the street just because they haven't gone to the same churches, haven't had the same god blessing their self-importance?'"

For the briefest second Peyrot looked more interested in her than in whoever was behind the door. "And what did this priest say?"

Elena laughed; she suddenly couldn't remember. Had it been Stela's usual thing about turns in the divine plan? Peyrot's undivided attention had erased her memory, made her feel silly. Had she ever even had such a conversation with Stela? She might have, she might not have. There was no reason for her to be embarrassed. "Does it matter, Signora? Don't we know the answer to that ourselves? Do we need a priest to tell us that religions don't guarantee morals?"

Peyrot looked disappointed with herself for having appeared interested. "I'm sure you are right, Signora. But I must get dressed and do some shopping for a vacation. So if you are finished with the water, I would really appreciate . . ."

There was a thread hanging off the ugly lounger behind Peyrot's thigh. Elena wanted to laugh again, this time at how literal a reminder she had of what she had just said. "You didn't ask me."

"Ask you what, Signora?"

"I mentioned what we call the troubles, but you didn't ask me what in particular I was referring to."

The woman sighed, but only after seeming to have to remind herself of having made a mistake. "I assume you're talking about the wars in the Balkans years ago."

"Yes."

"Then what's so strange? Please, Signora . . ."

Elena felt her strength returning. Did she owe it to the woman's transparent evasiveness? It didn't matter. One way or another, she was in a house of lies, it was really that simple. She had made excuses for Jovanka Popa even with her mother, but she had no reason to make them for Peyrot. They hadn't gone to school together, hadn't gone to bars together, hadn't attended weddings together. "Yes, I will be going," she said, relieved that her legs were again strong under her when she stood. "And I appreciate your patience. But there is one thing I must do first."

For the first couple of steps Peyrot was taken off guard, looked merely puzzled. Only when she understood the closed door behind the recliner was Elena's destination did she flutter her arms up in protest. "Signora!"

Elena refused to believe it was Philip listening to everything from behind the door, refused to believe he had traded away his mother for whatever confidences he had been sharing with a liar like Peyrot. And because she refused to believe those things, there was no reason to think about anything at all, just to get to the door.

"How dare you!"

Yes, she dared—the way she hadn't dared with Jovanka Popa. If only the woman would try to stop her physically, would decide that she was somehow vulnerable for leaving her bag on the couch, everything would be perfect because she would gladly knock her down.

But there was nobody in the small corridor behind the door. And there was nobody in the tiny bedroom to the left or the slightly bigger bedroom to the right. And certainly nobody could have hidden in the bathroom. There was nothing at all anywhere except a faint odor of camphor—people who had been packed away out of sight.

"I insist you leave, Signora!"

Elena was out of strengths. The woman looming at the end of the corridor in the living room might as well have been Goliath. Only petty things occurred to her. "Or what? You will be the one to call the police?"

"Yes."

That wasn't the answer she had wanted. Peyrot should have been afraid of the police, as she had been out in the hall. And what about the bedrooms? How could the woman act as though they didn't need justifying? If the living room looked thrown together from junk stores, the small bedroom to the left was barely above a monk's cell with its divan and empty book shelves. She hadn't seen all of the other bedroom where Peyrot herself presumably slept, but she had seen enough to know it hadn't been furnished the way magazines recommended, either.

"I *will* call the police, Signora. I have been very patient with you."

It was a terrifying thought: the woman had been telling the truth all along, *had* been extremely patient with the intruder. Where did she begin to apologize, comparing her to the likes of Jovanka Popa?

She was grateful for the sound of the front doorbell. It put off, at least for a few seconds, her need to stumble through an apology.

SIXTY-ONE

Warneke hadn't counted on Elena Cicut. For a hobbling moment at the door he wanted her to be anybody else—a building neighbor who had just dropped in on Peyrot, say. But it was in fact Elena Cicut, in a place she shouldn't have been.

And wouldn't have been if Sylvester—who else?—hadn't told her where to go to find her son.

"Here is your friend, Signora," Peyrot snapped, recovering from her surprise. "Now both of you leave."

Cicut's confusion crossed the room like a giant wave Warneke couldn't avoid. "I don't know this person."

Peyrot needed only a second for her own confusion to blossom into alarm. Warneke had no choice but to push himself inside and close the door behind him. If he had to force Peyrot to say too much in front of Cicut, that was how it was going to be. He hadn't asked the mother to be there; she wasn't even supposed to know he existed. The circus wasn't his fault. "Where is Leszek, Signora?"

"Who?"

"The priest who was with her son yesterday. Like you told me."

Her shrug of a lie dissolved the possibility she might not be part of everything. Cicut didn't have even that much doubt. Her dismay said she didn't know who he was but that she would deal with that later. "You tell different people different stories, Signora. Where is my son?"

Peyrot's big eyes ran to the shoulder bag on the end table. She might have worked with Leszek, but she didn't have his slickness. "What exactly has she told you, Signora?"

"That she hasn't seen him in days."

"The husband tell you that, too?"

"What husband?"

"The one who's in there dying. So sick she's afraid to leave the house."

"There is nobody . . ."

Warneke caught Peyrot's lurch, getting to the bag just as the woman's hands came down on its straps. He set himself for her swing, but she just sighed and dropped her arm behind a look of contempt. "You must be Warneke. I am surprised you would want another meeting with him."

Out of the corner of his eye he saw his name meant something to Cicut—again, who else but Sylvester?—but she didn't seem to know what and whatever it was could wait. Peyrot's disdain for him was total—professional, conspiratorial, anecdotal. She was not just window dressing for Leszek. She had shared a laugh with him over the debacle at the Via Nomentana. Whatever Leszek had done with the boy had been half her doing. And the open suit-cases on the chairs said she wasn't going to stay much longer to accept credit for it. "Where is he, Signora?"

"You have to ask him."

Elena Cicut seemed to gather her fury from the floor under her feet. She started across the room so blindly she didn't see the lounge chair in her path and gave her hip a hard whack.

"*Gospodza! Smiritye sye!*"

She was frozen by hearing her own language. If he had told her to calm down in any of the other thousands of languages and dialects in the world, she wouldn't have interrupted her charge. But she was startled to be reminded she hadn't been born in Rome when her son had been. And that she had just hurt herself.

"I ask you again," he said, tightening his grip on Peyrot's two wrists. "Where is Leszek and where is the boy?"

"I told you. Ask him."

He was distracted for a second by her wide, fat hands. He wanted to be distracted by them, to put off deciding whether he should have done what he would have done without Elena Cicut standing there. The most he could have accomplished by beating Peyrot? Getting her to blurt out that Philip Cicut was beyond his nobility, was already decomposing as a corpse somewhere.

"You have your goddamn diary! Why isn't that enough?"

Warneke didn't miss it. Peyrot looked over at Elena Cicut as though she had been addressed in more Serbian. If they had taken the diary, it was news to her.

"For the love of God, Signora!"

Cicut's cry was a mistake: Peyrot immediately went back to stone. "What god are we talking about now, Signora?"

Cicut began to tremble; the fury returned to her eyes in tears. Hip or no hip, she was ready to kill the woman.

Warneke tried to ignore the nausea rising in his stomach. He had missed his plane for a useless mission. Whatever had happened to the boy had been gratuitous because it certainly had nothing to do with the diary. And now he had put himself into a spot where he had to witness the mother coming to understand as much. That much he wasn't up for. That much he refused to add to his failures.

His swing caught Peyrot squarely down the right side of her mouth and jaw, making a light cracking sound against her lower teeth. For a second she struggled to stay on her feet, to keep her eyes open, to wrest her hands away from him. He didn't want to hit her again, he wanted to believe in her struggling as the chicken running around the farmyard after losing its head. Who was being gratuitous now? The question was even in Elena Cicut's eyes as she yanked at his hands. Whose side was she on?

Then the struggling stopped. Cicut was simply on the side of letting Peyrot go so she could slump to the floor with her eyes closed. For a second more only he could see the revolver that had slid partly out of Peyrot's bag.

SIXTY-TWO

It wasn't until Sylvester followed Emilio Tepedino's wave to precede him into the elevator that it fully dawned on him he was in the company of the man who had robbed him; robbed *him*, Charles Lawrence Sylvester, the only child of Joseph and Eileen Sylvester, fourth-generation heir of Carlo Silvestro from Bari. The diary had been in his safekeeping when it had been taken from the Reggio, and if he had interpreted Gaetano's hint right, it was the squirrelly little character with the graying mustache and squealy voice who had taken it away from him as surely as if he had played the lookout for a mugger in Central Park. Instead of playing reporter with the squirmy bugger, he should have been playing strangler.

"It has been years since your esteemed journal inquired about our activities," Tepedino said, pushing the button for the top floor. "Is there a special reason you want to do a story on us now?"

Sylvester recomposed himself to unspool the little speech he had prepared on his way over. He really didn't want to get down to hotel robberies until they were settled somewhere where another button couldn't be pressed to toss him back out into the street. Tepedino savored the bullshit. If Sylvester didn't mind his observation, in fact, it was about time the media paid more attention to what the Chamber had been doing for relations between the United States and Italy. Didn't Sylvester agree there was too much negative coverage of the occasional strains between the countries? Sylvester agreed, opening himself in the crawling elevator car and then down an echoing marble corridor to statistics on the Chamber's pivotal role in educational exchanges and trade flows back and forth. No need to jot down any of the numbers; Tepedino had them in detail in the office where they were headed.

The only face he recognized in the group photos blanketing the office wall was Colin Powell from his Secretary of State days. Tepedino was the third to Powell's left, trying to look both honored and important in his own right. *All* the pictures were of groups, even of the Tepedino clan going back a couple of generations and forward another one with a lumpy teenage boy. Emilio Tepedino had apparently never rated being more than just one of many. "I'm not certain what it is you would like to focus on," he said, ferreting through papers on his desk to find his threatened statistics. "Of course, if it isn't within my competence, I can direct you to the right person."

Out of elevators and halls, Sylvester had no more reason not to dive in. "I can't help thinking we've met somewhere before."

The brass wall plaque behind Tepedino's head reminding visitors what office they were in had more of a reaction than he did. "No, I don't believe so."

"Or at least seen each other . . . I know! I'm staying at the Albergo Reggio. I'm sure we saw each other in the lobby a couple of evenings ago."

As subtleties went, it wasn't, but it drew an appropriately scarlet color. Even the plaque looked more fidgety. "The hotel near Piazza Navona?"

"I could swear it."

Tepedino seemed to want to drop his eyes back to the sheets in his hand, but not at the cost of looking evasive. "Yes," he conceded. "That must have been the night I had to work late. I didn't feel like driving all the way home, then coming back early the next morning. I do that occasionally."

"They make you work late, make up for it with a little comfort."

"Something like that. Although I don't recall seeing you."

"Just in passing."

"Of course. You pass George Clooney, you pass me—equally memorable."

Sylvester needed a second to be sure he had heard humor, not self-pity. "No question. Same thing."

The little man looked satisfied. "They stop and stare at me on the street every day. But as I was saying . . ."

"You live out of the city?"

"Me?"

"Sounds like you have a long commute."

Tepedino didn't want to be irritated, but he thought about it. He wouldn't have minded somebody looking in on them from the hallway to interrupt the interrogation. "Not that far. But the traffic can make the shortest distance seem like a trek."

"The night you were there, wasn't that the night of the big commotion?" There was another level of red deeper than scarlet. "The robbery. Somebody broke into the hotel safe after an accomplice upstairs set off the fire alarm and the deskman had to run up to see what was going on."

A feeble smile. "I must have missed that."

"Lucky you. I thought they were going to evacuate the place. Cops marching around and knocking on all the doors."

"Now that you mention it, I might have heard something. I thought it was part of a dream. Once my head hits the pillow . . ."

"And especially after a long day behind those papers."

The sarcasm came out too much like sarcasm; Tepedino thought about ignoring it, but then dropped his reports. "Which you don't appear very interested in. Is there something else I can do for you, Mister Sylvester? Maybe the real reason for your visit?"

He hadn't rehearsed that part of it as thoroughly, and it had come faster than he had expected. Back to the eternal question: Because he had underrated Tepedino or because he had overrated Sylvester? "The fact is, Signor Tepedino, I'm trying to interview as many possible witnesses to the robbery as I can. For a story."

He really hadn't wanted his apprehension confirmed. "Yes?"

"Not that we're not interested in what you're doing around here, too."

"Of course."

"Kill two birds with one stone. And it turns out you're the stone."

That much bullshit he wasn't up to accepting. "A story for a New York newspaper about a minor hotel robbery here?"

"Not so minor, it seems. The police are making it a priority."

"Who told you that?"

"My sources. More than that I can't say. You understand."

He didn't know if he did or didn't. "But whatever for, this priority?"

Sylvester preferred the man's reds to his white; his dismay was far too genuine. Had they told him they were only interested in testing the hotel fire alarm? Was he only one of a mob when it came to robbing hotels, too? "That safe apparently contained valuables belonging to an important person."

More disbelief. "I've read nothing about this."

"And I hope you won't. I'd like to be the first to report it."

That much he was willing to believe, distastefully. "And that's so important to you you had to deceive me for the purpose of your visit? You might have just called me and said what you wanted to talk about."

"You're right, and I apologize. But I've learned to tread delicately where hotel guests are concerned. You never know why somebody has taken a room for a single night. People could get embarrassed. I think we avoided that by meeting personally and you explaining about working late. Again, I apologize."

Emilio Tepedino liked the idea of somebody suspecting Emilio Tepedino of having a hotel tryst and needed a moment to shake the fantasy. "I still find your interest in this robbery odd. But as I said, I was asleep when it apparently took place."

"So you didn't see anybody sounding that alarm as a diversion."

"If I was asleep, how could I see anyone pull an alarm?" He liked himself for that one; came close to dabbing at his mustache in triumph.

Sylvester remembered what Warneke had said about the safe-cracker—a parade of cutouts with nobody ever meeting anybody else. And nobody was more of a cutout than the one waiting for another lob he could swat back over the net effortlessly. "You really don't know, do you?"

"Know?"

"Who you were working with."

The expectant smile evaporated. "I am not finding this a pleasant meeting, Mister Sylvester. Perhaps you should talk to the other guests at the hotel that evening."

Dice rolling time. "I don't think many of them live a fifteen-minute walk from their office and claim they need a hotel room because of their long commute. You shouldn't have put your address in the White Pages."

"How dare you! Are you accusing me . . . . .?"

"As a matter of fact, yes. But don't worry about me. Your problem is the police asking you the same questions."

He looked miserably out toward the hall again; this time he didn't want anyone interrupting them. "I would warn you against libeling me, Mister Sylvester."

"In print? I don't even know if it's a story yet. But as a functionary like you knows, public scandal isn't always the worst of it. Sometimes the whispers circulate in the wrong places, and functionaries discover they're not considered so functional by the powers that hire and fire and make sure there is no more hiring."

"This is outrageous . . .!"

He reminded himself that he knew better, that over the years he had remained cool interviewing dictators, frauds, and all manner of sleazebags, and that Emilio Tepedino was nowhere in the league of most of them. But he still willed himself back into his mood in the elevator downstairs. He was still Charles Lawrence Sylvester, personal victim, who didn't need all that much encouragement to strangle the sniveling son of a bitch counting on his empty indignation to carry the day. "Yes, it probably is. But over there on your side of the net there are a couple of murder victims, and it's very easy to blame you for that as much as all the more important people you're used to obeying."

"Murder victims! You're ridiculous!"

"How'd you get your marching orders? A phone call? A coded e-mail? Or did you open those reports of yours and find a little note tucked inside?"

Tepedino took a deep breath, as much to show he had exhausted his patience as to calm himself. Sylvester hadn't seen that since he had told Nick he was grounded for the weekend for stowing Sylvester Sylvester in the hall closet to panic Patricia. "I think you should leave, Mister Sylvester."

"Did I mention the police have the name of the safecracker?"

More white, more patience. "I'm happy for them."

"No, you're worried you never met but he knows your name anyway."

"You're playing with fire, Sylvester."

"Oh? Flames? Big flames? Bigger than the police?"

Tepedino couldn't let it pass; there had been all those moments with secretaries of state like Colin Powell. "If you want to put it that way."

Sylvester didn't want to put it that way. The man was suddenly confident about more than educational and trade exchanges between the United States and Italy. The more he had felt threatened, the sturdier Emilio Tepedino had felt the ground under him. He might as well have been following the man's trail of breadcrumbs into the old witch's oven. But he still had to try. "Who we talking about, Emilio?"

Tepedino didn't mind the patronizing tone; he knew he had already won. "I'm sure one of your colleagues can tell you," he said.

Sylvester pictured mountain lions and rattlesnakes, and only some of them were in Oregon with Claude Applebaum and only some were real animals.

SIXTY-THREE

Govoni went from neo-fascists in Greece to separatists in Macedonia to super-nationalists in Lithuania. Actions, dates, official names of organizations, political importance—he rattled on with everything he had picked up from a couple of hours of phone calls and e-mails with Interpol. Every trail had been researched to infinite plausibility—and every plausibility was, well, infinite.

"I know you have a point here, Matteo," Gaetano said finally.

The sergeant was hurt at not being allowed to go on with what he had committed to memory from the paper in his hand. "Tomas Leszek," he announced reluctantly.

"Doesn't sound Greek or Lithuanian to me."

"Same kind of letter bomb, same kind of stationery." He surrendered his sheet of paper. "A contract killer. You provide the political situation, Tomas Leszek provides his solution. The Greek fascists, Macedonian separatists, and Lithuanian ultras have all found him useful. And that's just the three most obvious occasions. Interpol has been looking for him for years."

"I don't remember the name."

"We've seen reports now and then. No reason for you to remember. He's never been connected before to anything this far west."

Gaetano knew how to parse that: *"Maybe the Inspector doesn't have that steel memory of his anymore. Pity Sergeant Govoni for having to steer the old man through his daily duties."* "If there is a connection."

"I wouldn't rule it out. Letter bombs are his trademark."

"Trademarks are for toothpaste. Why call attention to himself if he has every interest in not being traced?"

"Vanity. Habit. Security in his tactics."

"And this bastard has been killing people for whoever meets his price?"

"It would seem, sir."

He could hardly decipher Govoni's scribblings. "Well, tell me this, Matteo. If so many people in so many countries have been able to avail themselves of his services, how is it that not one member of our vaunted Interpol has been able to find the same telephone number for locating him? Tell me how that is possible, Matteo."

The sergeant knew what he was being asked, and wasn't enthusiastic about being the first one to say it. Finally, though: "Somebody is protecting him?"

Gaetano tossed the sheet aside. "Bravo! Somebody is protecting this prick. And not just any someone! A someone who can have sauerkraut in the morning in Berlin, pate in the afternoon in Paris, and a Guinness ale in the evening in Dublin. Wouldn't you say? . . . So that leaves us where?"

Govoni didn't like that answer, either. "He doesn't seem to stay in one place too long. He's probably gone by now."

"That isn't what I asked. Gone or not gone, where does that leave us?"

"No closer to connecting Leszek to whoever might have hired him."

"Bravo again!"

"But I'm checking hotel registrations for the last month anyway. I know it's probably useless, but why overlook the obvious? My guess is that he's had an apartment somewhere in the city."

For the first time in several long minutes Gaetano felt he had something to contribute. "This Freedom Press, Minic's church, the congregation's more affluent members, check their house and apartment holdings."

"I should have thought of that."

Gaetano was sorry he didn't have a heavy object on his desk:
It would have been a test to see if he gave in to an impulse to hurl
it at the departing Matteo Govoni. *I should have thought of that.*
Chances were, the list had already started being compiled before
Govoni had come into the office. It wasn't much of a stretch to
imagine his retirement dinner when the humble Matteo would get
to his feet and, as part of his farewell toast, declare that "I have
learned so much working with Inspector Gaetano."

Gaetano wouldn't have minded if he had learned a little more
working with Inspector Gaetano, either.

SIXTY-FOUR

Warneke wanted to blame everything on the Cicut woman. He wouldn't have gone through two cigarettes if she hadn't sat there chain-smoking while waiting for him to do something. He could almost sympathize with Peyrot's complaints about the nicotine cloud in the living room. Cicut was making him feel responsible for things beyond his control. What else could he have done? He had skipped his flight home. He had taken Peyrot out of commission. Most of all, he hadn't told her what he really thought of her chances of seeing her son again. And still she sat in the lounge chair smoking, gulping from a bottle of water, and all but jumping up every time the elevator out in the hall whined up or down. She had no idea how much he didn't want to see Leszek walk through the door since the man would have almost certainly been alone. Who else's fault could it have been that he was waiting for what he didn't want?

"You could be here forever, you know."

On the couch Peyrot had stopped trying to wriggle out of the wire he had used to tie her hands behind her back; now she just wanted to show him how unimpressed and resilient she was. If he had been by himself, he could have shoved her taunting into the big suitcase he had tossed on the floor next to her and forgotten about her. But her contempt raised the doubts in Elena Cicut's eyes. "You are really convinced Philip will be coming back with this Leszek?" she asked him again.

Peyrot didn't understand the language, but she heard the plaintiveness. "Don't look to him, Signora. He is sure of nothing."

Warneke imagined Cicut getting up and cracking her water bottle over Peyrot's head. But the woman was too exhausted, barely up to the glare she leveled at the couch. "Why are you doing this? Philip has done nothing to you."

"Money," he said, making it sound like something exchanged in a universe other than his own. "It's their politics and their religion."

Peyrot pitied him, Cicut pitied Peyrot. That seemed to leave only Philip Cicut for him to pity. Instead, he took the small .38 he had recovered from Peyrot's bag off the end table, palming it as much as he could so the sight of it wouldn't excite Cicut all over again, and slipped it into his back pocket. Had he missed something on his first search through the rooms in the back? If he had missed an entire apartment the first time, how easy would it have been to overlook a telltale item in a single room? "Don't let her get off that couch," he said, returning to the back hallway.

He didn't wait for Cicut's reaction; better she just accept his implicit trust in her. But out of the living room, he saw only what he had seen the first time. There was still nothing in the small room except an ugly purple divan and a bookcase of paperbacks coated in months of dust. It might not have been smart enough for visiting religious dignitaries from Zagreb, but it would have done for kidnapped teenagers.

In the bigger room Peyrot's bed still hadn't been made, the toiletries and perfumes on her bureau still gave off a clotted sweetness, neither her drawers nor the two closets had any men's clothes, only Peyrot's silk robe hung from the back of the door. Again, he had found nothing so he knew he had found everything: Leszek had not only erased any sign of his presence, but also that of the Cicut boy. He had missed his flight home for being nothing more than a gravedigger.

And Peyrot's departure? They had obviously interrupted her before she had been able to start packing. Why couldn't Cicut understand the meaning of the suitcases and let go of any hope she had for seeing her son again? Why did it have to be him who would probably have to break the news in so many words to her? Leszek and Peyrot had completed their work, had no more reason for staying in Rome. Why couldn't Cicut admit that to herself and save everybody more exercises in futility?

He lingered over the perfume bottles on the bureau. Peyrot, kidnapper of teenagers and worse, had entered a store and bought them as casually as any other woman had. She had had moments of doing what women who weren't kidnappers and worse did normally. How was that interlude possible? It was the same dismay he had felt seeing Leszek walking down the street with Jackiw that first day outside the office of the Freedom Press. He didn't believe in multiple personalities, so how did human reason account for such shameless arrogance? He yearned for the abstractions of the classroom. As long as he was within them, he and everybody else seemed whole and logical. There was a path forward; not always conclusive, but forward.

"Warneke!"

He hurried back to the front room dreading that Peyrot had somehow gotten out of the wire. But no, she had just given up her sitting position to sprawl out on the couch, her hands still bound, her dress pulled up over her thick thighs all the way to the bottom of her white panties. Her smile was even smugger at seeing his peek at her crotch.

"It's the police."

Cicut was standing at the window looking down at the street. The alarm in her voice was a 180-degree turn from her first mention of the police a half-hour ago, seeing them then as the solution to everything. Stalled or not, he had managed to gain some trust from her. But the police were also still the police.

"They could be here for something else, yes?" she asked as he took in the two plainclothesmen and two uniformed officers sizing up the building and confirming that the address tallied with what one of the detectives had written in a notebook.

Warneke shook his head—the first decisive thing he seemed to have said to her since pushing himself into the apartment. "We can't take that chance," he said. "We have to leave, Madam."

Only after he said it did it occur to him how much he had tested her with the *we*. But by then she had overcome a momentary doubt about him and was across the room toward the front door, holstering her bag over her shoulder and leaving her water on the end table as she passed it. Peyrot couldn't have been happier. "You better untie me or I'll have to explain things to them."

"I don't think so. Tell them they interrupted a sex game. Unless you feel like telling them more ambitious lies."

He had been better off with her smugness; the spite that replaced it was unnerving. "You are a useless person, Warneke."

He was glad he didn't have time to debate the proposition. He had enough trouble knowing they would run into the police on the stairs or in the elevator. Snatching the water back from the end table, he pushed it back into Elena Cicut's hands as they went through the front door. She hesitated only for a second before understanding, some ancient experience in improvising clicking through the doubt in her eyes. She uncapped the bottle, took a slug, then put her arm through his, accompanying him down the staircase, a stream of excited Italian loudly and abruptly flowing from her about the vacation the two of them would soon begin in Paris. He had so underestimated the woman leaning on him she might have been a stranger. He got in an appropriate grunt as one of the uniformed policeman saw them coming down toward him and the whining elevator began its ascent with the two plain-clothesmen inside. She didn't miss that moment, either, with her deliberately startled *"Buon Giorno. Che c'e?"* The uniformed cop decided he had no patience for the curiosity of a passerby, and the elevator rose up past them with no orders from inside for them to be stopped. They were down at the street by the time the knocking started on one of the doors upstairs.

As soon as the uniformed cop left behind in the street saw them emerge from the entrance, he straightened up against the patrol car where he had been leaning, instant eagerness for accomplishing what those in the building had let get past. But even as Warneke was remembering the extra trouble he had made for himself with the gun in his back pocket, Cicut started growling at him about not reserving the right hotel rooms in Paris. He barely caught her drift in time as the cop started toward them with his hand already in the air; he lashed back that the hotel she had wanted cost too much. She immediately withdrew her arm from his in a snit. "Money, money, money," she huffed. "That's all you ever talk about. Money—it's your politics and your religion."

Warneke rolled his eyes at the cop, who had second thoughts about getting in the middle of a marital squabble and dropped his hand back to his side. He looked amused as he followed their bickering down the street.

Warneke's relief lasted only until the high rearview mirror of the van parked two doors down showed the cop resuming his slouch against the patrol car. He led Cicut around the corner where they could step up their pace until he found a taxi. "They're taking him back to my brother, aren't they?" she said, loudly releasing her nerves

"It's possible," he said, clinging to the word *possible* as not being a lie.

"Milo doesn't know Philip. He'll run back here the first chance he gets."

He didn't want to add to the brittleness that had suddenly overtaken them, so he only nodded, telling himself that finding a cab was more important. It was a mistake.

"You don't think he was taken back, do you?" She kept her eyes on the sidewalk patches she was eliminating under her sensible brown shoes. "You think they've done something to him. You think they might have killed him."

The accusation might have come not just from her, but from the woman emerging from the *salumeria* with her red net bag of cold cuts, from the parked cars, from the ornate marble plaque of some kind of calendar in the window of the furniture design store behind Cicut's shoulder.

"And I don't think you're even interested in Philip. I think it is this Leszek you really want to find."

If he concentrated on his reflection in the window of the furniture store, he would have had the perfect picture of hypocritical reassurance.

"I was better off with Stela Minic."

Warneke's eye moved away from the window. She was staring at him with some depthless sorrow and hurt that nothing from his mouth would make disappear. "Yes, I think you're right," he said, Peyrot's gun ever so lighter in his back pocket. "You *will* be better off with Minic. Both of us will."

SIXTY-FIVE

Gaetano admired the woman's boldness. She knew she was walking a tightrope and couldn't ease off her posture for a second. She offered explanations for nothing, and dared them to do something about it. Once they had freed her wrists from the wire, she just wanted them gone—no whats and whys about being tied up in the first place, no information on Tomas Leszek, no effort in denying the suitcases around her meant she was about to leave the city, all matter-of-fact hostility. They could stand in her living room all day, they could dream up some violation of her *soggiorno* for taking her into custody, or they could pretend she didn't exist. It was all the same to her since she had nothing more to say. When she announced she was going into the bathroom to pee, she paused a second to see if they wanted to go inside first to make sure she didn't have a guided missile in the bathtub. She resisted a smile when he nodded his permission for her to go, but as soon as she turned her back he smiled for her.

"She smokes different brands, but I don't see any cigarette packs," Govoni said, nodding toward the saucer of butts on the coffee table.

Gaetano had already noticed. It was no revelation the lady had had company, and from the smell of the ashtray probably the couple they had seen going down the stairs on their way up and by now long out of the *rione*.

"We could take her in," Govoni said. "She might not feel so secure at the office."

"For what? Somebody so *secure* won't have a traffic violation record."

Govoni detected criticism. "What would you call it, Inspector?"

Diversion, Gaetano thought immediately; he would call it *diversion*. But to what end and away from what? The woman's response to being tied up was just one anomaly. There was also the man who had tied her up with a piece of wire but who had also made sure the wire didn't cut into her flesh; that did not fit the personality of a letter bomber. And Tomas Leszek? She didn't say she had never heard of him, merely that he might have been one of the visitors who came and went regularly in the apartment next door; in any case, she had no information on the whereabouts of somebody with that name. Was it a crime to have just maybe—just maybe—heard of somebody?

Petrino stuck his head through the front door. "We have #8 open, Inspector."

Gaetano headed out, but Govoni hesitated with a nod toward the bathroom. "Just leave her here alone?"

"What do you suggest, Matteo? Analyze her pee?"

He could have done without the smirk from Petrino, but said nothing in case Govoni hadn't seen it. At that, Petrino's smirk wasn't much worse than the petulance awaiting him outside Apartment #8 on the face of the pizzeria manager who had turned out to have all the building's keys. Coming right down to it, was there anything at all lately he couldn't have done without?

#8 was everything #9 wasn't, starting with a jasmine-like scent over the living room. There wasn't a chair or table that hadn't come from some chi-chi shop in the Centro. The artwork on the walls might have been only prints, but he recognized Goya, Cezanne, and the one with the desperate looking people on a raft. The knick-knacks on the shelves had a polished brass look that said antique dealer more than flea market. "The bishops like their little nips when they come back from the Vatican," Govoni said with a nod toward the small bar in one corner of the room.

"Take a look in the back and see if our friend is hiding under a bed."

Govoni stomped off toward the corridor off the living room more heavily than was necessary. "I should get back downstairs," the pizzeria man said edgily.

"So go."

"But . . ."

"What? We're the police, man. Afraid we'll steal something?"

"No, no . . ."

"Thank you for your help. We'll be sure to mention it to the landlord."

The manager left without further protest, taking his sulk with him. But a bigger pout lingered after him. "You have a dog, Petrino?"

"Sir?"

"A dog. One of those four-footed things people keep as pets."

"No, sir."

"Then you don't know what a leash feeling is."

"No, sir. I guess not."

"It's where you get led around like a dog on a leash, and every time you stop to sniff something interesting, you get pulled away from it. It's like some sadistic game your master is playing with you."

"Sir?"

He could hardly explain it to Petrino when he didn't understand it himself. But standing where he was, he was tantalized by the fugitive feeling he was in the middle of more transience than that of an apartment for Minic's associates.

"Nothing you wouldn't expect," Govoni grumbled, returning from the rear of the place. "Two big bedrooms. Silk sheets, no less."

"You turned back the blankets?"

"Well, it was just a quilt . . ."

"No, no, Matteo. You were right. Well done." Govoni didn't know what he was being praised for, but at least his look of stupor was familiar. "I want a general alarm out on Leszek. Right away."

Govoni reached into his pocket for his radio with a nod that said he approved. "And the one next door?"

"She'll come with us. We'll see how secure she is when she has to think of something besides packing those valises."

"Good."

Gaetano ignored the condescension. He needed allies where he could find them.

SIXTY-SIX

bits were his specialization. Sylvester had Billy Pope to thank for that reminder. For more than seven years, everyone from Porterfield at the office to Nick at home had taken his mastery of them for granted. Not even Cynthia could contest that, though she was trying her best.

"You sure you know what you're doing, Charley?"

"Just send it to the copy desk at the last possible second. That means it'll go to Emery, and by then he's looking at the clock more than the copy."

"Even Emery will wonder about an obit a couple of weeks after the death."

"We do it all the time."

"Sure, when the nephew confirms that Uncle Hiram died in his mountain cabin alone with the bears. Cicut died publicly. The German papers . . ."

"The German papers didn't have our details."

"Or your imagination."

"You'd be surprised how much is fact."

He took her silence at the other end of the phone as his first serious test. If things broke right, there would be others over the next couple of days, but Cynthia was the first real challenge. "What do you want me to say?" she finally came back.

"I want you to say 'You're going to stir up a lot of hornets with this, Charley, and God bless you and Tiny Tim.'"

The *Post* kid Merriweather at the computer across the office sniffled a laugh. Cynthia didn't. "That graph about the diary . . ."

"I didn't make that up."

"Moving right along. I'm talking about the Foreign News desk. Somebody's going to red-flag that, and they'll be all over us asking where we got that information."

"Refer them to the Rome correspondent."

"Funny."

"Joey Bacsik translated that part for us before the thing was stolen."

"I must've missed that.'

"Before Joey was killed and before the Italians began investigating the hotel robbery. They want to infer that's all connected to Cicut's death in Mainz, let them infer away. We're just writing an obit."

"Yes, but whose?"

"Now *that's* funny. Get it through, Cyn. Any trouble, give me a call."

"If there's any trouble, it won't be me doing the calling."

"Just as a heads up. For old time's sake."

He hadn't meant any *double entendre*, and she let it pass. "Charley?"

"What?"

"What do you really think you'll accomplish with this?"

He recognized the tone from when she had warned him away from locking horns with Applebaum. "I don't need the protection, Cyn, and it's too late to give it to the people who did need it. Let's at least give the bastards a nightmare or two."

"And how will you know they've had one? When they come down on you?"

He couldn't think of a more likely alternative as he put down the phone.

"We do it all the time," Merriweather said.

"What's that?"

"Run obits after the maggots have had their feed."

"Nice picture."

The kid giggled and went back to his typing.

SIXTY-SEVEN

Warneke had tasted better vegetable soup, but he wasn't at the Cucina for its food. From his trestle table near the door, he watched Minic circulate among the refugees going at their lunch. The priest had practiced to a tic walking up between two of them, laying hands on the shoulders of both, and muttering something that forced them to freeze their spoons in the air. Most smiled politely, waiting for him to move along so they could get back to eating. Only a giant of a man with more holes than teeth in his mouth flared up at the hand on his shoulder; he looked ready to turn around and drive his spoon through the intruder before he took in the cassock. Busy saying something to the African sitting alongside, Minic missed the threat; by the time he paid attention to the giant, the big man was back attacking his bowl.

Warneke checked his watch. Elena Cicut was a minute late with her call. Had she developed second thoughts about trusting him? In her place he would have. He had been foolish to let her go home with a promise that she would rejoin him at the train station at the Cucina's meal time. In her place he would have been out of sight out of mind. He was a stranger who had been useless to her while the little man going from table to table in the name of charity was somebody she had known for decades. He hadn't been able to offer her even familiar lies.

But then Minic interrupted his patrol to reach into a pants pocket for a cellphone. He turned away from the door to say hello so that Warneke couldn't see his face, but there was a stiffening of his shoulders as he moved toward the rear counter where a couple of nuns were ladling out soup to late comers. Who else could have stiffened his shoulders besides Elena Cicut? The woman had kept her promise to meet again at the station. And indeed, when Minic did turn back, he squinted off in the direction of the terminal outside, considered the wisdom of leaving to meet with the widow, then clapped his phone back into his pocket with a sigh. He said something to the older nun behind the counter, she nodded, and he made more resolutely for the door.

Warneke waited until the little man had passed him and had opened the door into the brilliant sun before he got up from his table. He missed catching the heavy door before it slammed closed, but when he opened it again, Minic was still in front of the Cucina looking over at the terminal for a sign of Cicut. He was too distracted to worry about somebody coming up behind him.

"I have a gun in my pocket, Father. Do I have to take it out?"

The man adjusted quickly; he didn't even turn around. "You must be Warneke."

"We're going across the street to talk with the widow."

His neck reddened, but he didn't move. His Chakavian spittle was more noticeable when he sputtered, "I have said all I have to say to her, and she doesn't want to listen. If she is now in league with you . . ."

"We're going to talk about her son and Tomas Leszek."

He tensed all the way up to his neck; mention of a gun was nothing compared to mention of Leszek. "That would be a mistake," he said, an effort to his calm.

"You can be the one to tell her why. Move."

"You don't know what you're doing . . ."

"Go." He had to nudge Minic to the curb, and had a flitting dread of what he would do if the man bolted or cried out or did something else he hadn't planned for. But then some silent prayer or calculation abruptly revived the priest, and he strode across the street swiftly, like an independent porcupine. A new lie already in place for dealing with Cicut? Warneke was taken aback by the sudden sharpness of his anger. Up to that second he had never pictured himself actually using the small gun he was trying to keep covered with his palm. He wasn't somebody who held guns.

But then he hadn't been somebody who held wires against throats, either. And just the mustiness of Minic's cassock seemed like reason enough to behave irresponsibly.

Had he gone mad?

Sweat was prickling his skin as he left the street heat for the station's faint burning smell from the tracks. The two *carabinieri* stationed at the entrance didn't help his composure. Somewhere within a few steps he wasn't pushing Minic so much as being pulled by him. The gun, and it alone, was what remained of his control, but even thinking about it felt like an invitation to drop it in front of the policemen and get himself arrested. Then he had an idiotic thought, a religious one: He had given the priest the advantage by mentioning the gun. Now the man of vows was home in his spiritual garden, had nothing to lose but his life, so could reassert himself until that happened.

Elena Cicut was sitting in the promenade cafe squeezed between the ticketing lobby and the tracks, the only customer amid the half-dozen bare aluminum tables. She had changed from a blue to a brown blouse and washed her face on her visit home, and she looked less haggard than she had at Via Guido Reni. The waiter who had apparently brought her cappuccino was busy laughing on his cellphone over more entertaining matters than serving. Before she saw them approaching she was stretching her neck out toward the coming and going passengers from the trains, one last yearning for seeing her son among them. Warneke had a picture of Franjo doing the same thing at the Zagreb airport for him, and felt instantly cheesier for it. He was still alive and, he was sure, Philip Cicut wasn't.

Then she saw them and the yearning turned to stone as Minic reluctantly took a seat next to her. "Where is he, Stela? And no more lies!"

Her volume, her tone, or just her foreign language alerted the waiter to more than the conversation in his ear. Warneke glanced back at the entrance to make sure the *carabinieri* hadn't become curious about them; they were too busy directing a tourist to the Arrivals and Departures board. To keep the waiter from coming over, he signaled for two more cappuccini. The waiter said something to his friend on the phone about having to get back to work, hung up, and scurried inside to the bar.

"Slight deceptions, I admit," Minic nodded. "But you left us little choice."

"*I* left you . . .?"

Self-confidence had indeed descended over the little man while crossing the street. A blessing from The Madonna of the Taxis and Buses. "I'm sure this gentleman has filled your head with dark stories. How we abducted Philip. How we have held him hostage for Josef's diary."

"Milo said as much. You have, too."

"Because that's what you wanted to hear." He thought about reaching out for her hand, then took better measure of the ferocity in her eyes. "Nobody abducted Philip, Elena. He came to me because he wanted to go home and he knew you didn't approve and didn't have the money for the train fare anyway."

"This is his home."

"I'm sure that's how you see it and how you've labored to convince him to see it. He said he wanted my help for the trip, that I should have understood. And at first I thought I did. I was delighted he had made such a decision. He was a young man beginning to make choices of his own. But there was something in his manner that made me suspicious. When he went to the bathroom, I looked in his bag and found one of those pistols Josef kept around for no good reason. Philip was in no state to go anywhere, certainly not across borders where a Customs officer might ask about that weapon. How did I know he really didn't have the intention of harming Milo? I thought it imperative to get that out of his head even if it involved some temporary restraints on his movements. I regret not telling you this before, but I can't believe you would have preferred a dead brother and an imprisoned son. Or perhaps I'm mistaken. In any case, all that diary business was secondary."

"Once you couldn't get your hands on it, you mean."

Minic ignored Warneke. "It was Philip I was thinking about, Elena. In a way he's as much my nephew as Milo's."

She was so stunned she could barely shake her head. "There's no end to it, is there, Stela? Even now!"

"Maybe you should have asked Philip that. Should I say it? Maybe finally somebody should. The only time you and Josef ever saw others in the world was when you needed help. Once a long while ago you needed me to get you to safety. When you were back home, the two of you couldn't wait to turn your backs on our new beginnings to come here. When that failed, you spat at Milo's offer to go back and be part of something important. His whole life, Milo has cared about the children of our country. Why he has been a teacher and why he gives us hope today. Josef? I'm afraid I must say it, Elena: A terminal narcissist whose greatest achievements were international deceits written on paper that can be torn up tomorrow. And you the faithful collaborator until even you couldn't take it anymore. Where has that outlook gotten you? I can show you. It's right across the street at the Cucina. The continent's flotsam, people with no sense of identity, no spiritual peace, just an illusion they might buy it someday with a passport that says Italy or France or the United States of America. That is not what Milo represents, not what you should have poisoned your own son into believing."

"You hypocrite!"

Minic didn't flinch. "Inadequate, yes. Do you think I'm satisfied feeding those unfortunates across the street minestrone and pasta . . . ?

The slap echoed through the cafe and out into the promenade where two women heading for a train jumped in astonishment. If he had been on his feet, Warneke thought, he would have jumped with them. The *carabinieri* looked in their direction but a second too late to be positive the disturbance had come from them or even what it was. The waiter coming back through the door with the cappuccini looked on the verge of running back inside. Minic tried to give away nothing: He took the slap as if an overdue punishment, his numb smile chasing after his reddening cheek. She was the one who was distraught, playing back the last few seconds as somebody else's. Then she reached for the only crutch she had: "Where is my son right now?"

"I don't know. And I swear to you that is the truth."

She didn't believe him, but Warneke did. She couldn't afford to believe him, but Warneke recognized loss of control (it was only a call to Franjo away, wasn't it?). "You left him with Leszek," he prompted anyway. "The Peyrot woman told me as much."

She wanted to be annoyed that he was back to Leszek instead of concentrating on her son, but then she saw Minic's agitated reaction. "Tell me he's wrong, Stela."

The waiter couldn't deposit the cappuccini and the check fast enough to get away again. Minic watched him hurry off miserably. "I haven't heard from Leszek in two days. He was supposed to call me, but he hasn't. I have no idea where he is."

She couldn't deny it any longer, but that didn't prevent her from trying. "This Leszek has taken Philip to Zagreb, is that what you're saying?"

Warneke met Minic's timid look. He knew what reply was coming because he had already used it. "Yes, that is possible," he muttered. "But I was hoping to hear from him or maybe Milo by now. As I say, it's been a couple of days."

She looked at the two of them sitting side by side. She didn't think it odd they were together. She didn't belong to either of them or anything they represented so they were the same to her. "You have killed him, haven't you?"

"Elena!"

"I know death, Stela. Remember? And we are sitting here, the three of us with our little Italian coffees, we are sitting here in death. If not Philip's, whose?"

Minic was beyond pity for her: How could she accuse him of such a thing? Warneke felt weirdly liberated by the accusation. He didn't have to disguise anymore some sanctimoniousness he seemed to have been concealing even from himself. He looked at the sugar envelopes in the middle of the table. If he picked up a couple of them and tore them open for his cappuccino, he realized, he would have been acting as abnormally normal as Leszek walking down the street with Jackiw or Peyrot going into a store to buy toiletries.

". . . I did not ask Leszek to come here," Minic was saying to her. "I told Milo he was a dangerous man, has too many masters, and could only bring trouble. But Milo sometimes listens to people who play on his impatience."

She had stopped paying attention, was back to following the people hurrying for their trains but now only to confirm that she could sit there all day without seeing a familiar face. And meanwhile her own face seemed to divide in two, with the truth crowding under her eyes. She had kept it at bay in Peyrot's apartment, then in the street getting away from the police, but now it was rising toward eruption. "I must leave here," she said almost in a whisper, grabbing her bag from the seat next to her.

She had already blanked both of them from her mind as she stood up so she really didn't see Minic's raised arm to stop her from leaving. She didn't look at all in their direction as she worked her way through the tables out to the promenade, then fell into a more willed steadiness toward the street. Warneke had a picture of her going over to the *carabinieri* and saying something about the killers of her son. But she didn't, she kept going. And that much stoicism, even with a rush to get away from them so she could give in to the eruption under her eyes, sounded a small alarm, made him wonder if more than one member of the Cicut family was suicidal.

He was debating whether to run off after her and what good that would achieve when Minic picked up his cup. "Well, as long as it's here," the priest said. But the man's hands shook so much the coffee spilled over his fingers and he had to put it immediately back down on the table; its rattle was his. He gave himself a second before saying: "She didn't say anything to those policemen, but when she gets over the shock, she will go to the Questura. If I were you, Warneke, I would buy a ticket to go home. Whatever you fancied accomplishing here is just that—a fancy."

He didn't want to talk to the priest; any conversation at all promised to give the man a legitimacy. But neither did he want to get up to chase after Cicut and test his fears about her. "Why was it so necessary to kill the boy?"

"I know nothing of the kind."

"Yes, you do."

"I know nothing of the kind."

"Is that what you told yourself after that letter bomb, too?" Minic made a second, more successful grab for his cup. "What could you possibly gain from it? What could Jelic gain from it?"

"You've answered your own question," he said tightly. "Nothing." He took a big swallow, put the cup back down, dabbed his lips with the paper napkin, then rolled the napkin into a ball. "I have work to do," he said, pushing his chair back.

"Right. The charity room. How many compartments do you have in that head of yours? It must be tiring having to keep one closed off from the next one all the time."

"Your moral superiority is curious, Warneke. You have contempt for me, you have contempt for Jelic, you have contempt for Leszek. And yet if I were to call over one of those *carabinieri* right now, they would find a weapon on you threatening the same kind of mayhem you are accusing us of. What does that suggest to you?"

Warneke was aware of the smile on his lips, and of the heavy deadness in his chest that refused to let him say "Bodies—that's the difference, priest" because that suddenly didn't seem like such a huge difference to him, either. The smile and the deadness felt emptier and emptier as he watched Minic waddle back toward the entrance.

"Signore?"

The waiter was there to remind him that somebody had to pay and it wasn't going to be the people who had already left. Warneke fingered the edge of a bill beneath the gun in his pocket, hoping the note would be big enough so that he wouldn't have to dip again. Then what sounded like two shots rang out from the street near the entrance and people began screaming and running. Warneke's first thought was that he was the cause of all the chaos. His second was to get away before somebody else thought so.

SIXTY-EIGHT

Gaetano flipped his empty pouch at the desk, but as broad as the desk was, the plastic bag skidded off it to the floor. Sylvester leaned down from his chair for it and tossed it back.

"Pardon me. Thank you."

The American wasn't interested in apologies or thank yous and went back to frowning at the office window. The afternoon glare deepened his wrinkles, sentenced them to his face forever. "In the street. Just like that."

The stem of Gaetano's pipe reeked of old puffs, the most recent of them from an hour ago after Elena Cicut had been escorted out to a cell. "There were officers on duty, but it happened too fast. Minic stepped out of the station, she was waiting, two shots to the chest. She immediately dropped her weapon to the sidewalk and surrendered. The gun apparently belonged to her husband."

"Goddamn him!"

"God may be doing that to the Reverend even as we speak."

"I mean Cicut! Him and that junk collection of his! One gun to blow his own brains out, a second for her to kill Minic, and the kid runs off with another one. And I wondered why he kept the things around! The family that shoots together . . ."

"We have confiscated the others. They don't seem to be in working order."

"You say." He could only go so far with an anger that seemed directed at himself as much as at Josef Cicut; from the moment he had entered the office, he had been cursing someone in his head. "What about the son? Anything concrete?"

Gaetano consulted with investigative etiquette. The American might have been helpful and Elena Cicut had asked to see him anyway, but that didn't mean jeopardizing the inquiry with a prejudicial word. "She seems convinced Minic is responsible for the boy's whereabouts," he compromised.

"You mean she thinks Philip is dead and that's what Minic is responsible for."

Gaetano's eye drifted to the *verbale* in the cherry folder next to his computer. He didn't like Sylvester knowing its content without even reading it; it ridiculed the whole interrogation exercise. "You tell me. You've met the man. Do you really see Minic as homicidal? A propagandist of a crude, transparent kind, yes. But a murderer?"

"The kind with just enough guilt for rationalizations."

"Excuse me?"

"What a philosopher I met recently told me. Minic didn't kill anybody, but he'll be damned if he'll let you take away his vicarious guilt for it. A thrill is a thrill."

"You mean an accomplice after the fact."

"Before, during, after—something like that."

"You're being very cryptic, Signore. And the one who has done these deeds Minic secretly admires . . .?" Sylvester shot him an offended look; he didn't want apologies, and he didn't want disingenuousness about Tomas Leszek, either. It felt best to start again to have his confidence. "According to the Signora, Minic said this Tomas Leszek has left the country. That who you mean?"

One confidence deserved another. "That's the name," he nodded. "And why shouldn't he leave? After Claudia Ricci and the Cicut boy, he's earned a vacation."

"We are not yet assuming the boy has met foul play."

"Good."

"And as for the bomb . . ."

He went back to listening only to himself. "Good."

Gaetano wished bad things for the empty pouch in front of him; he really wanted to smoke. It would have been more practical than being insulted by Sylvester's tone and throwing the man out. "All right, let's say you're right. It's a hypothesis we have been looking into and will continue to do so. But the exasperating fact is that the more we seem to identify the who of these matters, the more elusive that who becomes. It's as though we have been made part of somebody's vanity game. Peek-a-boo, peek-a-boo, I believe you say in America. We reach out and grasp only air. At least with the Signora Cicut and Father Minic we have cause and effect, deed and consequence, perpetrator and victim. The weapon, witnesses, a confession—everything an inquiry demands. It's the kind of thing they pay me for."

"And what about the whys?"

"The first time we met, I told you I was charged with investigating the killing of Signora Ricci. Now it is Father Minic's death. My brief hasn't changed."

"And everybody else will be happy."

Another consultation: Did he let names pour out of Sylvester's mouth into who knew how many microphones or did he change the subject to the floods in Pakistan? He rarely read flood stories. "Everybody else?"

"Proietti, Jelic, Leszek, that chamber of commerce where Tepedino works."

"Assuming I knew what you were talking about, you'd have to ask them."

The big man got the hint, glanced around at the walls as if expecting to see some protruding device, but then abruptly unfolded himself from his chair. He could look threatening in his flaccid way when he loomed up, and Gaetano had a spasm of doubt about having closed Govoni outside. "You can't just let it go like this. Crazy woman shoots priest in despair. That's crap."

Gaetano held on to his silence until Sylvester came out of his crouch before the desk and swiped futilely at the air. It looked like some kind of baseball throwing motion he had seen on television. "If there's more to it, we have to have proof, and not even Signora Cicut is helping us there. Is there nothing you can tell me that might explain a little better what happened today? Something she has said to you?"

"Like what? 'I'm going to kill that bastard Minic?'"

"If she said it."

"What she said was that he once saved her life."

"She mentioned that. So all the more anguish involved in going from what must have been years of gratitude to today's events."

"The anguish was her son."

"What about this Leonard Warneke she said was with them at the station? She indicated you know him, as well."

He nodded. "He's the one who found out where they were holding the boy."

"Just that?"

"She didn't need Warneke to shoot the priest."

"But in view of the man's apparent associations in his home-land that we have uncovered, I can hardly dismiss him as just some casual third to their little coffees at the station. He was no neutral observer, Signore. Do you truly believe this Warneke was irrelevant to what occurred?"

"I wasn't there."

"And I repeat: Warneke was. From what you know of him, was he as irrelevant to matters as the Signora says?"

He conceded more thought to the question. "He seems to be a man of noble goals," he smiled haplessly. "Was he irrelevant? I'd like to say no."

"Is that what you are in fact saying?"

"What I'm saying is that if he was with Elena before the shoot-ing, yes, he might have prompted her more than he was aware. Minic had never saved *his* life."

"So not totally irrelevant, then."

"Like you say, ask him."

Gaetano dropped his pipe on the desk; for some reason it didn't roll off onto the floor, too. "Unfortunately, yet another who has been eluding us. He checked out of his hotel this morning. We have an alert for him, but he has undoubtedly already left on the wings of a carrier pigeon."

"Sorry, I can't help you further."

He was sorry too, Gaetano thought. He had pulled up more than one curtain for the American newspaperman to take a peek, with nothing more than truculent evasions and indignant criticisms to show for it. Whatever he had been expecting had been much more than he had gotten. "Then perhaps I should call in the Signora. I cannot give you more than ten minutes."

Sylvester allowed another tentative smile. "Your favorite number. First at the paper's office, now here."

Gaetano got up from his desk under an irritating reminder of the incompetence around him. The imbeciles at the Termini dozing while a shooting took place under their eyes. Petrino allowing Cicut and Warneke to proceed down the staircase past him. And the other fool who had let Sylvester dance away from the crime scene with unrecorded folders. "And when you are finished," he said, stuffiness in his voice even to his own ears, "I would appreciate a list of those files you removed from your office. In the interests of the paperwork that is our only concern, you understand."

He went to the door without bothering to see Sylvester's reaction.

SIXTY-NINE

Elena walked through the office door followed by a police-woman and Gaetano's assistant Govoni. She met Sylvester's eyes directly. If she had spoken, he thought, it would have been something to yank his tail ("So what do you think about this, Charles? I'm in a real mess, no?") But she said nothing, just pressed her lips as though regretting even the thought of a flippancy and then slumped over to one of the tall chairs in front of Gaetano's desk. She had already acquired the constrained pace of a prisoner. At the door Gaetano motioned for the other two to proceed him outside. When Govoni's frown said he didn't think that a great idea, Gaetano motioned more emphatically for him and the policewoman to get out. His concession to his assistant was to close the door only three-quarters of the way behind him.

"I suppose you do not have any cigarettes."

Her dry voice in the oversized room was like a whisper in a church, embarrassing for singling him out for attention. "You need Gaetano's rank to smoke in this building, and even then you're not supposed to know about it."

She hadn't expected any other answer. "He's dead, Charles."

Sylvester took the chair next to her. He knew she wasn't talking about Minic and that it wasn't the priest who was responsible for the greater puffing of her face and the nervous lacing and unlacing of her fingers over her stomach. "Nobody knows anything for sure, Elena."

"I do. Milo was a liar even as a boy. How could the people who speak for him not be the same?"

On the way to the Viminale he had rehearsed for both her and Gaetano—smart answers to what he was certain would be asked, evasions to what he didn't want to share with either because he didn't want to be brutal or because what he knew was nobody's business but his own. But only a few feet away from her he could think only as the friend—the solicitous friend—she must have considered him for asking to see him. "You have to think of your situation right now. This could mean the rest of your life in prison. For starters you need a lawyer."

She smiled at the idea from that Cicutland distance where just because human beings in other parts of the world acted in given ways didn't mean the natives had to. "To say what, Charles? That I did not shoot Stela? Even if I wanted to say that, dozens of people saw me do it."

"Not whether you shot him. Your state of mind when you did. That makes a big difference for any court anywhere."

She didn't blink. "My state of mind was that he conspired in killing Philip and I detested him for that. All the way out of the station I kept telling myself that, legally speaking, I had probably missed my chance by not shooting him at the bar where we were sitting with his lies, that if I did anything now there would be an element of premeditation. But then I realized I had lost credibility for an impulsive act anyway by stopping off at the house for one of Josef's guns before going down to the station. So I had nothing to lose by waiting for him outside, do you see? Legally, it would not have mattered if I shot him at the bar or where I did."

"Who have you been talking to for all these legal distinctions?"

She shrugged almost comically. "I watch all your American police shows. They are always talking about those distinctions." He was supposed to smile with her, but he didn't feel like being responsible for *Law and Order*. "You must understand, Charles. Without Philip does it really make a difference if I live in a prison cell or in that apartment with all its shabby memories? What would a lawyer accomplish? Dragging everything out with objections and motions and one postponement after another? There is nothing left to postpone."

He knew he should have had an answer to that, but his mind was blank. And then it wasn't, and he wished it had remained so. "I should have never rung your bell that day. Maybe none of this would have happened."

She was baffled. "Why ever do you say that?"

"I don't know. It just feels like it all started then."

She thought he was funny. "You will have to explain that to me. Josef was already dead. Philip was already gone. Stela was already plying me for that diary on Milo's orders. Even that Leszek was already planning to kill that poor woman in your office. What exactly is it you started, Charles?"

He shook his head. It felt like the closest thing he could do to not feeling small and mean and with it all also presumptuous. She aimed her pensive smile at the window—at the outside, he realized, she wouldn't be seeing too much more of. "You do not want responsibility for death, Charles. You do not want it, either, for that deadness before death. It is not a badge of honor. It does not make you wiser and more mature. It certainly does not make you anybody's hero. I am sure you have your own problems to take care of back in New York. Have your vacation here and then go back and take care of them. I am sure there are people back there who will appreciate your help more than I am in any position to. No?"

Her finality seemed to leave him nothing to lose, and the question—one he had never really wanted to explore before—spurted out of him. "Why me, Elena? Of all the people he could have sent that diary to, why me?"

She really wasn't all that interested. "That letter you showed me—didn't he explain it there? You being a journalist?"

"And he never met any others in the last god knows how many years? Did my name ever even come up in your conversations with him since I left Italy?"

Her eyes admitted something was off—and if she had nothing else to think about, she would focus on it. "Not very often, no. You knew Josef. When you were not there in front of him . . ."

"No, I did not know Josef. That's my point. Why me?"

"Is it so important now?"

"To me, yes."

She shrugged; in some crucial way he had already left the office and she was back to being alone. "I do not know what to tell you, Charles. Perhaps because you were the first journalist to occur to him, nothing more than that. And perhaps he told Gruber that he was going to send it to you, which meant that Milo and everybody else would find out soon enough. Josef had come to despise my brother, Charles, and also to fear him. I wonder if he had any company at all near the end but that contempt and that fear. Maybe you reminded him of better times, like you reminded me of them. I cannot apologize for him, but you were his weapon. Was he so wrong?"

There was blank and there was blank. And then, Sylvester thought, there was the vacuum he was suddenly flailing in. What had Bruno said about his doctor? The more you let people talk, the more you wondered why you did?

SEVENTY

As soon as Bell saw the obituary, he knew his day, his week, much of his foreseeable future had taken an awkward turn. What passed for consolation was the odds he wasn't alone. If Broderick hadn't already rousted him out of bed, it had to be because he was busy stammering to pinstriped suits in Washington about the little piece of creativity that had undoubtedly sprung from the word processor of Charles Sylvester.

Diplomatic circles have been stirring with rumors for some days that Ambassador Cicut took to his grave documents indicating that a prominent politician in the Balkans today played a major role in one of the region's bloodiest atrocities during the wars of the Nineties. The evidence was said to be in the form of diaries maintained during the Balkan hostilities by Ambassador Cicut himself and others. There has been no official confirmation of the existence of these diaries or how and where they might have been compiled, let alone of the charges said to be contained in them.

Bell swallowed more orange juice pulp and studied the three sentences again for internal contradictions. He didn't see any. "Diplomatic circles" were invisible bullshit. If Sylvester said his "rumors" had come from them, there was no way short of rocketing up to the ozone layer to inspect all the exhaust there for puncturing his claims. And that "prominent" Balkan politician? Gee, who could that be? And the "others" touch was good, too. Who knew how many still living Josef Cicuts were roaming the globe ready to swear they had witnessed bloodbaths ordered by Milovan

Jelic? Best back away from the butcher before one of them came forward with the grisly details supporting Cicut.

Who had never recorded anything in the first place.

Bell put the paper aside on the kitchen table and went over to the coffee maker for his second cup of the morning. He really had nothing better to do except drink coffee, see what other inventions he could find in the paper, and wait for Broderick's call. With Catherine off to work, there was no hurry to shower and dress and head off her cracks that he was too ripe by half. He could be a man at leisure with nothing more dramatic before him than *Perry Mason* reruns. That might have been what Broderick and the pinstriped suits had in mind for him anyway and for more than a single day, so maybe he should get into practice. Gratitude for past accomplishments was just that—in the past. For sure, they would find a way to fault him for Sylvester's lark. Something to do with the secretary maybe, how he had persuaded himself too quickly that she didn't speak Serbian, couldn't translate the diary, and represented no threat. He didn't know what that had to do with anything, but in Broderick's place he would have explored that territory for possibilities. A waste of time pointing out that the diary had contained no genocide accusations or that Cicut hadn't taken anything to the grave with him or that those so-called diplomatic circles weren't talking about anything but the next Olympics; reality represented only insubordinate argument. No, if he was going to object to any reprimand he heard on the phone, it would have to be with the same *Alice in Wonderland* gusto with which he was condemned. What had that cake said? "Eat me?" How about just "Fuck me?"

At least the sugar gods were good to him: They waited until he had stirred them into his coffee before allowing his phone to buzz. He waited three, then opted for four, buzzes until he was convinced Broderick was beet red. But when he picked up, he was the one caught off guard because it wasn't Broderick.

"Have you seen it, Walter?" an apoplectic Applebaum demanded.

The wonders of the Internet, Bell thought. It allowed people to be annoying even when they were three thousand miles away in the pre-dawn hours.

"This is Sylvester. Bet on it."

"Relax, Claude. Who reads obituaries?"

"People who're going to die, that's who! This wasn't supposed to happen, Walter. You know it wasn't supposed to happen."

"No, it never is."

"What? What's that mean?"

"Things are never supposed to happen. I wonder how many civilizations down through history have had that same complaint."

"I'm not up to being witty, Walter. There's no way the Foreign Desk isn't already squealing about this and that's going to come back to me."

"Take your foot off the gas pedal, Claude. You're not their first concern."

"How can I not be, for Christ sake? My title is Roving Correspondent. It's there under my byline every edition."

"Oh, *that* Foreign Desk!"

Silence, then with more strained patience: "You're not reassuring me, Walter. Porterfield's going to want to know why I didn't hear these same so-called rumors in these same so-called diplomatic circles."

"Let me count the ways. How about because you're on vacation on the Pacific Coast, the rumors have only circulated in the last couple of days, there are no rumors to begin with, and these diplomatic circles are just in Sylvester's brain. Think something in there will get you off the hook with Porterfield?"

"In a word, no! The least he'll want is for me to make some calls."

"Well, there you go, like Marshal McCloud used to say. You can go back to him and say it's all bullshit."

More silence, then what sounded like a dying man's last sigh: "You're not following me here, Walter. As soon as I make a single phone call like that, there *are* rumors. They're nine hours ahead of Oregon time over there. Think they haven't already seen this and aren't scrambling? Think the German foreign ministry isn't wondering why the ambassador from Lichtenstein has heard what it hasn't heard? The ambassador from Spain isn't sulking that he's not on the grapevine like the ambassador from Portugal? The second I start calling around, it becomes fact for everybody. This is a goddamn snowball coming down the mountain and guess who's standing at the foot of the mountain. Give it a shot, Walter. One guess."

Bell would have said himself, but he also couldn't dispute the man's paranoid logic. He probably would have heard the same panic eavesdropping on Broderick's meetings with the uber-Brodericks in Washington. "On the other hand . . . I hear your frustration and I sympathize, Claude. But what is it you're asking? I can't delete the Internet and I can't go around buying up every paper on the newsstand."

"I know, I know."

"So give me a request I can pass along."

"Goddamn it, Walter. There's got to be something you can do."

"And I'll put my mind to it as soon as I hang up. And I expect you to do the same thing. Grab that rod and reel of yours, go out on your lake and meditate on the problem while you wait for those salmon to grab your line. Call me as soon as you come up with something. I should be home all day."

He clicked off Oregon and all its early morning darkness and returned to his coffee. It didn't taste as sweet as it should have. The sugar gods weren't as pleased with him as he had thought. He felt only a little better reading about the attorney and the rodeo cowboy who shared the Obituary page with Cicut. Being frazzled by Applebaum wasn't much compared to the mourning in the households of the lawyer and the cowboy. There were probably even kids crying in those houses.

When Broderick finally called, he didn't sound much different from Applebaum except for one thing: he had a definite request to pass along. "Call off your friend over there. It'll only aggravate matters."

"I'm pretty sure that horse is out of the stable, Frank."

"Well, damn it, find out!"

"I already know."

"You've heard from him?"

"*Not* heard from him. If there was a problem, he would have been in contact. Otherwise, assume operation completed. The guy likes to work in negatives. You can see where that would make him comfortable."

"This is bad, Walter. Very bad."

"Yeah, I can see that."

"With that crap in the paper this morning, absolutely everybody is going to be adding up two and two and pointing toward our friend. Any hope of having exclusive leverage with him . . ."

"Gone."

"You don't have to sound so smug about it."

"I'm just sorry I wasn't more persuasive talking you out of the idea."

"Good try, Walter, but this isn't being recorded."

He doubted that; maybe not recorded by Broderick, but there were a lot of Frank Brodericks. "You know I wasn't enthusiastic, Frank. But forget that. The question is, what now? There's always another door, right?"

Broderick sounded almost appeased. "Good. Unlike your friend, let's accent the positive here. And there's more than one presidential candidate there."

"Yeah, but this one has a temper and has already sent one message that he didn't like being dicked around with."

"The brutal act of a terrorist, and we have a policy against terrorism in this country. And that doesn't apply just to the ones who read the Koran . . ."

Bell stopped listening after the second word he anticipated from Broderick's mouth. It was depressing having a conversation with himself. As he put his cup back down on the table, he thought of how excited he and Catherine had been when the marble slab had been delivered from Carrara. Anyone who visited the Bells had to be dragged into the kitchen and hear the story of how they had run into the Carrara importer and talked him into half his usual price for the table. No question, the Bells had been insufferable. For weeks they had been squeamish about even laying plates on the thing so as not to ruin it . . . No, not exactly. It hadn't been about not ruining it, but about not showing it enough respect. Dirty dishes or clean dishes had made no difference.

There was a regal style to the slab that should have been uncluttered, pure, visible to everyone only for itself.

Luckily, they had gotten over that intimidation. Sometimes he wondered whether deep down Catherine didn't miss the old Formica table. He had been tempted to ask her more than once, but had held off in case she gave him the wrong answer.

SEVENTY-ONE

Sylvester pictured the *Post* office mobbed with dozens of Merriweathers. The more he filled the emptiness around him to fantasize about competitors peeking over his shoulder to see if he had details they didn't, could imagine their groans of envy, the less he had to think about what he was evacuating in the late afternoon heat. He didn't want to be alone typing out the journalism school verbs he always taunted Patricia about (something else he had to stop when he got home). It was spooky. Facts had never felt so much like laboring up one desert sand dune only to find another awaiting. The Stazione Termini? Yes, that was the place where trains came from and choo-chooed off to near and far places on the continent. Piero Gaetano? Yes, that was the name of the Italian police official handling the investigation into the shooting of Father Stela Minic. Cicut? Yes, that was also the name of the one-time ambassador whose death in Germany had stirred so many of those special rumors in diplomatic circles. Were the deaths of Cicut and Minic related? It couldn't be ruled out; only further developments would tell. Was Charles Lawrence Sylvester suggesting his imagination could be those further developments? No, he wasn't suggesting that. He had exhausted that vein. That had been part of the parallel life he led thinking he was achieving something while those having to survive within the earth's dimensions had been carrying on with their shootings and surrenders and imprisonments. For himself there was merely carbon monoxide hypocrisy—colorless, odorless, completely undetectable, but still toxic. He just wasn't sure where it was coming from.

The End.

Finito.

30, as the old newspapermen had written at the bottom of their copy.

His walk back to the hotel felt like a perp walk: He waited for somebody to shout out an aggressive question that would ricochet around in his lungs to remind him why he had become a center of attention. He liked the sight of Romolo scurrying over to the desk to hand him his room key—one person in Rome who had as much to be embarrassed about as he did. He made sure to keep it that way by pretending not to notice the man's extra-toady smile. He was so good at ignoring it that he reached the staircase before Romolo's call penetrated. The piece of paper being waved after him was a message that had been left for him.

The note was unsigned, and that arrogance immediately equaled Warneke. All it said was: "I TOO MUST GO FURTHER THAN JOHN WARREN." What was that supposed to mean? They had talked about the English don John Warren in the car outside the house where Philip Cicut had been held. He had told Warneke the story about the stillborn obituary, and Warneke had told him he had been made for fools' errands. And then? Then chitty chitty bang bang, something about having to do more with his life than John Warren had managed in life *or* death. And so? So now Warneke was going to do more with his life than John Warren had? Good for Leonard Warneke. Maybe John Warren would give him a passing grade.

The phone in his room gave him only until he had closed the door behind him and dropped the key and the note on the bureau. Porterfield had evidently skipped one of his fund-raising evenings at the Met for staying at work to read dispatches.

"Is this for real, Charley?"

"You prefer fiction?"

Wrong crack. "There's some thought that's what the obits have been lately."

"I'd hate to ruin old Claude's fishing."

"First things first. She shot him in the middle of the train station?"

"More or less."

"And it's the widow of . . ."

"From the obit, yeah. You should get the Foreign Desk on it."

Throat clearing. "One guy from the Foreign Desk seems to be on it already. And with a lot more detail than I've seen on the wire services. All they have is the names."

"I mean . . ."

"I know what you mean. It's yours."

"What's mine? The rest is going to be by the numbers. Trial dates . . ."

"And connecting all the dots to the bombing?"

"If there's a connection to be made."

"Huh! I wonder where I got the idea somebody thinks there *is* a connection."

"Why you should have the Foreign Desk on it."

"How much more can they be on it than you are? What do I have to do—ask you in Italian? You want to make that favor you're doing me a little more open-ended?"

"You asked me to fill in for a few days, Kev. That's open-ended enough. And you also have a correspondent here."

"Stop dicking around. The next time Roenicke goes back, it'll be to pack up his furniture. We both know that. Stalled enough now to give me an answer?"

Porterfield was right: Having to think, just having to admit he had to think, was stalling. Flopping down on the bed, a bone-deep weariness seemed to have been waiting for him to surrender to it.

"I've got to know, Charley."

It was in front of him. Joey Bacsik had been the first to ask, eons ago when Joey Bacsik had still been on the planet, and now at last he could have answered the old son of a bitch. "Ever get tired of that incomplete past hanging over you, Kev?"

"I'm more worried about the incomplete present right now."

"Stop being a hardass."

Porterfield braked down. "I guess."

"Well, sometimes circles need to be closed. I think that's why I'm here instead of France or Disneyland."

"Let me take a wild guess. Felicia."

It didn't sound as embarrassing coming from someone else. "Never toast your marshmallows with martyrdom. The damn fire never goes out."

"I haven't seen that."

"Of course not. I'm suave and responsible. But at some point you have to stop blaming the other guy for what you've done or not done."

"And I thought it was just me you were blaming for Applebaum."

"Yeah, that's on my list, too. Things I haven't done and should have."

Back to the accelerator. "Okay, this is all great for you and your middle-aged awareness. I hope you have a big truth session and it all works out. In the meantime, you have a few bodies and a lot of geopolitical insinuations around you. Insinuations you've been the first to make. Is this really the time for therapy confessions?"

Yes, it was, he thought. The hypocrisy wasn't all *that* colorless and odorless.

Porterfield heard the silence. "Okay, it is. And I'll indulge you for another second, like I have nothing better to do but worry about your career. You can't tell me you don't think you're running in place back here with the obits. How many dead people you going to say the same thing about?"

"Some are worth remembering by more than their friends and families."

"And we can do that without you supervising it. Think about it, Charley. Let's say for another 48 hours. Then I've got to move. I've got too many candidates for too many posts and I'm beginning to hear the murmuring of a lynch mob outside my office door. In the meantime, a follow-up tomorrow and the next day. I want to stay ahead of the wires and your office host over there."

"For the website?"

"That's up to you. You're not Roenicke."

"I'm not Applebaum either."

"Okay. Now you're negotiating. He stays out of it."

"Now, next week, and next month?"

"Now, next week, and next month.'

"That a promise?"

"When he comes back, he can worry about Norway."

"You're not answering me, Kev."

"Yes, it's a promise. We can talk about it when you wind up things there."

"That's not an answer, either."

"Jesus, if I didn't know you better, I'd think you wanted something."

Sylvester sympathized: He didn't know himself too well, either. When was the last time he had wanted something? "Enough of Applebaum's bullshit, Kev. Is it really doing you all that good at this point?"

Silence. Then: "You can benefit from anything if you have the stamina."

"If you want to keep running on fumes. Take it from somebody who knows: Feeling that tired all the time just isn't natural."

Silence again. Then: "You hold up your end and we'll talk in 48 hours."

He sat staring at the phone after he hung up. He wanted to be thrilled. He wanted to be thankful. He wanted to feel like a shit. *Some*body had died for his sins. Stela Minic? Claudia Ricci? Joey Bacsik? Josef Cicut? Maybe Elena in jail or Eddie Roenicke back in New York or Myra Roenicke having to choose between packing up the furniture or getting a divorce. There were so many candidates he felt universally sponsored.

Or he just needed the company of all of them, as he had needed a mob back in the *Post* office doing his story. The living, the dead, or the fantastical—whoever was available. He didn't want to be alone as he punched out Cynthia's cell number and debated whether Patricia or Nick should get the call after that.

SEVENTY-TWO

etrino had never seen a dead body before, not one with its throat slashed anyway, and he had to call on all his fortitude to stand erect over the blood puddle while the medical examiner went about her computations. Sensing an imminent retching, Govoni cleared his throat for the officer to look his way for permission to go back up to the roadway. Gaetano wanted none of it. "Leave him alone," he muttered through his pipe. "If he can't deal with corpses, let him grow vegetables."

Govoni looked disappointed—humanly disappointed—in him, but Gaetano didn't care much about his feelings, either. He was back to being the dog resisting uselessly against his leash. He had no doubt about the identity of the young man curled up under the billboard and already saw himself in his office waiting for Elena Cicut to be brought to him so he could break the news to her. She had been only too right about her son. Did that make shooting Minic self-defense or revenge or something in between in the penal code? He didn't know. Fortunately, that wasn't part of his job.

"There's this, Inspector."

The medical examiner Vannucci came out of Philip Cicut's jacket pocket with her tweezers holding up what appeared to be a letter on a sheet of yellow legal paper. She deposited it in a transparent envelope so it could be read through the plastic, zippered it across the top, and passed it up through Petrino. Even before taking it, Gaetano knew it was another board game piece, the way the body itself was one in having been dumped off a roadway but not *that* far off so it wouldn't take forever to be discovered. All that was missing from the scene, he thought, was a pair of dice to get the game under way. What he could make out of the crabbed handwriting through the plastic, he was sure, they had been supposed to find. Why else would it have been in Italian?

> *Mother, I have gone to Zagreb. I cannot let the man who is responsible for father's death get away with it because he claims family ties. When has that ever mattered with us? . . .*

And nothing more. A jagged question mark to make it seem as though Philip Cicut had been interrupted and had barely had time to pocket what he had written. No wallet, no bus pass, but a half-letter the killer had implausibly missed. A half-letter from a Croatian son to a Croatian mother in Italian. Even for a mocking game, it was insulting.

"That politician Jelic is his uncle, isn't he?" Govoni, hovering over his shoulder, asked. "Think he means him?"

Gaetano handed the envelope to Govoni without answering and took another look at the billboard above them. It was intensely lacking in irony. The brunette with the tits peering through the sides of her black strapless dress for Parmalat might have been aiming for subliminal breast-milk associations, but there was no suggestion of the world Philip Cicut and Tomas Leszek inhabited. Surely there had to have been some new film with a title like *The Ambassador's Son* or *The Dead Foreigner*. Had Leszek been in such a frantic rush to dump the body that he couldn't find a more sardonic billboard or did the man simply lack a sense of occasion?

"We'll have to show this to his mother," Govoni said. "To be sure he wrote it."

"Go to the apartment first. See if there's any sample of his handwriting around. I'd like to know the answer before I ask her."

"But we already know it, right?"

"What we know is never enough."

Govoni's expression said he didn't understand, but he slipped the envelope into his pocket and glanced around like somebody who thought he had seen everything there was to see and wanted to get on to something else. "Start back?"

Gaetano was about to say yes when Vannucci stood up from the body and tore her Latex gloves off. She was tall, thin, very leggy, not unlike the Parmalat model on the billboard above him. There was also something familiar about her light blue blazer and jeans, but it refused to identify itself in his brain.

"You don't like going around killing priests," Govoni said, leading the trudge through the weeds back up to the car, "but this Minic had a few things to answer for."

And then the thought dawned. "Bravo, Matteo!"

"What did I say? About Minic?"

"What I've been trying to figure out. Why priests look more like priests in business suits than when they're wearing cassocks."

Govoni made an effort to look interested. "Why's that, Inspector?"

"Because when they wear cassocks they look like what we expect priests to look like. We can forget about them, stick them into their little corner in our minds. But when they wear a layman's suit, it's always ill-fitting and emphasizes what little fashion sense they have. They pound it home how unfit for the world they are!"

Govoni played back the words, confirmed that he had understood them, then still looked baffled. "And so?"

Gaetano waited for the man's bafflement to ease. But it didn't. He could have stood where he was all day before the same expression of bewilderment. He had to try again. "People shouldn't come out of their pigeonholes, Matteo! It only makes for a lot of commotion and in the end makes everything worse! False first impressions, illusions, deceits, all those diversionary things. So much time wasted when the truth is so simple. Cassocks for everybody!"

Govoni thought another second, then glanced furtively toward Vannucci, Petrino, and the others still around the body. "I got it," he said lowly. "A homicide is a homicide. It has nothing to do with anything else. Count on me."

Gaetano started to shake his head before the man's obtuseness. But it refused to shake. It was as though his head had been severed from the rest of him.

SEVENTY-THREE

"Gianni is very annoyed with you about that obituary."

"I didn't know he was a reader."

"Things are brought to his attention."

"What's he got to be annoyed about?"

"Some people think he's the 'diplomatic circles' you mentioned. Naturally, they suspect some labyrinthian Italian political objectives."

"Deep thinkers."

"It hasn't helped Gianni."

"What can I say?"

"Why did you do it, Charley?"

"Do what? I wrote what I heard."

"What your left ear heard from the right one?"

"A very reliable source."

"Between us. For the sake of argument."

"For the sake of argument?"

"If you had to have a flight of fancy, say."'

"Well, let's think. You knew Cicut. He had a broomstick up his ass. What better legacy than sticking it up other people's?"

"I see."

"For the sake of argument."

"That hasn't changed—the more uncertain you are, the cruder you become."

She might have been inventing that, maybe not. Either way, he had foreseen her long-suffering looks from the second he had

accepted the invitation to be a guest of the Proiettis at the Senator's favorite Tuscan restaurant; there would have been no Felicia
without them. And how could Da Arnaldo *not* have been the Senator's favorite Tuscan restaurant? The lighting was fashionably
dim, the menu didn't stoop to the gutter practice of listing prices,
and the pervasive aroma of refrigerated cold cuts and artichokes
felt monitored by a state-run thermostat. Most of all, the place
was only a few doors down from the Senate, making it natural for
Proietti to be on display as much as the boar heads on the walls.
In fifteen minutes four people had come over to pay respects to
the Senator and his elegant wife. One of them had even disguised
his curiosity about the American sitting between them.

"I think they're talking about you."

Sylvester glanced over at the nook in the rear where Proietti
was still bent over to catch the muttered wisdom at the prime
minister's table. Protocol had demanded the Senator be the one
doing the table hopping where the head of the government was
concerned, and he had been getting an earful for his courtesy.
Even Mrs. Prime Minister and the others at the table had tired of
waiting for the audience to end and had rippled off into their own
conversations.

"I have more readers here than in New York."

"And for what? For pigeons in the piazza, nothing more. You
clap your hands and they all go fluttering up in the air for a few
seconds. Then they come down again and go right back to pecking
around the way they had been. So what have you accomplished
with your little noise?"

"And that contents you?"

"I'm just being realistic."

"Of course you are. But I wish every once in a while people
would say, I don't know, 'I'm just being a rug merchant,' But
never. It's always 'I'm just being realistic.'"

"Experience is experience."

He could have let it go. He should have let it go. And that
seemed like two good reasons not to let it go. "How do you do it,
Felicia? Is it really all polished coffee tables and matching coast-
ers and the right anecdote for the right guest?"

"If you need that caricature."

"I used to think that was just a shell you'd lose if things got serious."

"How nice."

"I could yell, 'Hey, come on out, Felicia. This is really serious. Pay attention.' And you would! Not a second thought about how begonias brightened up the living room."

He had his crudity, she had her neck roll. "We can't all be successful missionaries. Forgive me for disappointing you."

"Come out, come out, the real Felicia! Come out, come out!"

"When the crude doesn't work, the clown does?"

"I'm versatile."

"And predictable."

Even to himself, he thought. "But back when, we both had our hopes, right? For what exactly? Do you remember?"

"I don't see the point of this conversation, Charley."

"Was it for the usual things—we'd grow, prosper, and do everything you're supposed to do for a better tomorrow for us and the kids? Or was it just the hope that someday we'd be able to overcome ourselves?"

She winced. "That's a new one."

"But it's true. We were always letting ourselves get in the way of each other and then going off into a corner and regretting it, promising not to do it again. We were going to be perfect people, for Patricia and Nick as much as for ourselves. But in the end we both accepted us as us. I even got the kids out of it."

"Back to being crude."

"I benefited. I'm admitting it."

"So why question it now?"

He wouldn't have minded having Porterfield back on the line so he would feel less embarrassed about telling her why. "Ego, I suppose," he said instead. "You were more you than I'd counted on."

"Even more charming than advertised?"

"Much more."

She hadn't wanted that answer, even sardonically. She swept at invisible crumbs in front of her. "You're talking—at least I think you are—about yesterday's vanities. By the time you realize that's all they are, it's too late for anything but to keep going. So don't get stalled now, Charley. It won't get you anywhere."

"I like to close circles."

"I think we have."

"No, because underneath all the bullshit I still don't understand it and I know sure as hell Patricia and Nick don't."

"Don't be so sure about that. We've talked about it more than once. I don't find either one of them stunted."

"I'm not talking about a quick lunch with them in Rockefeller Center every couple of years. They're your kids, Felicia."

"And I don't love them any less for that. I gave them what they needed when they were young enough. If they need more now, they should be adult enough to ask me for it. They have their telephones and computers. But they should also be grateful I never allowed us to use them as an excuse for the two of us becoming miserable."

"And no chance we wouldn't have?"

"You want me to say no after all this time?"

"No."

"Good. That will make this dinner less awkward."

"And Patricia and Nick . . .?"

"It's always been about us, Charley, not them."

"For Christ sake, they weren't just glasses on the table."

"No, and that made it hard. But one of us had to make a decision, and you weren't going to leave them. So I made the decision. For them as well as us."

"And we were doomed just because you decided we were?"

She had to be sure they weren't being overheard from the adjoining tables. When she looked back, his disingenuousness had won her more space. "What does the ostrich see when it buries its head in the ground?" she asked icily. "You never told me. But no matter how much you may have wanted to deny it, you were relieved, too. You didn't have to pretend to respect me anymore."

"Those magazine . . .?"

"I'm not just talking about what you called my fluff writing. There was a whole world of . . . lack of respect behind that.

Respect for me as more than the person who shared your table and bed and children. There were the serious people up here and then there was Felicia and her kind down here. They were colorful, taught you things you would have never thought about otherwise, but at bottom . . . what? Local color. Cultural adventure. Helpful insights. You detested the Applebaums and didn't think much more of Roenicke, but even they were up here in a way because they worried about what was in the head of the president of Moldova and I didn't."

"You've sure made up for that."

"Yes, I have. But stick to the easy version, Charley: How I wanted to move on with my life and how that didn't include you, Patricia, and Nicky. We need our enemies. It makes everything easier."

"Not for the kids it doesn't."

"Get out of their way and let them tell me that." For the flash of a second her eyes softened in dare, trotting out the wary foxes she had once loosed in bed waking up in the morning. Then they looked away from him to focus on the arriving Proietti. "Marco doesn't have cabinet meetings that long, Gianni," she rasped.

Proietti sat down and flapped his napkin over his lap too forcefully. "Marco doesn't like disorder, and he thinks Charley has caused some."

"Not to worry. The pigeons always land again."

She shook her head at Proietti's quizzical look and he didn't insist. "A good Brunello, no?" he asked, retreating to his wine. "There are better, but why let pretense spoil satisfaction?" He was satisfied enough with a sip to get to the message he was carrying. "Never underestimate the twists of the Italian political mind, Charley. What you maybe saw as a little fiction writing about Cicut, the gentleman over there views differently. Two calls with Washington can do that for you."

"We all seem to be assuming I write fiction."

"Yes, let's assume that, okay?"

"Because old Marco's so on top of reality?"

"He likes to think so."

"For the sake of argument, Charley," she purred.

She had won the first round and she knew it. He didn't have to be a bad sport on top of everything else. "And how does Marco see things?"

"He thinks it was Washington that put you up to that obituary."

"Of course he does. To accomplish what?"

Proietti shrugged; he hadn't gotten that far. "Do the specifics—what policy, what image, what country—matter in the end? Why I feel a great relief when I burrow into the banal excesses of the seventeenth century. Blackmail, extortion, guilt—things you can put a price on. Today it's all abstract posturing, the potential power to control energies. Like an electric utility. You can't see it, just feel it."

She put her wine glass back down on the table with a thud. "If you don't want to be understood, Gianni, say so and we'll order. But Charley involved in some palace intrigue is ridiculous. I hope you told Marco that."

He *hadn't* invented their marriage, Sylvester thought: It had been a long time since she had replaced the foxes in her eyes with wolves and made it clear to outsiders that she wasn't going to take prisoners.

"Of course I did. I assured him Charley was not for sale, even for a few sentences. I was right to say that, wasn't I, Charley?"

"Don't start doubting it now."

"Then tell me how you are so well informed. I don't think you're psychic."

"You lost me."

Even in the restaurant's candlelight dimness Proietti paled. There was an announcement coming, and he gave away its source by having to stop himself from glancing behind him to the back table. "They found the Cicut boy's body this afternoon," he said falteringly. "There will be a press conference at the Viminale tomorrow."

Sylvester registered Felicia's look of horror and then her *"Dio!"* It was better than paying attention to the frisson in his forearms that wasted no time spreading up to his shoulders. "They're sure?"

"Yes."

"How can they be sure?"

"They're sure. Believe me."

He didn't know why he should; if he didn't believe it, he wouldn't have to picture Elena being delivered the news in some grim dank cell. At best he was hearing things third hand, wasn't he? "Where did they find it?" He told himself the *it* was a detail and his job was details. There would have to be a call to Gaetano first. He couldn't just take what he was hearing on the word of Proietti or of a prime minister

Then again, he wasn't paying much attention to what Proietti was jabbering on about in reply. Just more details—so many particulars that his prime minster friend Marco had imparted before ordering his pheasant.

"Charley?"

She put her hand out atop his. Exactly what he didn't need. When had her freckles started looking more like liver spots? His body felt like it was in one dimension, hers in another, and he didn't want reminders of either. It *wasn't* them against all outsiders. It hadn't been in a very long time—back in the years when Philip Cicut had still been alive and had been playing on the floor of Nick's bedroom with his trucks and making crashing noises with his mouth and not knowing how soon he would be dead. And Nick being so close to it? How much of a crapshoot was it that they were talking about Philip instead of Nick? That was another reason for wanting to give in to a shiver. "I'm okay," he said, not moving his hand until she withdrew hers.

"But you expected something like this," Proietti pressed. "Wasn't that what you were trying to say that night in my study?"

The Senator wanted to look solicitous; a little encouragement and his eyes would have teared. Her look, though, was an accusation. He had known something that might have prevented Philip's death? "Was I?"

"I think so. And I should have listened."

She couldn't countenance the idea that he had done less than he might have done, but she still wanted a target. "I knew that boy an hour after he was born, Gianni," she said almost in a hiss. "When the nurses brought him in to Elena. How can you talk about him like he's only some . . . political oversight?"

"*Per piacere, Felicia.*"

His brusqueness froze her. She waited for an apology, at least a look of regret, but neither came, just a pained show of impatience behind another sip of wine, a pregnant invitation to sit quietly or leave the table because he had gotten to a crucial question for their guest and didn't want to be interrupted asking it. Her glinting eyes needed only another moment to decide what to do. Reminding herself of the ears at the nearby tables, she straightened her shoulders to regal dignity, palmed her bag off the table, and stood up. "Excuse me, *signori.*"

Proietti knew better than to object, to confirm for the curious that there was an argument going on. He looked after her until he was sure she was heading toward the back; there could be no gossip about her going to the bathroom. "That was insensitive of me," he conceded. "Of course she's shocked. I forgot how long she knew the boy. But there's more involved here, Charley. Nobody wants other people's wars being fought in their country." He was being so earnest he didn't see Felicia take a U-turn at the bathrooms and head back toward the front door, the stateliest of acknowledgments for somebody who greeted her at one of the tables she passed. "Yes, I should have paid more attention to what you were trying to tell me and Gaetano. All those people in the house that night distracted me. But is there anything else we should know?"

"Why ask me? First I've invented things, then your friend over there is happy inventing bigger things. Go ask him."

"I didn't say I agreed with him."

"You haven't said you don't, either."

"Seriously, Charley."

He tried to picture where *Seriously* was. In a cavern under Da Arnaldo? In an attic above it? Or maybe outside where Felicia was going? He should have made an effort to find out; for sure *Seriously* wasn't in front of him. "Give me a minute."

"Where are you going?"

"I knew Philip, too. Same hospital room."

Sanctimoniousness was owed its due.He assumed the eyes that had followed Felicia to the bathroom were on his back to the front door and that they weren't looking at a friend. He hoped so, anyway.

After the chattering and air conditioning of the restaurant, the muggy night quiet outside was like falling into a vacuum bag. Felicia was across the street accepting a light from a couple who had given her a cigarette. She looked fragile in her lemon dress getting the light from the man's unsteady hand. Sylvester waited until his insides resettled and the couple passed on before crossing over to her.

"You shouldn't be out here," she snapped, puffing but not inhaling. "It looks bad."

"He'll get over it."

Her eyes glistened in the street light; one thing she would never get over was being cavalier about her reputation. But then she remembered why she had marched out of the restaurant. "What in god's name did Philip get himself into?"

"He thought he owed somebody for the way his father ended up, and they saw him coming. He never had a chance."

"Just like that. Alive and then dead."

"With a lot of useless hopes in between. Mine, too."

She didn't want to think about what that answered. "Did the whole family just go crazy? They weren't like that when we knew them."

"That was a long time ago, Felicia."

"But there should have been *some* sign of all this madness."

"Maybe there was. Did we want to see it? Would we have recognized it for what it was if we did see it? Or maybe somebody just threw a new stick of dynamite through the window. Yesterday isn't today."

"Very philosophical."

He thought of sitting in the car with Warneke and talking about John Warren. John Warren had led to nothing twice: first back at the office doing the obituary and then looking for Philip Cicut on Via Guido Reni. He didn't want to be philosophical. A third fiasco wouldn't have been a charm. "Any calendar will tell you the same thing."

She blew more smoke angrily into the night. "I can't imagine what it's like to be Elena now. First that insane thing she did, now this." She handed the cigarette to him before he had to reach for it. "I would go see her, but I would have nothing to say and I'm sure she would resent it after so long."

His lungs could have done without the drag, but it was too late to complain after the fact. He seemed to have had that sensation a lot lately.

"Do you think I should visit her?"

"No."

She hadn't expected so much finality. "Because it would upset her?"

"That's what you just said, isn't it? Why else?"

She scrutinized his face for the else; she found it fast enough. "You don't believe me. You think someone in my place wouldn't dare visit her, that I'm just talking."

"I thought we were talking about Elena and Philip." He gave her back the cigarette, averting the petulance she was aiming at him. "You're right about Gianni. We shouldn't leave him hanging out to dry like this."

"Will you visit her?"

"I already have. But probably again, yes."

"Because it's part of your job for Porterfield?"

"Yeah, that dirty thing."

"I didn't mean . . ."

"Yes, you did, and why not? What other interest would I have? Who the hell are we, Felicia? Two people standing in the street who want to have great, swelling feelings for things but who between them can't even smoke a cigarette. So what do we do? You'll work it out for yourself like you always do. Me, it's doing what I do best, the only thing I know how to do. And even that I've spent years putting into holes and graves and tombs and mausoleums and just memories. So maybe it's time to get back on track, find out what living people want and scheme for and despair over not getting. Some of them will be bullshitters and dreamers, and the rest may be altogether dangerous, but maybe I should at least find out and let others in on it and hope they give a damn."

"They won't."

"I know. You're being realistic again. And probably you're right. But at least mark the starting line and let everybody go from there."

It took another moment for her to understand. "You're leaving New York!"

"Like you said inside, finally getting out of the kids' way. I talked to them last night. They can't wait to get me out the front door."

"To go where?"

"Don't worry. Not here. This is just a chit I have with Porterfield."

"He should give you whatever you want."

"That many Pulitzers I haven't won."

"But you have him over a barrel and he knows it."

"I wouldn't go that far."

He felt X-rayed by her stare. "That's why you came, isn't it?"

"You looked upset."

"I don't mean out here to the street, I mean Rome. I really wondered about that. You had such a burning desire to see Bruno Lepri? You couldn't buy him a plane ticket and put him up for a couple of weeks? Then inside with all that talk about getting out of your own way. You're finally divorcing me, aren't you, Charley?"

"You never got your copy of the papers?"

"I mean *you* are finally divorcing *me*."

"I never thought of it that way."

"No?" She tossed away the cigarette. It bounced off the cobblestones, barely managing to keep its frail light. "How did you think of it?"

She was right, of course; right to the end. "A debt. Something you could owe me. First in my name, then in the kids'."

She nodded; she had known that all along, too.

"We're lucky, you know. We're obtuse and vindictive and just plain hateful at times, but it hasn't cost us a fraction of what it's cost other people. So maybe we should get over all our wailing. We're not the ones who invented suffering and pain."

She forced a smile. "There's the theme for your columns when you replace that hypocrite Applebaum. The bodies we bury in the name of living. Who's better qualified to talk about that from both ends?"

"Nobody said I was replacing Applebaum."

"Then you'll just be negotiating poorly again. Do it right this time, Charley. It may be your last chance at it."

"A parting shot?"

"Of course," she said, sliding her hand through his arm. "You didn't expect me to let you have the last word, did you? Now let's go inside and have dinner. I'm very hungry and Gianni will be thrilled with our announcement. And maybe when we go home tonight after getting rid of you, we'll really make love."

He wasn't *that* mature, Sylvester thought, leading her back inside to all the noise and artificial air.

SEVENTY-FOUR

Elena needed rules for when Tiziana started shrieking from the end of the block corridor. They didn't have to be severe rules (she would need latitude for when she wasn't feeling energetic), but there still had to be a standard of some kind. She settled on Tuesdays and Thursdays for translating the woman's ravings into French and German, on Mondays and Wednesdays for her own language and Hungarian, and on Fridays and Saturdays for English and Spanish. On Sundays she could make up a language, a mishmash of African tongues with a name of its own, or, if she felt like it, she could steal one of the languages from the other days of the week. Nor was there anything to prevent her from ignoring the lunatic's rantings altogether on Sundays—to make it her personal Sabbath. As long as she didn't abuse the privilege. Being flexible couldn't be a license for being irresponsible.

The other prisoners, the guards, the outsiders who dropped in with their legal questions or prayers or charitable impulses, they were a harder challenge, but Tiziana offered help there, too, with her screaming out of names that immediately lost meaning for coming from a crazy woman. To hear her, the names had loved her, they had stolen from her, they had died on her, or they had left her for dead, but as long as they existed only in her madness, they didn't have to exist for Elena. Any reality they might have had once upon a time as people weak or cruel or well-meaning, as parents or lovers or accomplices, had evaporated in coming out of Tiziana's mouth. So why couldn't Elena treat those who bothered her similarly, but merely by disposing of them in her mind? Since when was shrieking the only valid passport for being sure others didn't exist? Her whole life she had been most effective when she had shared as little as possible.

Most of the rest of her daily routine was easier to control. By herself she would have never gotten up at six o'clock for lukewarm coffee and a day-old brioche, but six was no great sacrifice after years of getting up just shy of seven anyway. The same with the eleven-thirty lunch and seven o'clock dinner, or for what passed for lunch and dinner. For these inconvenient hours and taste-less meals, she could be thankful for her time in the hills, when gourmet eating hadn't even been a fantasy. And how different was having to deal with roaches in her cell from having to stomp on the centipedes and chase off the rats that had scurried around in every cave she had slept in? Even the toilet smell reminded her of the makeshift latrines in bushes and creeks. It was as though the years had waited for her to realize how useful her time on the run had been.

The most serious obstacle to some peace of mind were the drug deals, fuckings, and other hallucinations past and future that echoed up and down the block from morning to night. Making it clear she wanted no part of these conversations, let alone answer questions about why she had shot a priest, had brought her nothing but insults and disdainful mockings of "the queen." Her isolation hadn't been isolated enough. She still had to over-hear the others, still had to be on guard against the worst of the dykes in the shower room. In Tiziana's place she might have used one of her meal spoons to puncture her eardrums, but she wasn't in Tiziana's place. She had to find a better solution for fortifying herself against all the intruders around her.

Reading had helped. Busoni, the sour lawyer the American had insisted on sending to her, had sidestepped her request to go to her apartment for some of her favorite books, but at least he had made the effort of looking through his own shelves for some-thing he considered appropriate for her. Nothing about violence or love or really any personal human emotions at all. Language books she had read more than once, those he had deemed safe;

and studies of polar bears and seals endangered by the melting ice cap. However tiresome the books were, once inside their pages she could wall herself off from the chattering along the block. Within them she could even allow herself a stray thought about what had gone into Busoni's selections. She should worry about shrinking icebergs where she was? That was a funny idea, but it also gave her a moment imagining Busoni reading the same things in his living room. She pictured a wife walking through the room and rolling her eyes at his obsession. Then there were Busoni's children: They were too young to read the books, but they saw the pictures of the endangered animals on the cover and asked their father to read to them. Busoni? He would have told the children to study hard in school so one day they would be able to read the books for themselves—if they hadn't already drowned by then. She found it easy to identify with those children because in the end Busoni would be leaving her on her own, too. How could a judge or jury not have sensed that kind of bloodless personality and given her the maximum sentence?

But that was out of her hands. The important thing was that no matter how long she had to follow the orders of the prison system, she would not be defeated by it. She was still herself, still arranging ahead of time what to allow in her mind. And as with translating Tiziana's rants, she had to be careful not to be rigid for the sake of being rigid. Even what she knew was a self-delusion, that Philip might still be alive, could be comforting. How could she *not* be mortified when the guards announced that he was waiting for her in the Visiting Room and she had to walk outside to have every word of their conversation monitored? How could she *not* be simultaneously elated and embarrassed to see him growing older, to hear his announcement that he was getting married, to see his joy that he was about to give her her first grandchild, to see his agitation about why his wife never wanted to come along on a visit and know that the woman would never allow the child to come visiting, either? There was so much confusion in thinking of such things, and she always dropped off to sleep wondering if they would become any clearer if she stayed awake for another few seconds.

Tonight she fought her drowsiness. Before going off to sleep she insisted on seeing what her grandchild looked like. Was it a boy or a girl? Just to get that piece of information out of Philip made her want to reach across the Visiting Room table and slap his face. He could be so much like Josef when he decided she was better off not knowing something. It wasn't as though she had the money to buy the child something and needed to know if it should be for a boy or girl. What was the matter with him? Did he count on her spending the rest of her life in prison so that she would never be able to see for herself? She wouldn't put it past him. Josef's idea of protectiveness had always carried a whiff of imprisonment, too.

As she grew angrier, the threat of sleep receded. For once the murmuring from the cells across the corridor wasn't her principal enemy. She sat up on her cot to be closer to it and further away from the misery of what she had been thinking. She welcomed the clang of the corridor door down near Tiziana's cell. It was unusual for the guards to be moving around at such an hour; or maybe it was a nightly routine that she had missed because of sleep. But what was definitely unusual was the sound of a second person—for certain a visitor. And she knew immediately who the visitor was and that he was there to see her. It was the policeman who had been asking her all the questions since she had been arrested, the same one she had seen the evening outside the hotel where the American was living. She was sure of it because she heard the slight drag on his foot—the hitch she had seen as he left the hotel before slamming at his car.

Elena knew why he had come, why his approach had made it impossible for her to drop off as she had been doing. She knew it so completely that it felt natural to shriek as loud as Tiziana, not caring in what language it came out.

SEVENTY-FIVE

On the third day Leszek began to feel like a tourist. From the beach in the morning to the casinos at night he had acted the part since arriving, but he had been wary of taking too much for granted. It was the fourth time in nine years he had come to Dubrovnik for relaxation, and that habit carried a warning. Was some overeager member of a police bureaucracy capable of projecting Tomas Leszek's behavioral patterns and, without going through superiors, alerting the locals or, worse, dispatching stingers from some beehive that didn't exist officially? The possibility was hardly science fiction. It wouldn't be the first time the convenience of computers preempted understandings. By his third evening under the old city's placid terracotta rooftops, though, Tomas Zhivkov, toy manufacturer from Sofia, was willing to feel at ease in his surroundings. Nobody had been paying suspicious attention to the rude Bulgarian who had been making a show of ugliness in dealing with incompetent hotel clerks, slow waiters, and aggressive souvenir sellers; those he had trafficked with just detested him, pure and simple, no manhunt agendas involved. If Tomas Zhivkov was seen as typical of the toy trade, the people he had put in his cross hairs had by now sworn to buy their children socks for Christmas. Rather than being in a hurry to reach for a phone to report his presence, they were elated just to see his back. They would remember nothing about him except his surliness—not the manner of a wanted man. It was the first time Leszek could remember Bulgarians being useful for something.

He sipped his vodka tonic and took in the gallery of Germans, Americans, and Italians sitting around him in the Stradun cafe. There were no undercover policemen or stingers in their worlds. They couldn't be more satisfied with the setting sun, the stone walking street, and their umbrella drinks. He envied their mind-lessness—not just in spending their kunas frivolously because that was expected of vacationers, but in their ignorance of the working universe they had taken leave of for a few days. How could anyone live as obliviously as the German father at the next table wiping the ice cream off his son's shirt while his wife watched with more paper tissues at the ready? They didn't have the tiniest inkling that the father's corporate bosses back in Frankfurt or Berlin, the ones who had provided the salary for the family holiday, were at that very moment seeking introductions to somebody like Tomas Leszek for a delicate project aimed at protecting or increasing their profits. Why did he admit a sliver of envy for such ignorance? He had never believed in innocence; naivete and stupidity yes, but not innocence. Maybe because he wouldn't have minded a moment every once in a while of having to think of nothing more urgent than wiping ice cream off a kid's shirt? It was possible. Lucky for him, the thought hadn't occurred to him disposing of Cicut. He already had a quiver of squeamish-ness remembering the loud crack of that kid's neck.

For now, though, in his tourist's frame of mind, his most pressing business was deciding whether he wanted to go to Sveti Vlaho for the evening concert or to the courtyard just outside the walls of the old town for a film. He was leaning toward the cinema. Not only was the concert indoors, but it featured two pieces by Sibelius, a composer whose melodies agitated him with their heroic romanticism. The film, on the other hand, would be outdoors, enabling him to enjoy the evening's soft breezes regard-less of whether the Italian clown Benigni, the advertised star of the picture, was funny. The Benigni film it was, then.

His watch said he had 35 minutes to get over to the courtyard for the show. Subtracting five minutes for catching the attention of the waiter and settling his bill, he would still have twice the time he needed to get where he was going. He could use it. Sanguine or not about going unobserved, it didn't hurt to be doubly and triply sure, to stray here and there for a few paces to see if somebody followed him. He would have done it anyway, but it seemed extra advisable with the daily headlines in the Italian papers screeching in the kiosks and from the desk of his hotel about the Cicut disposal. The Italians might have only been kicking futilely at walls, but noise had a habit of waking up people across borders who were better off left sleeping. And on top of that there was the loud silence about Peyrot. She had been arrested, that much he knew for certain. And that was all he knew for certain. His sources had suddenly become blind, deaf, and dumb. There had been a shift that made them uncomfortable to be associated with him even for a few seconds of texting from an untraceable distance; the inevitable shift of political calculations after every little public stir. Might Peyrot have begun to doubt herself after they had shown her pictures of Cicut's body? He had never detected that weakness in her, that was why she had come so highly recommended, and she had known very well what his task had been when he left for the last time with the boy. But who knew what could happen under police questioning? He was just glad he hadn't mentioned Dubrovnik to her as pillow talk and had been noncommittal about a rendezvous with her once they had gotten out of Italy.

There were enough clocks in the store windows and on the church towers not to draw attention by looking at his watch again as he ambled over the Stradun's white marble toward the cinema. He gave the city sweepers high marks for keeping the street clean; half the cities in Europe could have used their skills. He smiled at the child who ran a balloon right into his knee and waved off the apology from the embarrassed mother; her big thighs (smelling of mint?) reminded him of the best parts of Peyrot. A smirk was more in order for the vendor who lurched out in front of him with his broken English to hawk wall rugs, belatedly recognized unfriendly toy maker Tomas Zhivkov from their dealings that morning, and hastily stepped back again with a scowl. Disturbing the hustler was the least he could have done in the name of civilization. When he had first come to the city, the Stradun hadn't been such a carnival of greed. Even the souvenir peddlers had been reserved, all but puzzled when somebody entered their shops or approached their stands to inquire about a price. National pride had dictated that outsiders weren't needed for local survival. But that attitude had crumbled under the waves of tourists who year after year swamped the city as destructively as the Serbians and Montenegrins had dreamed of doing in the war years. Now the place was just another Latin bazaar, an eastern version of Rome and Paris. He doubted he would make a fifth visit for a respite.

He had used up most of his 35 minutes by the time he got to the cinema. Abrupt detours into a couple of side streets and reflections from store windows had been to no effect. More important, his instincts detected nothing out of the ordinary. He was no Leonard Warneke, the idiot who had tried to be so clever with him and Jackiw in Rome. The man had been an amateur, trying to learn on the job. Even Jackiw, no prince of intellect, had spotted him in his car outside the Freedom Press offices.

Which raised another worming detail: If he had been right not to have arranged a rendezvous with Peyrot, had he been careless in not cleaning up Jackiw before leaving Italy? It was a wonder the Pole didn't have a kiosk on the Stradun selling information to anyone who passed by. Who else had known about the house where they had kept Cicut? Only the priest, and that dwarf was past worrying about. Had he said anything at all to Jackiw that might prove troublesome? He didn't think so, he had never trusted him and had always been on his guard, but it was irritating even to have wonder about it. He should have worked out his logistics more efficiently on his last day in Rome so he would have been able to leave Jackiw in the same ditch as Cicut.

There were more people on line in front of the cinema than he had anticipated. Most were Italians—something he should have figured on for a Benigni film. He was annoyed for having forgotten that. Not that the 20-year-olds with their peeling beach tans, spaghetti straps, and sandals looked like police recruits sent across the Adriatic after him, but the oversight accused him of having gotten a little too comfortable. If he had thought ahead the way he should have, he would have chosen the Sibelius concert, romanticism or not.

Changing his mind and walking on, though, threatened to make him only more conspicuous, so he paid his admission and followed a giggling couple inside. The boy's hand was so glued to the girl's ass without any protest from her he doubted they were going to be watching much of Benigni over the next couple of hours. At least the inside was the same outside from his previous visits—bleacher seats within a courtyard horseshoe of the rears of scarred apartment buildings, with the fourth side off the entrance passageway allotted for the big screen. Scores of people were waving fans and newspapers to drive away not just the heat but the sour goulash of smells coming down from the kitchens all around them. The building tenants who had made the odors were already in place at their windows for the free films they got to see every night. He had to choose between wedging himself into tight spaces midway up or climbing all the way up to a couple of benches unoccupied in the last rows in front of the raised projection platform. He dragged out his decision to make sure nobody already seated was interested in him as more than an idiot who didn't know where to sit. Registering no one like that, he climbed up to the back. If memory served, the closer he was to the projector, the more grating the sound of the film being unspooled, but that seemed like a reasonable tradeoff for being able to survey the latecomers coming through the passageway next to the screen. As innocuous as they might have been, he had made enough hasty mistakes on the day.

No sooner did he camp down in the empty last row than the lights hanging off the walls of the apartment buildings dimmed and the old man operating the projector just above his head set it to whirring. He had the crazy impression whole seconds elapsed between the start of the projector and the first flickers of film on the screen. Did sitting up so high next to the projector give him a vantage point that went beyond basic physics? That made no sense, of course, but the feeling of a gap between aiming the projector light and having its images appear distracted him as the screen went into an advertisement for a Croatian refrigerator in English. And that was the second thing that made no sense. What American or Englishman was going to buy a kitchen appliance during a vacation and then pay freight charges sending it home? Had America run out of refrigerators? The audience splayed out on the rows below agreed with him in its laughter and buzzing talk. He welcomed the reaction; he didn't like being the only one aware of bizarre things. They were confusing, unnerved him. He told himself to stop thinking about them before they just rattled him more. An old woman at a top floor window in the building to his left bit into an apple as she watched the screen. He hadn't been able to bite into apples since he had lost his front teeth and been fitted with a three-unit bridge. Something smug in the woman's face said she knew that.

He had made a mistake.

The certainty of it instantly smothered his chest. His breath had to struggle to rise to his throat. Prickles under his skin goaded him for not having gone to listen to Sibelius. His impulse was to stand and run over to Sveti Vlaho before the concert had advanced too far, but he couldn't do that without attracting attention, so he dropped his head down to his legs and inhaled as hard as he could, telling himself the water-logged ground under his shoes was radiating refreshing mint water specifically for him to sniff up. Natural things had not totally abandoned him. They just insisted he pay more attention to them. He promised he would.

The refrigerator commercial made way for one for a soap detergent. He recognized the sound of a glockenspiel. People were happy, saying bright and happy things about cleaning dirty clothes. But he kept his head down until he was sure the seizure was over. The detergent advertisement was also in English and it too drew laughter from the audience. He began to breathe more easily, but he was sweating—across his forehead, on his arms, on his back. He found it ridiculous. It wasn't like him. If anyone was watching him, he couldn't help but suffer professionally. The word would go out that he had become unstable. And there were still so many opportunities for work. He pictured some manufacturer in Dubrovnik—one who had both refrigerator and detergent factories—contacting him and paying a tidy sum to eliminate rival refrigerator and detergent manufacturers. No experience in industrial projects? No problem. The objective was the same, and the bottom line had better be the same. He wasn't available for just anybody at any price.

He thought about meeting the fidgety manufacturer in a room without furniture. The manufacturer had insisted on no furniture because he was afraid of being recorded for extortion purposes, not realizing that wasn't a possible outcome, that the only possible outcomes would be that he either paid what he promised to pay or that he would be dead, no need to concern himself about blackmail. It was a calming thought. Finally, the strain on his lungs subsided. He didn't know how many minutes had passed, but when he looked up again, the scarecrow thin Benigni was driving a bus and chattering on in Italian with English subtitles. The audience was tittering, but wanted an excuse to roar. Benigni wouldn't give it to them, he was on his own schedule. He could work for audiences without caring about what they wanted, what they considered important. His monologue went on and on and the English subtitles couldn't keep up with it.

He looked over to the woman with the apple in the window, to see what she thought of the actor's arrogance. But she wasn't there. She wasn't like him: not only could she chomp into apples without worrying about her teeth, but she could come and go from the film as she pleased in her own apartment, keeping an eye on what she had on the stove, going to the bathroom, disturbing nobody.

"It gets much funnier. I've seen it before."

The loud whisper startled him. He darted a look up at the platform, but the old projectionist was immersed with a pencil in one of those newspaper number puzzles; the voice hadn't been that old, anyway. Then he saw the head bob on the far side of the light funnel from the projector. Not only had somebody slipped into his row from the far end, but the man had slid in well past the center. And he hadn't noticed!

"He builds it up," the hoarse whisper said again. "Then you get everybody in the audience howling. Wait till you see."

He felt like an idiot trying to lower his face below the light funnel to get a better look at the man, then like a double idiot when all that got him were splotches in his eyes.

"You haven't seen it?"

He shook his head. If he couldn't see who was talking to him, he couldn't have been seen, either. Let the man imagine his response.

He had made a mistake.

The Swiss Army knife pressing on his thigh from his pants pocket was useless. By the time he got to it the stinger on the other side of his splotches, if it was a stinger, would have been on him. And if it was a cop? Was he going to start stabbing policemen? He wouldn't have gotten out of the courtyard, let alone Dubrovnik. He wasn't just badly armed, he was unarmed.

He had made a mistake.

"Enjoying your vacation?"

He didn't know the voice, he couldn't have since he and Jackiw hadn't given the man time enough to speak, but he recognized the amateur as Leonard Warneke carefully lifted himself under the projector light to resettle right next to him. He didn't have to guess at what he was holding in the pocket of his windbreaker.

"I know you?" he asked anyway.

Leonard Warneke smiled through another glance at the screen. "Here's where it gets funny when he falls off the bus. What they call slapstick."

He made another mistake. The roar from the audience jerked his head toward the screen where Benigni was all arms and legs as he toppled off the bus into the street. The noise in the courtyard was deafening. For a second it seemed to be the reason for the sudden searing at the side of his chest that suffocated him more than his breathing fit had. And this pain he didn't have to sit with because it propelled him off the edge of the row into the wooden steps, his arms and legs jumping around even more uncontrollably than Bengni's. But how much of the roaring laughter was for him? Not even the two men at the edge of the row in front of him turned their heads to see how funny he was. They were too engrossed in the nonsense they had paid to see.

"A gift from John Warren, you bastard," the voice said.

He didn't understand the amateur's tone of contempt. They had been content to mock Leonard Warneke and drop him in the empty apartment when they had caught him in Rome, hadn't they? Why so much hatred in the man's voice?

The old woman back at her window didn't seem to understand, either. She just took another bite out of her apple. Did he imagine her grin?

www.ingramcontent.com/pod-product-compliance
Lightning Source LLC
Chambersburg PA
CBHW020838020726
47497CB00005B/1161